# SPLINTEGRATE

## ALSO BY DEBORAH TERAMIS CHRISTIAN

*Mainline*

*Kar Kalim*

*The Truthsayer's Apprentice*

# SPLINTEGRATE

## DEBORAH TERAMIS CHRISTIAN

**TOR**

A TOM DOHERTY ASSOCIATES BOOK · NEW YORK

SPLINTEGRATE

Copyright © 2019 by Deborah Teramis Christian

A Tor Book
Published by Tom Doherty Associates
120 Broadway
New York, NY 10271

www.tor-forge.com

Tor® is a registered trademark of Macmillan Publishing Group, LLC.

The Library of Congress Cataloging-in-Publication Data is available upon request.

ISBN 978-0-7653-0047-8 (hardcover)
ISBN 978-1-4668-3713-3 (ebook)

Our books may be purchased in bulk for promotional, educational, or business use. Please contact your local bookseller or the Macmillan Corporate and Premium Sales Department at 1-800-221-7945, extension 5442, or by email at MacmillanSpecialMarkets@macmillan.com.

First Edition: December 2019

Printed in the United States of America

0  9  8  7  6  5  4  3  2  1

*To Shawn, who inspired it.*
*To Celeste, who helped shape it.*
*To my sister, Chris, who supported it.*

# PART

## ONE

# 1

**TRYST.**

Polished black plassteel façade, muted reflection of hot red neon glowbars marking sign and playhouse door. Shimmerscreen across that portal, hologhosts moving in shadow-embrace within it, hinting at the fantasies that lay beyond. A high-end ride in the closed world of the Enclave of Port Oswin.

Tryst was the draw leader for erotic entertainment in the pleasure districts. Not simply because it was a house of domination—there were other, older playhouses in the Enclave—but for the talented dominas within. And for one in particular, embodying control and sex and fetish, archetype raised to high art and turned into marketing tool.

Believe the verts, the Winter Goddess made her home at Tryst. You could see her on the feelie channels, cold cyberwind ruffling her long mane of snow-white hair, arch your back as her sharp claws scratched your chest. Catch a whiff of her perfume—or were those pheromones?—a musky spicy scent wafting on the ether of the net. She was the avatar of Pain, direct from the realm of ancient Calyx legends, the Sa'adani tales every child grew up with. The beautiful but harsh goddess who brought proud men and women down and kept them in her torturous, icy grip forever.

See the vert and ask yourself: Could you dance with the Queen of Winter and leave her domain after?

Would you want to if you could?

Many came to find out for themselves.

**A MAN KNELT** before the Goddess in a small reception room inside the playhouse. They were alone in an octagonal bubble of contrived reality within the fantasy land that was Tryst. Black marplast walls melted seamlessly into an expanse of red-and-black striated marble flagstones, smooth and cold—and in its center, Janus, naked but for his codpiece. His arms were bound behind him with rough hachach rope, his head bowed, eyes studying the toes of the domina's white spike-heeled boots before his bended knees.

Fashions came and went across the worlds; clients' fetishes echoed the variety of the many cultures spanned by the Sa'adani Empire. But some preferences spoke strongly to archetype, and those were the tools that Kes, as Winter Goddess, preferred to work with. When the client's mind was human, a certain length and shape of heel would always signal "phallus," "power," "command": a resonance she well knew how to use.

She set the ball of her foot on the man's thigh, pointed toe near his groin, stiletto heel pressing a whitening indentation into his skin. She leaned forward, just so. The heel dug deeper as her toe brushed against the leather codpiece. The scrap of garment moved, nudged by his swelling flesh within.

"You are leaving Lyndir for a while," she remarked coolly. "You come to serve me one last time before you go." She shifted her toe so that it pressed more firmly against the codpiece. "It doesn't please me that you go, slave. I won't have you around to toy with for far too long."

Her voice, that practiced instrument, went hard and low—a foreboding emphasis with a dash of regal petulance. She punctuated the sentence with pressure from her boot: heel taking more of her weight, toe pressing against leather and the flesh beneath. Janus twitched reflexively, breath hissing inward. Yes. That caught his balls, a discomforting threat. There was a fine sheen of nervous sweat on his smooth skin. The white-haired domina smiled to herself.

"What have you to say for yourself?"

The question rapped out sharply. It was a measure of Janus's nonplussed state that he stuttered before answering.

He could not be recognized in that moment as one of the triumvirs of the Red Hand cartel, former boss of the Maze Rats derevin, an ambitious street gang. He was a man of wily cunning and far-reaching power—though now, he was nothing but her toy. Oh, true: a toy that paid well for the privilege of being there at her feet, collared and bound, eager to serve the Winter Goddess for the evening on a rainforest planet innocent of any season of cold. It was the illusion he savored, the pretense of being stripped of control, reduced to the erotic reality of the moment as he trembled beneath her searing gaze. For if it had been other than mutual pretense—had he truly lived the life of a slave of the House, or elsewhere in the Sa'adani Empire—well, he was the stubborn type, who would resist his fate until his spirit was crushed or he died trying for freedom.

But for a time, in this playhouse fantasy of suspended disbelief, he surrendered and did her bidding, and Kes took her pleasure in commanding him in ways that were very real in that moment.

"B-business calls me away, Goddess," he stammered. "If I could stay, I would."

"How long will you be gone for?"

"Perhaps twelve weeks, if it pleases you."

He spoke in the submissive protocol she had trained him to and sounded guilty while he did it. His averted gaze did not catch the downturn of her ruby-painted lips.

"It most assuredly does not please me." And those months of absence would not please Helda, mistress of the House, either. Janus paid well to reserve sessions with the Goddess five times a month, a far more expensive proposition than most clients could ever afford to contemplate. He had been a regular for the last year, ever since his business had brought him to Port Oswin, the sector capital, and he had dared to enter Kes's lair, the hottest attraction in the Enclave. It was a lucrative booking as predictable as the Ward Commissioner's monthly "donation" shakedowns, and a bonus Kes had grown accustomed to tucking away in her outworld investment funds.

Though, to be honest with herself, she would miss a bit more than Janus's money. He had his own small redeeming qualities, as clients went. There were reasons why he returned again and again to this particular woman among all the professional entertainers in Port Oswin's licensed quarter. Only the Winter Goddess read him so well, and took such personal pleasure in the torments she inflicted upon him. There was a chemistry between them that transcended his usual experience of common houses, and her experience of common clients. He engaged a sincerity in her dominant nature that few clients could elicit, and they danced the dance of pleasure and pain, command and compliance, unusually well together.

He knew that as well as she did. It was evident in his eyes as they sought hers, brows furrowed with discomfort as he dared to glance up without permission.

"I'll count every day, Goddess, until I can serve you again."

A common avowal, from clients aroused and anticipating the session that stretched ahead of them, but with Janus it meant something more. His enthusiasm, she knew, did not wane when the session was over. At least, it hadn't so far.

Yet she let displeasure show in her expression. "Then I shall have to use you thoroughly while I have you, won't I? Before you are gone for so unseemly long."

There. The right note of unhappiness, so he would strive harder to please her; the right threat of erotic torments to come, to titillate him. On some level it was true: she wanted to use him hard before he left. Let her inner Beast loose, and play with him as she would play with a partner in her personal life. No more consideration for the professional niceties that constrained her: the need to craft a session that was part theater, part psychodrama, that kept her clients enthralled but never pushed them too dramatically beyond the limits of their own comfort zones.

She wanted, for once, to bite until she drew blood; to spank him so his behind would be marked for days, not merely hours; to use the instruments of torture that only the most hardy masochists could endure, and Janus no masochist. . . .

But, no . . . that was not how the game was played. Clients were clients, and had to be treated differently.

If Janus knew how she played in her private life, he would run screaming from the room. And that would be bad for business.

So instead of continuing the pressure at his groin in a way that would double him over in pain, she withdrew her foot and set it deliberately on the floor. "Kiss it," she ordered coldly, and her slender captive bent over obediently, pressing his lips to the toe of her boot. He straightened up, eyes again diverted downward.

Kes stepped back, the white shimmersilk robe diaphanous about her form, revealing cleavage, a hint of thigh, the silver-and-white leather of her halter. She turned arrogantly on one heel and strode to the side door, an open portal cloaked with hanging silken veils. "Follow," she commanded, tossing the word over her shoulder, certain that she would be obeyed.

Janus clambered awkwardly to his feet, without the use of his arms for balance, and stumbled quickly in the wake of the Winter Goddess.

HELDA SAT IN the twilight confines of the control room that was the electronic nerve center of Tryst. From the external lighting of neon glowbars to the clandestine recording of intimate encounters, it was all observable from right there. Spyeyes and house AI and neural systems interwove the structure of Tryst, turning it into a nearly living interactive sphere of involvement.

Her personal slave, Pol, the supervising stimtech, ran Control on this shift, assisted by two other house slaves who were also technically qualified. They had given no special acknowledgment to Helda when she entered Control, for protocol was suspended in certain working environments even for owners and dominas. But they quickly made room for her at the console, and Pol vacated the command seat so his Domna could take advantage of its strategic systems.

Like most shigasu, Helda eschewed obvious cyberware, but a Dosan needed certain capacities to interact with systems of the establishment for which she was housemother. The rigger jack at the base of her neck was concealed beneath her collar-length brown hair. Now a lead trailed from it into the headrest of the command chair that cushioned her body with morphfoam.

The monitor bank shifted displays, nudged by her thoughts and inquiries: guest count at the door; duration of stay; moment-by-moment cost/profit ratio at the Mix bar where clients ordered designer drugs and drinks to go with their evening's entertainment. House slaves and stimtechs working behind the scenes in the fantasy house were tracked as they maintained the ambiance of the club, as were the shigasu working the floor and those whom they escorted— for, unlike holodens and sense parlors, no client moved unattended through a playhouse.

In this rarefied environment, erotic fantasies were crafted for the client or client group. For that was the specialized art of the shigasue, the entertainer class of Sa'adani tradition. Whether providing dinner conversation at a banquet hall, serving raffik in a classic tea house, or directing ecstatic exploration of the senses in modern sensoria, the shigasue crafted scenes that appeared spontaneous, yet followed basic dramatic elements of proven effectiveness. A skilled entertainer established rapport, created and built tension, brought that energy to a climax that dissolved in resolution.

It was a classic, simple formula that lent itself to endless variation, from the witty repartee of a tea recital that dissolved in laughter over punning humor to the psychosexual drama of sensation play, domination, and stylized submission that Tryst specialized in.

There, in the elegant, ominous torture chamber of the Winter Goddess, Kes approached the dais, setting the stage for the more intense encounter that was about to unfold. Helda smiled and leaned into the monitor screen. It was nearly as great a pleasure to watch Kes work as it was to be the subject of her personal attentions. She was a master of her craft, thoroughly wasted under her former contract to the Icechromers. Helda congratulated herself again for scoring such a prize for the House, and turned her rigged attention to the scene before her.

**KES SWEPT VEILS** aside and strode, white heels clicking, across a black marble floor. She took her seat on a throne-like chair of ice-blue steeloy and glittering chrome. She was lit from above and below by electric-neon gels that gave an unearthly cast to her features. The domina was a study in light and shadows with the merest hint of color: pale skin; snow-white hair; white halter, thong, robe, and boots; full red lips, red nails, and dusk-shadowed eyes. The refined planes of her face changed in the shifting blacklight that turned shimmersilk luminescent and lips black, then red again.

A subliminal vert flickered in the air, lost in the interplay of light around her: the glimmer of the throne, the sheen of silken draperies billowing softly behind it. The vert was a subtle holoprojection with no purpose other than to underscore her presence. Her own considerable aura took on layered meaning in the observer's eye in this way: a significance Tryst's housemother had carefully crafted into their virtual campaign two years before, when Helda first decided Kes should be a presence to be reckoned with.

"The Avatar of Pain," one of Helda's more popular sensie-verts had portrayed her. With sublims of lust and compliance, it was designed to snag the attention of the submissively or masochistically inclined. That message danced now at the subconscious edge of Janus's perception, evoking Sa'adani mythology about one archetypal ruler of the icy Underrealms. The programmed illusion veiled, yet revealed, the flesh-and-blood Kes much as the shimmersilk did her body. It was a media construct, yes, a packaged impression, but also something more. It was an aspect of herself that would sell, forming the believable seed of reality tucked within the layers of subtle suggestion.

That was one of Helda's gifts, recognizing attributes worth working with. She had nurtured that seed, then plucked it, packaged it, and sold it and Kes together, bundled as one. Now world-class masochists came routinely from five subsectors to avail themselves of the Winter Goddess. But pain was not the only tool in her repertoire. Far more often, clients sought from her that intangible quality that few shigasu really offered: command. The sense of a woman in control, a woman who owned her power, whose unshakable authority could reduce them to a quaking, uncertain shadow of themselves with a word, a look, a tone of voice—and then use them, erotically or otherwise. Clients imagined, in that fleeting moment, that she desired them like they desired her.

It was unlikely, of course—Kes's genetic orientation was towards women—but a client pays to believe that he is wanted, that he is the coveted prey of the Goddess incarnate. And what kind of a House entertainer would she be if she could not foster and maintain that illusion? It was easy to help people believe what they wanted to believe. What they paid a thousand credits an hour to believe.

She beckoned Janus to her, pointed him to kneel on the step below. She leaned forward, then, and traced one long, scarlet fingernail around the data-port on his temple, protected by a small button, gleaming as red as the lacquer on her nails. "There," she said softly, resting one finger atop the port. "I want inside your head. Into your deepest, darkest fantasies. What do you share with no other, Janus? I want you to share it with me."

He tensed at her whispered suggestion, drew back a fraction of an inch. Her nail traced down his cheek. "More intimate than sex, isn't it?" she murmured. "Letting someone into your mind. . . ."

His brow furrowed; his lips parted. Kes laid a finger upon them, stilling his protest before he could voice it. "Think about it. Think about how you want to be possessed by me." Her voice hardened. "I want all of you, slave: all that I can have. Your body. Your heart. Your imagination. *Mine*. Think about being taken by me, there." She tapped his brow.

His expression changed then, minutely; so small a shift that a less attuned observer would have missed it. Kes read the energy in his stance, how he leaned into her once again. A smile quirked her lips. He was doing it to himself, arguing, persuading, his imagination following the seeds of suggestion she had planted. He wanted to be possessed—or to have the illusion, at least, that she possessed his innermost thoughts and being.

Not that she ever would; no man chipped and rigged like Janus would dare let her into sensitive areas of his brain. But he also had the wherewithal to create a safe playspace in his neural circuitry, a portico where their thoughts could mingle and the rest of his guarded knowledge would remain behind unbreachable barriers—if he trusted her enough to let her in at all.

It was about the trust. Would he go there with her? Their play required it. Did he want to trust her more? Obviously. Would he make himself more vulnerable in consequence? In time, he would. Kes smiled at the certainty of that process. This sort of dynamic she could predict very well: push here, get that result there.

"That is for next time." She granted him a slight reprieve. "I expect you to come prepared to be . . . explored."

She straightened; then her hand slipped down to the medallion around his neck, the double-twined dragons of the Cho-sen sect. That a cartel boss should have religious leanings amused her, especially towards a sect she despised. It made it more piquant that he wore the medallion always; there were so many levels to play on when her whipping boy also embodied things she scorned. She gave the chain a half twist around his neck; drew him closer to her. "But for now . . . I think something more immediately pleasing to my senses, yes?"

She stood, drawing him to his feet by the chain, her boot-heeled height putting her eye to eye with the tall man. She strode to the static field against one of the hexagonal walls, feeling him stumble to match her pace. She turned Janus's back to the wall and pushed him against it with one flat hand. He stuck, captured wherever he touched it by the energy field that ran across its surface. Instant bondage, far quicker than all the other ways she had at hand to restrain a client.

Janus stood, torso at an awkward angle from the way his bound arms were pinned behind him. It forced his back to arch, chest shoved forward. She traced her nails across his skin as her other hand gestured skyward. A snap of her fingers—along with an invisible trigger on a neural cyber relay—and a panel descended from the ceiling. She spared it no glance, its contents memorized, but saw Janus's eyes widen as he took in the implements of torment and pleasure that hung upon it. She reached directly to her side and took a powerwand from its holder, violet sparks of static electricity shimmering about its tip. She stepped forward, letting the sparks dance lightly over her subject's breast. He gasped.

"Now," she said. "Let us begin."

HELDA SCOWLED IN the dim twilight of Control.

Kes's client now huddled at her feet blinking away tears. A catharsis had been reached, the conclusion of the drama the shigasa had orchestrated for him. Long minutes later, he stood, she dismissed him, they parted ways.

The Dosan watched his slender form pass through the iris door in real time as she rapidly scanned back through the spyeye log of this session. She noted again how Kes had escalated tension with her client. She paused playback, frowning. Dangerous tactic. One she wasn't sure she approved of at all.

Helda unplugged the lead in her rigger jack and stood, pausing a moment to reorient as her senses focused on her physical surroundings. She left the control room to Pol, ignoring his bow as she departed, and turned her footsteps to the shigasa's changing room.

Kes was at her dressing table when she opened the door.

"Not smart." Helda pronounced judgment from the doorway, leaning against the jamb, her long, quilted azure robe softening her wiry form and nearly concealing the tension in her body.

Kes caught the housemother's eyes in the mirror on the wall before her. She continued to remove her makeup with precise strokes of a cleanwand. Ions loosened and particulates lifted from skin, consumed by the device's self-fueling energy field. The post-session routine was habit, no concentration required. She kept her gaze on her Dosan in the doorway.

"Are you in one of those moods again? Second-guessing how I work a client?"

Helda shook her head impatiently. "Work them how you like. But there are some places you shouldn't go."

"Oh?" One white eyebrow arched, just so. Kes bridled any time Helda tried to direct her domination of paying clients. Let the Dosan spit it out, whatever nit she wanted to pick today.

"You know it. Asking a client to let you in his head? What were you thinking?"

Kes shrugged elaborately; her dark red brocade robe slid down and partly off one shoulder. "I've done it before. It captivates them. Do they dare? And once I'm there, will they be safe?"

"Not a gambit for that one. He has secrets he'd kill to keep. Don't step near them."

The shigasa's brows drew together. She put the cleanwand down on the table, hard. The clack of it punctuated her motion as she swiveled about in her chair to face Helda.

"You know what I hate about domming for hire." It was a statement, not a question. The Dosan nearly winced. "That's right," Kes continued. "I won't serve *them*. If it must be a transaction, it will be one where the power dynamic pleases me. Pleases *me*, Helda." She jabbed her thumb towards herself. "If you want a service domina, use Noriko. Use Coel. Use any shigasa you've taught to go through the motions. But if you want a real domina behind the set-dressing of your Goddess of Winter, then she'll have real demands on her session slaves. Real trust. Authentic control. Not that playacting the others do." She'd come to her feet in the middle of that assertion. "I'll do this my way, or not at all."

Helda spread her hands in a placating gesture. "You hate the work of traditional shigasue—"

"That's right."

"—so what else would you do? You're very good at this, Kesada. But best to do it wisely."

"If this work isn't enjoyable for me, why should I do it at all?" It was a sharp retort, nothing more, but Helda's lips thinned. The domina raised one finger to cut her off. "Don't start with me about duty and obligation. I have exactly two weeks left to my contracted service, and then I'm my own woman again."

"You're adopted into this House, now," Helda countered stiffly. "Your contract is a mere formality. You are family-bound here. As long as you're with Palumara House, you will do what the House requires of you. It's your oath, and it's your duty."

Kes stepped closer, her height and presence imposing on Helda's space. "Believe it or not, I still have my adoption oath memorized—mine, yours, and Clan Mother Bejmet's. I haven't forgotten what's expected of me if I want to stay part of this clan. But I will serve this House on my own terms."

"Or not at all?"

"I didn't say that."

"You think it, though."

Kes stepped closer still. The two women were a hand-span apart. "You infuriate me sometimes," she breathed, her voice low and tense with self-control.

"You owe the House," Helda said, retreating to the defense of her position as Dosan. "You owe me."

Her defense did not prevail. Kes darted out a hand, grabbed Helda by the hair at the nape of her neck, and pulled her closer. "I'll show you what I owe you," she said in husky tones—but it was an erotic threat, as the hand in Helda's hair forced her to her knees before the domina. Kes leaned into her erstwhile superior, dominating her with strength and leverage. She bent the Dosan's head back, causing her to look up. Their eyes locked. "I think I owe you a beating. And then you owe me sexual service. Don't you, kushla?"

Kushla. Old Sa'adani term for girl; for favorite; for a person who was a sexual plaything or a concubine. Helda flushed; she could play the top or bottom side of this dance, but with Kes, somehow her sexual submission always came welling to the fore—not in business, but in bedroom play. And as the beautiful shigasa's gaze held hers, all thoughts of business fled.

"Yes, Domna," she whispered.

Kes's lips met hers, and their discussion about how to dom clients was forgotten.

# 2

METMURI ESIMIR POPPED a tab of Serafix, or "mentaid" as it was called on the street. His addictive drug of choice dissolved in his mouth, the cool pink froth of it melting across the back of his tongue and sliding down his throat. Absorbed through mucus membranes, the juice hit his system at the predictable speed of molecular transport rates. He had been tense before, a little twitchy and scattered as this morning's dose metabolized out of his system. But at this point in the afternoon it was easily time for round two of the day. Maybe there would be a round three, if he were up late, just enough to grease the skids of social coping and his work. Oh! His work . . . !

"Dr. Metmuri?"

It was Terel, his intern assistant. Descendant of old Tion bloodlines, attached to Esimir's post because of the doctor's presence there—that, and clan obligations to Esimir's family. Terel's clan was slightly lower ranking, intermarried, once partners in medical practice with the Metmuri four generations ago. Strong honor bonds remained between their families.

Not that Esimir needed an assistant, really—it was far better not to have anyone too close to his work—but if the Director of Special Projects must labor with interns underfoot, better someone biddable, and as trustworthy as honor-bound duty could create. The alternative was the Imperial Navy support staff who peopled the research station. And they were entirely too eager to horn in on his work, elbow past his security-locked doors, snoop on what he had under development.

No. Better Terel. Esimir could invoke roi'tas, honor-debt, and shut him up if he needed to. Or have him shipped back to regal, crumbling Tion, home of nanotech and ancient monumental architecture. It would be a living death to an aspiring biotechnician's career, unless he specialized in nanotech. And Terel did not.

Ah, but now his assistant was looking anxious. Time to humor the boy. Well, not boy, alas, not that fresh-faced youth he once must have been. He was just old enough now, just educated enough, to seem nearly manly, affecting the mustache and side-clipped hair of his elders back home.

"Dr. Metmuri?" he persisted.

"Yes?" Esimir turned and looked at him full on, blinking as the mentaid flooded his system, accelerated his synaptic responses, gave him a mental clarity and sharpness of movement that passed for nervous tension. He blinked until his slightly watering eyes cleared. "What is it?"

"It's time, sir. In the chamber. They're waiting for you."

"Ah." The doctor's hand strayed reflexively to his brow, rubbing the spot between his eyes as if soothing away tension. That gesture could not smudge the rus laserscribed there. The half-green, half-blue elongated diamond symbol of psionic skills marked his status as bioempath. It also marked him as an adept of arcane healing energetics and held him to a higher code of ethics than others.

An ethical man about to kill his fourteenth experimental prisoner this year.

He turned his footsteps down the hall and considered the peculiar situation he was walking into. A bioempath swore never to put his hand to a weapon, never to personally take a sentient life. Esimir had never done those things; he had honored the oath of his caregiving profession to the letter. That his subjects were condemned to death was not his decision to make. That his work was furthered by the execution of imperial justice was something he had come to terms with, for what he strove to accomplish was . . . essential. Noble, even, if it met with success, as he was so very close to doing.

The source and fate of experimental subjects was not something he had given much thought to when old Prevak had brought him in on the Splintegrate project. Learning how to splinter a personality and reintegrate selective parts of it came at a cost, he saw that now. But didn't all the great discoveries require some experimental fodder before they achieved success? These test subjects were provided by their imperial sponsors, and without such support it would be impossible to do this project at all.

When Prevak left the team, Esimir had campaigned for this position leading this research—for it embodied his quest and perhaps his salvation in one. So if this work compromised his principles—and his professional oath—in service to a greater good, well . . . he had to find a way to live with that, didn't he?

Oh, but that was a foolish direction to send his thoughts in today, with mentaid giving laser-sharp focus on any subject that crossed his mind. His stomach roiled in rebellion. Esimir wrenched his attention away from his personal demons and back to the matter that awaited him in the chamber.

Terel followed him down the hall, through bulkhead doors that could seal airtight in case some nasty bug got loose from Phages, or a cyberdrone from Systems stomped down the corridors, mindlessly limb-rending. Once or twice such things had happened, though not in Esimir's tenure there. Imperial Naval Weapons Research Station 207 had a better security record than most. Necessarily so, given what they worked with behind closed doors.

The chamber was an octagonal room used for high-level control and observation of certain experiments within the Special Projects division. The far third of the space was walled off with transparent blastplas in reinforced bulkhead framing. An armored hatch, closed now, secured the entrance from this side of the room. Beyond the plas, a similar secure doorway on the far side of the test chamber opened into the containment area.

This was the splintering chamber, where they performed the first and most dramatically visible part of the splintegration process. Esimir loved this room, built as it was to his own specifications. It was a mutable workspace, and right now it was optimized to splinter the personality out of a test subject.

On the near side of the plas, control panels and tech stations ringed the faceted walls, with seating for observers and science staff in the center. There, he could do the work of a god.

The Serafix was coursing through the doctor's system quite nicely by the time he stepped into the chamber. There was one obligatory observer already seated there, the Justiciar from Lessing who must witness this legal execution. Beside him sat Ugoli, adjutant to the station's commander, who would attest to the results from this iteration of Esimir's experimentation. Three technicians and Ferris, his best research assistant and medtech, held their positions at control stations around the room.

Faces turned towards the bioempath as he entered. His eyes were still watering, just enough to blur his vision a bit. He blinked some more, then turned his hyperacute attention on Ferris.

"Systems ready?"

"Yes, sir," she replied.

The dim lighting on the other side left the plas a dark and reflective pane cutting across the room. Esimir walked towards his reflection, a middle-aged, moon-faced, sandy-haired figure in the aqua service tunic and striped leggings of his profession. He waved his hand past a wall sensor and the lights brightened on the containment side of the chamber.

He studied the distraught man restrained there.

The prisoner was screaming something, to judge by his open, working mouth. His face was flushed red and tendons bulged in his neck. No word carried through the plas, though, not even the faintest hint of noise. Static bonds held the subject snug in the trode chair where monitor leads ended in delicate microprobes in his flesh.

They were monitoring, sampling, maintaining biofeedback—and most important, those in his skull were mapping brainwave activity at the various levels of neural matter they were interested in.

That much of the process, at least, was painless. The brain had no nerves to transmit pain. Perhaps the flesh intrusors were a bit uncomfortable—but no. The subject was not cursing because of the probes. He just seemed upset on general principles.

Esimir wagged a finger at him and turned away from the plas.

"We're sure this is Biancar Prime, yes?"

"Prime," agreed Ferris. "The original one the sentence of execution applies to."

"His clones all sedated?"

"Yes. Secured in holding for now."

Esimir nodded to himself. He ignored the assemblage that awaited his orders and turned back to study the convict.

Few prisoners came to such irreversible straits as a death sentence. Most beings who committed heinous crimes chose slavery or a brain wipe to expunge their offense upon the body social. Neither of those were a viable option for Biancar, violent serial rapist and slayer of children. He refused the wipe, and it was deemed that he did not have enough honor or impulse control to adhere to even the basic terms of voluntary slavery.

Esimir watched the rapist rage in sound-insulated silence. The man did go on, as if all this were somehow unexpected.

Maybe, to his limited imagination, it was. "Remanded to Resource Disposition" did not convey a great deal of finality to the uninitiated. Perhaps Biancar had never quite realized that he would be serving imperial justice not only with his body, but with his life. For all subjects who became part of the Splintegrate program, would, at some point, lose their life.

For the court, that satisfied the terms of the sentence. But they could not have known that a cloned subject must lose his life again and again before being wholly dead. And here Esimir stood, ready to do it again.

He reminded himself of the bigger picture, then looked over his shoulder to Ferris. "Synaptic mapping engaged?"

She nodded. "Already recording."

"Position the flexor."

Technicians complied. A hemisphere of plas densely populated with sensors, a cortical array, neural transducers, and AI links lowered in an arc over Biancar's head.

The flexor resembled the brain tissue regenerators used in specialized surgery, but the purpose of this creation was not at all reparative. Instead of healing the brain, this device would leech the electrical flow of cortical activity away from the brain mass, mapping and decoding as it read—and destroying as it read as well. That flow of energy and information was a one-way street, channeling everything into the AI banks of the Splintegrate project. It was adapted from imperial mind-wipe technology, but yielded a result far more revolutionary.

"Systems aligned," reported Terel.

Esimir nodded. "When you are ready, Ferris: begin."

She nodded and engaged cortical scanners, keyed a comp sequence that started the human core-dump process. "Scan engaged," she reported.

Biancar's face went slack; his mouth lolled open. Esimir stood by, watching the subject of his handiwork relax into the deadly embrace of the core-dump technology.

No more the predator but the prey, he thought. I helped put an end to your perversions. Just as you will help put an end to mine.

# 3

**THE ALERT THAT** the head of Political Division was arriving at Lyndir did not come until her ship was already in orbit around that jungle-wrapped globe.

Commander Obray knew the expression "his jaw dropped," but he'd never experienced such a thing until he'd jacked into his morning reports and the magenta holocode of PolitDiv blossomed before his eyes. It took a minute for the unbelievable reality to sink in.

The Emperor's right hand was here, in the capital of the Confederation of Allied Systems Sector. Here! Of all the eleven sectors of imperial space, the second-most-powerful person in the Sa'adani Empire was about to walk through the doors of Internal Security in Port Oswin.

Into *his* office.

Excitement and dread warred within Obray. He worked on shutting his gaping mouth while he rushed to change into a fresh set of service whites. It wouldn't do to meet this personage in his workaday decker's jumpsuit. Internal Security work on Lyndir was a job of netrunning and cyber-sleuthing. Exciting as all hells from inside the infosphere, but from the clothes to the duty—done while sprawled on a netrunner's couch—all pretty pedestrian-looking to outsiders. Definitely not impressive.

And he couldn't help himself. This was one person he wanted to make an impression on. The Kingmaker could make or break his career.

His mouth snapped shut on that thought, and he readied himself for her imminent arrival.

### "ILANYA CASANI EVANIT."

The chief of Internal Security's elite Political Division introduced herself with full clan names to Commander Obray. Her datapad was a formality of identification, extended in such a way that the twining ochre and gold clan sigil laserscribed on the back of her left hand was also visible. It was an indelible emblem that spoke of her Gen'karfa caste, the warrior-bred aristocrats second only to the noble Lau Sa'adani in status.

She did not need to rely upon such obvious signs for her credentials, of course. The tailored charcoal-gray service jacket over gray bodysuit, the red-and-gold flash of rank at her collar, made her standing as Arcolo, division leader, evident.

And everyone in the imperial security apparatus knew her name.

Obray knew better than to actually examine her documents. He also resisted the perverse urge to call her "Eva" to her face. It was well known in the service that she permitted that familiarity to those who worked closely with her. Perhaps she did not know that throughout IntSec she was also known by that nickname—by far the most benign of the many things she was called. It was a way to make the prickly thing approachable. And there was no lack of people who wanted to be closer to the peculiar vortex of power that was Ilanya Evanit.

Intuitively, Obray took in her energy. She moved like a prowling jeegar, ready to pounce, and all his inbred caste instincts kicked in at once. It would be meticulous manners and formal address for this one. She was as imperious as any high-born he had ever met, and self-preservation dictated how he must behave with this officer beyond what IntSec paramilitary courtesy required.

"Domna Arcolo" it would be. Like "Lord General" in local CAS Sector space, no one could fault that style of address. Even though her rank was more like a Cassian colonel than a general—but then, no rank did justice to her role as Nalomeci's chosen agent on secret business for the throne. Unless she expected to be called something else . . . ?

As Obray agonized over formalities and wondered what he should say next, Eva relieved him of those concerns.

"Sit, Commander." She ordered him back into his chair and remained standing before him. He should have felt authoritative, ensconced behind his control consoles. He did not. He felt pinned to the spot by his visitor's intense scrutiny.

The woman was a trim figure of nondescript middle age. Her hair was red, short and stylish. Her eyes were a cold blue; her chin pointed; nose a bit longer than what qualified for beauty. Her gaze missed nothing and was unsettlingly direct. Her air of entitlement and easy command was what he expected from the highest ranking of Sa'adani aristocracy. It was still not pleasant to have it directed at himself.

She raised a finger and her escort came near. Unintroduced and unobtrusive, the man wore high-collared service grays without rank insignia. Ilanya's armed escort remained outside; this one had followed her in. He moved deftly, holding himself two steps behind and one to the side of wherever the lady placed herself.

He leaned forward now, ear angled to catch her soft-spoken words. His head was shaved and eyes concealed by a slotted, silvered visor band hardwired into his temples. Military-issue rigger jacks were visible at temple and brow, and a jaw-mounted monitor tab pulsed in coded chromatics. The man was chipped and jacked right now into some encrypted system through tightbeam relays. The sensors in Obray's desk top confirmed that much.

That, and the man's skeletal reinforcements, subdermal armor, at least three concealed weapons systems . . .

Ilanya Evanit caught Obray studying the man by her side. "This is Teo," she volunteered. "My matasai."

Matasai, matasai . . . explanation and befuddlement in one. It was an Old Sa'adani word that the woman from the capital world tossed out as if everyone sprinkled their talk with archaic terms. Although born in old Empire space, Obray was more fluent in Common these days, the polyglot tongue spoken throughout the CAS Sector, not the pure strains of Qualuni he had used in his youth.

His nervous fingers chorded a query into his deskcomp, below the Domna's line of sight. He read the display and glanced up, right into Eva's piercing blue eyes. Matasai, a word from old folktales. Slave-assistant-escort-bodyguard. An aide who was owned, expected to provide for every need of his owner, and die if necessary to protect him. Or her.

And in this case, to judge by the room sensors, he was both walking data-bank and cyborg-quality arsenal as well. The visible cybermods were just the tip of the iceberg.

Ilanya smiled, an expression that did not touch her eyes. "Display." She spoke into the air; her matasai understood it as a command. He snapped to attention, then stood at parade rest, eyes front. A holocaster in his visor beamed forth, and an image formed in the air between Obray and Ilanya.

It was someone Obray recognized instantly from the smuggling affair on Selmun III two years ago. The holo showed a tall, slender man in an expensive but understated suit; long auburn hair tied back at his neck, hairline just starting to recede. The lacquered red button of a single neural implant or rigger jack at his left temple. The lack of caste marks on skin or clothing proclaimed him to be a CAS Sector native. The image closed on his face: high cheekbones, aquiline nose, brown eyes.

"This is Janus," said Ilanya. "One of the three triumvirs of the Red Hand cartel. I believe you've crossed paths before."

Obray nodded sharply. "Though he wasn't a triumvir back then, or even a derevin boss. Just a lieutenant."

"He has risen to prominence since. Now he makes his headquarters right here in Port Oswin."

"Oh!" Her news startled the blurt out of him. He had no idea. Should they have been tracking the man . . . ?

"This man has become a liability to imperial interests," the PolitDiv chief continued, "and it would further those interests for him to be eliminated. Soon. Unfortunately, his security is better than we anticipated." She waved a hand sharply and her matasai cut the display. She began to pace.

"We've tried to take him out twice now. Those failures have chased him away from business elsewhere to go to ground here, in his home territory, where he thinks he's safe. That's why I've come to see to this personally. Our inability to hit him with a routine assassination is a failure that cannot be tolerated."

Obray blinked. That was a disturbing thing to hear, on several levels. Janus must have great protections in place to avoid "routine" assassinations instigated by PolitDiv. Or great luck. And then there was this display of zeal, with Ilanya Evanit coming in person to Obray's own doorstep. That was worrisome. Word was, the PolitDiv chief was fine at delegating—until she homed in on a "special project" and made it her own. A grisk with a bone had nothing on her when she decided a situation deserved her undivided attention.

Suddenly uncomfortable, he remembered something a mentor told him years ago: whenever the Kingmaker was involved personally, a gambit was being played in the Great Game. A coup, an assassination, a genocide: whatever it was, it would set a chain of effects in motion that would ripple across the Empire and align something, somewhere, in favor of the Emperor.

And now she was here, to make her play on his watch, at his field station. He shifted uneasily as she interrupted his train of thought. "To start with, I require you to establish surveillance on our target. Thoroughly. I want to know his patterns in intimate detail so that we can pick the best time, place, and manner to deal with this outstanding matter."

Obray was fascinated and perturbed at the same time. Internal Security policed imperial regulations and searched out domestic threats. Their work did not slop over into things like assassination—that was the purview of Polit-Div, along with all their other invisible machinations. It was not a level of gamesmanship he'd ever wanted to participate in, even though such things were sometimes necessary for the welfare of the Empire. Yet as commander of Lyndir field station, he knew there was no permanent PolitDiv presence here. It must be something extraordinary that lured the Kingmaker out of her spiderweb and all the way to this provincial capital, to turn her obsessive attention on her chosen target. When this jeegar went on the hunt, they said, she would not come home without her prey.

Obray didn't think this was a game trail he wanted to be on, but given her position, he had no choice. She would move her castle-stones on the board, and for now he was one of the game pieces. To comply was his duty.

"You'll be wanting surveillance around the clock, then," he offered.

"No, Commander." Ilanya spoke curtly. "I don't think you understand me. I want category ten surveillance. I want gnat-cams on his clothes, his household staff infiltrated, satellite and security cams tracking his street movements, and everyone he talks to tagged and traced. I want to know what he has for dinner and whether it is his favorite food. If he takes a leak, I want to know it, and I want to know it in the hourly update you'll be linking to Teo."

"How long do you want this continued for, Domna Arcolo?"

"Until I tell you to stop. Teo will downlink the target's present location to your systems. I also want Janus traced in your local infosphere. We need his footprint, his patterns. I need to be able to anticipate his moves so we can strike in the right way. If we fail again, he'll know he's not safe at home, and then he could flee anywhere. I can't take that chance. We're running out of time."

Obray noted the tension in her voice. "My best decker will spearhead the operation," he promised. "He can find anyone and anything in the 'sphere."

"Just what I want to hear."

"As to workspace—will you be our guest here in Vael, or will you be using Sector Security offices?" If he could divert her to local sector functionaries, they could dance attendance upon her and he'd be free to—

"I'll stay here," she said, crushing his hopes of autonomy. "Besides, I don't trust these provincials to manage something so sensitive. I'll commandeer their security service if I need their resources, but let's start with our own people. Impress me, Commander Obray."

In some back room of his mind, a much younger Obray, unused to dealing with the high-born, quailed for his future. But the commander was older and wiser now. Ilanya might play the Great Game, but he was on her team. He wanted to serve the Empire; she lived to serve the Emperor.

"As you say." Obray chorded directives into his console. "Cat ten prep is commencing. If I may have your files on Janus?" He looked questioningly at Teo.

"Downlinking," the matasai replied. Obray saw secure circuits engage on his monitor board, and he met Ilanya Evanit's eyes.

"All will proceed as you order, Domna Arcolo."

"See that it does." She stood, self-contained and erect, yet poised as if she would spring into action in the blink of an eye. "Hourly updates, Obray. We have a liability to deal with, and this time he won't see it coming."

She and her matasai left, and he watched the door slide shut behind them.

Yes, he thought. Definitely on the hunt.

# 4

**KES DID NOT** spend the night with Helda. Never did, alluring as the older woman's submission was. After an intimate encounter, they became Dosan and shigasa again. The tension that always lay between them drew them close until the inevitable spark leapt the gap, igniting passion and power. When the first flush of that exchange burned itself out, they separated again. They never kissed when they parted ways. That was not the kind of understanding that they had.

The domina stretched languidly, then threw the quilt back and rose naked from her bed on the floor. She padded across the bleached white pammas matting that covered the floor, natural reed fibers soft and yielding beneath her feet. Clients would be surprised if they could see how the Winter Goddess lived in real life. Entertainers wove their illusions of beauty and decadent comfort for clients in spaces created to showcase such things. How she lived behind the scenes was very different: in a modest four-mat room of old Qualuni style, cabinets to hold bedding, walls covered with pithpaper and wood lattice, an alcove in the east wall for altar and meditation.

The domina's professional wardrobe was in her dressing room, near the client chambers of the fantasy house; here in her personal space, modest chests and concealed cabinets sufficed to hold her belongings. Her favorite robe hung behind a dressing screen painted with flying red-orange grieko, symbol of good fortune. Before it, cushions welcomed guests to seating on the floor at a low black-lacquered table.

It was like something out of a history sim, the simple dwellings of the shigasu dictated by tradition and sumptuary laws appropriate to their caste and profession. That had been one of the first things that surprised Kes about this lifestyle. Unlike the entertainers who started out as the young service girls called benko, she had come to this work late, only two years before, through a convoluted path of misfortune and debt servitude. Helda took pains to make sure that Kes learned essential customs and traditions promptly. She would fit in with the requirements of Palumara House, the shigasue clan that owned Tryst, or she could return to the derevin-run brothel Helda had bought her contract from.

It was her choice, said the housemother—but really, it was no choice at all. To be used sexually at the whim of a street gang that had a legal debt-claim over her, or have the chance to gain her own small measure of autonomy in the realm of the shigasue? Helda had known what she would decide.

And so Kes learned the behaviors and basic skills expected of an entertainer, and complied enough to satisfy the minimum requirements of the House. It was never enough for Helda, the exacting perfectionist running this little piece of the Palumara empire, but it was enough to get by. No wonder Kes cared a little for the Dosan who had freed her from complete servitude—and resented her overbearing ways, as well.

But not for much longer, Kes thought, and felt a thrill of joy course through her.

She slid back a lucent panel in her wall and scooped up the purf from its nesting box on a shelf there. The geneered symbiont was a recent Name Day present from her girl, Morya. It thrummed a greeting, twining its feather-light body around the woman's wrist until it resembled a fluffy white bracelet. The purf felt radiantly warm; she stroked it absentmindedly as the creature adjusted to her. It wriggled a bit, muscular grasping of delicate snake-like skeleton beneath feathery hair, until it settled into a comfortable position. Its audible thrumming ceased.

"Is that better or worse, Frebo?" she asked her pet, stroking it again. The symbiont's color shifted, white infusing with green until it stabilized in that color range, shot through with gold, a streak of pink, and flecks of dark orange.

Kes contemplated the purf's display. Frebo was picking up the baseline energies of her aura, echoing them in its chameloid integument. The symbiont could stay that way—thinking it blended undetectably into the human's predominant energy field—or it could help alter the dissonant energies of its host, bringing that person's basal vibration into a more harmonious range. Not everyone knew what a purf's display meant, but Kes was careful not to wear Frebo around other people. She had learned to mask her true feelings and reactions. She would not be sharing visible clues to the storms of conflict that often raged within her.

They said the green reflected growth, and the gold showed insight or enlightenment. She'd grown and changed through trying times these last few years, and gained some wisdom out of it, that much was true. The orange flecks corresponded to the resentments that niggled when she let them, not uncommon after an encounter with Helda. Or before, for that matter.

Well, that wasn't surprising, either. There were many things about her circumstances that were beyond her ability to change or influence. It almost made her feel trapped—but, if so, at least now it was a trap of her own choosing.

Helda had freed her of debt-slavery when she'd acquired the domina's contract, but in some ways Kes was more constrained now than if she wore the distinctive neck tattoo of a chattel servant. This very month she had finally done what no slave was allowed to do: with her apprenticeship behind her, she'd been legally adopted into Palumara House, and sworn an honor oath pledging her loyalty to this shigasue clan. They were now her legal family, in place of the one she had lost. And when she paid off the balance of her debt contract—which she could do after her next payday, just two weeks away—she would still be part of Palumara House. She would always have a home right there, either at Tryst or somewhere else among the shigasue of the Enclave.

She felt butterflies again just thinking about it all, and Frebo's orange flecks shifted towards acid yellow. On the surface, the adoption represented what she had desired forever: to be acknowledged and embraced by a Sa'adani clan. It might not be one she was born into, but at least it made her more fully Sa'adani, like her long-vanished mother. She had not hesitated to say yes to the offer. It gave her what she'd sought her whole life: a place to belong, no questions asked.

Still, she had not been raised within the confining structure of a clan and extended family. She'd grown up with her own aspirations: to fly to the stars, to leave sweltering Lyndir far behind, perhaps to seek out her mother on some distant world. . . .

Dreams.

Palumara House would not let her leave Tryst to start some new career, not when she was of such value to them and they'd taken her into their bosom. Maybe she wouldn't mind being so tied to them. She loved her work, for now. And she loved Morya. At long last, she was getting to a place where she could bring her love to live with her, have the life she wanted. Make a home.

Yet she still had her dreams.

With Frebo snug around her wrist, Kes snagged her white lounging robe off the screen hook and wrapped its soft folds around her. Opening another wall panel, she sat at her deskcomp and, with murmured voice commands, began her morning routine.

Others might look at news first thing in the day, or check personal coms. Not Kes. She pulled up a chart of Lyndir's star system: six planets, one gas giant, an orange-yellow primary. Layer by layer she added data to the map until a full astrogation display was before her. Gold-blinking spots marked transport lane beacons; orange flashes traced imperial courier routes above the elliptic plane in space off-limits to civilian travel. Naval corridors in red; a yellow no-fly zone around the Lesotrope orbital research station. More data, from shipping lists to hazard reports, scrolled on side and bottom.

Kes took in the status of local space with a practiced glance. There was nothing unusual in-system today. She zoomed the image out to reveal all eight populated star systems of Lyndir subsector, hazard and astrogation reports scrolling to the right. A stellon encounter was reported on the main warp lane to Chorb, cleared by naval patrols last night; a gravity anomaly was developing in real-space near Selmun; there was the solar wind report for the asteroid races at Merion.

So if I were going to see the races, she thought, how would I get there from here, off-lanes?

She called up an astrogation utility, plotted the course with simulated point-of-view star readings, avoiding known hazards. Five Standard hours, the run would take.

It was a short hop, as her armchair astrogation went, but she wasn't in the mood for anything more complex this morning. She checked her work with the Net's astrogation AI, a service she paid to use. It was a moderate expense, but guaranteed her work was right. She had to check it somehow, since she had no specialized astrogation comp to run these self-set problems on.

As usual these days, her calculations were correct to five decimal places. She smiled to herself. She'd ace the certification test if she took it now.

And then what?

Her smile faded, and she cleared the board with a single command. On to finances.

Sometimes that was much more uplifting than the star charting that took her nowhere. The purf would eventually cajole her out of any lingering moodiness, but she found looking at her nest egg was also a quick way to lift her spirits.

*This way out,* her balance proclaimed. It was her ticket offworld, if she chose to use it that way—her chance for bigger opportunities.

The account had begun as a way to shorten her term of service to the Ice-chromers. Faced with ten years or more of low-paid debt slavery, Kes knew clever investments could change all that. She intended to buy back her contract when she had enough—but Helda's fast dealing had short-circuited that plan, helping and hurting her at once. Kes had come out of sex work at the Salon and into a shigasue apprenticeship contract that had to be worked through before her debt balance could be bought out.

Still and all . . . it was a better situation than she'd started out in. And her investments were doing well. She noted that options on Tion nanotech were up this morning, smiled, and issued a sell order.

It was one thing her father had ground into her: the rules of proper invest-ment. The way you built stability and kept yourself safe. Even though what he taught and what he did were two different things.

Yellow flecks on the symbiont shifted back to orange and red, and she blanked the financial display with a gesture. She would not let memories of a dead man ruin her mood. One day soon, this bankroll could be her ticket off Lyndir. Or maybe she'd go for that astrogation cert at last. Or, hells, maybe she'd stay with the Palumara until the work just wasn't fun anymore. The House loved her, the public loved her, and there was plenty of money to be made at Tryst still, if she wanted to work for it.

Very soon, she'd be free to make all those decisions for herself.

And as for Morya . . .

She felt a thrill again, and did a quick mental calculation. If she didn't get that cert or go offworld, she had enough to pay off her own contract, *and Morya's, too.* Kes could free her love from the grasp of the Icechromers at last, bring her here to live with her, and give them both the fresh start they deserved.

The pink streak on Frebo grew, along with nervous yellow. Her thoughts danced up to the edge of her grand plan, and skittered away again. She had the money now. In two weeks, she'd have the freedom. And still she hadn't said a word to her lover. Didn't want to jinx it. She wanted her girl with her, but would Morya agree to Kes's vision of their future together? The secret thought flitted through her mind again, and again she shied away.

Ask her to marry you . . .

It was too big, and once she said it, it would be too real. But the time was coming fast when she would have to spit it out. She couldn't bear to spend a day as a free woman and not know her love's answer. She had her life to re-claim, and her girl had to be a permanent part of it. She was pretty sure she knew what the answer would be—but she had to find some courage to ask that life-altering question in the first place.

Kes bounced to her feet, driven by a bloom of nervous energy, and peeled a bright pink and yellow Frebo off her wrist.

It was time to start her day.

# 5

KES REMEMBERED HER father, Hinano Bren, as a man with the chiseled good looks of a vidstar wrapped around the grasping heart of a Darvui-caste merchant. Vain, temperamental, and controlling, Bren was also clever enough to build a fortune on the appearances and illusions of beauty he held so dear.

He had modeled briefly in his youth—at first for Lena, his half-Sa'adani grandmother, at her Emporium in the Southbank artists' ward. Later he moved on to sensie-feelie productions that needed hot SeF-equipped body models for sense recording. Bren was not averse to trading on his looks, but he saw the fleeting spike in income it provided, credflow that would last only as long as bodysculpting and fad interests kept one in the public eye. He wanted something more enduring, something he could build that would keep him in style: not as a face, but as a man who owned the faces, and the fashions they wore.

That leaning did not surprise his grandmother Lena, herself known to have the blood of a merchant-caste family. Retail clothing sales made her a modest living, though Bren scorned her stock in trade. "Common imports," he criticized, "when it could be originals. My artist's eye is offended."

"Lyndir is not a hotbed of fashion," the old woman told him dryly.

"Not yet," he replied.

Upon her death he inherited the store he had begun to manage for her. Clothing outlet became boutique; boutique became design house; designs became fashionable exports. The Emporium was forgotten, and Hinano Limited became a small fashion house with trendsetting styles that swept the sector.

That was long before Kes's birth, of course. Bren was an established figure in the fashion world by time he met her mother at a reception for the commander of the sector's Imperial Navy task force. Rhea was a striking officer: tall, pale blond hair braided back, almond-shaped violet eyes speaking to rare Àstarethi bloodlines. He noticed her across the room and lost no time making her acquaintance.

"I don't go for uniforms," he used to say, "but for her I made an exception."

Kes became cynical about that when she grew older. Of course he would go for her: she was a weapons officer on the task-force flagship. When the admiral moved on, she'd be gone as well. That was the kind of dalliance Bren preferred— one that would be over when it was over, and not come back to haunt him.

How discomfited he must have been when the Sa'adani officer returned months later, unannounced—along with the infant she bore, who was more than unexpected. By his own account, Bren looked on mother and child speechlessly.

"There's no room for her on a ship of war," Rhea had told him. "You take her, or the crèche gets her."

Bren told his daughter he welcomed her with open arms. But Kes had seen him with other children and knew she was not hearing the whole story.

"Why did you take me?" she had probed when she was ten. "Why not leave me with the crèche?"

Was she looking for reassurances? If so, she had asked the wrong question, or perhaps the wrong man. A shadowed expression crossed her father's face. It was a look young Kesi could already recognize: it meant that what followed would be tailored, revised to fit Bren's version of history as it should have happened. Her heart sank before he uttered a word, but she tried to listen between the lines, to understand the truth behind it all.

"Your mother was concerned about your well-being," he said slowly. "She couldn't keep you on a warship. Her family wouldn't recognize you, she claimed. If a Sa'adani clan wouldn't take you in, you would have to go to a crèche. Or to your father. So she brought you to me."

"Did you know about me before?"

"No, she didn't tell me."

"Did you want me?" Kesi asked, with the blunt frankness of a child, and heard the hesitation before he replied.

"You're my daughter. How could I leave you to grow up in the commons?"

The Empire idealized the extended families and tightly ordered clan networks of the Sa'adani, tolerated the casteless contract families popular in the CAS Sector, and grudgingly provided for those who fell in between: the orphaned, abandoned, the unwanted who grew up in casteless communal environs. Such persons were destined for a dreary future in low-status jobs, unless they chose the escape offered by conscript service, or disappeared into the street gangs of the derevin underworld.

"That wasn't going to happen to *my* daughter," Bren declared flatly.

Kesi heard that well enough. No one would say that Hinano Bren had consigned close blood kin to the oblivion of the crèche commons. He had done it simply to rescue his self-esteem, not the daughter he had been ignorant of.

She didn't ask about it again.

ILANYA EVANIT GLARED at Commander Obray.

"I don't believe I heard that right."

Obray cleared his throat and repeated his unwelcome news. "Janus has left Lyndir on a private ship for an unknown destination."

Eva's eyes narrowed. "Are you sure he isn't fleeing us? He doesn't know we're watching him?"

Obray shook his head. "From his household com chatter, this was planned for some time. We just didn't know about it before. He must have been packing his bags at the same time you were ordering the cat ten surveillance."

Her thoughts raced. "When is he returning?"

"We're working on that, and continuing infiltration of his household. The usual procedures."

Ilanya gave a grudging nod. There was no point in returning to Calyx; the imperial homeworld was a two-month journey away, and she'd already been on Janus's trail for weeks. Killing him in his home base would send a multilayered message to the rest of the Red Hand cartel, one they would not dare ignore.

"I want his behavior profile updated as you get intel," she told Obray. "What's his pattern? His weaknesses? I want to know before he returns."

Obray was about to reply when a static burst from his desk console drew all heads that way. *"Hiya, Boss Man,"* came a synthesized voice from the speaker. *"Gotta newsflash for the Boss Lady."*

"FlashMan," Obray muttered in acknowledgment.

*"Pardon me for listening in,"* said the netrunner, *"but if you're trying to get a handle on our man, you might want to check out his local friends. I'm still uncovering his contacts. Man doesn't have much of a social life, so it's slow going. Work, backstabbing, work, extortion, more work. Very boring. I'll feed you what I get as I get it. But one thing I know right now: it seems he has a lady-love stashed away. Betcha she'll have some interesting answers to the right questions."*

Eva sat up. "Janus has a partner?"

*"I didn't say that. I said a lady-love. Unless a shigasa is his mistress? Who knows. I don't think he's keeping this one, though. Anyway, check out Tryst in the Enclave. Last thing he did before he caught a skimmer to the starport was order a big arrangement of crystal lilies to be sent there."*

"You've been busy," remarked Obray.

*"Let's just say I think to look in the right places. Petty cash accounts can reveal so much, doncha think? The card sent with the flowers said, 'I hope you enjoy these until my return. Your devoted servant, Janus.'"*

"How classically romantic," Ilanya said acerbically. "Who did he send that to?"

*"An entertainer named Hinano Kesada. You might know her from local verts as the Winter Goddess."*

"Verts for what?" Ilanya demanded.

"For a fantasy house in the licensed quarter," Obray explained. "High-end erotic encounters."

"Ah."

"*Well, that's my good deed for the day,*" said Flash. "*I'm off for more cash accounting. Seeya.*"

A static burst marked his disconnect. Ilanya regarded Obray with disapproval. "FlashMan's your civilian contractor? The one you say is your best netrunner?"

Obray nodded.

"Same one who cracked the Red Hand on Bekavra?"

"Yes."

"It seems like you leave him a very long leash. Am I to understand you let him eavesdrop on your office conversations through your desk systems?"

"I've given him permission to come and go through my interface as he needs to," Obray replied in a measured tone, "unless I have the system locked down in secure mode. He respects that."

She studied Obray for a moment, all short dark curls, square jaw, unflappable demeanor. Her lips thinned. "That may be, Commander, but I don't want him listening in on my briefings with you. He can know what I give you leave to tell him. All of our conversations will occur under security lockout. Do I make myself clear?"

Obray paused a moment before responding. "Yes, Domna Arcolo."

"Very well, then."

"If you like," he said, changing the subject, "we can issue a warrant and bring in the shigasa for questioning."

"No. I don't want her suspicions aroused with a detention order, or Janus tipped off that his activities have drawn undue interest."

"Do you want the cat ten extended to her, then?"

Ilanya drummed her fingers on the arm of her float chair. "Have you dealt with licensed quarters, Commander? Personally, or professionally?"

"Occasionally." He shrugged. "But not much."

"An Enclave can be incredibly touchy to work with. The fallout, should you cross the wrong persons . . ." She shook her head. "Their network of connections and favors owed is far greater than you would think. Every client who has ever had a favorite in a tea house, every patron who has kept a shigasa as mistress, every enterprise that hopes to gain face and influence by doing social business in a licensed quarter—they are all invested in protecting their interests in their favorite entertainment House."

"Yes." Obray was aware of those facts. "But that doesn't stop us from questioning whoever we must during an investigation."

Ilanya gave a snort of amusement. "That is a nice IntSec party line, Commander. But to question one shigasa is to risk offending her entire House. Do that, and the House's patrons—across many worlds!—will close ranks to shut you out in the most unlikely quarters. The Sector Governor's staff will somehow cease to be cooperative; reports will be lost in fail-safe retrieval systems;

persons you plan to arrest will mysteriously vanish when you go to find them. All because you have alienated an entertainment House that you thought inconsequential."

Obray considered the Arcolo's words. Perhaps that was why IntSec so rarely approached the licensed quarters as a matter of policy. It was notoriously difficult to secure their cooperation, and investigations in those districts rarely made significant headway. A self-fulfilling prophecy?

"So no, Commander, neither you nor local security will descend upon the Enclave to winkle out information."

"How, then, do you want us to handle this, Domna Arcolo? If we can't question Janus's woman, and you don't want us to approach the shigasue directly?"

A faraway look came into Ilanya Eva's eyes. "That is something I'm thinking about. Meanwhile, give Teo access to your Enclave data files. We'll talk more about this soon."

# 6

KES CHANGED FROM her white robe to loose indigo workout trousers and tunic. Then she left her room and walked the two flights of stairs to the roof of Tryst.

Outside of client areas, the shigasue built along simple, traditional lines; there was no lift shaft or bounce tube to speed her ascent. Speed was not of the essence, anyway, at this leisurely late-morning hour. After a short trek, she approached the top landing, where pithpaper window squares glowed with sun-bright luminescence. She rested her hand on the doorplate until she heard the latch click open with palm recognition.

Kes pushed the faie-wood frame open and stepped out into the roof garden complex. She stood there a moment, breathing in the fragrance of flowering lavender tersia vines trailing along the street-side balustrade. For a moment she was transported back to the penthouse garden of her youth, her childhood refuge and playground. This was far grander, though, than anything Hinano Bren had envisioned outside his doors.

Here were sprawling city blocks interconnected through an elevated urban wilderness: countless nooks and crannies hosting exotic plants and strange small creatures that kept the ecology in balance—an adult-sized playground and arboretum to enjoy and explore.

Tryst was located in the Shelieno, the river garden district, the oldest of the three licensed quarters of Port Oswin. Collectively they were called the Gantori-Das, the Enclave—an administrative designation for regulation and tax purposes. But each of the entertainers' wards was a discrete unit located within gated neighborhoods scattered throughout the interlocking domes of the city sprawl.

The Shelieno was located four lazy bends of the river upstream from the delta flats where Port Oswin's earliest structures rose. The sandbar-studded waters of the Dryx cut through the white chalk riverbanks of the garden district. The gentle slopes above were once covered with native growth that had expired when climate-controlled domes cooled and dehumidified the native Lyndir air. The Shelieno took its name from a type of imported groundcover planted there in rambling parklands. The district was a once-exclusive residential area that had given way to riverside entertainments and the encroachment of new housing as population swelled in the city.

During Lyndir's independent existence, the Shelieno had been an unlicensed freewheeling center of nighttime amusement. After annexation by the Empire 150 years ago, the area had become an official part of the Between-World of the shigasue, with ceremonial gates erected to mark the entrances, and non-shigasu business owners compelled to sell out or subcontract to the controlling Houses. But even under new management, the basic nature and appeal of the district remained the same. The Shelieno was still renowned for its gardens and parklands. It was a favorite place for tourists to visit during the day, and lovers to stroll in the evening on the river walk above the warm steaming waters of the Dryx.

The pleasure gardens were echoed above the city streets in the rooftop realm of the shigasue. The buildings of the licensed quarter abutted one against another, forming a terrain of neon façades and rooftop greenery in a vast network two or three stories above the ground. Arching walkways and overpasses linked roof arbors and flowerbeds, reflection ponds and rivulets, in a continuing maze that nearly spanned the length of the district. Even trees were supported, planted atop specially constructed earth-berm retaining walls, their hybrid root systems trained to grow inside the structures themselves.

If she wanted, Kes could walk the entire district via its rooftops, visiting other shigasue establishments through roof access and leaving again, without ever passing clients on the streets.

That was, in fact, one reason for the interconnectedness of the garden complex. Shigasu did not need to leave their closed world to walk, to exercise, to enjoy the outdoors—or as outdoors as one got in Port Oswin without a cool-suit. The entertainers did not risk losing their glamour by mingling too closely with ordinary folk on the public streets or parkways.

Kes had discovered the roof gardens on her second day at the Salon. She did not have free run of them, then; she was no shigasa, and as an indentured sex worker on Icechromer debt contract, there was a sharp limit to where she was permitted to wander. She had access to the orchid gardens atop the brothel, to the reflection ponds above the chai house next door, and to the grassy meditation square above the dance hall behind the Salon. Other gates and walkways were barred to her palmprint, as was the case for all the Icechromers' indentured staff.

Her move to Tryst had opened up the rooftop wildlands to her, a realm she delighted to lose herself in. This was so much larger than the place where she had spent her childhood leisure—and here there was no house AI to track her every move. It was a feeling of liberation she'd never had as a child.

She smiled to herself, and set off in the direction of the Salon.

IT WAS EARLY, yet, for the joyboys and -girls of the Salon to be up and out of bed. Morya roused herself with difficulty. She'd much rather sleep until mid-afternoon, as the others would—but this was the day of her weekly rendezvous with Kes.

It seemed best to keep their meetings to once a week, at a time when she could easily avoid watchful eyes. The Salon stayed active until the last clients were seen out the doors at the crack of dawn; only then did the house staff seek their own beds. The housemother, Dosan Kiyo, was asleep now, so this was the best time to head off to the dance hall garden. Not that the excursion would be forbidden, but Morya would just as soon not invite questions about her regular visits to the meditation square.

She yawned, brushed long black curls out of her face, tugged on workout clothes, and fumbled with the drawstring of the baggy indigo trousers before the fit was snug enough. Into sandals, out the door, as if she had every right to go practice laufre exercises so early in the brothel day.

She shook her head to herself. Of course, she *did* have every right. Icechromers owned her body-service, but she wasn't a slave, and she still had a right to spend her free time how she wanted, within certain limits. Davin guarded the front door and palmlocks and gate sensors secured the rooftop egresses, so she wouldn't be leaving the premises without permission. Reassured by that knowledge, Icechromers and their managing Dosan let the joy-girls and -boys have free run of the House and its immediate environs.

Sometimes she encountered one or two others from the House doing laufre in the garden as well: the androgynous hermaphrodite Liesa, or nervous Varl, who seemed more collected after he'd worked energy for an hour. This sort of coming and going was routine.

Morya had to remind herself of that when she saw Franc's blocky form sitting on a stool at the foot of the stairs in a half doze. He was a lieutenant of Gistano's, the Icechromer boss, and ran part of their debt-service business. Yet, like all street-ready 'Chromers, he occasionally did stints of house duty. He must have been puttering about all morning. A cup of kaf sat cold on the table beside him. He looked like he'd plunked down to rest for a moment and fallen into a doze right there.

Morya's footsteps slowed. To get to the roof she had to walk right by him, and Franc was the worst of the derevin crew. He'd hand-picked half the joy-house workers, angling to get their debt-contracts picked up by the House. It left him with a peculiar sense of entitlement in his dealings with staff.

She braced herself and strode ahead, eyes on the stairs, ignoring the dozing Icechromer.

His beefy hand shot out and gripped her arm as her foot touched the first step.

"Up awful early, aren't ya, pretty thing?"

*Pretty thing.* Ugh. Franc knew her name; he'd bought her contract, when this had all started. His speech was affectation, and he sounded like all the other 'Chromers. A real name for a sex worker would be too personal, now wouldn't it?

She turned her head, her blue eyes catching his appraising look squarely. "Good morning, Franc." She let her gaze move purposefully down his arm, to his pale hand on her naturally tan skin, then back up to his face. She raised one eyebrow. His hand did not loosen its grip.

Well. That tactic used to work for Kes. It had been worth a try.

"What?" she demanded.

His eyes remained half-lidded beneath heavy dark brows. "I got in too late for any fun last night. Glad to see you're up and about."

Morya got his meaning instantly. "What can I do for you this morning?" she asked, at once the compliant joygirl.

It was a well-practiced role, easy enough to slip into, for free service to derevin members was in her indenturement contract as barter for room and board. She was obligated to sexual service; they, to material support. If Icechromers defaulted or abused her, her contract was void and her debt considered paid.

She fantasized briefly about telling him to go fuck himself, but that would trigger the thorny part of that contract: if she refused service, she made herself liable for sentencing as a slave. Imperial justice was very clear about little details like that: you worked off a defaulted debt with a service contract, or as a debt-slave. At least with her contract she had security. Slaves could end up anywhere, doing anything. Both paths offered reparation in the government's eyes, but it made a big difference to the person serving the debt sentence.

So it was not unhappily that she followed Franc's smiling gesture and knelt before him. The first thing most newly contracted joyboys and -girls experienced in the Salon was sexual training directed by Dosan Kiyo. Morya had been surprised to learn that one could be eroticized to literally anything. She had come to find many aspects of her compulsory work palatable, and some downright enjoyable.

She was irritated by the delay Franc caused her plans, but not at the activity he asked her to do. Not at all.

When she was done, she asked permission to go.

"Yeah. Leave," he told her. He looked more ready for bed than ever, but didn't miss the chance to pat her on the ass as she walked by.

Three years, two months, five days left on her contract. If someone touched her uninvited after that, she'd break fingers. Until then . . .

It was easy to forget about debt-work in the meditation garden. It was a small grassy square half-hidden behind a border of red-flowering stavis and spiky green-white leander fronds. A broad-canopied faie tree stood on the eastern side of the square; beneath its shade stood a shoulder-high jumble of butter-yellow brae stone, native to Lyndir. Water pooled in an artificial basin atop the rock, cascading in a burbling watercourse to the catchpond below. Brae stone spread out from that pond, trailing in a way that seemed natural and eventually became artifice, as flagstones were placed to ring the entire grassy court.

It was not until she stepped past the leander fronds that she saw Kes was already there. Her long white hair was tied back and she was sitting in the center of the lawn beginning the first series of laufre warm-up stretches. They had the square to themselves at this moment, though that was sure not to last for long. Morya took advantage of the temporary solitude and trotted over to the domina, plunked down on the bluegrass beside her. She sat with her trousered leg pressing against Kes's in a pose imitative of her stretch.

"Need some help?" She grinned and pressed closer. "Need some room?"

Kes gave a low growl; she twisted sideways, put a hand to Morya's throat and pressed her backwards until she overbalanced and fell back laughing into the grass. They kissed and lay there for a moment, Kes's long leg thrown over her, pinning her to the ground.

"You're sassy this morning," Kes said, leaning on one elbow.

"Yeah." Morya studied the violet eyes in the fine-lined face above her. "I can't help it. I miss you."

Kes's brow furrowed. "I miss you too, kushla." Her face dropped closer; they kissed again. "But you know I can't visit."

Morya gave a nod. She could not leave to visit Kes, and Kes was not welcome to return to the Salon. She'd been a disruptive influence, Dosan Kiyo had declared, and the housemother had been glad to be rid of her in a trade she claimed was beneficial to all concerned. Kes had been loved or hated by clients—telling them what to do, and how to do it. The contract trade had certainly benefited the striking woman, who was far better suited to being a domina at Tryst than a sex worker at the Salon. And if she was not allowed to return—well, it spared the Winter Goddess from being recognized as a former derevin joygirl. That could tarnish her mystique.

That it also cut her off from Morya, her devoted sometime-lover, was something no one seemed to consider. It didn't seem to bother Kes much, anyway. Or maybe she just didn't let on.

Morya wriggled away from her grasp. Don't go there, she thought. That's a mood that will bring you down all day.

"Hey. Let's start, all right?" she prompted. "While it's quiet here."

It was always quiet in the meditation square, but Kes seemed to catch the undercurrent. Kes gave Morya an odd look that she could not decipher, seemed on the verge of saying something—and then did not. Instead, Kes simply nodded assent.

Morya suppressed a sigh. They were so close, and yet so far. The domina had offered more than once to stop these weekly visits. "If it's too painful—"

"No," the joygirl had insisted. "I would rather see you sometimes, know you're all right, than never see you at all. That wouldn't solve the problem."

They had found no other solution to their dilemma, though.

Morya went through the motions of laufre, grounding, centering, running chi energy through her chakras in time with the ancient movements of the discipline. Her form mirrored Kes's, the two pacing in slow harmony through the ritualized gestures of the exercise.

That's how I want my life to be with hers, she thought. In harmony. Together.

Was it merely their circumstances that kept them apart? Couldn't Tryst's star shigasa exercise a little influence, see her more often, or more privately, if she wanted? Always they met in public, around other people. Never close, since Kes had been banned from the Salon. Never close enough to do more than tease, or flirt. They didn't share a life, or intimacy anymore. Only moments. Fleeting moments.

I won't push her, Morya thought. Juro take it: I *can't* push her, even if I want to. Because of how she is. Because of our situations. Everything. Dammit.

She faltered in her motions, losing that quiet place of calm that usually came over her. She lost the rhythm with Kes, then caught it again.

Just be here now, she thought.

Small comfort, but it was the best way she'd found to cope. With her indenturement; with the absence of the woman who had won her heart. Her protector when she was new to the Salon; her seducer; her dominant lover. Now maybe only her friend, though she felt like so much more.

By time they finished the exercise, there were three other people in the square, one pacing the flagstones on the meditation path, the others warming up for laufre. As usual, Kes did not kiss her before the eyes of others. They parted ways with a hug, and a long touch of hands. Again that odd hesitation, and a lingering look from Kes. Then Morya watched her go through the north gate that remained off-limits to her, back to Tryst. Back to people who shared her company on a daily basis, as Morya once had.

When she could no longer see long white hair, she turned her back on the gate.

So much for keeping that mood away, she thought glumly, and turned her steps reluctantly homeward.

# 7

DR. METMURI PAUSED inside the door of the neuralforming lab in Section Four.

Ugoli was an unexpected presence at Med 2, idly watching what data feeds were visible to those not jacked into the AI. Beyond him the med bay beds glowed in their soft blue aseptic fields, recumbent forms of the Biancar multiples visible atop them. The doctor was eager to deal with the clones, but the adjutant stood, literally, between him and his work.

"Simikan? What can I do for you?" Esimir asked. Ugoli's rank meant "raid leader," a designation that suited his martial bearing and air of disdain for the scientists he helped manage. Esimir tolerated him because he was the eyes and ears of the station commander, not because his presence invited cooperation.

The simikan moved to the control island and stood by the interface station, casually blocking Esimir's access to the command chair. Ugoli was a short-necked, red-haired, ruddy-faced man, trim in navy blacks, standing straddle-legged in a way that felt confrontational. The bioempath reached out with a tendril of psychic touch, just enough to taste the mix of emotions in the officer. Defensive arrogance, unease, a hint of self-doubt . . . He nodded to himself. Ugoli was new, and surrounded by brilliant scientists engaged in projects he barely comprehended. Esimir had a mental image, suddenly, of the man working doggedly to master warp drive physics in the Imperial Naval Academy, resenting his brighter classmates to whom such discipline came easily. He craved action, not the mental exercise that made him feel less worthy than others.

The doctor rubbed the blue-and-green rus on his forehead as the imaginary moment faded. No telling if that was a true vision of Ugoli's past or merely a fanciful one. In his experience it was just as likely to be either, but it gave him an empathic connection with the simikan nonetheless. The adjutant was the kind of man who was distrustful of what he did not understand, and in the realm of applied research, there was a great deal that he did not understand.

Esimir made a sudden decision. It would be better to have Ugoli as an ally, to help him grasp what must appear arcane. Build up a little rapport, even. In recent months there had been a certain lack of administrative sympathy for the Splintegrate project, and Esimir was increasingly frustrated by admin's unreasonable demands. But if he could get Ugoli on his side, the man could advocate for the Splintegrate project. A little time invested here could be well worthwhile.

The doctor relaxed and saw Ugoli glower. The officer was not used to civilians

standing down when his posture was intended to put them on guard. Esimir
smiled to himself. It was time to change the rules of engagement.

"So, Simikan," he repeated, "how can I help you?"

The officer cleared his throat. "You've put in a request for field testing," he
said, his tone accusatory.

"I have," Esimir replied complacently. "We're finally ready to test our splintegration results in the real world." He sidestepped the adjutant, put a hand on
the back of his command chair.

"You're claiming there's no more you can accomplish under laboratory conditions," Ugoli grumbled. He jerked a thumb over his shoulder at the multiples
in the med bay. "But it's apparent you're not done with all your lab work yet."

Esimir took his place before the control console. "That's a different phase
of the work." He nodded towards the slumbering clones. "We can imprint the
personality aspects we desire into our subjects. Beyond that—what can they
do here? We can't give them an ordinary life in a laboratory." He shrugged.
"Certainly nothing that will let us judge how a personality fragment will operate in society. That is our essential next step: to assess a tailored persona in the
real world."

Ugoli's brow creased. "You've reported that the splintering procedure is
successful. Is it, or isn't it?"

"To answer that, Simikan, I need to talk a bit about clone imprinting. And
while I do that I need to power up these console systems. Would you mind having a seat here while I do? You're blocking my access panel on the interface
board."

Ugoli blinked, stepped away from the console he stood by.

"Please." Esimir gestured to a chair. "Join me while I run through the systems checks." There; that was better, to have the adjutant seated in a compan-
ionable way nearby, rather than looming in a confrontational stance. The doctor
began systems prep, bringing data traces online from the interface board. The
AI could have handled it, but the manual routine gave him something to do,
let him draw Ugoli into his work in a nonthreatening way.

"I worked in the imperial clone labs on Corvus for several years," he remarked, bringing the medical data feed alive on the board. "You know the
difference between body clones and vivified clones, yes?"

"Of course," the officer replied testily. "Organ replacement versus live human
being. Different legal categories entirely."

Esimir nodded. "The ones destined to come alive are created only in strictly
controlled conditions under imperial license. Not a simple process. Expensive."

"Not too expensive to stop them from being used as soldiers," Ugoli grunted.
"There are clones in the Imperial Marines. I've served with some on board ship.
Don't a lot of them come from Corvus, where you were?"

"Indeed." Esimir stifled his usual lecture on the economics of custom-bred warriors versus natural-growth recruits. "The Emperor favors certain warrior types as shock troops. That is the kind of work I did."

"Oh?" Interest tinged the officer's voice.

"Yes. I was involved with the full spectrum of clone growth. A viv cloning has six stages of processing. We're in the fifth right now." He gestured to the med bay floor. "Did you know it takes five weeks to grow a body to adolescence? Though the clones don't grow a brain in that time, or not what we think of as one."

"They have gray matter, don't they?"

"Oh yes, but barely any neural pathways, you see. The brain is not formed by childhood experiences or emotions, so there are no engrams." He caught Ugoli's blank look. "Memory traces," he amended. "Without them, no personality evolves. If we left the body like that, we'd have only an organ-bank-grade clone."

"That's not what you're creating here."

"True. To create a clone with a personality, we need to reproduce the neural pathways of the original. A cortical array can do a brain scan, record neural activity, play it back later. That gives us a blueprint, but the map is not the terrain. To create that terrain, we add NNs to the mix. Nanoneurals."

"I've heard of those."

Esimir nodded. Popular science on the news these days talked about NNs used to repair brain damage, an increasingly common healing technique. "Nanites are injected into a developed brain; they wed with neural chemicals, track the flow and behavior of this chemistry at the molecular level. Once they've mapped the original, we extract them and inject them into the clone. There, they duplicate the patterns they have just learned. They remap the brain so that it mirrors the original. We call that neuralforming. Like terraforming, in the gray matter itself."

"Ah."

Esimir could read nothing from the simikan's expression. He extended a tendril of empathic touch and felt the officer's queasy fascination with the concept. "That's phase four of cloning: neuralforming replicates the original's cognitive functions and motor control."

He gestured to the Biancar clones in the med bay. "For the Splintegrate project, we do this with LNNs—limited nanoneurals. They're smartchems that don't remap the brain massively. They leave it in a half-finished state—still open to new mapping, as it were. At the end of this stage, the clone is not yet highly neuroactive."

He sensed Ugoli's confusion. "It's like shaping a mass of clay," he added, "but not detailing the sculpture." Esimir pointed to a brain trace on the board. "The biostate is like that of a person in a coma."

"I see." Ugoli looked at the display he doubtless could not interpret.

"Today we start stage five of the process: neural maturation." Esimir engaged AI systems, calibrating smartchems that would soon flood the craniums of his subjects. "We let LNNs create neural pathways in memory recall areas. This makes a brain landscape that can support the cortical and synaptic data we'll activate later."

"The playback phase." Ugoli perked up. This he knew about.

"Er—yes." Esimir smiled condescendingly at the slang term. "Precisely."

Ugoli nodded to himself, satisfied.

"Here is how splintegration differs from traditional cloning: There is one vast difference with our neural maturation."

"And that is?"

"The LNNs we use are sorted and controlled by Prevak, the project AI. Prevak separates out the personality pattern we want to duplicate in the clone. Undesired behavioral pathways are just not copied at all."

Ugoli looked confused.

"See, limited nanoneurals map only what we want them to. This is how we splinter a personality—we reproduce just a select part of it. Then we create clones with only the aspects we desire to see."

Comprehension dawned. "Ahhhh. . . . This LNN step is what your report was referring to when it said the project was a success?"

"LNN mapping is one part. The other is the 'playback' you referred to. Prevak isolates the personality fragment we want out of the original engram set and cortical map. Our AI is the intelligent designer; a filtered cortical dump is the motive force; the LNNs are the scribing medium during imprinting, and the brain is the already-prepared canvas ready to receive the work."

Ugoli studied Biancar$_1$ in the closest med bed. "So you are duplicating brains, but only partial brains. Or is that partial personas?"

"That is one way to say it. The brain is whole and functional, of course. We're introducing limited aspects of the whole into the clone. Then there is the final step, the awakening, that is like calling someone back from a coma to reinhabit the body. The ensoulment, if you will."

"And you and Terel do that?"

"Dr. Avenoy has only a modest capacity to sense life," Esimir said tartly, "not the skills to call a specific soul fragment. That is my task, since we wish the clones to be as much like their original as possible. That is what I did on Corvus, as well. The birthing."

Esimir looked away from his console and caught Ugoli staring at him. Unease showed on his face. The abilities of a bioempath to affect the life-force of an entity were the stuff of mystery and folktales. Seeing Esimir on a daily basis had demystified the doctor, made him seem a mundane aspect of the Naval Weapons Research Station until something like this came up.

He watched the officer's assessment of him shift in that moment. Ensoulment.

Coma revival. Nice tricks, if you could do them, and Esimir could do them very well. It was why Prevak had requested him for the Splintegrate project five years ago.

He smiled at the adjutant, a polite expression that did not touch his eyes.

"You were asking, Simikan, if we have been successful with splintegration, or not. This is our last test batch, the final run we need to validate our results. We've had no aborts for six series now. Fine-tuning, yes; significant problems and mis-maps, no. In that regard, splintegration is successful."

"No more psychotic breaks? I heard about the biotech who was killed by one of your clones last year."

Esimir shrugged. "That was the result of incorrect aspect filtering before the imprint process. It was not a problem with the process itself. We've corrected for that. As I said: six series, trouble-free."

Ugoli shook his head. "This work is impressive, Doctor, but I'm still not clear what you want. Do you mean you want to release the Biancars when you're done with the awakening?"

Esimir shook his head quickly. "Not at all. In laboratory conditions, Biancar$_2$ and Biancar$_3$ interact sociably enough—"

"Of course they do. Biancar$_1$ contains the predator aspects of the original personality."

The doctor frowned at the interruption. "Yes, and that is not a persona I would release into the world, ever. But we can't tell how completely we've filtered these aspects until we observe their real-world behaviors, correlate them against the mapping schema. If we're mistaken, we could be putting clones on the streets that would perpetrate crimes again."

"Is that likely? With these nanoneurals you use?"

"We filter as strictly as we can, given this stage of project development. But this *is* development, and I cannot guarantee the results. Hence my need for a field test."

Ugoli regarded the doctor soberly. "You refuse to use convicts for this test, but convicts are really all we can supply you with."

Esimir pulled a rigger lead out of the headrest of the command chair and paused with it in his hand. "Our dilemma is this: we need to splinter someone who is not a criminal—or not so criminally inclined that they've acted on the impulse. We need a clean control subject to validate our personality redesign."

He inserted the lead into the base of his skull, leaving systems idling, and regarded the adjutant. "*Can* a splintered clone function as an independent unit at all? It is our belief that they can, but we need to test that with a non-pathological subject. If that works, then we are very near success."

Ugoli tilted his head. "And what does success look like to you, Doctor?"

"Like it always has, Simikan. When we can strip unwanted personality aspects from a person, combine the remaining threads into a new whole, and have that individual function well in the world, then this will be a proven technology for eliminating pathological behaviors."

The officer sat expressionless for a moment before a faint look of amusement came over his face. "A commendable goal, I'm sure. Station Commander Olniko will be glad to hear the Splintegrate project is nearing completion."

Esimir shook his head sharply. "We're not that near. This project has been underway for five years. This is only the splintering process you see here; we haven't perfected the integration phase yet. That's the bit where we recombine desired aspects back into a single body."

"Meaning, you integrate your clones back together into one person?" Ugoli clarified.

"That's the goal."

"Why do you even need to do that? Surely your AI can pick and choose the aspects you want, and put them into just one clone the first time out, yes? Since it manages to parse out the personality threads in the first place, it seems a waste of time to strip clone minds to combine them back into one person."

Esimir bit back a retort, and reminded himself that he was dealing with a layman. "Of course it would be ideal to have all of this handled by the AI. It would be best if we were only imprinting one perfectly tailored personality into one clone. But we're years away from that yet, Simikan. The AI is still learning how to manipulate personality engrams. This is easier done with an external vehicle—multiple clones—until we figure out all the challenges involved. But we are much closer than ever before. You can tell the commander that from me."

"I will certainly do so, Doctor." The adjutant stood abruptly. "And I will recommend your request for field studies be approved." He gave an uncharacteristic smile, nodded sharply, then left the lab.

Esimir watched his retreating back. Ugoli positively radiated smugness, and the doctor had no idea why. But there were more pressing matters at hand. He shrugged it off and returned to the splintegration process before him.

# 8

SO MUCH FOR the big bad domina. Hinano Kesada, you are a coward.

Kes berated herself all the way back from the garden. She was never short on words when they needed to be said, but looking at Morya, knowing she couldn't give her refuge yet . . . The words had died on her lips. She couldn't ask her anything, much less declare her love for her.

And what if her girl's feelings had changed since they'd been together? It had been so long.

She knew this line of thought would drive her crazy if she stayed with it. By the time she walked into her room she was ready for any distraction, and two greeted her eyes in short order.

The first thing she saw was an arrangement of crystal lilies in the center of the lacquered black table. Transparent stems, delicate petals like sheets of sculpted mica refracted the light, all frozen in a wild array that glittered and trembled gently with the movement of air in the room. As she approached them, her eye was drawn from alien flowers to the naked figure of a woman in the chamber beyond. It was Desta, her assigned house slave, who was tidying up the sleep area, stowing Kes's bedding for the day.

House slaves were a common enough domestic occurrence, not only in the Between-World of the shigasue, but in the households of the aristocracy and the well-to-do and many other places throughout the Empire. Desta's nakedness while serving was a different matter. That was not a common state for slaves—most tasks required some degree of clothing for warmth, if nothing else—but in the body-casual and sexually charged atmosphere of erotic houses, nakedness was often the order of the day, as it was at Tryst.

Though Desta was a woman grown, like all sentient property, she was referred to in the diminutive. The girl's willowy figure was lithe, and Kes let her eye be drawn by her seductive grace.

Her motions were economical, the curves of her body and neck accentuated by the black scrolling lines of the property mark tattooed around her neck. Her upswept hair showed off slender sprays up each side of her neck nearly to her ears. The symbolic collar was a traditional symbol of slave status, the design unique to the owning house. Some slaves were oblivious to their markings, or resentful of them; some, shamed by them. Yet others wore the mark like a piece of fine jewelry. Desta was one such, a born slave whose parents were also House

Palumara property. The marks were not only part of her person; they were part of her identity, one she seemed quite comfortable in.

Not for the first time, Kes wondered what transpired in the mind of a slave, how she embraced her place in the household and the clan she was attached to. Kes had tried to find that mindset with the Icechromers for all of ten seconds, and succeeded at it not even half that long.

Desta felt Kes's gaze upon her and glanced up to see if her owner needed her attention.

Kes gave her a half smile. She liked to watch her girl work; she had the poise of a dancer and that hint of innocence that appealed to the predator in Kes. But for all the distraction Desta offered, the slave's presence was expected here, picking up the room at noon—what counted for early morning in a shigasue household. Not so, the flowers. They were the real curiosity of the moment, and Kes's eye traveled back to them.

The domina reached beneath blossoms that looked like spun sugar to remove the note affixed to the vase. She read it quickly, smiling to herself. Janus. She had remarked once that she liked unusual flowers. Since then, her favorite client had sent her something monthly, something alien and expensive and lasting. Never the same thing twice. And this, a remembrance until he returned. Good. It was good to know he was coming back. You never knew with clients; they could be so transient. But not Janus.

She dropped the card on the tabletop and turned to Desta, who was just sliding the pithpaper door shut on the last folded blanket. "Is my bath ready?" she asked, already disrobing, dropping indigo tunic, trousers, and sandals in a heap for the slave to deal with later.

"Yes, Domna, it is." She plucked a robe from the screen, held it open for her mistress to slip into. Without further conversation, Kes went to the door and left the room, conscious of the girl following behind. She turned left in the hall, went two doors down to the semi-private bath she shared with two other shigasu. A gust of warm steamy air welcomed her as she stepped inside.

The floor was water-resistant red talus wood, the tub black brae stone, large enough for three. A sheen of bath oils glistened atop the water, and the relaxing, energizing scent of bayim herb filled the air. Without looking behind her, Kes shrugged the robe off her shoulders and felt the slave's waiting hands take the garment before it could hit the floor. She stepped into the tub, the water just this side of too hot, and breathed out a sigh as she sat and stretched her long legs out completely. Her hair trailed in the water as she entirely submerged. When she surfaced, Desta was kneeling by the tub, soaps and shampoo and brushes to hand, ready to tend to Kes's needs.

There was an ordinary fresher in her own room that served for toiletry and quick showers, but Kes had fallen into this weekly ritual bath after seeing Morya. A time of relaxation and pampering, and the welcome distraction of the slave if the sexual tension was too much to tolerate. That was the problem with seeing her girl weekly, but not seeing her, really. The lust. The desire to take her, right there on the grass of the meditation square. The need—sometimes urgent need—to hurt her, hear her cry out in pain and pleasure and see her beauty transform into something exquisite with the intensity of sensation shared between them. Knowing that Morya craved her touch, that they both wanted more.

And why not? she asked herself as Desta's sure hands rubbed soap into her hair. We were so good together, while I was there at the Salon. And we will be again. If I can only find the right way to tell her. . . .

Kes frowned. The slave came around the side of the tub, pulling the rinse line out of the wall to cleanse the soap from Kes's hair. She reached out idly as Desta leaned over her, grasped Desta's nipple between her long nails, and pinched, hard. The slave gasped, but knew better than to interrupt what she was doing. She ran water and pulled a hand through Kes's hair while the domina tightened her pincer grip even further. The girl moaned but continued her work, her body squirming sensuously with the effort to stay still, to keep herself available to her owner's touch.

Desta finished the rinse. Kes smiled to herself and released her grip. It was a sure thing the slave was aroused. If Kes was going to languish with the slow burn of lust, by the gods she would not be doing it alone. When the girl reached for a sea sponge, Kes grabbed her wrist and drew her closer. "Come in," she said, pulling the slave into the tub with her.

Desta did as she was bid, the surprise on her face giving her a charming expression. She had rarely been in the tub with her owner before, but she knew what was coming.

Kes stretched out her arms to either side of the brae-stone basin, leaned against the cushioned backrest, spread her legs so they were straddling the slave's thighs. "Do me," she commanded. Water would complicate things, but make them that much more sensual as well. Slick skin against slick skin, the probing touch of fingers and hands . . . why languish, after all, when there was a slave to do your bidding? Desta knew how to serve her mistress well.

The slave's hands slid up Kes's thighs, her lips caressed Kes's breast just beneath the surface of the water. The domina closed her eyes and lost herself in the sensations of heat and flesh and the rising flush of orgasm.

The image of Morya pleasing her did not intrude until the very end.

# 9

KESI TOOK ALLIE'S hand and dragged her, giggling, under the concealing overhang of powder fronds. Ducking beneath feathery leaves, squeezing between sapling trunks of curling brown minum bark, the girls wriggled into the heart of Kesi's favorite garden hideaway. Thick yellow-leafed casca shrubs opened around them in a natural clearing, small and secretive in the heart of the rooftop grove. Questing root tendrils broke the surface here and there before burrowing again beneath the browning leaves that matted the loam. A cluster of casca trunks grew intertwined to one side, their root runners forming a hollow with a natural seat. There Kesi sat, then motioned Allie to kneel before her. Prisoners always knelt to the Queen; it was one of the rules of the game.

In other rooted nooks and crannies were some of Kesi's favorite things that she liked to keep here: a blanket for when the ground was damp; fruit rolls from the kitchen—scout trooper trail provisions, like Commander Kolo on the Simnet ate when he was stranded in the Alloy Desert, chased by Boru tribesmen and forced to trek across the wasteland to the nearest imperial outpost. There was water to drink—only water, for Bren refused to stock Nutriquell, the drink of champions, and adventurers risking their lives on alien worlds would not be caught dead drinking lacto or fizzies. Beneath the root knot that edged the seat was a scrap of waterproof camotarp, acquired through a complex series of trades with her classmates on the Net, containing the most precious items of her stash. She pulled the tarp out now and spread it on her lap to reveal the hidden things it contained.

She unfolded it slowly, watching Allie's face as she unveiled the treasure she had hinted at for days. A final fold of cloth turned back to reveal a vibroknife and two bundled lengths of prickly hachach rope.

Allie had brought the rope herself, weeks ago; it was the same as the uncomfortable restraint used on prisoners in the Commander Kolo series. The knife, though—that was new. Kesi touched the ivory hilt of the weapon, raised it into the sunlight, where the reinforced monofilament blade appeared like a fine wisp extending from the hilt.

Allie's eyes widened. "That's what Commander Kolo fought the bolgers with in the Merith swamps last season."

"Yeah." Kesi turned her wrist; the wire blade vanished from sight, too fine to see when it was not at the right angle in light.

"Does your father know?" Allie whispered, thrilled and nervous at once.

"Shh." Kesi hushed her friend, glancing reflexively to the side of the clearing where the lavender tersia bloomed. There was the AI spike, its data pickup obscured with leaf mold and sweet sticky sap from the tersia blossoms. It could almost have happened naturally. The gardener bot cleaned the data pickup weekly, as it was one of the many eyes and ears of Lena, the house AI, throughout the penthouse and rooftop grounds. And weekly, Kesi cluttered it up again.

There were certain fun and games they played in the heart of her secret preserve that she might not get in trouble for, but she did not want to test Bren's tolerance or the limits of Lena's discernment programming, either. Sometimes the AI sounded too much like the grandmother it was named after. But Kesi and her friend were unmonitored for now, and safe. She relaxed and turned back to her friend. "Of course he doesn't know. He wouldn't let me keep it."

"Where'd you get it, then?"

"I have ways," Kesi said mysteriously. She thought of the series of trades she had orchestrated to free this from Lonzo's uncle's workshop junk drawer. A devious smile spread slowly over her face. Allie didn't know that the knife did not work. The hilt mechanism that would vibrate the monofilament thousands of times a second, slicing effortlessly through almost anything, was broken. Still, it was enough that they both knew what this slender deadly wisp of a wire could do. . . .

Kesi held the blade in the sunlight again. Allie stared at it, fascinated. "Today," Kesi announced somberly, "we're going to do the rope game. We'll play Camisq and Spacer. I'll tie you up just like before. But this time, the camisq are not going to torture the spacer with tersia thorns. This time they'll use their real vivisection tools." She twisted the blade in the sunlight and Allie's eyes widened.

Her friend got very quiet, so quiet Kesi heard her swallow past the tightness in her throat. Slowly, Allie nodded, eyes never leaving the inert blade. This, at last, was the game they had both wanted to play, that they had constructed in bits and pieces as time and imagination allowed. The camisq, fearsome alien vivisectionists, had preyed upon spacers until the Empire had put an end to their torturous habits—based on history, and repeated monthly in the *Best of Commander Kolo* outtakes on the Net.

Here in the Queen's Lair, though, no Imperial Marine would arrive and rescue Allie the Spacer from the attentions of her chitinous captor. Not that the spacer needed rescuing: she had been the one to bring the rope, and showed Kesi the two hunters' knots she'd learned to tie. Early on in their games Kesi had wanted to be the spacer, until she realized that the aliens got to do much more interesting things. Once or twice they had switched roles, but Allie had tied her up too tightly, and hurt her with a thorn scratch. It was very irritating, and they had never switched again.

Besides, Kesi really enjoyed tormenting her friend. And Allie liked it, too.

"Where do you want to tie me up this time?" Allie asked eagerly.

"Lay down in the middle," Kesi gestured. "I'll tie your arms and legs to roots."

Her friend complied. Hachach rope stretched from wrists to root runners, from ankles to casca trunks. Kesi stood back and regarded her handiwork: prisoner, secure. Allie had that look about her of resistance and anticipation that meant Kesi could do whatever she wanted to her captive. Oh, she would struggle some, no doubt—but when the torture started, Allie would lie still for it and moan like a wounded spacer in the most appealing way.

"You are mine, human vermin," Kesi declared, quoting a camisq character she'd seen on the Net. "Today we shall see what it takes to make you cry."

"I'll never cry!" retorted the prisoner.

Her captor smiled wickedly, and brandished the vibroknife in the air. "We shall see!"

She knelt beside her friend and leaned in closely, holding the barely visible whisker of a blade before Allie's face so she could see what was about to hurt her. It was play, of course; Kesi would never hurt her friend in ways she didn't want to be hurt. The bruises from buddy-punches, scratches from their wrestling, and the thorn-torture of the vivisectionist aliens—all of that was well within bounds. But Allie still did not know that the knife did not work. For all she knew, this was a weapon that could sever her arm from her body in the best camisq fashion. Uncertainty flickered in her eyes as she considered the danger, and how far she could trust her friend.

Kesi felt that flicker like a rush of power. Her best friend, helpless before her because she trusted her that far, and now . . . wondering if she should trust Kesi at all. Fear and power and trust, a stew Kesi savored but had no words for. She felt it in her body like a physical urge.

She leaned over and kissed her captive full on the lips.

Allie, startled, hesitated a moment. The camisq had never kissed the spacer before. Then she responded in kind.

A moment later, Kesi pulled back. The girls stared at each other, tension and indescribable feelings thick between them like a static bond. Kesi took a deep breath. She did not break the spell with words, but turned her focus to Allie's arm, her hand and blade poised to begin cutting.

This was the heart of the game. It had started with Allie's desire to be tied up and scratched with thorns, captive in the grip of controlling tormentors. But now, the torment was real.

This blade would really cut.

Kesi had learned that the hard way when she tested the monofilament on her finger. The slice was so fine that she'd felt no pain, but she saw blood well up along the narrow slash the inert blade had opened. It was then that she realized that this was just as good as a vibroknife that vibrated. Better, even:

there was no risk of doing very serious damage, not if she was careful with it. Even playing with thorns, she was careful: she didn't want to hurt her friend too much, didn't want to puncture her, or scratch too deeply, or do it in a place where veins came close to the surface. Common sense, Kesi had in abundance. Sure, there was some danger . . . but that's what made the game fun.

More fun now, with a real blade.

She angled the monofilament towards Allie's bare forearm. With the sunlight falling just so, it was possible to see approximately where the end of the blade reached. She knew not to start probing with that tip—a monofilament could penetrate inches of flesh instantly, since there was no resistance to reveal how deep one had gone. She'd learned that slicing cheese in the kitchen. A vibroknife made a great cheese slicer—and left deep marks in the cutting board, if you pushed too fast.

She didn't push against Allie too fast. Just laid the blade against her skin, and pulled.

No obvious cut. No gaping wound. A moment or two later, though . . . blood welled up along a line finer than the finest razor could leave. Just a little. Less than a thorn scratch, really. It had just been enough to break the skin, though if she pushed just a little deeper, she could cut muscle. . . .

Allie felt nothing, but saw the expression on Kesi's face change. She lifted her head, glanced down along her arm, and saw blood. She moaned.

Kesi cocked her head. That sounded very theatrical, but Allie was not the kind of spacer who moaned theatrically. She cut her again, broke skin along the length of half her finger.

Allie glanced at the cut and moaned again. An overdone, unconvincing moan.

Kesi sat back on her heels. "What's wrong?"

"What?"

"You're faking it. What's wrong?"

"Am not."

"Are so. You never moan like that."

Allie hesitated, frowning. "Well, it's not the same."

"Why not?"

"Don't get me wrong, I like the knife! But . . . I can't feel it. You know. Not like the thorns. I feel those when you scratch me, the pressure, the line of pain. This is too, too . . ."

"It's scary, isn't it?"

"Yeah. But it doesn't feel the same."

"Of course it doesn't. It's a knife, not a thorn."

"I guess I like the other better."

Kesi sat for a moment, perplexed. She had savored the fear, the anticipation, the threat that the knife presented. But that feeling bled away as the cutting did not have the effect she'd hoped for. What she really liked was the squirming.

When they got going with the thorns and scratches, Allie squirmed and moaned—really—and breathed hard, until sometimes Kesi had to throw the thorns away and abandon the camisq role and lay atop her captive friend just to quiet her down.

If the vibroknife wasn't going to produce those results, she didn't want to play with it. "All right," she said, setting the knife to one side. "We'll do thorns, then. I want you to really be tortured, you know."

She was pulling barbs from a tersia vine overhead when Lena's muffled voice came into the clearing. It was audio from the closest unobscured data pickup, near the walkway. "Kesada, you are wanted in the house by your father. Come in quickly, now. He has guests who want to meet you."

Kesi stamped a foot. "I'm busy," she shouted towards the AI.

"You're to come in now, he says, or he will come out to get you."

Kesi's brow furrowed. Maybe he couldn't find her secret clearing by himself, but Lena would surely direct him close to her whereabouts, and then he might discover this place she wanted to be her own. Better not to have him out here at all.

"I'll be there," she shouted grumpily, and turned back to her bound friend. "Sorry," she said. "You heard."

"Yeah." Allie held still while her wrists were untied, then undid her ankles while Kesi returned the blade and rope to the camotarp bundle and stashed it away.

"Kesada, guests are awaiting you," came Lena's nagging reminder through the casca shrubs.

"Coming!" Kesi led the way back out of the grove and trotted to the house with her friend close behind her. When they crested the short slope that edged the garden plaza, they sighted the house. Allie halted in surprise at the edge of the bluegrass, studying the fashionably clad strangers lounging and drinking and laughing in clusters along the arched gallery that flanked the house and opened into the mosaic square.

"Where'd they all come from?" she asked.

"Around. They come for lunch on Bren's party days, stay through dinner, then go out in the evening."

"You didn't mention they were coming."

Kesi shrugged. "He doesn't tell me, usually. If you weren't here, I'd stay in the garden all day until they were gone."

"We could still. Stay in the Queen's Lair."

"Naw. If Lena says he'll come after me, he will. It's show-and-tell time."

Allie looked quizzical.

"You'll see," Kesi told her, and started across the plaza towards the house.

They made their way past exquisite women and handsome men in glamorous fashions. Some smiled upon them condescendingly; some moved aside as if their dirt-streaked clothes and leaf-scattered hair would rub off in passing. Nearly all recognized the face of Hinano Bren's daughter, who just last year had debuted as a child model for spydersilk saris. But they were not here to chat with a child, and it would be uncouth to appear to be currying favor with Hinano senior's offspring. No one spoke to them as they wove through the crowd and into the multilevel maze that was Bren's Rivercrest penthouse.

They found him in the multimedia room, holding court amid a handful of admirers. He stood by a holopedestal raised to eye level, the vert on it featuring an auburn-haired woman in revealing windblown robes of russet and gold. It was a clothing commercial for his newest line of fabrics, and the woman in the vert was the same as the one standing at his side, his arm wrapped proprietorially around her waist.

"Ah! Kesi! There you are. Come here."

She entered the room with Allie in tow; Bren's lips turned down as he took them both in. "You've been making a mess of yourself. And your little friend—Alix, is it?"

"Alees," she corrected him.

His eyes narrowed slightly, in the way that meant he did not expect to be contradicted. Kesi squeezed Allie's hand, tugged her a bit behind as she stepped forward. "You wanted to see me?" she asked, drawing his attention back to her.

He motioned her to him with one hand, the other embracing his interest of the day. The woman smiled down at her as if they were old friends. Kesi stared at her flatly. Bren's hand came down on her shoulder, gave her a warning squeeze that meant "behave."

"This is Asaro, our newest rave for the Sheer Passion line. You've seen her on verts."

"It's lovely to meet you, Kesi."

"Pleasure, I'm sure." She echoed the words she'd heard her father use often, but stripped of inflection. The model's green eyes cooled.

Bren laughed flatly. "She needs some polishing, as you can tell." He spoke to his friends as if Kesi were an object. "But she was charming in the sari verts."

"Charming!" voices agreed.

"When she's not trying to emulate a dirtcrawler, she cleans up quite nicely."

"I'd say so." Asaro offered another smile, less warm than before. "She has those high cheekbones." A hand with slender fingers reached down, tilted Kesi's head up. The woman studied her appraisingly. "Eyes naturally violet?"

"Her mother was from New Arilèé, on Calyx. As pureblood as one can be, these days."

"Ah. Old world genetics. One of the five classical looks."

If Kesi's head had been free she would have shot her father an angry look. Her mother was from Calyx? That was more than he had ever told her before—like she had no interest? Instead she scowled at Asaro, who released Kesi's head from her grip and snuggled closer to Bren's side. "Not very sociable, is she?" she remarked.

"She has her rough edges." He pushed Kesi back a step, moving her more to the center of his gathered friends, then released her shoulder. "Be nice to our supermodel," he admonished, "or she won't tell you about her homeworld. She's from Corvus, you know."

Kesi turned her expressionless gaze on her father. He was mocking her, now, mocking her interest in other planets and her armchair star travels on the Net. She had made the mistake of mentioning Corvus to him already: that, and the four other worlds in the CAS Sector where Imperial Navy task forces were head-quartered. Each with flagships; each a possible duty station or base for her mother's warship. What she was doing eleven years ago when Kesi was born might no longer be relevant, but if she were a career officer and still serving in this sector, it seemed a pretty sure thing that she would cycle through one or more of those stations sooner or later. Kesi had them all marked on her per-sonalized star chart in her Net account.

"Kesi fancies herself an astrogator." Bren laughed heartily; his sycophants joined in on the merriment. "But I think she'll have enough to do, recording this next vert with you."

"What?" Kesi exclaimed.

"You're doing another vert, with Asaro. Sheer Passion scaled down for children."

"I don't want to."

She blurted it without thought, and bit her lip the moment after. Bren had his company face on, so his expression did not change, but she caught the shift in his eyes. He gave a small laugh that sounded natural; only Kesi recognized that he had forced it. "She's as stubborn as her mother was," he said to his audience, "but she'll do it."

Kesi shook her head, took a step away from him. "I told you I won't do it again. I hated it."

"You don't know what you're talking about. The verts were a huge success."

"I don't care." She'd made her stand, now she had to brazen it out in front of these onlookers. She folded her arms across her chest. "I hate the cameras and the clothes and everything else about it. It's stupid."

They'd had this conversation before: Bren planning her modeling career, Kesi saying that once was enough and she wouldn't do it again. He laughed off her protests, dismissed her moods as childish—but never before had others witnessed this exchange. An awkward silence reigned for a moment as every-one in the room watched her and her father. Then something changed in Bren. She saw it in his eyes first. Anger, maybe, buried quickly beneath a layer of ice, then that distance he had. Cold, lofty.

He sneered at his daughter, a curl of the lip that could almost be taken for an ironic smile. "If you feel that strongly about it, then I'll find some real talent for the job. I can only coach you so far, and when it comes down to it, I don't need a surly, ignorant child with no appreciation representing my art."

Kesi's defiance faltered. She wasn't surly, she just didn't like being pushed in that way that only her father could push her. She opened her mouth to protest.

"Besides, I need to find someone who excels at this. Who doesn't need the instruction you do. A natural. You don't have what it takes." He shook his head at her. "You're not good enough." He turned to Asaro and smiled. "Real talent is born, not made. I recognize it when I see it."

He kissed the model and dismissed Kesi with a gesture. She felt all eyes upon her, and turned, red faced, to leave the room while he was occupied. People moved out of the way for her in grudging small steps, studying her discomfort—reluctant to let her leave, but unable to make her stay. Then Bren said something lighthearted and all attention was upon him again. Kesi became invisible to the crowd and slipped free. She walked rapidly down the hall, Allie close behind.

"He's mean," her friend offered.

"I don't want to talk about it."

"Why doesn't he think you're good enough?"

Kesi wiped hot tears away before they could spill down her cheeks. "Don't want to talk about that, either."

# 10

ILANYA EVA PROWLED her Port Oswin office. Janus offworld, his infosphere barely subverted, his household only five percent infiltrated—Obray was working as fast as he could, but it was not fast enough to suit her.

She forced herself to sit in the floatchair her matasai held out for her at the desk. No need to fret about business, she thought. Let's go at this properly.

She closed her eyes, breathed deeply, centered herself. With a thought, she flipped a cyber relay that brought her Tolex implant online. It was a wetware comp within her medial temporal lobe, her resident population of LNNs keeping it programmed and on track. The equipment was highly classified, available only to selected politicos, high-ranking military, and heads of the intelligence community. In use, the Tolex felt like acute memory blended with instant association of facts. Online now, it brought issues and updates to the forefront of her mind in a way that felt like sharp memory recall.

"Give me your sidelink," she said to Teo. He obeyed, and updates flooded her Tolex and were sorted just as quickly into mental storage. With him by her side, she was never far out of touch with the data- and infospheres that were the backbone of her work for the Emperor.

She browsed a subset of that infosphere now. Here, fresh in her mind, were her daily hot list and status updates. Eva dispatched orders as she reviewed ongoing issues: send a new lover to subvert the Dalukin ambassador; arrest a mutinous general in the borderlands; tell blackmail-compliant Lord Umato to hold his Imperial Council vote in reserve and not speak publicly about the succession yet.

The succession. The ever-present concern that furrowed her brow while she dispatched the last urgent items of the day. She wiped that data with a dismissive reflex and called up the mental construct she thought of as Raem the Taskmaster.

Raem was a version of her first ethics professor at the Academy on Locanan: querulous, argumentative, always ready to play devil's advocate. An insightful and provocative gadfly. Over the years, Eva had lost the company of any peers who would challenge her thought processes and decisions. She'd outranked them, or destroyed them, and who dared question her now? Since few could challenge her in that way, she had to provide it to herself. She knew Raem the Taskmaster was partly an aspect of her personality, but he nearly felt like an AI. It seemed that Raem had equal access to the Tolex, and could draw upon the same data, but drew different conclusions from it. He challenged her natural progression of logic, forced her to think outside the box.

It was an irksome but valuable gift.

Eva conjured Raem out of nowhere and felt the presence of a different personality in her mind. Maybe the Taskmaster was a figment, but that did not stop him from speaking acerbically to her.

*Dawdling, are you?* The sneer was audible in the voice she imagined in her head.

"Not willingly, old man."

*There is so much more you could be doing.*

"That's what I've been telling myself."

*Telling is not doing.*

Eva sighed. Self-flagellation, she did not need. "There's only so much I can do, with Janus offworld. It's being handled."

*He could be gone for months, and Nalomeci could die at any time.*

"Don't exaggerate. Doctors estimate he'll live for months yet."

*He'll abdicate before he becomes completely incapable, and he might do that at any time.*

Eva shook her head. "He won't commit to that before his daughter has support."

*Rishan has support right now,* Raem snorted. *Just not enough to carry the Council vote that would ratify her as his heir.*

A female heir to the throne. In the centuries since House Adàn had come to power, there had been only a handful of empresses among the many rulers of the Sa'adani, and those had served far back in time. A woman had not sat on the Dragon Throne for over four hundred years. Rishan was next in line, following the assassination of her brother Esker three months before. Hers would be an historic ascension, if it occurred. There were many committed to seeing that it did not.

*Nalomeci is old, ill, and has lost his will to lead,* Raem said. *If he dies before you can arrange the ratification votes, we will be plunged into civil war. The Outlord faction will ensure it, if it will let them return to power.*

"So? Nothing has changed. You know why we settled on the Red Hand cartel for our strategy. Squeezing others would not yield the same results. This is the right pressure point to achieve our ends."

The construct gave considered agreement. *With cartel assistance, Lord Shay will have the means to bring the independents in line and ratify the Empress.*

"Precisely. Stability will be ensured."

*That is not the only reason you wish to see Rishan swiftly on the throne,* Raem said pointedly.

Eva clenched a fist. What did it matter why she worked to assure the succession? As long as her efforts were not in vain.

FAR AWAY IN the Emperor's Palace, Rishan held the hand of a dying man. Her father's death was not imminent, but it crept steadily closer, as unstoppable as the deepening freeze of a Cascan winter. The med bed that sustained his life could only slow, not stop, the ravages of the alien parasite that destroyed him.

Since his son's murder, his state had worsened. "He no longer cares if he lives," Halani, her father's mistress, explained. "No parent should have to bury their child, and he blames himself. If he had not announced his intention to abdicate, to leave the way clear for Esker's ascension, your brother might still be alive. He lingers now until your place is secure, but I fear his heart is no longer with us."

Rishan embraced that insight. It helped make sense out of her brother's death and her father's steep decline. It was not the first time Hali's wise observations revealed facets of human nature to Rishan. She had much to learn from the older woman, and it was important that she make a point of doing so.

Halani sat across from her now, holding her father's other hand as he dozed in a twilight state. She did not notice Rishan's gaze; she was looking lovingly at her bed-bound companion, stroking his forearm with a gentle touch. They looked like a scene from an ancient Matsu frieze: the caring companion, the dying lover. Like a piece of fine art, Hali was. Her stunning beauty had grown only more marked in her middle years, her once jet-black hair touched now with gray at the temples, and left uncolored at Nalo's request. He was endlessly in love with the unretouched reality of Oshida Halani, his mistress and companion since the death of his wife years before.

Hali held a unique position in the Emperor's household. For half of her near-twenty years, Rishan had known this woman as part of her father's life, overlapping with her own. She did not fill the role of a mother to her—no one could do that—but the beauty known as the Blossom of Calyx was a friend and a role model in other ways. A professional entertainer and sometime courtesan, she epitomized social grace, political savvy, and astute observation. Her shigasa skills and privileged position allowed her to flawlessly navigate the complexities of court life, all while avoiding the ire of potential rivals and political enemies.

It was a skill set Rishan desperately needed to master for herself. She saw the sharp glances and the circling wolves outside her doors, and knew there was little time to prepare for a position she had not been bred to. Never had it been imagined that she would one day become the heir.

Part of her was eager to take on such a challenge, but the other part regarded it with trepidation. When Esker had been killed, she'd pleaded with her father to spare them all the turmoil. Why oh why did he not just clone himself and put an end to this misery? If they could do it for the most valued officials, surely when it came to the Emperor—

Nalomeci had tolerated the question from her only once before reminding her of truths she was trying to ignore. "Cloning cannot guarantee that the identical soul fragment is returned to a given body," he said. "That is never certain once a soul has returned to the lau, the All from whence we came."

Rishan waved a hand in frustration. "What does that matter? You'll still be you, with the memory imprint."

"But my soul would not be," he said gently. "Ruling this empire is a soul-choice, Rishan, just as you have chosen your entire incarnation: your body, your family, your skill sets. If someone has died, their clone may carry the same memories, but there is no way to be certain it carries the same soul. Therefore, it may not legally rule."

She looked at Nalomeci now, careworn and asleep, and blinked back tears. That conversation had been her last attempt to get him to take a radical step to preserve his life. She hated that he would not, but what Hali had told her then was true: she had to prepare herself not only for his passing, but for what would happen to her next.

"You are unready for the Game of Houses," Hali had observed, "much less the Great Game of which it is a part." Her position and their long association allowed her to speak with unusual frankness to the Emperor's daughter. "I can help you remedy that, if you will accept my assistance. It would require that you apply yourself diligently. We haven't much time."

Rishan looked at her friend now, for friend she had become in these last months. They were no longer child and adult, but seeker and mentor. Rishan was learning, growing, and changing as she must to meet the challenges of the times.

Her father's eyes fluttered open. "Have we heard back yet from Ilanya Evanit?" he asked in a hoarse whisper.

"No, Father," she replied. He was disoriented, still in a drug dream. Rishan knew who Ilanya was, but she was not privy to whatever grand strategy presently occupied that secretive woman. She could tell her father nothing about his trusted right hand.

He squeezed her hand. "Never mind. She's reliable. All will be well."

She returned the squeeze as he drifted back asleep. She exchanged a questioning look with Halani and saw puzzlement there to match her own. Whatever that business was about, they might never know.

Nor could it possibly matter.

# 11

EVA HAD NOT initially intended to hunt Janus. His cleverness and success in his upward climb were traits she admired, in principle. Only after it became necessary to leverage the Red Hand did he become a target. His death would strike to the core of the cartel, show them they were not impervious to the long arm of the Kingmaker, and that the cartel would be safe only when they acquiesced to her wishes.

His demise would achieve a specific result—a very carefully calculated result, as precise as the sociometric predictions of Raem the Taskmaster and her augmented intelligence could make it. Her tactics were in keeping with her—their—philosophy and strategy of selective action.

It was that strategy that took her so far from home on her various self-assigned field missions. "It's like a child's game of castle-blocks," she'd explained once to Teo. "A structure may look elaborate, but remove just the right piece, and all the blocks shift position. In predictable ways, if you plan carefully enough."

"Or they come tumbling down," he said dryly.

"A possibility." She shrugged. "But not likely, if one plays deftly. Some blocks are foolish to move; others are irrelevant. Push the right one in the right direction, though, and the others will fall into line. You will win the game."

It was a good metaphor for the game she played so well. It was one of her gifts, that ability to perceive which building block to move in order to rearrange the entire heap in proper order. It was why she saw to certain things personally. Only she could sense the shifting currents, calculate how to act in the moment or change leverage to achieve her desired ends. On the most important matters, it was not something that could be left to subordinates to do.

For that reason, she had journeyed to Bekavra weeks ago to nudge things in the proper direction to ensure Rishan's succession. Approaching old-line organizations was out of the question. Corporations, Great Houses, Sa'adani derevin cartels: any group with the massive resources she required was also tangled up in old Sa'adani factions and alliances. They would be more difficult to coerce, and their positions could change unpredictably because of hidden faction interests and influences.

Only here in the CAS Sector, culturally different than older Sa'adani space, were there relatively independent groups. And of the leading cartels in Cassian space, Internal Security had the inside scoop on the richest of them all: two years before, a raid on Bekavra had laid critical parts of the Red Hand network open to scrutiny. Now, as time pressure grew, Ilanya Evanit knew exactly where to go, who to talk to, and how to reach them.

Her target chosen, she had asked the triumvirs to a meeting. It was time to nudge the cartel in the direction it must now go. Would inevitably go, when she was done with them.

SHE HAD MET the bosses of the Red Hand alone in a park on the outskirts of Bekavra: Sefano and Mika in the flesh, Janus a life-sized virtual representation standing on a holopad Sefano had brought with him.

Eva was comfortable with the relative isolation of the meeting. Teo recorded it and monitored her from a hillside one klick away. He could shoot the eye out of any one of the bosses at that distance, and though she was out of range of his sidelink to her Tolex, she felt nearly as physically secure as always. No doubt the triumvirs were equally protected. A sense of security allowed one to focus on the business at hand.

Mika seemed to be the spokesperson for the trio. She was a broad-featured woman with short gray hair, a square jaw, and an unblinking dark-eyed gaze. Her high-collared, stiff-shouldered tunic emphasized the blocky lines of her body, giving her a gender-ambiguous, faintly military air.

"We're surprised that you pressed for this meeting," she said, pointedly leaving Ilanya's names and title out of her speech. "IntSec has made it clear that we are watched. We've grown accustomed to such a frivolous use of imperial taxes." She shrugged broad shoulders. "We make sure to toe the lines that IntSec requires we observe." She smiled ambiguously. Eva filled in the subtext as the woman spoke. She might as well be saying, *We don't get caught doing anything that would get us in overt trouble.*

"In short, then: we see nothing we could possibly have to talk about that you cannot get from IntSec files."

"Nevertheless, you are here," Eva pointed out. The Red Hand knew very well who the Kingmaker was, just as she knew of the web of trade and influence this cartel managed. "It is not security files that interest me, but what you can do to assist me."

Mika actually blinked. Sefano looked surprised. Janus betrayed no reaction, but forced himself to stand even more still. Eva smiled to herself. There. That got their attention. She continued with the tactics she had resolved to try first.

"You know who Lord Shay is, I presume."

She expected them to nod; instead, blank looks met her own. Her brow furrowed. "The Yellow Sa'adani leader of the Reconciliation faction on the Imperial Council," she supplied.

Mika spread her hands. "That is Sa'adani business," she said apologetically. "Such matters don't touch us here in the CAS Sector."

Eva took that in. Of course Council dealings impacted this sector. The Red Hand could claim disinterest, but that was a lie. This cartel traced its directorship all the way back to an ancient order of assassins that had originated on the motherworld of Ástareth, in the once-empire of Urshad. That brotherhood of death still existed there, and its derevin descendant had played a persistent role in the Empire's criminal underworld. The Red Hand had flourished in Sa'adani space long before its migration into the confederation sector over two centuries ago.

"One of you, at least, must know of Lord Shay," Eva persisted, locking eyes with Sefano. "He is, after all, a famous distant kinsman of yours, is he not?"

The triumvir had a fringe of close-cropped white hair above prominent ears and a pleasant, nondescript face. He could have been a senior bureaucrat or a well-off retired citizen in his plain tunic of expensive zio cloth.

Sefano returned her gaze with a neutral expression. "Is he?" he asked blandly.

Eva quirked a lip. This crime boss was a Darvui-caste merchant, born and bred in Sa'adani space. His kinship was distant from Lord Shay, not in the dishonored den-miri sense, but through accidents of marriage and migration that had diminished his family's status from once-noble roots over many generations. Until two years ago, IntSec had been ignorant of this connection, but after the netrunner known as FlashMan had infiltrated Red Hand systems, Sefano's biofiles and history were now part of IntSec's dossiers. The cartel boss knew his ancestry. And now, so did she.

Let him play coy, then. She diverted the conversation to a new path. "Lord Shay holds considerable influence on the Council, but his faction is sometimes . . . divided in opinion. For him to secure unity and bring his allies to the table with one voice, he needs greater resources." Eva had been speaking to them all, but she addressed her words now to Sefano. "That is why I'm here. I am asking you to donate resources to your kinsman."

The triumvir's brows shot up and he burst out laughing. The others joined him in merriment. "*Donate* resources to Shay?" he chuckled. "Do I understand you correctly? You want us to just . . . give . . . support to your pet nobleman?"

Eva did not respond to their laughter. She let the question hang on the air until they quieted to hear her answer. "I am asking you to put significant resources at the disposal of your kinsman," she affirmed coolly, "so he can do what he must."

Janus snorted; Mika grinned. Sefano looked at her speculatively. "Whyever would I want to do that?"

Ah, she had him engaged now, dropping the corporate "we." Sefano was the senior of the triumvirs, and she had no doubt that his decisions often ruled how the organization ran. The rest of this conversation would pay courtesy to the illusion of three, but the words would be framed for only one.

"The Emperor requires the minister's aid, and all the backing he can muster through his allies. If you give Shay the means to rally this support, the Red Hand will have the favor of Nalomeci III, as well as that of the minister."

"Imperial favor." Sefano fell silent for a moment, seeming to think it over. "In exchange for what, exactly?"

"Between the three of you, you control the economies and resources of at least twelve subsectors."

"Fifteen," Sefano corrected her smugly, "but only in the gray market, of course. We do not usurp official channels in those regions."

She dipped her chin. "I would say half of that should be sufficient to help Lord Shay accomplish what he must in the short time remaining to us."

"Half—!" Sefano's eyes widened in disbelief. Mika shook her head. Janus studied Eva with narrowed eyes.

"This minor gratuity in return for imperial favor?" Sefano waved a hand. "Such generous terms you offer to bankrupt us. No."

This, too, Eva had anticipated. Time to shift tactics. "The Emperor will make it well worth your while."

If they would not do it out of a Sa'adani sense of familial duty, they would certainly do it out of self-interest. This cartel already controlled more wealth than all but a few noble houses or trade consortia, and none that she knew of had the bloodline connection to a royal councillor to excuse or facilitate an influx of wealth from unexpected quarters.

Eva was preparing to explain Nalomeci's terms when Janus spoke up. "If the Emperor is so anxious to fuel this lord's activities, why not let him contribute from his own purse? Oh!" He snapped his fingers. "I forgot: the privy purse is intentionally small, so the Emperor cannot overtly buy Council favors." He shook his head. "How unfortunate for the Emperor. And for you."

Eva glared at the man for a second before she could soothe the challenging expression off her face. "The Emperor does not ordinarily offer amnesty, trade licenses, special charters, and patronage for organizations with activities as questionable as your own. I suggest you think carefully about this offer, and how it will benefit you."

Mika looked skeptical, glanced at Sefano. The boss folded his arms on his chest, cocked his head with a look of interest on his face. Only Janus remained unaffected by the sally.

Eva spoke again. "Lord Shay would, of course, recognize his cousin, if acknowledgment would suit that cousin's purposes."

A flicker of interest showed in Sefano's eyes. Of course legitimacy would tempt him, perhaps as much as imperial privilege. That was Raem's analysis of the man as someone who could be bought by rank and privilege. It rang true.

But it was Janus who spoke into the lull. "You offer us dependencies, Domna. You offer us to be compromised and accountable."

His interruption was unwelcome. She replied more curtly than she intended. "I offer you the chance to expand your business into legitimate channels, and to operate without restriction or repercussion even in your gray-market undertakings. No derevin cartel has ever received such a charter from the Emperor."

"You offer us the death of the Red Hand," Janus retorted. "First by paupering ourselves, then by a bastard agreement with the Emperor that sooner or later he could not afford to honor." Janus shook his head. "So kind of you to go out of your way to meet with us today. How unfortunate that yours was a wasted journey."

He turned to his compatriots. "There's no deal to be made here. I oppose it."

Sefano hesitated. "There might be ways—"

"We do not deal in exchange for imperial favors. It would compromise us too much."

Sefano locked eyes with Janus, then nodded once. "As you say."

Eva saw they would be having words on the matter, but it would not be in front of her. Sefano glanced to Ilanya, an ambiguous message in his eyes, but his words betrayed nothing. "Come," he said to his companions. "We're done with this." He picked up Janus's holopad; for a moment the slender triumvir towered over the others in midair. "The Red Hand is not for sale," Sefano said, "not even to the Emperor."

With a tap of his finger he shut the pad off, and Janus disappeared. He and Mika turned their backs on Eva and walked away on a winding park pathway, soon vanishing from sight.

She watched them go in disbelief, then cursed them soundly. Sefano had been on the verge of agreement. It was Janus's resistance, alone, that had spoiled the play.

She had other ploys, other offers, but they did her no good, for the trio refused to see her again, or even receive communications from her. Other cartels had ties to opposing factions, or lacked the resources needed to put votes solidly in Lord Shay's hand. This was the only avenue that would serve, and the door to it was shut, even as the Emperor's health worsened.

AFTER THAT MEETING weeks ago, Eva had spent long hours in conversation with Raem, analyzing the interactions of the triumvirs. Little was known about Janus, who had been a lowly derevin lieutenant when IntSec had acquired the Red Hand intel. But Raem's take on Sefano was correct—she had read that much from the man's aura while offering the bait. If unopposed, he would reach for legitimacy and recognition by House Shay. It was equally obvious to her that Mika would follow the consensus of the group.

The obstacle was Janus, and to this hindrance there was but one solution. The Kingmaker must reach behind the closed door of the cartel with a hand of violence, to destroy the obstacle and send a message with two meanings: that Sefano was free to deal how he saw fit, and that not even the Red Hand was safe from the grasp of the Emperor, if they were not his friends.

Sefano had been a street enforcer in his younger years, working his way up the ranks. The sudden death of this one truculent partner—in a cartel thought inviolate by backstreeters—would get his attention and force that door open again. If Janus were out of the way, Sefano would bring the cartel to the table out of self-preservation, as well as self-interest.

During the next round, Sefano would play this game her way, and the castle-blocks would fall where she wished them to.

# 12

TEO WAS DELIVERING a routine briefing in Obray's commandeered office when his sudden tense hesitation warned Eva of something unexpected in the update. "What is it?" she prompted.

He paused before responding. "You know security sends out look-alike decoys when you travel, Domna, to obscure your trail and protect you from hostile parties. They often follow your regular routes of travel, or variations close to them."

Her lips thinned as she sensed where this was heading.

"One of those decoys journeyed to your vacation retreat on Desle." The retreat was a sprawling lakeside cabin in the midst of a secure royal hunting preserve in the homeworld cluster. Ilanya felt a sinking feeling in her stomach. That was not merely a vacation home. It also served as artist's retreat for her sister, reclusive Lajeen, who wanted nothing more than the solitude in which to create her raku weavings and parch paintings. Some of these she displayed in the best galleries; others she gave away on a whim to strangers.

Eva got to her feet, turned her back on her matasai so he would not see her tears.

"After the decoy party arrived, a low-flying zipdrone evaded perimeter defenses and bombed the cabin."

"Survivors?" The word was a harsh whisper.

"Two of the security escort who were checking outbuildings. One winged the drone, and a fragment was recovered. It was a device of Briel manufacture."

Briel, a military concern that supplied only the Cashnacarra and their close allies. They were a Green Sa'adani faction wavering between rebellion and loyalty, with splinter groups that would only be reined in by wholesale and autocratic clan allegiance to the Dragon Throne. Allegiance that Lord Shay could make happen, with the right support.

Support he would have marshalled by now if she had secured the cooperation of the Red Hand. Instead she was waiting for Janus to reappear, marking time while her family was murdered.

She slammed a fist against the wall, and Teo fell silent.

This was the other reason why she'd approached the cartel. If the succession was secure, there would be no further point in her enemies harrying her. Her death would not give them any political advantage when a fit and healthy

Empress was in power. She felt guilty that her personal concerns played a role here, but why should her family be at risk because she was serving loyally? There had to be an end to this. Only if Rishan were crowned would this sniping at her and her loved ones cease.

She took a deep breath and collected herself. Eva had resolved to let Janus's death speak for itself before she approached the triumvirs again. When such a blow struck out of the blue, the survivors would learn to fear her, and be more compliant in the end.

And yet . . . there was one other way, one that could turn probability into certainty. She'd attempted it early on and failed—there had been too many technical obstacles, and Janus a distracting target that demanded pursuit. But the death of her sister provoked her, and constructive action seemed more imperative than ever. She wanted surety, and wanted it now. And finally, the right tool might be to hand.

"Get me that netrunner IntSec likes so much," she said over her shoulder. "I want FlashMan on the com right now."

FLASHMAN'S LIGHTNING BOLT–SHAPED form stalked unhappily down a corridor of red light, the straightforward channel in to Red Hand systems on Bekavra. He'd been there before, a couple years ago. Only then, he'd been decking on-world, so he could shave nanoseconds of response time against the hunter-killer defenses at the access points.

He had no safety in proximity this time—Ilanya had yanked his chain hard about gaining instant access to Sefano's com system. "Drop everything," she demanded. "I want him on the line right now. After all, sneaking around com systems is one of your specialties, is it not?"

Did Ilanya know that he had left back doors aplenty in the cartel network when he'd done his previous snoop and run? Most were gone now, as they would be, after a system was so thoroughly compromised and then restored. But some of the primary systems seemed so simple and so essential that they had been reincorporated into the new, improved Red Hand networks. Leaving odd little entry points like this one.

Flash stooped in the hall, running his spiky fingers over a maintenance hatch in the wall. It should be nothing more than an infrastructure port, transitioning high-level interface data to machine-level language, but the edge marks he'd left on the virtual port cover told him this was one of the entries still coded to his own cypherlock routine.

He inserted pointy fingertips into a pattern in the virtual hatch. They might be natural divots in the metal—or might not. He let current flow through him, carrying electrons and bit-level commands. The hatch popped open, and he regarded the machine language interface behind it with distaste.

Nothing like small, cramped, primitive, dank code layers to go creeping around in. Like sewers beneath a city, they'll take you anywhere, but do you really want to use them to get there?

He sighed and shrank his sim-form as he stepped into the maintenance cubby. Pulling the hatch snug behind him, he peered into the maze of pipes and port tubes aglow with their own low-level light. He no longer had a master map of the Red Hand systems, so there was some question where all this would lead. All he knew for sure was that it was part of Sefano's com network.

He gave one portal a squinty eye. Its funnel-shaped mouth gaped back at him unexpressively.

What the hell, he thought. That's as good as any.

Flash derezzed and flowed his electrons into the gaping maw of a machine-layer subsystem.

SEFANO LAY ON a massage table in his office. The floatboard bobbed ever so slightly under the masseur's firm pressure into deep tissue. The cartel boss drifted dreamily, enjoying the treatment, which was both therapy and relaxation. It was a brief interlude in his day that was his own time to shed worries and be relaxed in his body.

The ping of his conference com channel was therefore all the more incongruous. No calls were put through to him this time of day. He cracked an eye open, glancing towards the wall viewer that was in his direct line of sight. The screen was a-blur with a test pattern or a static pulse. What the . . . ?

"*Send the massage guy on a break,*" a synthesized voice spoke from the vid unit. "*This is private. You don't want other ears in the room. Trust me on this.*"

Sefano bit back a curse. Who was this? Whoever it was, it was a major breach of security. Alerts should already be shutting down the system, but the telltales over his desk remained inert.

Who wanted a private word so badly?

Curiosity won out over anger. He glanced over his shoulder and nodded dismissal to his attendant. The athletic man left the room as Sefano leaned up on one elbow.

"Who are you? What do you want?"

A thin cackle came from the wall vid. "*I'm just the gatekeeper. Here's your real fan club.*"

The vid screen rezzed into image. Sefano inhaled sharply and sat up, fumbling for a towel.

"Sorry to catch you at an inconvenient moment," Ilanya said, "but you've left me little choice. You haven't been answering my calls, so I decided to be a little more direct."

The cartel boss hoisted himself off the floatboard, padded on bare feet up to the conference vid.

"You compromise me," he snapped. "We don't deal singularly with outsiders like you. *Especially* not like you."

Ilanya waved a hand in dismissal. "Perhaps because in the singular you would deal with me more rationally? I'm running out of time to play games with you, Sefano. Believe me when I tell you this: nothing is more important to me right now than securing your cooperation."

The cold look in her eyes convinced him of her sincerity—and the lengths she would go to get her way. The look put him in mind of Adahn Harric, Janus's late predecessor. An unsettling analogy, that.

"I had the impression you were interested in coming to terms with us," she continued. "Was I wrong?"

Sefano crossed his arms on his white-haired chest and stood there like a gruff bear. So much to say; so little to say that was safe. He felt balanced, suddenly, on a precarious knife edge. "If we're going to talk business," he equivocated, "give me a minute."

He turned his back to the screen, walked to his green silk lounging robe, and donned it. He eyed his neatly stacked clothing for a moment, but relished the thought of dressing in front of Ilanya's scrutiny even less than the thought of dealing with her in his robe. He stepped into slippers instead, and turned back to the wall unit.

"I can't help you, Domna." He layered his negative statement with deference that implied a willingness to help. Would she read what he could not say outright? "The time is long past that one person alone dictated the actions of the Red Hand. There are two votes against your proposal of cooperation. I must abide by the will of the triumvirate."

"I need to know where you stand, Sefano, so let me lay it out for you." She studied him coolly. "If there were only two votes on the table, and the other one opposed you, whose vote would prevail?"

He bit back an oath. Only two votes on the table? The woman had no limits. He knew her reach was long, but did she really think she could threaten the power structure of sector-spanning enterprises like his own . . . ?

The two kept silence as they took each other's measure. And then Sefano realized the answer to his question was yes. He knew backroom tales about the Kingmaker, shared among the derevin only. She could, and did, manipulate power structures like his every other week. Surely there were ways to stymy her—

—but did he really want to? Perhaps he stood to gain more by playing this her way.

Another moment of calculation, and he finally replied. "I am the senior triumvir. If there are only two votes, mine prevails."

Ilanya's head dipped once, slowly, as if affirming something to herself. "And do you, personally, have interest in operating under the Emperor's carte blanche?"

What an incredible opportunity. He'd known it the moment she'd said it in the park before Janus nay-sayed it, the protective, short-sighted response of a guttersnipe out of his league. Mika, always conservative, erred on the side of caution. As always, Sefano must rely upon his own vision for how power should be played at the top.

He gave a single sharp nod to Ilanya, not trusting himself to speak.

"I know derevin honor is . . . strong." *Touchy,* she might have said. He would not have disagreed. "So I must ask you a hypothetical question. If one of your number were to perish, would this in some way prevent you from conducting business with outsiders?"

Ah, so now they were down to it. Those lines were not difficult to read between.

He would not want Mika gone. She'd proven her worth over years of service. She saw the downside to things first, but heeded business realities in the end. But how would he feel if Janus were out of the picture? The junior partner had come to rank by inheritance of position in crisis, not by planned triumvir selection. The least productive of their number. The one with the most demanding scruples. Problematically so, even.

Janus was not a triumvir cut from the cloth of the great assassins and machinators of old, definitely not. He was of that new breed of cartel bosses here on the frontier, a casteless man risen from the ranks of derevin without the history and traditions of the great crime families of old Sa'adani space. His business acumen was good, even exceptional, but to this day, Sefano had never quite warmed to the upstart who had chanced to fill Adahn's shoes.

"The loss of a senior partner would prevent me from conducting business at all," he said, as if musing out loud. "The more senior they are, the more value to me and to the cartel. But if a more junior one were to go . . ."

He walked past the floatboard and took a seat on the couch that faced the wall vid. "Let me explain our honor code to you. If a Red Hander is intentionally slain, honor and custom require that we avenge that death. If the death is the action of a sole individual, vengeance is against that one person. If the act of a family or house, we destroy that family or house. If the blood feud of a clan, we destroy the clan. We eradicate the source of the offense, you see."

"When Adahn was killed in the raid on his Bekavra complex," Ilanya interjected, "you did not eradicate Internal Security."

Sefano chose his words carefully. "There is a certain economy of scale beyond which it is not worth our while to go. We cannot fight entire imperial bureaucracies, so we do not try. Sometimes a cartel member is crushed beneath the wheels of an inexorable machine, and we consider that part of the price of doing business. Although, I should point out . . ."

"Yes?"

"If we were to, say, lose a member to abduction or assassination sponsored by law enforcement, it would not be possible for me to turn around and treat with the entity responsible for that attack. Even if there is merely well-founded suspicion of official involvement. Our honor forbids contact of that sort, and our constituent derevin would not allow it. I would lose all support if I tried to extend that particular olive branch."

An unreadable expression flickered across Ilanya's face. "I see," she said slowly.

"It is the more personally motivated offenses that we avenge in time-honored manner, and which still leave the door open for business." He went on. "An eye for an eye is quite simple. Clear-cut. If someone kills one of our number, we kill them in return. We are obligated to do so. Personal vengeance operates under different rules than do our run-ins with official entities."

Silence prevailed between them for an extended moment.

"I understand," Ilanya said finally. "And the impact of personal vengeance on your business dealings?"

"Negligible. We are meticulous about exacting blood debt. Once that is settled, it is settled. We do not let it derail our good business decisions."

"So if a triumvir were slain for a personal matter, and you then destroyed that killer, your need for vengeance would be satisfied?"

A humorless smile touched his lips. "Exactly so."

"And you would then be free to conduct business as you saw fit?"

"In this hypothetical situation we are discussing? Yes." He hesitated. "Naturally, I could never nudge events in this direction. But if they were to fall out this way of their own accord in a hypothetical world . . ." He shrugged. "We could carry on with business in the normal manner afterward."

"Naturally. Then I think we understand each other," the head of PolitDiv said. "I will need a swift response to my offer, when I put it to you again, and we must move ahead rapidly at that time. Are you comfortable with those terms, Sefano?"

His head inclined on a bullish neck. "I say again, I cannot discuss 'terms' with you, Domna."

Her lips pursed. "My mistake. I should have said, 'In a hypothetical future, were your circumstances different, do those sound like conditions you could live with?'"

Sefano wrestled down the urge to pick nits with that restatement as well. Dice the words how they might, they both understood they were making a deal on the side.

He nodded agreement.

"Very well, then, triumvir. When the obstacle to your hypothetical cooperation is gone, I'll contact you again. We can continue this discussion at that time."

The screen went blank as abruptly as it had gone live.

Sefano sat in contemplation on the couch for a long time after that.

# 13

WHAT EVA HAD learned from Sefano left her in a bind. She brought her Tolex online to explore contingencies.

*There's nothing wrong with your strategy for dealing with the Red Hand.* Raem interrupted her analysis. *What's wrong are your tactics.*

"How so?"

*It appears that simply killing Janus will not open the way to the deal you seek. You dare not assassinate him in the usual manner.*

"I don't see how else we're supposed to get to him," she countered. "My best assassins can set things up so it looks personal. They're good at staging a scene. Investigators will read it as we desire."

*The Red Hand has its own investigators. Can you take the chance that no one will see through your ruse? Besides, your best assassins are in the Outlands stalking seditious lordlings. It would take months of travel time to import the kind of talent that might help you here.*

"Still, that might work . . ." Eva mused.

*It dangerously extends your timeline. Remember, this target is from a derevin with a tradition of contract killing. They are the hardest kind of target to hit, much less sell on a cover narrative of personal quarrel. Witness our earlier failures with Janus. It is no wonder his protections are exceptional.*

"And thank the gods for that favor in disguise!" Eva exclaimed. "I wanted to send a message, but that would have slammed their door in our face." She felt uneasy at the near miss. Not even the Kingmaker was infallible.

*There was no way to know. That kind of subcultural code is not documented in anything we acquired from their systems on Bekavra.*

"How do we move ahead, then?" She remembered dealing with Lord Wagate's seditious and paranoid grandson. Only after half a year of household infiltration was a faux bodyguard able to remove that malcontent from the Game. Raem was right: it *could* very well take a long time to take Janus out. And every week that ticked by put them that much closer to the Emperor's looming death, and the end of their window to guarantee the succession of his daughter.

"We need a faster and more certain way to get close to Janus and hit him when he returns. Suggestions?"

*You may not like it,* he replied in a droll tone.

She sighed. "Let's hear it."

*Janus is close to this shigasa he sent flowers to. He is vulnerable when she dominates him. Let us, then, co-opt her. Let her be our tool. The personal factor is already present.*

Eva's brow furrowed. A roil of conflicting emotions washed through her.

Raem addressed her unspoken thoughts. *Yes. Exactly. You have an in to the shigasue, if you choose to use it, but it is a galling one to employ, is it not? Those sad souls who went astray how many generations ago? Unmarried pregnant daughters turned out in righteous rage, and the Between-World where they found safe harbor. Who would have thought Ilanya's Gen'karfa blood would take root in shigasue soil?*

She stiffened. "It is an enduring stain on our clan's honor. I don't need to admit to any blood ties there."

*But perhaps you do. A data trace shows you have remote cousins present in Lyndir's Enclave. One is especially well-placed to help you gain access to the shigasue.*

If Raem had been present in person, she would have given him a scathing look. Instead, she walked the floor, disgruntled.

"I see your logic about using someone already inside, but it's unlikely to work. True, Janus won't expect a threat from his pet dominatrix. She'll easily get close to him, and his guard will be down with her. Agreed on those points. But then we coerce this shigasa to do . . . what? Poison him? Stab him? And just hope she'll carry through with it effectively? No matter how we pressure her, you know how risky it is to rely on coercion alone to effect assassination. If this fails, our hand is tipped and we lose Janus again. And with him, our chance to secure the Red Hand's resources."

*Why not just plant someone in the house of domination, then? Janus can succumb to a quarrel with a jealous lover, say.*

"Too much time involved. An Enclave is not someplace a plant just strolls into. They need to really become part of the Between-World to pass there."

*Ah, yes. Sacrosanct as they are.*

"Hmph." The Between-World operated under special dispensation from the Emperor. It followed its own rules, had its own laws and law enforcement, and was in many ways untouchable, even to such an entity as Political Division. She knew from previous efforts that infiltrating the Between-World with her own people would take months or even years, if it was possible at all. It was not a solution for short-term needs.

"I see no answers here, Raem," she said sourly. "You're not as helpful as you could be."

*Well, then, perhaps you should review your business-social invitations,* the Taskmaster said.

The non sequitur took her off guard. "What?"

*You've been invited to tour Naval Weapons Research Station 207. You really should scan your incomings more often.*

"Is there something there I need to know about?"

*Maybe. There is something that niggles. You should look at it more closely.*

Ilanya Eva stopped in her tracks. Raem did not often advise her on a direct course of action. When he did, she paid attention. "What?" she prodded.

*I'm not certain. But there is something about their research projects that might be of use. Another way to work the shigasa angle.*

"You think so?"

Raem shrugged. *Call it intuition.*

She laughed out loud. Her intuition, having intuition. That was the sort of sidewinding insight she prized the Tolex for. She pulled up the classified briefing on the weapons research station, scanned it rapidly. Her files were not complete, of course—no human brain could hold a complete infosphere of a planet, nor even a significant subset of intelligence activities. But what she read was enough to start her musing. She saw why Raem had "niggles."

"Teo," she said after a while, "downlink the whole file on RS 207 from our archives. Sidelink to me when you have it."

"Yes, Domna."

Somewhere along the way, Raem slipped offline.

An hour later, she confirmed an appointment with Station Commander Olniko.

**COMMANDER OLNIKO SEVARO** Tai walked with a stiff limp, the result of a cyborg-quality prosthetic left leg poorly adapted to by its human host. Ramrod-straight back, short-cropped gray hair, deep-set gray eyes, he was a quiet man with an aura of authority about him. He had chosen to leave a whitened scar upon his brow and right temple: a visible reminder, if his gait was not, of what he had experienced, and why he did the work he did at Naval Weapons Research Station 207.

Ilanya Eva shook Olniko's hand upon their introduction: an uncommon gesture of peerage from the head of PolitDiv, but one warranted by the commander's status. She took him in with a glance, eyes lingering on the crimson and blue Gen'karfa caste mark on the back of his left hand. Her Tolex chip held his dossier in foreground storage, including caste; it was another thing, though, to get the measure of the man face-to-face. Olniko was a decorated hero of the first siege of Armajad, once a strike-force commander, and a rare survivor of that fatal naval nightmare, an engine-blasted vessel suffering catastrophic implosion of drive crystals in space.

When the gods want to preserve your life, Ilanya thought, they will preserve it against all odds. "Commander," she said, "it's an honor to meet you. Thank you for the invitation."

"The honor is mine, Arcolo." Olniko's voice was gravelly, deep in pitch. He gestured her to the plush leather floatchairs in his debriefing lounge. They would not sit across his desk, like officer and staff, but assume the casual formalities that prevailed between Gen'karfa. They took their seats at the same time, her matasai assuming his usual place behind and one step to the left of her. Eva reached out with her psi sense—a wild talent PolitDiv had trained her to use in her early days in the field—and smiled in satisfaction. Olniko radiated respect for her, but did not hold her in awe or fear. It was the ease of association she had come to expect only from ranking Gen'karfa and Lau Sa'adani, those who imagined they had power bases of their own that were impervious to Polit-Div's machinations.

She accepted a cup of kaf proffered by the commander's service mecho and raised it to her host. "In health and service," she said, invoking part of the loyalty oath taken to the Emperor. Olniko murmured the same over his cup, and the pair made small talk until the mecho had laid out a tray of pastries. As it retired back to its cubby, Eva set her cup down, leaving the food untouched.

"I've been over your quarterly reports," she said. "You have one project in particular that intrigues me."

"Yes?"

"The Splintegrate project."

"Ah, yes."

A moment of silence prevailed. Olniko had no doubt planned a station tour or some other routine dignitary treatment for her. She sensed him switching gears to accommodate her pointed focus.

"What exactly interests you about that project, Arcolo?"

Eva paused. "We are speaking securely here, I take it?"

"We are."

"The strategic plan notes the uses of splintegration for weapons purposes. Loosely speaking."

The commander nodded. Weaponry produced by the NWRS installations often took organic forms.

"I'm not clear, Commander, how clones of limited aspect can serve as weapons. Explain that to me."

Olniko dipped his chin in acknowledgment. "One of the personalities that we separate out consists of what you might call the aggressive and sociopathic aspects of a subject—the parts that make for a killer without qualms."

"Surely you're not mass-producing murderers? Though obviously you're working with them as subjects."

Olniko quirked a dry smile. "No, Arcolo. The objective is to isolate a personality type, or collection of aspects, that make for that rare warrior personality—directed and disciplined, of course. You know of the clone banks on Corvus, where warriors are bred and shock troops are produced?"

"Of course."

"One thing they have found in the Corvus program is that the personality traits of the clones do not stray far from those of the organic original."

Eva dredged through related data stored in her Tolex. "Meaning, the quality of the warrior clone depends on the chance development of the original?"

"Correct. We train and breed individuals so that they can reach their fullest potential—but if that endpoint is as fierce, as determined, as bloodlusting as we desire, that has been determined by innate personality factors that we could not control. Until now."

Eva nodded slowly. "So the Splintegrate project will let you single out aspects you wish to combine in the ideal warrior."

"Yes. The plan is to imprint clones only in that optimal mold. One that holds the harsher attributes that we require in front-line soldiers, but do not necessarily want to see in our civilians."

"Ah. The old 'universal soldier' template." She alluded to an ancient warrior ideal, the soldier who lived only to kill, an unstoppable fighting machine perfectly biddable by his masters. It was the myth of a precision tool of destruction, not truly attainable en mass with frail human psyches—until now, perhaps.

She smiled at Olniko. "I'd like to see this project firsthand, Commander. Can we arrange a visit?"

"Certainly," he replied. "Let me speak with my adjutant." He pardoned himself, crossed to his desk, and summoned Ugoli into the room.

As he did, Ilanya brushed the edges of the Raem construct in her mind and congratulated herself.

*You old bastard. I think you were right.*

**DR. METMURI JAMMED** the rigger lead into his jack and engaged the AI systems with three short jabs at console controls.

"Report," he growled into the com set. Technicians came online one after the other, their positions greening on the status board. He glanced into the laboratory bay before them, where Biancar$_3$ lay on the rightmost med bed, the last of the clones needing engram and cortical imprinting. The bioempath raised his eyes to peer unhappily at the elevated observation gallery. There sat Olniko and Ugoli in navy black, and two figures in service grays whom he did not recognize. The simikan caught the doctor's eye, raised an imperious hand in his direction, and brushed fingers at him as if to say *Run along and get on with it.*

*Let the show begin, my ass,* Esimir snarled mentally. *Enjoy your "show."*

He spoke to his staff with the audio relayed to the gallery as well as tech headsets. "Med 1, 2, online. Condition?"

"Stable," reported Bero from Med 2.

"AI, report."

"Prevak online, in monitor standby," said Ferris curtly.

"Imprint?" Esimir continued with the verbal checklist. This was all for show: the doctor at Control and Terel at Interface could see the total weave of the datasphere through their rigger jacks. Vocal check-ins were redundant and glacier-slow compared to the nanosecond pace of the AI-coordinated system. But visitors wanted a Juro-taken show, so they could imagine they were watching what was invisible to the human eye. Olniko's bright idea.

Fine. Have some mummery.

"Inducers synched," reported Imprint. "AI interlock in place."

"Interface?"

"All systems in flow, streaming infoscape to Control—and gallery." That was Terel, prioritizing the datasphere. He channeled an entertaining light show to the observers' gallery, more set dressing for the theater they performed.

What stupidity. As if an imprint process offered anything for unrigged observers to see. Ignore the schedule, Ugoli had ordered. Give them a demo. Turn this serious work into a sideshow for some VIP's entertainment. High-handed, ignorant sons of—

Esimir wrestled his temper down and sat for a moment, breathing deeply, slowly, bringing his adrenaline-speeded pulse back under control: a rapid adjustment, for a trained bioempath. This was no time to let emotion cloud the attention he needed to pay to this task.

No doubt these visitors would be bored with this "demo." So be it. The successful imprinting of this last of the Biancar subpersonalities was more important. That was his real priority, as it should be for all of them. With the skill of long practice in compartmentalization, he walled off his irritation and bent his attention coldly to the task at hand.

The procedure unfolded just as he had described it earlier to Ugoli. A cortical array dropped down over the skull of the sleeping clone. One feeder thread pierced the brainstem to emerge beneath the thalamus, traced fissure paths to penetrate deep into the cerebrum, and leaked programmed limited nanoneurals into the subject's frontal temporal lobe.

In that region with greatest control over personality and sense of self, nanites bonded with neurochemicals to build new neural pathways. Soon they would be as defined as if Biancar$_3$ had thought that way for a lifetime.

The array came online. Through induction, it replicated a certain set of bioelectrical patterns from the original man. Synapses fired in the clone's gray matter and pathways recently laid down by LNNs filled with the chain-reaction energy of thought.

Esimir watched the clone's brainwave traces shift and smiled to himself. The filtered core dump continued: "playback," as Ugoli had so crudely put it. Finally the point of critical density was reached. The bioelectrical storm of activity became self-sustaining and patterned. LNNs were extracted, the probe tendrils withdrawn, and finally, systems disengaged.

Biancar$_3$ slept on, still comatose, his brainwaves now significantly altered. It remained for the spark of ensoulment to awaken the clone, but that was a step not even Olniko could precipitate before its time.

Esimir looked up to the gallery. "That's it," he said tersely. "Imprint successful."

The visiting officers looked his way, and one stood. Lights from the med bay caught her sharp features as she walked to the end of the gallery and down the stairs, out onto the lab floor. She came directly to the doctor where he sat jacked into the command chair. He glimpsed the others trailing behind, but something about this woman drew his eyes to her face and kept them there.

"Thank you for doing this on such short notice, Dr. Metmuri."

Her words disarmed him. He sputtered for a moment. "Um, yes. As you say." Who was she? They had not been introduced, and he did not recognize the uniform or the rank tabs. Just that they were not Navy.

"The clone will sleep until he is enlivened, is that correct?"

"Yes."

"But you are certain that a different personality has been imprinted from that of the original."

"Different . . . no."

She raised a questioning brow.

"A subset," he added. "All elements were present in the original."

"I see. But it is effectively different, yes?"

"Without the other subsets to counterbalance in various ways . . . yes. That is our experience."

The woman turned and looked into the med bay, the lower bay floor lighting casting her face into sharp profile. "And you control the aspects that come alive in a clone."

It was a statement, no response required. Esimir sat silent. She turned back to him. "I met Biancar$_1$ a few hours ago. He seems like an ordinary person to me. Surly. But not a killer."

Esimir clenched his jaw. Met his clones, without his permission or escort? And he hadn't been informed? He threw a stormy glance at the officers gathered behind her, saw them watching him intently for his answer. He met her eyes again.

"Antisocial personas don't usually appear different to the casual observer. Leave him alone with some children, and we'd see his true colors come out pretty quickly, I'd say."

The woman pursed her lips, looked Esimir over as if she'd heard something distasteful. "Are you absolutely confident that you can separate out the destructive aspects?"

The bioempath began to answer with the same line of science he used on every layperson, from the station commander on down. He opened his mouth to speak about disassociated personality traits, and shadow-side aspects that bring balance to a whole and so must stay present—when he felt the stray quest of a psychic probe.

It was subtle, so very subtle, but she was close enough that he sensed the shift in her aura as she extended energies to probe him. It caused him to shut his mouth again, nonplussed, and guard his thoughts. Yet even as he did so, he sensed it was not a deep probe, but a mere riffling of the surface. A touch that could sense his truthfulness, perhaps, or his sincerity—but so unexpected, from one who did not wear the rus of the psychically adept. He regarded her warily.

"I'm sorry?" What had she just asked him?

"You separate out the killer?"

And now just as her psychic finger lay upon him, so had he, also, a finger on the core of her interest. It was a two-way channel between them now, though his touch was so gossamer-thin that he would wager not even another bio-empath would sense it. And now he understood her question. She did not care about psychological nuances. She wanted to know if fundamentally destructive elements could be separated out of a core personality. He nodded emphatically.

"That is the whole point of this work. To splinter off what causes people to harm others." He said it in all sincerity, for that was what he and Prevak had envisioned from the start. She must have sensed his conviction, for she smiled to herself. In that moment she went somewhere with that thought that left him cold.

"And you can package that all up in another." She nodded to herself. "I'm sure we'll speak again, Doctor."

She turned on her heel and walked away.

Esimir looked in her parting direction long after the door closed behind her entourage.

# 14

THE CLAN MOTHER of Palumara House, Eosan Bejmet, lived in a quiet corner of the Shelieno, on a terraced bluegrass hillside shaded by cracklebrush trees overlooking the steamy Dryx. The official residence of the Mother of Palumara House on Lyndir was elegantly modest, a single-story structure built with clean lines of native faie-wood to a traditional floor plan. Three wings surrounded an enclosed garden courtyard; the rear gates could be opened onto a view of the misty river and the Southbank artists' ward on the far shore.

In the ordinary course of events, Bejmet's world was self-contained. She answered only to the mother house on Calyx. On Lyndir, she was supreme authority to all Palumara House shigasu, and all local Palumara business was controlled and directed by her, or by her leave. The sensoria, the dining houses, the exotica offered at Tryst, were all her responsibility. Her house's war of constant competition with the economically powerful Ikoi House was hers to direct, while the irritations presented by Shonei House—with their cheap imitations of Palumara attractions—were distractions to be ignored, or thwarted where possible.

Management and intrigue on that scale came with the title of Eosan, and were things Bejmet was well used to dealing with.

This day, however, was not an ordinary day, and the intrigues it presaged were enough to unsettle the most poised of entertainers. Already Bejmet's visitor awaited her in the garden. She had heard footsteps along the gallery moments before, as a housegirl led the newcomer to the pavilion by the garden's miniature lake. Bejmet felt the urge to rush through her preparations, and resisted it with effort, using precious minutes to collect herself before the awkward meeting that loomed.

Looking in the mirror, she smoothed her pale yellow crepe undergown, retied the belt of the green brocade over-robe for the third time, and eyed her graying blond hair, piled ornately atop her head. She inhaled deeply and gathered herself to her full height—a modest height, but made more imposing by her traditional dress and her formal carriage. With any of her shigasu, she would have worn an air of authority as well. She checked herself in the mirror again. To her dismay, she could not tell if authority seemed present in her at all. All she noticed were tired lines at the edges of her eyes, and the downturn of her lips where a frown kept creeping unnoticed upon her face.

This would not do.

You are no benko, she reprimanded herself. No unschooled apprentice, to lack such self-control. At least compose the mask you will present to this visitor.

She stared in the mirror again, willing herself to a centered state, permitting the muscles of her face to relax until the only lines there were natural signs of age, not of distress or worry. No need to let this one read too much from her visage. She closed her eyes for a moment, using the old shigasue trick of memorizing how her face felt in that moment, so that the expression of openness, faint hint of smile, sincerity and respect could remain just so in the meeting that was to come. A mask, indeed.

She flicked her eyes open to regard her expression. Satisfied at last, she turned and walked out onto the gallery and down steps into the garden.

Through the latticework walls of the pavilion she saw the housegirl was serving her guest. A chuckling brook concealed their words, if any were being shared; by the time she stood in the arched doorway, the slave was bowing her way out, and a place awaited her across from the woman who had come to call.

"Domna." Bejmet greeted her with an obeisance, a dipping motion between a bow and a curtsy. The woman accepted the gesture placidly, held out a hand to motion Bejmet to take a seat in her own pavilion. She did so, kneeling across from where Ilanya Evanit sat upon plush cushions, a demitasse of chai held loosely in one hand.

"Cousin." She nodded to the shigasa. "Thank you for seeing me on such short notice."

"I am honored," Bejmet replied. "But I confess I am . . . surprised. What can I possibly do for a dae Ilanya?"

"Dae": a "great" one, meaning a legitimate one of full Ilanya bloodline, not dishonored, not disowned. It was blunt admission that although blood of the same ancestors flowed mutually in their veins, their status and standing in the clan were vastly different. Rarely did a dae of any clan bother to interact with those who had gone astray, who had fallen into the realm of the den-miri, the dishonored.

In Bejmet's case, strong clan identification in her family lay two centuries in the past. That she bore the same Ilanya surname was not definitive proof of blood-bond. It was only through gene tracing that the relationship could be established unequivocally.

Ilanya Eva had shown her that gene trace on the net this morning, when they had first spoken. Their blood kinship was irrefutable. That relationship brought with it considerable obligation as well, should dae choose to call upon den-miri. The prospect had hung like a shadow over Bejmet all day.

Could there be any other purpose for this stranger's visit here? It would be too rude to ask directly. Bejmet let her opening question hang on the air and noted with discomfort that her guest was in no hurry to answer it. The imperial officer drank from her tea cup, set it slowly down on the broad arm of her chair. It was almost as if she were reluctant to speak of what brought her here. Or maybe she was unsettled, speaking with a den-miri cousin? Surely she was no more practiced than Bejmet herself . . . ?

Eva's words interrupted her musing.

"You have a dreamflower who works for you." She used the shigasue's own euphemism for one who entertains. "I have a particular interest in her, and I require her services."

Bejmet kept the practiced smile on her carefully made-up face. Eva was not that simple. Services could be discreetly arranged through any of the Palumara houses in the Enclave. It was more than that which brought this distant relative of rank to her inner sanctum.

"I need her for an extended period. When I am done with her, I will return her to you. Should you lose her services at some point, I will compensate you for her loss."

Bejmet regarded her caller, those unblinking blue eyes holding her own. "I'm afraid I don't understand. What kind of service do you wish my dreamflower to perform for you?"

Eva busied herself again with the tea cup, cradling it in her hand. "You don't need to understand, Cousin. That I ask it should be enough."

Ah. So that was how she wanted to play this game. The woman was probably intent upon some arcane perversion, and wanted a toy she could use and return—and much the worse for wear, if there was a chance that they would "lose her services." There were places to arrange such entertainment, but Palumara House was not one of them.

"I'm afraid without knowing the purpose for which you desire a shigasa, I cannot provide you with one," Bejmet said, letting an apologetic tone creep into her voice.

Eva studied her silently for a moment, then smiled unexpectedly. "Perhaps you misapprehend me, Cousin. I need a dreamflower for a purpose that furthers the interests of House Ilanya. I wish your discreet aid to this end. That is why I have not simply walked into one of your establishments and dealt with a shigasa in plain sight of all."

"Is that so?" said Bejmet.

Eva's eyes narrowed slightly. "That is so."

Bejmet took a deep breath. "Forgive me, Cousin, but I still cannot help you. There is no Ilanya vassalage binding the shigasu who are my charges. Their allegiance is to the house that feeds and shelters us all. While I may choose to also work on behalf of Ilanya interests, I have no power to compel my subordinates to do so. I'm sure you understand."

An odd expression crossed Eva's face: disbelief, it seemed, at what she was hearing. She set her tea cup down on the table with more force than was necessary.

"I take it you are familiar with the Political Division of Internal Security?" she asked curtly.

Bejmet felt tension knot her stomach. Secret enforcers of the Emperor's will—who did not know of them? She nodded response to the question.

"You're looking at the uniform." Eva gestured to herself, her words clipped. "I need your cooperation for a matter that touches upon the security of the Empire. I am enlisting one of your shigasa to help us. You'll be well paid for her time, of course."

Her words had gone from a request to a statement bordering on an order, and Bejmet schooled her expression with an effort. This woman had no right. The shigasu were the Eosan's to order, no one else's. No matter the rank or how high in the government, no outsider dictated their business. Those with legitimate need for shigasue cooperation approached the mother house first—surely even PolitDiv knew that. If Ilanya were that interested she should be in conference with Dae Yoku on Calyx. Bejmet could not commit her shigasu to clandestine aid of any faction, and no outsider could demand it.

"I'm sorry to disappoint you," she said coolly, "but my answer is no. Not unless I know the use, and unless I approve. There are some requests we receive for services so unusual that even I cannot give them my blessing. I can refer your request to the mother house on Calyx, if you would like. I can't promise how they will decide."

A moment of silence stretched between them, Bejmet sitting properly correct, Eva coiled in tension or anger. The PolitDiv officer spoke first. "I take it you do not follow much political netnews."

Bejmet knew plenty of political news, most of it from the pillow talk of clients. What need to follow net headlines diligently? They rarely held the true story, anyway. "No," she confirmed. "I don't watch much."

"Has your reading of recent history, then, given you to understand that the head of PolitDiv is the right hand of the Emperor?"

No need to listen to netnews or history for that. That was common knowledge, a trivial data point in how the world worked. "I'm aware of that, yes."

Eva produced a datacard from her pocket, flicked it towards Bejmet with two fingers. The Eosan picked it up from the floor, hesitated.

"Go ahead. Activate it."

She thumbed the tab that illuminated the card, let it display whatever information it was preprogrammed with.

The card rezzed into a miniature holoplane, an identifying headshot of Ilanya Eva revealed within, along with a stream of related information: rank, title, security status, command priority, and more scrolling beneath. The Emperor's personal seal was watermarked in the data stream. Bejmet studied it for a full minute before thumbing it dark, and lowered the card with trembling hand.

"I had no idea, Domna, that you, that you . . ."

"Keep the card. You can verify the information on it with your house systems later."

Eva leaned forward suddenly. Bejmet recoiled a fraction and dropped her eyes, finally losing the mask she had so carefully maintained.

"I preferred to work with you as a cooperative kinswoman on this matter, Eosan, but you have eliminated that gentle alternative for me. Now I will tell you frankly how it's going to be. I am not approaching your house through official channels, so your Palumara House superiors need not be informed of our business. This is our private understanding, just you and me, as cousins. Do you understand me?"

Bejmet kept her eyes lowered respectfully. "As you say, Domna."

"You have a shigasa named Hinano Kesada working at Tryst. You will instruct the Dosan there to make that woman available to us. I have agents who will visit discreetly and remove her from the premises. Not permanently; we'll return her in about two months. When she is back, I expect that the Dosan and all others in that house will conveniently forget that she was ever gone from their midst. It will not be a topic for discussion, under any circumstances. Is that clear?"

"Yes, Domna."

"Her house will be paid for her time, her usual rates, and a large gratuity to ensure discretion." Eva stood abruptly; Bejmet came quickly to her feet as well. "I want you to set weregeld price for her also. For our records."

"Weregeld?" Bejmet's voice cracked. That was the price owed in reparation for someone's death.

Eva gestured with a finger, and a man in service grays and a silvered visor stepped out of the greenery along the garden path. He had been standing motionless a short distance away, lost from direct sight behind screening powder fronds. Bejmet started at his unexpected presence. He came to stand beside and behind Eva.

"This is Teo," she introduced him. "He'll be in touch with you regarding these details. And yes, I said weregeld. Don't worry, Eosan, we don't plan to kill your shigasa. It's . . . protection for us both, in case anything unforeseen happens. If so, we've taken care of this little detail before the fact, when emotions are not inflating values. Understand?"

Ilanya Bejmet nodded mutely, in contrast to the storm of protest she held within. As if she sensed the unspoken resistance, Eva took a half step closer, riveting her with the intensity of her gaze.

"And Cousin? If you disobey me in the least wise—if you reveal this to others, if your shigasu do not give you, and hence me, utter obedience and utmost discretion . . . if you interfere with my plans, rest assured: I will destroy you."

Bejmet paled beneath her makeup.

"That is neither jest nor idle threat." Eva pointed at the datacard the Eosan still held in her hand. "Study file ten on that card. It contains a summary of punitive actions I've taken in the last year. All verifiable in your infosphere."

Eva's cold blue eyes held hers. "If I take that path with you, there will be no Palumara House on Lyndir, and no mother house left standing on Calyx. If you betray me, I will crush all you hold dear. Don't doubt that I can do it. Is my meaning clear?"

"Yes, Domna," Bejmet forced out.

Her thoughts raced. She had no doubt based on the tales she had heard that the Kingmaker was that ruthless and that powerful. But why was this unusual demand for a shigasa worth such weighty threats? Bejmet was not so powerless that she could only bow before this arrogant Gen'karfa's whim. She had ways to discover information, or to stymie this woman's machinations, if she must. The Sector Governor himself came to Tryst, and he owed her favors. She would talk with him, privately—

Eva turned a quarter-turn away, paused. "I know," she spoke into the air, "how very well connected shigasue are. What pillow talk garners you for alliances and spy capacity."

Bejmet started, guiltily. It was as if Ilanya had read her thoughts. The woman locked eyes with her again. "Do not think to invoke this network against me," she said. "I will count that as the gravest of betrayals, and the Emperor listens to my advice about such things. If you do not aid imperial interests as required, and honor the need for strictest confidence, then you stand in opposition to the Emperor's will."

Eva turned back to face Bejmet squarely. "If Emperor Nalomeci does not wish your adopted clan to exist, Den-mira, then their very foundations will be ground to dust and a retrovirus tailored only for their bloodlines will be loosed to obliterate them all."

A cold fist clenched in Bejmet's guts. She knew with certainty that what she heard from the head of PolitDiv was absolute truth. Ilanya Eva would snuff Palumara House without blinking, if it served her purpose.

"That you exist at all is at the leave of the Emperor. Do not make us make an example of you to the other shigasue."

Bejmet sank to her knees, and bowed her head to the ground at her cousin's feet.

Eva left without another word.

# 15

KES LAY FACEDOWN on her bed, naked. Desta straddled her hips and leaned into her back, fingers kneading tired muscles, massaging away the stiffness that had settled there after Kes had administered a strenuous flogging the day before.

"Hethbert will be the death of me yet," the domina mumbled into her crossed arms. "He responds to sensation about as well as a dolophant."

"He likes you, though," said Desta.

"Of course he likes me. They all like me. But giving him a beating he can feel through all that blubber takes the aim of a marksman and the endurance of a . . . of a blacksmith."

The girl's skillful fingers dug into her right biceps and shoulder, working to loosen muscles that were nearly as hardened as a smith's. "If anyone can do it, you can."

"He says it's his monthly massage."

The slave giggled. "It can feel like that. The thuddy sensations, you know? They get to deep muscles, loosen them up." She emphasized with a dig of her fingers.

Kes glanced over her shoulder at the girl. "Don't tell me about thuddy sensations. I do it right—you won't have skin left on your back."

"Domna—!"

"It's true."

"I wouldn't like it if you played that way with me."

"I would only do that with someone who invited it, and that doesn't happen very often. I sure can't do Hethbert like that. Thing is, he actually *wants* a massage. Floggings are relaxation for him. If it was torture, he'd run the other way."

"He's not a pain player."

"No, not many of them are. Not like my Morya."

Desta spread more lotion on her hands, moved to the left shoulder blade, began to rub tight muscles there. She was silent for a bit, worked her way to the upper arm. Kes sighed in pleasure.

"You miss her, don't you."

"Who?"

"Morya."

Kes was silent. Desta dug fingers more deeply into muscles that had tensed up again.

"It's all right, Domna. I'm sure she misses you, too."

The tall woman turned her face to the other side, where she could not see Desta easily. "Doesn't matter." She shrugged against the expert fingers that worked tension out of her deltoid muscles. "We can't spend the kind of time together we'd like."

Desta's brow furrowed. "You sound frustrated."

Kes's muscular shoulders heaved in a prone shrug. "It hasn't been the same since I left there."

The slave shook her head. "I'm sorry, I don't follow. Why do you say that?"

Kes blew air through her lips, exasperated. "Because, silly gritzl, Morya can't leave and I can't visit. Dosan Kiyo forbade me entrance."

Desta's hands stopped moving, rested with warm palms atop Kes's shoulder blades.

"What?" The domina twisted her head about, to glimpse the quizzical look on her slave's face.

"She can't do that."

"Well, she did."

"No—I mean, she *can't*. It's not allowed to bar shigasu from shigasue establishments. Not once you're clan. And you've been adopted."

Kes froze beneath her. When she spoke, her voice was strained. "Are you telling me that as a joygirl she could tell me to keep out, but as Palumara House kin, she has to let me in?"

"Maybe not to visit, not if it's disruptive—"

"That's what she claimed. I'm out."

"—but she can't refuse any entertainer who walks in the door as a client of her house unless they've created disturbance there as a client."

Kes was silent.

"You ever been banned as a client at the Salon?"

The white-haired head shook in the negative.

"Then you can go in as a client."

"In as a client."

"Sorry, Domna. I thought you knew that. I thought you were staying away on purpose."

"On purpose."

Kes rolled over suddenly, throwing the girl from her back and onto the pammas matting beside her. She pounced atop her, grinning fiercely. "I can go in as a client? You're sure?"

The slave nodded.

"If you're right, girl, I'm going to give you one of those floggings you like. The relaxing kind."

Desta grinned back at her. "I'll be looking forward to it."

Kes knelt up, threw her head back, and laughed. "Client? Oh, Ashani's tits, I have to plan this visit just right." She poked the girl in her ribs; Desta squeaked. "Get up, you lazy thing. I need help getting clothes together."

A SARTORIAL CRISIS delayed Kes's departure from Tryst. Dressy but casual clothes were her preference; she could change quickly, go across rooftops, and descend into the Salon through the entertainer's entrance. But then she would be slinking back into that place as if she had something to hide, like kitchen staff that came and went away from public eyes. Or Icechromer eyes.

On the other hand, to approach from the street meant mingling with clients and the public who knew her from vidverts. She could not walk the streets of the Shelieno like any other passerby; she had learned that in the last year, when shopping trips and journeys into other districts had become noteworthy for the groupies that followed and the brash tourists who thought they could approach her. If she took the street route it mattered very much how she dressed and conducted herself because out in the world she was—as Helda always impressed upon her—a walking advertisement. It would not be Kes who stepped out the client door of Tryst, but the Winter Goddess in streetwear.

Seemed like an awful lot of trouble to go to, just to see her girl. But the alternative of slipping into the Salon incognito, as if she were sneaking, was even less in her nature.

She settled on a white silk blouse, flowing sleeves caught tight at wrists, open at the chest to reveal a full bustier of white leather and silver metal stays. She wore white clingpants of pressure cloth like spacers' shipwear, fabric hugging the line of her long legs; around her slender waist she wrapped a belt of silver links a handspan broad. Finally she stepped into white canvas and chromed metal knee-high boots of the thick-soled industrial style fashionably called Urban Combat Gear—not suitable for combat at all, of course, but with lines reminiscent of military styling, with plassteel toes.

Suitable for kicking ass, she thought, which is just as well, considering where I'm going. Icechromers. Feh.

When she stepped out the door, she was a monochrome fashion statement from boots to white mane, the only color her bloodred lips and red nails. She knew her look was distinctive enough no matter how she dressed—truth be told, she enjoyed playing it up, enjoyed the attention it garnered. But today her thoughts were elsewhere. She was nearly blind to the admiring glances that came her way on the street outside Tryst. She had a mind only for her destination: the Salon.

The building looked as she remembered it from her arrival there three years before. Three stories tall, a plaster-smooth, windowless façade designed to draw the eye to the broad door frame of the entrance. That frame was the traditional emblem of a joyhouse: faie-wood paneling an arm's length wide edged each side of the entrance, ornately carved with figures in sexual positions or caught in hedonistic scenes of celebration. Kes approached that distinctive doorway with slowing footsteps. She noted clinically that her pulse was racing now, just as it had when she first crossed that threshold. She collected herself for a moment, then pushed the door open and walked into the dim light of the foyer.

"You!" Franc was sitting door duty, and complete surprise showed on his face. He came to his feet. "You know the rules." He blocked her path, arms crossed on muscular chest. "Turn around and walk out before I have the pleasure of throwing you out."

Kes looked down her nose at the man a handspan shorter than she. "I always knew you were dumb, Franc, but I thought you could read."

"Leave." He pointed a finger.

"Haven't read the house rules lately, have you?"

He hesitated.

"You better refresh your memory about admission of shigasu to shigasue establishments. In case you forgot, the Icechromers sublet this operation. The license is held by Dosan Kiyo. That makes this a shigasue business."

"So what?" he snapped.

"So you can't keep out shigasu. Hadn't you heard, Franc? I'm Palumara clan now." She hooked a finger under the cuff of her right wrist, pulled the cloth back to reveal a short silver thread that followed the line of her tendon. It was the data-encoded tag shigasue clanmates wore to identify themselves to each other and to entertainer houses when they traveled from home.

Franc's heavy brows drew together. "Wait here."

He called upstairs; moments later Dosan Kiyo joined them in the doorway. Her confirming glance at Kes's wrist was perfunctory. "I heard Bejmet adopted you." Kiyo was related to Ikoi House, but the grapevine of news in the Shelieno kept no event of significance hidden for long. "I wondered if you'd come back sometime."

"Just here to enjoy the pleasures of your establishment," Kes smiled at her. "You do run such a lovely brothel, Dosan." She let the smile fade. "I trust you have no problem with me paying for services here?"

Kiyo's eyebrows crept up her forehead. "No problem. You're welcome to spend your money."

Kes tilted her head in acknowledgment.

"But leave the Icechromers alone, will you? I don't need more trouble from you. You start, and you'll be banned, paying client or no."

"I understand you, Housemother," the domina told her. "Now if you would kindly have your muscleboy step aside, I'd like to come in."

Kiyo gave Franc a sharp look. "Same applies to you. Don't you start with her."

"Start what?" he grumbled. "That's a nice piece of ass we're missing, but if she's on the paying side—"

Kiyo rounded on him instantly, jabbing his sternum with one finger. "*That* has you off the door and on report to Gistano. What relationship you had with your indentured debtor is past. This is a client, and you know house rules regarding how we treat clients. You *do* know them, don't you, Franc?"

"Yes, Dosan." He studied the floor as he replied.

"Get yourself to Gistano."

He slipped away from her angry scrutiny to report himself to the boss of the Icechromer derevin. Kiyo regarded Kes wryly. "Well, at least you didn't start that one. I'll take you around and give a few reminders about clients and house rules. I'm sorry to say I think it's necessary. I'm not sure the boys have missed you since you've been gone, but they surely haven't forgotten you."

Kes smirked, and followed Kiyo into the lounge of the Salon.

MORYA SAT AT her dressing table rearranging her hair. She had two hours before she needed to be in the lounge, and that left enough time to experiment with some other way to put her dark curls up.

Someone scratched at her door. "Yes?" she called out. In the mirror she saw Dosan Kiyo open the door.

"Your shift just changed," the housemother announced. "You're on duty right now."

"I am?" Morya turned, one hand holding hair coiled atop her head, the other fumbling with a clipstic to weave through and hold it in place. "Now?"

Kiyo gave her a cryptic smile, and stepped back into the hall, someone taking her place in the doorway.

Morya gasped. "Ah!" she cried, jumping up. Abandoning curls and clipstic, she dashed to the door and into Kes's arms. "Oh! You! Whatever are you doing here?"

Kes silenced her with a kiss, then pushed her back into the dressing room, shutting the door behind them.

"I'm your client, kushla."

"How can that be?" Morya asked, astounded.

Kes sat on her dressing stool and patted one thigh. "Come here and I'll tell you about it." They sat, arms around each other, while she filled Morya in on her welcome discovery of shigasa perquisites. Kes ran a hand through Morya's tumbled hair. "So for as long as I hire your time, we can spend time."

Morya beamed. "I don't know what to say."

"You don't need to say a word." She grinned devilishly. "Maybe do a little screaming, but words are optional. Take me to your room."

Morya hesitated. "You don't have toys with you. Do you want anything? We can use the playroom. . . ." That was the room reserved for sexual torments and certain kinds of rough play. Most brothels had one, nothing on a scale to compete with a place like Tryst, but adequate for commonplace kinky amusements.

In reply Kes kissed her, caught her lip between her teeth, then slowly bit harder and harder until Morya moaned in arousal.

She released her grip. "I have everything I need," she said softly. "Let's go."

Without another word, Morya stood and, taking her lover's hand, led her down the hall and up the stairs to her room.

# 16

HELDA JOINED BEJMET in the reception chamber of her residence. "You wanted to see me, Eosan? You said it was urgent."

"Thank you for coming so quickly." Bejmet took Helda's elbow, steered her towards the gallery door that opened on the inner courtyard. "Come, let's walk in the garden and talk."

As they descended the steps, she fidgeted with a datacard in her hand. She gestured with it towards the stream that meandered through the garden landscape, led them to its source in a small waterfall constructed near the pavilion. "Here," said Bejmet. She sat on a stone bench beneath a feather leaf tree, where the burbling rush of water was loud enough to conceal their words from chance ears of household staff. Helda recognized this as one of the Eosan's favorite spots for sharing confidences. She sat beside the senior shigasa, and waited for her to tell her why she had been summoned.

Bejmet played with the card she held and did not meet Helda's eyes. She seemed unable or unwilling to begin. The Dosan rested her hand on Bejmet's thigh. "What's wrong?" she asked gently.

Bejmet forced out a brittle laugh. "Right about now I'm supposed to be dictating to you how you are going to cooperate with an outsider who has chosen to intrude in our business."

"Eosan?" Shock and puzzlement were evident in Helda's voice.

"If we cooperate with her, we are bowing to outside interests, doubtless at cost to our own, and I suspect we're falling into some Lakshan-cursed imperial intrigue in the process. It's an intolerable precedent to set, and it will cost me my place and future if the mother house learns of it. If we do *not* cooperate with her, she will destroy Palumara House out of spite. Not just us on Lyndir, but the entire House."

Of all the possible reasons Bejmet might have called her here, this was the last thing in the world Helda was prepared for. She could scarcely believe her ears, but the Eosan was near tears and her distress quite real. She had never known her to take wild flights of fancy or exaggerate circumstances. She shook her head in disbelief. Destroy Palumara House?

"Who would want to do that?" she blurted.

In answer Bejmet pressed the datacard into her hand. Helda studied its contents and then sat still, her mind racing.

The pillow talk that came to the ears of the shigasue included a great deal of political intrigue, whispered from Enclave to Enclave in the rapid sharing that had characterized entertainers since ancient times. When such intelligence spread through their network, once in a great while Helda heard the Kingmaker mentioned. Never as an immediate contact, but as the spider in a distant imperial web, pulling strings with far-flung consequences that sometimes drove a client to the Enclave to seek solace from his worldly woes. The head of the Emperor's political police was a shadow figure, a faceless bogeyman; everyone knew he existed, and like the bogeyman, hoped they would never encounter him.

Or her. Helda was surprised to learn that a woman was head of Internal Security's political police. She had never thought about it. She paid attention to the government players on distant Calyx only through the grapevine of shigasue gossip. It had not been relevant to her life . . . until now.

She felt for Bejmet. This much official scrutiny was at best uncomfortable; at worst, fatal for their business. Entertainers of the Between-World might associate closely with favored patrons or clients, but they stayed scrupulously out of politics, favoritism, faction intrigues: away from anything that could put their autonomous status at risk. Gods forfend they should become distrusted, or perceived to be some group's tool. Clients aligned with opposing interests would fall away, all shigasu would be suspect, everyone's business would be hurt.

Surface neutrality was the hard-and-fast rule for entertainers. They might bend that rule when it suited them—to serve an honor-debt to a client, perhaps, or gain obligation that would help the shigasue strategically. But never would they compromise neutrality in answer to the needs of outsiders.

Out of this doggedly neutral stance came other codes of conduct, foremost among them that no house allowed clients to dictate staff or business decisions of any sort. Clients were just that, and no more, outsiders who stepped upon the stage of the Between-World only for a time, while it was the shigasu who must live there, always.

Now here came the ultimate outsider, the Emperor's shadow enforcer, the Kingmaker herself, daring to dictate terms where even the ruling Lau Sa'adani nobility stayed scrupulously hands-off.

She didn't know if she was more affronted by the gall of the woman, or worried by the threat to them all.

Bejmet was both. "It's dangerous to defy her," she said. "This is the one who arranged for the extinction of the entire kin network of House Aneo, after the Aneo Rebellion was put down. She has the capacity to carry out her threats, and she won't hesitate to do so."

"What is it she wants that's worth such consequences?"

"Not that much, relatively speaking." Bejmet avoided her eyes. "It must be a move in a bigger game, one she'll kill to keep secret. That is why I don't take her words as threat, Helda. I take them as promise. She made clear the consequences of defying her or betraying her."

Helda shifted uncomfortably. "Are you betraying something by sharing this with me?"

Bejmet laughed bitterly. "No. You're part of it."

"Oh?" She handed the datacard back.

"She wants one of your girls for an extended period. She won't say what for. Then she'll return her to you. But she also wants us to name weregeld price, in case we 'lose the girl's services,' as she put it."

Helda's brows drew together. "She's doing something that might kill one of my shigasa."

"Apparently so."

Bejmet and Helda shared a look. It reeked of secret schemes and machinations; a precarious business, if they allowed it. Yet with Ilanya's . . . promise . . . hanging over their heads, how could they not permit it?

"Ashani guard us," Helda breathed. "This is awful."

Bejmet nodded.

"Does it matter what girl I give them?"

The Eosan did not answer her, but studied the stepping stones at their feet.

"Bejmet?"

The older woman sighed. "Hinano Kesada."

"What!?"

"They want the Winter Goddess."

"What in the seven icy hells do they want with her?" Helda's voice rose. Bejmet raised a cautioning finger and motioned her to moderate her tone. Her own reply was a harsh whisper.

"Now you know all that I know. And I tell you as your Eosan that you are going to cooperate with this Juro-cursed woman, and we will pray that no harm comes to Kesada. I've been over this a million times, and it's the best we can do."

Helda came to her feet, fists clenched, then unclenched. She could not defy her Eosan. She could not put Kes at risk. She distrusted PolitDiv; to imagine Kes in their clutches was unbearable. To imagine her House destroyed, even more so.

She shared a long, bleak look with Bejmet. Unable to speak beyond her turmoil, she gave a deep bow and took her leave.

# 17

HELDA FOUND DESTA in the slave quarters. "Where's Kes?"

"She went to the Salon, Domna."

"She did?" She blinked in surprise. "What for?"

"To see her girl there."

Helda shook her head. She needed to find Kes, talk with her about her sudden engagement . . . Desta was making no sense. "What girl?"

"She had a lover when she was there. That girl. Morya."

Helda's fingers tightened on the door frame. Kes had never once mentioned a lover left behind in the joyhouse. Helda was the only one the domina had here at Tryst, and as far as she was concerned, Kes could have a lot more of her.

Seeking out a forgotten lover at time like this? Helda bit back anger and a sudden surge of jealousy. "If you see her before I do, tell her to come speak to me," she ordered, and shut the door as the slave was replying.

Retiring to her rooms, Helda called Bejmet on the com. The Eosan looked tired. "Yes?"

"When are we supposed to do this . . . thing . . . with Kesada?"

Bejmet glanced off-screen, then back to Helda. "Tomorrow, noon. They're sending two men to get her. No uniforms, I'm told. They'll identify themselves to you at the door."

"They could have just contracted for her services," she snapped, "instead of creating all this disruption."

Bejmet sighed. "Would you have let the Winter Goddess go for some unexplained purpose for two months or more? I wouldn't have. I told Ilanya no the first two times she asked me."

"Our regular clients—the bookings already committed—"

"I know."

"Tomorrow's too soon."

"I know that, too."

They fell silent, regarding each other through the net. Any time would be too soon. There was no right time to do this at all.

Helda released a long-held breath. "I'll tell her tonight. She'll be ready tomorrow."

Bejmet nodded and broke the connection.

Helda slammed a fist on her desktop and cursed until she was out of breath.

Then she buzzed Thea, one of her two personally-owned slaves. "Bring me a tab of Glitz from the Mix bar."

"Yes, Domna."

Good girl. No hesitation; no reminder that this was against the Dosan's own rules, that shigasu of her house did not take euphorics and mood alterants. They were for clients only.

But not today.

KES AND HER girl lay entwined in bed, sweaty, tired, disheveled. Morya traced the domina's white eyebrow, ran a finger down her cheek. "It makes you look so different than you used to," she murmured.

"You liked my blond hair better?"

She shrugged. "It's just different. I hardly recognize you on the verts, but you sure do look good."

"And not in person?"

"You . . . !" Morya's lips pressed against Kes's. "You're even better in person. I've gotten really tired of looking at your verts."

Kes propped her head on one hand, wrapped a raven curl around her finger. "Yeah, about that. I guess you'll see me more often now. Maybe a lot more often."

The statement was quiet, matter of fact. Dark blue eyes sought her own. "Do you mean that?"

Kes studied her girl's face: luscious lips, the slightly dimpled cheek where her smile quirked habitually to the side. Fine brows, furrowed now with the earnestness of her expression . . . a sudden teariness in her eyes.

Gods, thought Kes. It really matters to her.

She felt the nervousness in her own gut that said it mattered to herself as well.

"Yes, I mean it," Kes told her. "I'd like to . . . well. We need to spend more time together. So we'll do something about that. All right?"

Morya grasped her hand, kissed her fingers in reply. She lay there thoughtfully for a moment. "Can you afford this, though? It's awfully expensive to book a girl for hours."

"Expense is relative."

"No, really."

Kes chuckled. "You cost a hundred creds an hour. I clear three hundred an hour after house cut, more with tips. Trust me. I can afford it."

Morya kissed her again, quickly, and shrugged off her pensive mood. She got out of bed, poured two glasses of fenberry juice from the service cubby, and returned to the bedside with the drinks. "What are you grinning at?" she asked.

Kes gestured with her chin. "Your backside. Bears my marks."

"Ah." Morya looked behind her, glimpsed enough to see marks from Kes's handiwork. "Souvenirs. You warmed me up nicely." She sat on the edge of the bed and passed a glass to Kes. "And yes, before you ask—I'm acutely aware of them when I'm sitting. I'll remember you've been there for a while." She grinned mischievously.

Kes squeezed Morya's thigh in a possessive grip. "Mine."

"I suppose Kiyo charged you extra, to leave marks on me."

"Of course."

"I can't imagine you playing without marks, though."

"Not with you. You make me want to play hard." She sat up, finished her juice. "I have to get going. I have work tonight. And before you don't ask, I'll tell you: I'll be back. Tomorrow."

Morya leaned her head on Kes's shoulder. "Thanks. I wasn't going to ask."

"I know." She kissed her cheek. "Look: I have something I want to talk to you about. Something important, for both of us. Maybe we could talk some at laufre tomorrow, all right? It's our usual date, anyway."

"Ooh. I don't know." Her brows pressed together. "Sounds serious. Should I be worried?"

Kes pushed unruly curls aside, cupped Morya's cheek in her hand. "Nothing to worry about. It's good. I want to talk about our future together."

The breath caught in Morya's throat. "Do we have one?" Her voice shook. "Together?"

"If you want it, yes."

Morya's answer was in her kiss. When they broke apart, she had tears in her eyes, and Kes did not trust herself to speak.

"I'll see you tomorrow, then," Morya said.

Kes nodded and busied herself, collecting her things to leave. By time she trusted her voice again, she was halfway out the door. She paused.

"See you at noon, kushla."

The door shut behind her, and Morya collapsed in happy tears.

KES DIDN'T WANT to deal with the public. She returned to Tryst through the rooftop gardens, her mind racing with a thousand thoughts as she walked the familiar pathways.

It's all right that you didn't ask her tonight. It's too soon. We needed that time together. But tomorrow . . .

She smiled. She no longer had any doubt how Morya would answer The Question. And her contract—it would take a while to work out the details, but in the meantime, she could still see her girl, even spend the night there if she wanted. . . .

She allowed herself a smile. Desta had been right: her entrée to the Salon had been a given. Now, what kind of flogger would give the best thud, to reward the house slave? She considered that as she took the stairs rapidly down to the backstage dressing levels of Tryst.

She nodded to Pol in passing, the slave heading for Control for the early evening shift. "The Domna wants to see you," he said.

Kes nodded. She entered her dressing room, already stripping her street clothes, and talked to the wall comp. "Give me the Dosan," she told the house com system. It tracked Helda's whereabouts, connected the two. "I just got in and I'm running late," she said. "Would you like to join me down here or shall I come up?"

There was brief silence on the com, then Helda's voice came in a breezy inflection. "Oh, we can't keep clients waiting, now can we? I'll come down there."

Kes looked askance at the speaker. That was a strange tone to hear from the Dosan. Flippant. Helda was many things, but seldom that. She shrugged, donned her red dressing robe, sat at the table to apply her makeup. Moments later Helda entered unannounced, shutting the door behind her.

Kes caught her eyes in the mirror; the Dosan leaned against the door, studying her with an odd expression on her face. "What's up?" the shigasa prompted.

"I hear you went to the Salon."

Kes nodded, holding her mouth just so while she ran a color wand over her lips.

"I didn't know you had a lover there, Kesada. You're holding out on me." She said it lightly, as if it were a joke, but Kes didn't like the sound of that comment at all.

"Then I suppose Dosan Kiyo didn't tell you every little thing about me when you traded for my contract. She's good for saying only what she has to, that one."

"This isn't about Kiyo." Helda stepped closer.

Why was it they always managed to have confrontations in this room, before sessions, or after sessions? Was that why Helda was taking that tone with her? Did she want to be taken down again, here, now? Kes wasn't interested, not after an afternoon with Morya.

"What *is* this about, Helda?"

The Dosan ran her hands through her unruly hair. "About things that are over your head, Winter Goddess."

Kes put the static tube of powdercoat down and swiveled around to regard the housemother of Tryst. The woman couldn't meet her eyes; something was definitely wrong. "What are you talking about?"

Helda burst out in a laugh of hearty amusement. "Puppets of the gods, you know? Like that old poem, *lives arranged in ways that only gods perceive, you live your days upon a hidden string . . .*"

Kes eyed the other woman. If she didn't know better, she'd say Helda was on something.

"You have your secret love and I have my . . . secrets. We all affect each other's lives profoundly, don't you think? In our little ways."

Kes shook her head. "I don't have time for this. If you have something to say to me, spit it out."

Helda *tsk*ed at her. "And that is not the proper stance to take to your Dosan, either, junior shigasa that you are. When you treat me with proper respect and are honest with me, maybe I'll do the same with you."

Kes turned her back on Helda and picked up the cosmetic stic again. "Suit yourself. I have a client in half an hour, so pardon me while I continue getting ready."

Helda bridled, put hands on hips in that way she had before she loosed her temper. Kes deigned to ignore her angry reflection. Finally Helda laughed again and broke the tension. "There's plenty of time tomorrow, oh yes, plenty of time. I'll talk to you then." She left without another word.

Kes was glad to see her go. If she was going to carry on like that, tomorrow would be more than soon enough.

# 18

KES FOLLOWED HER ordinary routine in the morning, sitting with Frebo, checking her net accounts. She noticed the purf showed more pink and gold today, joyful colors to match her mood. The few orange spots there broadened on the symbiont's feather coat as she thought of her strange run-in with Helda the day before.

I'll talk with her after laufre, she told herself. I'll be more calm and centered then, anyway.

She started an astrogation problem, flubbed it, tried again, then gave up halfway through. She couldn't concentrate; her mind was already at the meditation square with Morya. She put Frebo away and changed into her workout clothes, eager to get on with this very special day.

She was about to walk out the door when she heard someone scratching on it. She opened it to Helda standing there with a grim expression on her face.

"Going somewhere?" the Dosan asked, pushing past her into the room.

"Laufre."

"No, you're not."

"Yes, I am."

"No. You are not." The tension in her voice gave emphasis that halted Kes's protest mid-breath. She cast a glance towards the door she had just entered. Kes followed the look and saw two strangers in the hall, nondescript men in business-cut tunics who might be clients. They waited right outside her door.

"Who are they?" she demanded.

"Shut it," Helda said to them. "We need a moment."

The taller of the two nodded and closed Kes's door.

"I should have spoken to you last night," Helda said, "but I was . . . in a mood, and didn't."

"Is this an apology?"

"I don't have time for apologies, and you don't have time for laufre. Pack a bag with essentials in it. You're going with these gentlemen on a little trip. Right now."

Kes's mouth opened; Helda came close to her, put a finger on her lips. "Please, Kes. Please. Don't argue, don't fight. Just listen. This is by order of Eosan Bejmet. It is something special you must do for the sake of our house. Remember your oath. That's all I can tell you."

"Go where? Why?"

Helda shook her head. "You'll be gone for two months—"

"Two months?!"

"—maybe more. Consider it . . . a lengthy booking, if you will. We're receiving full price for your time. Cooperate. Be the gracious shigasa you were trained to be."

"I'm a commanding domina these days, not a gracious chai girl, or did you forget?" Kes hissed angrily. "I will not be sent off like this. Are you mad at me about the Salon?"

Helda winced. "This has nothing to do with the Salon, Kes. Truly. These arrangements were made by the Eosan on very short notice. We had no time to prepare you."

Kes stood stiffly. "Do you at least know who the client is?"

The Dosan hesitated. "A government official. A very high, royally favored government official."

Kes glared. "Now? Right now?"

Helda nodded.

Kes riveted her with a look, eyes sparking with barely restrained temper. "You can't tell me more?"

"I don't know more."

"Then you promise me, Helda, that you will tell Morya at the Salon that I'm called away, and when I'll be back."

The Dosan nodded.

"Right away." Kes clenched her arm, squeezed it. "You swear it?"

"Of course." Helda pulled away. "Now hurry. These men won't wait."

In a quarter hour she was packed and dressed again in the white clothes she'd worn on the streets to see her girl. They were close to hand and no doubt dressy enough to impress this client, no matter how imperially favored.

She left with the men flanking her, an escort that reminded her of professional bodyguards. She put away her misgivings and gathered her power to her. By the time they left the building it was not Kes they escorted, but the Winter Goddess who led them.

NOON CAME AND went in the meditation square. Morya waited, then worked out by herself. She had the self-control not to cry until she was back in the privacy of her room. Then she dried her tears and chided herself for being too emotional.

Something came up, that's all. I'll hear from her soon. She's supposed to see me again today.

It was a comforting thought and helped ease the rest of her day.

———

HELDA SAT COMPOSING a note to be delivered to the Salon. She didn't care to talk to that girl directly—that was entirely too much contact with her—but it wasn't right to relay messages through Salon staff. Words were too easily twisted that way. She needed to say just the right thing to her. . . .

After a few tries she threw her stylus to one side. Nothing was coming out right. What did you say to your lover's lover? She was too sick with worry about Kes to be able to concentrate on a note to Morya.

She would take her time, think of something. She could send it a while later. Maybe in a day or two, when she felt less raw.

She considered another tab of Glitz, decided against it, and settled for a drink instead.

# PART

TWO

# 19

FLASHMAN DRIFTED INTO the central node of Janus's com network disguised as an audit ping. His loose collection of electrons appeared to be just another low-level cluster of infobits, routine traffic that Red Hand defenses didn't look at twice.

At the portico to Janus's household systems, he dropped his masquerade. He coalesced back into his lightning-spiked sim-self, set pointy arms akimbo, and gazed up at the massive routing nexus that towered overhead.

The mass glowed a dusky purple, its asymmetrical bulk looming like an inverted pyramid buried peak-first in the dataplane of the call center. Dataports punctuated the nexus two thirds of the way up the outward-sloping sides. They looked like broad round portholes glowing molten yellow. From each, a line of coherent light streamed outward like a beacon, parallel to the "floor" of the dataplane.

The beams glittered in the void like chaff-filled streams, rushing data into and out of the cartel boss's systems. This was the main gateway between net infrastructure and Red Hand household—not the sole route, but the one most commonly used. He could have flowed right through one of those golden portals—but if he tried it, he'd have a fight for his life on his hands. Bugrunner probes showed hunter-killer defenses inside the nexus, the kind that pursued relentlessly once they engaged a target.

Time for other tactics, Flash thought, patting the neon-pink satchel that hung across his chest. And fights were off-limits here anyway. A cat ten was a delicate thing to pull off. It reminded Flash of some of the touchy jobs he'd done for the assassin Reva, an old client of his.

He morphed his sim hands and feet into bonding pads and started up the backwards-inclined ascent. He chafed at the pedestrian but safe approach, but Obray was paranoid about not leaving a trace, even so much as a netrunner signature. Flash was nominally under contract, but at times like this, he was reminded that he wasn't all that free yet, after all.

When he was done sulking about Obray's over-cautiousness, he dealt with the problem the commander had set him. If he couldn't go in and risk his usual flashy data infiltration, then he'd find some other way to play info-tag with Janus. With a little unwitting help from Internal Security—they never noticed when

Flash did some judicious borrowing of code segments from their routine library—the decker had cobbled together a unique creation.

Clever me, he congratulated himself. If anything like it exists I've never heard of it before.

The satchel hung behind him now, swinging with the motion of his ascent. The bag was heavy with the weight of the worm he had created. Or tapeworm, as he had introduced it to Obray. They had met in cyberspace recently so he could show off his coding.

"Why tapeworm?" the commander asked, taking the ropy, wrist-thick length of the construct into the white wire-form hands of his officer's sim.

"Because it's a self-replicating parasite. It can split off—and the fragment has a life of its own. Step one: when Janus enters his com system, the worm infiltrates his wetware through the rigger jack in his head."

Obray grunted surprised approval. That alone was an unusual approach to things. Cyberdeckers focused on the virtual worlds of the net and the 'spheres; few mucked around in the delicate chipware that enabled cyberinterfaces.

"Step two: a piece of the worm stays behind in whatever standalone system he connects with. It'll monitor the info there, then rejoin the main worm when he taps that system again. Whenever he jacks into a clear com channel later, the worm will dump data to us."

"Selective infection and data dumping. Nicely done." Obray handed the semi-sentient, squirming thing back to FlashMan. "I still think it's a shot in the dark."

"Of course it is." Flash shrugged as he packed the worm back into its bag, a virtual storage place in his cyberdeck. "But you know I must be right."

"That his Red Hand systems are not on the net?"

Flash nodded.

Obray shrugged. "Maybe. A standalone system is so unwieldy, though. So limited. Who would want that?"

Who but a security-paranoid Red Hand triumvir who knew that any system with standard net access was ultimately vulnerable? The cartel boss was wired in all the ordinary ways, but nowhere, yet, had they found a crumb of Red Hand data to keep the Kingmaker happy. That conspicuous absence positively screamed "secret hiding place." Janus, this wily ne'er-do-well, must have done that most unthinkable of virtual atrocities: created a system that held his most precious data completely offline.

Blasphemy. But clever.

"Creepy-crawly in your ear, you'll never know that we are here," Flash nattered to himself as he climbed higher with his sticky-padded grip. Soon, whenever Janus accessed this com net, a piece of the tapeworm would ride that wave and take up residence inside the triumvir's personal cybergear. There was just one tiny drawback to the plan, something Flash had neglected to tell Obray.

A little piece of Flash's cyberconsciousness had to ride the tapeworm as well.

He reached the collar of the port, squinting against the near-blinding radiance of its data stream. Morphing one hand back into digits, he reached behind him and fished the worm out of the satchel. The coil twisted like a live thing, eager to bore into the systems it was coded for. Holding it against the lip of the port, he activated it with a command in his cyberdeck. The worm crept inside the nexus, working slowly against the blitz of data rushing into and out of that orifice.

As coils slid from the bag, over his forearm, and into the com center, Flash repressed a shudder. His work on the worm had been quick, without refinements that more time would have permitted. It lacked enough discrimination routines to make the assessments Flash thought essential to this operation. He didn't want a tapeworm that was noticeably intrusive to the person being infested; he didn't want it dropping off in the wrong systems, or failing to pass data correctly when shunting from standalone system to Janus's wetware.

The only way he'd seen to fix those problems was to piggyback on the code, as it were, to ensure its proper function. The process seemed straightforward enough: he would split his consciousness in cyberspace—a trick he had long ago mastered—and leave that scaled-down bit of fractal awareness bonded to the tapeworm. It worked when he ran simultaneous sim-selves; it worked with the tapeworm on his trial runs, too. This should be a walk in the park.

He collected his nerve, preparing to infuse the tapeworm with a bit of himself. He would stay linked to it through a trickle transmission from his base deck at all times. Still . . .

It was kind of like leaving brain cells behind, he thought. Yech.

He tried not to dwell on it too much, or the possible brainburn consequences if he lost part of his consciousness permanently in virtual space. Why dwell on the unlikely? On the plus side, he was doing something no one had done before. His street cred would go through the roof with this one.

Afterward, when it was successful, was soon enough to tell Obray.

As the tapeworm probed the sparkling data stream, he closed his eyes and switched progs in his deck. He experienced the brief moment of vertigo that came with split cyber-focus as his electrons flowed into the worm construct. When he opened his eyes again he had to blink: his sim-eyes saw a data stream, while his worm-body felt it as a flood-tide of energy. Interesting, that. The tapeworm was more sensation-oriented than a sim-self. Might make for an unusual ride.

When the last of the worm's tail vanished into the routing nexus, FlashMan shook his head to clear it. The vertigo was worse with it in there and him out here. He started to climb back down the tower. The split sensation should lessen the more distance he got from the worm, the more time he had to get used to the shift in perspective.

That was the theory, anyway. When he left cyberspace, Flash was sweat-soaked and dizzy. The feeling lingered even outside of the net's infosphere.

He tried to ignore the discomfort and was glad his report would be devoid of this information. There were some things Obray was better off not knowing.

# 20

"**THE STYRCIAN LEAGUE** is a thorn in my side," Janus complained to Karuu. "They have been since they moved into Red Hand space, and most of their activity is in *my* territory, not Sefano's, not Mika's. They're obscenely wealthy—nearly on the scale of a cartel—so they can buy entrée where most derevin can't. They're actually beginning to compete with us. With me. Like here."

He sounded offended as he flicked a hand towards the viewscreen showing the benign cloud cover of Luus. The capital world of the tri-pedal brodien sprawled below, home of creative inventors, clever devices, and manufactories that, until recently, had shipped goods exclusively in hulls belonging to the Red Hand. He stared unhappily at the forested world below. "Now I'm going to have to teach some lessons that I'd rather not. If one Triskelan breaks an agreement without consequences, the others will follow suit. I can't have that. I can't *afford* that."

Janus turned a dour gaze on his lieutenant. "What do you know about the League that I don't? I want to nip this in the bud."

Karuu sucked air between his lips and tusks, a noisy indicator of serious concentration. "No telling what you are knowing, Boss, but I share what is in my head." Again the short-furred Dorleoni sucked his substantial teeth, collecting his thoughts. "They are wealthy only in the last two or three years. Out of nowhere. Trading something very small and valuable, they are, to the Imperials. Some commerce done with various House armies, hub planets, the Navy—but mostly with the Bureau of Mutagenics."

"Psionics?" Janus quirked a questioning look.

"Something to do with that, yes. No one knows details, or I have not yet found lips to be loose on the subject."

Janus mulled that information for a moment. "I never heard of the Styrcian League before this last year. What did they do before they got in so good with the Sa'adani?"

Karuu wrinkled his muzzle in mirth. "Smugglers."

"Did you know them?"

"No. But that scale of work we both know, yes? Certain I am not, Janus-Boss, but a smuggler group with same geographical footprint was called the Mardin Band. Simple name for simple operations. Confederates with ships, doing hot cargo drops and hijacks, hiding from naval pursuit between runs in a most interesting place."

"Where was that interesting place?" Janus supplied the obvious line.

"Funny you are asking." Karuu tossed a salt fish fingerling snack in his mouth and talked around it. "They were thought to have a base in the Claw Nebula. No one ever found it. Navigation is badly awful there. Long- and medium-range sensors do not work. Many nav hazards, stars not visible for astrogation except from edge of the nebula—very dense cloud it is."

"Navy never ferreted them out?"

Karuu shook his head. "Ambushed naval patrols, they did. Pickets started waiting for them outside the cloud. Suspected they had a wormhole there—sometimes Mardin Band raided subsectors far away, while no rats from the hole have peeped."

"Interesting." So they were clever and cagey. "How'd they turn into the Styrcian League with a legit imperial business front?"

The Dorleoni spread his hands. "That far the oracle does not reveal, Boss."

"Karuu," Janus chided. "Poor time to lose the thread of the tale."

"Faint, delicate rumor I can offer. Best word to my ears now is this: they found a star system lost in that nebula, or at the end of their maybe-wormhole. That is where they take their name from, a world called Styrcia. A hidden backwater personal empire for pirates, yes?"

It wouldn't be the first time people on the outside of the law had taken some place over and made it their own. "So this Styrcia is their base, but no one knows its location."

Karuu nodded. "I am thinking that is where they found whatever keeps the Empire so happy. After legitimate trade started, the picket ships were recalled from the nebula."

"So they are rich and in so good with the Imps that a blind eye is turned to their other ventures. Like their continuing criminal activities that are starting to really piss me off."

"Um, yes, Boss. Exactly so."

"Then it seems pretty simple to me. With connections like that, I'd be stirring a hornet's nest if we destroyed them or put them out of business."

Karuu blinked in surprise. "You are not going to destroy them?"

Janus shook his head. "Sounds to me like crushing the Styrcian League will upset some big players, and that will bring the Imperials down on us. There are some forces we don't want to get on the wrong side of. No more than we already are, anyway."

"Then how will you deal with them?" Karuu looked puzzled.

"Simple. I'll take them over."

Karuu shook his head. "How you going to do that, Boss? No one even knows where their base is."

"That's simple, too." He eyed the Dorleoni. "That's your new project, Karuu. You're going to do it for me."

The old smuggler squeaked in dismay.

"How many operations have you co-opted or taken over in your time, my furry friend?"

"I do not know. I do not remember."

"You can't count that high. You know all kinds of ways to crack this sort of nut."

"That kind of nut they are not, Boss."

"I'm not convinced of that. You see what you can come up with and run your best plan by me."

"You do not be knowing what you are asking, Janus!"

"I be knowing, Karuu. And we have two months to get this accomplished. I would be a much happier man if this were all taken care of by time I return to Lyndir. I'm not willing to spend more time than that on this project."

"That's impossible!"

"You know what I like about you, Karuu? Every time your back is to the wall, you find a way to do the impossible. I trust you won't disappoint me on this."

The Dorleoni sat unhappily in his chair and twitched his flippered feet. "Why me?" he lamented.

"Why not you? You're the one with the talent in this direction. But look on the bright side."

"That is?"

"I'll be here to help." Janus flashed a smile and stood. "Uplink your files, will you? I want the data dump on the League."

"Yes, Boss."

Karuu watched the tall Red Hand triumvir leave the observation deck. He popped another salt fish in his mouth and chewed it slowly. One of these days he would get out of this business. It was too high-stress. Take over the Styrcian League in less than two months? Of all the unrealistic, wild-eyed fantasies . . .

Yet as he uplinked the data files, some of the sub-entries caught his eye. He read a little, rejecting his wild ideas out of hand. His mind wouldn't let it rest, though, and late that night, when he got out of bed to reread the file, he had to admit Janus was right.

He definitely had a talent in this direction.

KARUU FLOATED IN zero g in an empty cargo hold of the observation platform. He pushed off from surfaces with a gentle flex of his flipper-like toes, setting himself to sail through the air in a long, straight line, hands by his side, until he neared another surface. Then he curled over in a ball, somersaulted deftly about with the momentum of his tuck, and extended his legs to push off again in yet another random direction across the hold.

He called it "swimming." It was the closest thing to a leisurely plunge that he could take in this place without bodies of water, a self-soothing habit he shared with most of his fellow natives of Dorleon. The gently repetitive motions felt almost like coasting through water after a hard thrust with flippers. It put Karuu in a meditative trance, a state reserved for his deepest introspection, or when a problem eluded his best methods of solving it.

The Styrcian League was the problem that niggled as he swam through the cargo bay. Urgent inquiries among his private intelligence network confirmed that the Mardin Band was indeed the same group as the League. Unfortunately, that was both answer and quandary.

Most gray-market cartels had a derevin background. They grew out of urban gangs that began with small local crime and eventually morphed into something organized and big. The best of those were big to the point of affecting entire economies, like the Red Hand, but such a progression was rare for smugglers. Their organizations were more compartmentalized. They liked to work independently and scorned the constraints of a larger group. Yet the Mardin Band was trying to make exactly that transition with their transformation into the League. New name, new ventures, new ways of doing business.

They might succeed, and they might not, but their smuggler-quirks that handicapped them in cartel business also made them impervious to Karuu's machinations. They were incredibly insular and not well networked with outsiders. It was difficult to get inside their organization or their operations.

No, he corrected himself. Make that impossible. Exhausted my network of contacts, I have, and all I have confirmed is that Pers Mardin bosses the Styrcian League. More, I do not know.

Karuu tucked and pushed off a glow strip. He closed his eyes as he coasted across the hold.

Without information I am powerless to squeeze them. Cannot threaten, if I do not know where they are vulnerable to threat. They have no business partners, no obvious weakness. . . .

He shook his head. It was a foolish seapup trick, to keep coming at this from the old angles. With Janus needing answers immediately, there was no chance to infiltrate and snoop as Karuu would have with an enemy of his own. Surely there was an answer here right under his nose, if only he could think of things from another angle. The right other angle.

That's what a zero g swim was good for.

He opened his eyes as he approached a wall surface, did his tuck and turnabout, stuck his feet out once more. The external bay door passed beneath him, as if he were looking down at a pond that reflected stars overhead. A screen field held atmosphere within the hold, and the field of stars beyond the bay was slightly shimmery with its distortions. It took some getting used to, this feeling of drifting near an airless void, but a year's worth of extended visits to the orbital station at Luus—and periodic weightless "swims"—had helped Karuu acclimate to the odd perspective.

The Dorleoni did not ordinarily spend so much time in space. He was much more a dirtside wheeler and dealer. Even so, this base location was a useful jumping-off point for his work expanding Janus's interests. It was amazing how open gray-market businesses could be to cooperative ventures when approached by a respected and well-established cartel. As a smuggler, he had never wielded so much clout. For that matter, some operations came under Janus's wing voluntarily, simply because the business advantages were so superior.

The thought stunned Karuu with its simplicity. He blinked eyes wide in surprise; lost in a furious chain of free-association, he ran headfirst into a wall while gazing out at the star field before him. He bounced off, jarred, and drifted in a random direction, rubbing his head.

His swimming trajectory was ruined, but his inspiration was intact. "Business advantage," he muttered, as he tumbled slowly through the hold. "Of course! If the deal is sweet enough then quietly will they come!" Stars rotated past his field of vision, coming in from his lower right, sweeping past to his upper left. He shut his eyes to the distraction, pursuing the trail of inspiration he was hot upon.

If the Mardin Band was like most smugglers, what they lacked was real diversification. If they wanted to reinvent themselves as this semi-sanctioned League doing business with Imperials, they needed . . . everything. To play at a higher level they'd have to grow their infrastructure, get more distribution, more storage. They had to be short on these things. And certainly short on security, or Janus never would have uncovered their competition.

And what could the Red Hand offer the Styrcian League? Why . . . all of those things, of course. Everything they lacked. Coverage, distribution, security, protections for cash flow, intelligence, and more, much more.

Karuu's coarse mustache bristled in a fierce, tusky grin. Oh, they might want to remain independent, but they could be co-opted after they were in the bag under a cooperative agreement. Or better yet, a subsidiary agreement. Let them have carte blanche to branch out, and let Janus help them do so.

The Styrcian League would be a . . . a *franchise*! They would gain all the benefits of being Red Hand cartel, without being Red Hand cartel. But they would *appear* to be, to outsiders and to the cartel itself—because in exchange for all those benefits and all that influence and all that room to operate in— they would have to agree to be, however nominally, part of Janus's operation.

"Ha!" Karuu let out a triumphant cry at his burst of genius.

He fetched up against something that was not a wall, that clung to him with a static-electric feeling that bristled the fur on his body. His eyes flicked open.

"Ack!" He seemed to be in space, with nothing but star-specked void before him. He had drifted into the screenfield, and its containment aura was just sufficient to hold him tackily to its surface.

"Station!" he called out. "Grav plates on."

With a stomach-churning sensation of sudden weight, Karuu plummeted to his right and landed heavily on the traction padding of the bay floor.

He got up with a groan, nursing a bruised shoulder. He should have looked where the floor was, before that order. But he had more on his mind than gravity orientation at the moment.

"Station!" he called out again, waddling towards the door. "Invite Janus to conference. I have a plan to tell him."

# 21

**A SLEEK STEEL-BLUE** Zevan luxury aircar awaited Kes and her companions outside Tryst. She glanced from the vehicle to the taller of her escorts, her quizzical look prompting him for a word of explanation.

Most private transport inside the domes of Port Oswin were ground-effect vehicles or floatcars using repulsor pads, not flight-capable aircars; the inter-locking domes that created human-norm airspace on Lyndir were spacious, but not spacious enough to support much air traffic. Only government officials, the high-caste, and those with wealth enough to buy waiver permits owned and flew aircars within the domed cities of the CAS Sector capital.

She should know. Hinano Bren had owned two such vehicles, and she knew what it took to get one. She'd inherited and flown one herself, before the Ice-chromers had put an end to that lifestyle.

The tall man returned her gaze impassively and held the door open for her. No explanation would be forthcoming from this one, she saw. She turned from him stiffly and got in. He followed after; his companion entered from the opposite side so the pair flanked Kes in the rear compartment. The driver engaged the liftpads, elevated the vehicle above the garden rooftops of the Shelieno, and put it in flight mode.

Their transit was direct: out of the garden district, over the industrial flats where the Dryx flowed into the Destiny River, then through four Old Town domes to the offworld nexus. They slowed to low-elevation hover mode as they negotiated an airlock, one of several transit tubes that gave egress to and from the open planetary atmosphere of the starport and adjoining airport that served travel between Lyndir cities.

The Zevan moved leisurely over the out-dome Shipping Warrens and into an airport traffic pattern. The air transit lanes between cities were beacon marked but not heavily traveled. Most Lyndir natives preferred the transcontinental bullet train network for their inter-city travel.

The astrogator part of Kes's brain calculated their departure vector, their orientation over the Destiny River and the Dolos Ocean behind them, glimpsed airspeed over the driver's shoulder, and came to its own conclusions about their destination. "What's awaiting us in Lessing?" she demanded suddenly of the shorter, blond-haired man on her left.

He looked at her, startled. "Uh—"

"Dain." Tall and Dark spoke the man's name curtly, shook his head, and the other fell silent.

"I'm going to find out anyway when I'm there." She locked eyes with the tall one. "What's the big secret? Afraid you're going to ruin the surprise?"

"Sarit," he addressed her, "we're under orders not to speak with you. Your host will explain all when you are safely delivered." With that he turned eyes front and shut her out.

She rolled her eyes. "Sarit." That was a bureaucratic Sa'adani word that loosely meant "citizen." It was neither derogatory nor honorific: it was what you got addressed by in your tax bill.

She was now "Citizen." Terrific.

She matched her escorts' silence for the remainder of their trip.

KES RECOGNIZED THE skyline of Lessing as they approached. It was the only Lyndir city built atop a mesa, raising it above the densest of the rainforest growth around it. The ancient volcanic plug was draped in the persistently encroaching vegetation of this land; its height made the domes of the city appear to be floating above the surrounding sea of green.

Her astrogation interests made her familiar with every major transit port on Lyndir, both star and planetary. Lessing held an airport and a small freight service starport. At the point where the traffic control beacons directed in-bound travelers into the local landing pattern, the aircar she was in banked and proceeded northeast, away from the city and into the wilds of the Harvest Range. She craned to glimpse the distinctive lighting of the guidance beacon in the forest beneath them. It was a Trac-4 vector marker, the kind reserved for military use. She pictured the continental routing map in her head and leaned back stiffly in her seat.

She knew where they were headed.

The activities at Naval Weapons Research Station 207 were not the stuff of netnews, but the large swath of no-fly airspace that marked its perimeter was known to every rated pilot and planet-wise astrogator on the globe. The installation was located beyond the highest crest of the low verdant mountains outside of the university city of Lessing. The site lay at the tropical edge of the rainforest zone: defoliated, leveled, and excavated in a quick, efficient incursion into the hyperactive growth of the jungle fringe. Construction industry buzz held that it contained four subterranean laboratory complexes and four levels above ground in a featureless command hemisphere. That half-sphere and outlying service domes were visible on satscans and marked in detail-free outline on flight charts.

The aircar banked past the end of a forested ridge and angled lower towards a cluster of opaque domes. There was no obvious military perimeter in sight— that would be concealed in the riot of vegetation on the ground—but the duradome outlines perfectly matched the charts Kes had committed to memory. Inspired by her mother's link to the Navy, she could plot courses to every major and minor naval installation within eight subsectors, including fuel depots and rumored munitions dumps. In younger days, she had spent many idle hours figuring where among those many duty stations her mother, Rhea, might be posted, or might have business. For a moment she enjoyed a wild fantasy that her weapons officer parent was stationed here, had learned of her existence in Port Oswin and ordered her brought for a reunion.

She indulged herself with the thought, a pleasant if foolish distraction. Otherwise she would have to start worrying about who wanted her company for weeks, and who would start that visit at a secure weapons research facility.

She kept her knowledge and speculations to herself as the vehicle descended to a landing target and passed through an atmosphere lock into an enclosed parking field. The handful of grounded vehicles suggested the military nature of the place: there were two army-style cargo haulers, a scattering of self-contained jungle-crawlers, and a cluster of aircars with the bland uniform look of government service vehicles.

Her escort guided her to an airlock into the building and Kes glimpsed a plaque by the bulkhead door: a stylized starburst in gold etched on black—the Imperial Navy sigil—above the number 207. She nodded to herself and led her escort within.

# 22

METMURI, OLNIKO, AND Ugoli occupied seats before Ilanya's desk. Teo stood discreetly behind his owner, who held court in a borrowed office.

"Good news for you, Doctor," Eva addressed the station's Director of Special Projects. "We're giving you a test subject you can release into the world."

She studied Metmuri's round face. The doctor was still absorbing their introduction. He had not realized until this minute who he was dealing with and what authority she held. Now, while he was off-center with that realization, she dangled the enticement that should win his cooperation. His round face lit up enthusiastically. And before he leapt to too many conclusions—

"This offer comes with a few limitations I must impose, and I'll tell you why. Your project is timely, for Political Division's purposes. You should consider this a field test under real field conditions. To that end, I must learn from you how tractable these clones are. Can they be ordered to behave in a certain way? Will they do my bidding, like clone-bank soldiers on Corvus would?"

The bioempath looked completely confused. She had expected that, and in that moment she reached out with a gentle psychic touch. She needed to monitor his true reactions closely. Would he rebel at the interference with his plans? Could he be persuaded to do his duty? Or would she have to compel cooperation?

The expression on his face sobered. "We essentially filter personality aspects here, Arcolo." He was shaking his head. "We don't remove volition. They are ordinary people. They're as biddable as ordinary people."

Which is to say, "not very," she thought, unless self-interest was served or devotion was involved.

"Nevertheless, Doctor, I have something I want one of these splintered clones to do. What is the best way to achieve that?"

Metmuri blinked, startled. "That's—that's not what this is about," he blurted. "With all due respect, that will ruin the field test. We need to see how they behave independently, without expectations or instruction sets of any sort. That's the whole point of this experiment: to gauge their capacity for self-directed functionality in the normal environment. If you try giving the clones orders, that's an entirely different set of variables."

Ilanya glanced at Olniko, who had already cautioned her that Metmuri still thought of this as a project with therapeutic uses. "Discarding dissonance," his project brief described it, "tailoring personalities and making minds whole." Both he and Prevak before him had been kept in the dark about the strategic uses long planned for their technology. After all, those plans were strictly on a need-to-know basis, and Metmuri had no need to know.

She turned back to him smoothly. "I understand your reservations, Doctor," she replied. "That's why I said there are special limitations in this case. You will still have opportunity to test general functionality with clones made from this subject. But I need your special help in creating a biddable mindset in at least one of them."

Metmuri's eyes narrowed and she sensed his growing anger. "Then I think you should tell me what, exactly, you want to accomplish," he said curtly.

Ilanya's voice hardened. "I've told you sufficient information for your purposes. I plan to give orders and I need to have them obeyed."

Metmuri made a sound very near to a snort; Ugoli stiffened. The doctor pointedly ignored him and spoke only to Ilanya.

"This isn't Political Division, Arcolo. If you want specialists in behavior modification, you already have them: destroy these pathways here, get that behavior there. That is not what we do with our clones."

Eva regarded him calculatingly. "I know you were assistant director of the clone banks on Corvus."

"I was."

"You created obedient clones there. How did you do that?"

"That was different. The Primes we cloned were soldiers already trained to obedience, with those habits already mapped into their brains. Imprinting that personality into a clone was simple wholesale replication of unaltered neural pathways. If they didn't have those behavior patterns already, their multiples would not have been inclined to follow orders."

Eva raised an eyebrow. "Yet you're plucking apart the very psyche of the Primes you work with here, and I read that some of the clones you produce are extremely biddable."

Metmuri shrugged. "The Secundus series are often entirely compliant—in the sense of being passive and directable by others. Many of them lack decisiveness or a matured sense of self. Without powerful motivation from within, they respond to motivation from without. If *that* is what you desire, that I can provide. It is not the same as someone who hears an order and willingly, creatively, industriously obeys it."

Eva suppressed a sigh. The contents of Metmuri's lab reports resided in her Tolex now, but parsing science jargon in an arcane specialty was not her forte; she had not yet assimilated the information to a point where she understood the nuances of it. For this interview, she relied more on the verbal briefings she'd received from Olniko. Perhaps her ignorance of the project was hindering communication here. But she knew a way around that.

"Let me phrase this a little differently for you, then." She shifted tack. "I hear you telling me, 'this can't be done'—to awaken a clone who is not a soldier and have them be obedient. So I want you to figure out how it *can* be done. It's that simple."

Metmuri took that in in silence.

"You will start the cloning process today. Then you'll have seven weeks while the subjects are fast-grown in vats and then some time beyond that while we age them to resemble their original. During that time you can find a way to create a biddable clone. If you need to call on resources from Corvus, or elsewhere outside this station, let me know and I'll arrange for it."

Metmuri looked pained. "That does not follow our protocol. We've never done . . . These are not soldier clones I'm working with here! What makes you think this is even possible?" he sputtered in frustrated indignation.

Ilanya barked a short laugh. "Because I already have ways to ensure obedience, and I'm fairly certain they're far less pleasant than anything you could devise. You know what solution comes most quickly to my mind, Doctor? I would implant a detonation chip and warn the subject that disobedience will be punished with instant death. Then I would demonstrate that with one of the clones, so the others don't think it's a bluff."

The bioempath recoiled as she continued. "If I want a more happily cooperative subject, I would have a pleasure center wired for externally controlled stimulation. Then obedience swiftly becomes an addictive sensation, and any deviation from my orders brings the loss of pleasure. Which becomes quite unbearable, I am told, once a body is addicted to the pleasure factor. Eventually disobedience becomes inconceivable."

Metmuri looked at her as if seeing her for the first time, and she sensed dismay and horror in his aura.

"That approach takes time, though, and I don't have as much of that as I would like. So I am hoping you can come up with a better solution. Otherwise I shall have to rely upon my own alternatives. They may be crude, but they are also effective."

She gave him a humorless smile. He paled and she felt his emotions shift.

"I'll see what I can do," he mumbled, subdued.

"Good man."

Commander Olniko addressed them both. "Your test subject is here, I'm told." He tapped his ear, referring to his com implant.

Ilanya stood; the others came to their feet as well. "Then our business here is concluded for now. Start your splintegration process, Doctor. And when the cloning is well underway, let me know what you come up with to assure obedience to orders."

"Arcolo." Metmuri ducked his head and left the room hurriedly ahead of the rest.

**IT DIDN'T LOOK** like a prison cell, but it might just as well have been one. Kes paced the floor of the small windowless room she had languished in for hours. It contained a table, two chairs, a couch, and a service cubby—it was a meager conference room, perhaps, sealed behind an iris-valve door. That style door was common on board imperial vessels, she knew; the construction assured rapid closure to create air-tight compartments. She had never seen one in person before, and the way the portal's interleaves had widened to admit her had drawn her eye in fascination.

It was the last fascinating thing she'd seen all afternoon. The valve irised shut behind her and did not budge again.

There was not so much as a vid term in this room, or not one she recognized. Kes finally abandoned the restless prowling and lay down to lounge on the couch, which was too short for her height. Maybe she could take a nap and pass the time that way. Better that than the endless, pointless speculation that had begun a tail-chasing circuit in her head.

She was succeeding in drifting off to sleep when the door irised open and someone walked unannounced into the room.

At first she thought he was just a funny-looking little man: graying lank blond hair, round face, a teal-colored tunic that did not complement his pasty complexion, white-and-teal-striped trousers of an odd cut that hugged his calves. Then she blinked and sat upright, and really registered what she was looking at.

The half-blue, half-green diamond-shaped rus in the middle of the man's forehead said it all. This was a bioempath. A doctor, of course, but not just by virtue of medical training. Anyone who wore that laserscribed mark had years of training in psionics and energetics. This man had dedicated decades of his life to the study of disciplines that to Kes's understanding essentially comprised one large mystery school.

There were few bioempaths in the CAS Sector—they were more common in Sa'adani space—but every citizen recognized that rus. You saw it on the evening news when some deader at the scene of an accident was revived unexpectedly by a bioempath, or an impossible cure was effected by their disciplined use of energetics.

She'd never thought to meet one in person. What was a doctor of this rare breed doing in a place like this? Surely he was not her client? Or was he?

She collected herself rapidly, coming to her feet to take advantage of her presence and stature to make herself imposing in that space.

"Sarit Hinano." He greeted her and gestured to the nearby table. "Please. Have a seat."

There were guards behind him in the hall: the two who had brought her here, and two naval security in black fatigues. They stayed outside but had a clear line of sight to her; she saw sidearms at the hips of the uniformed men.

Her lips thinned. She remained standing while the doctor took a chair. Only then did she sit opposite him. She still had not said a word.

That silence seemed to disconcert the good doctor. He clasped his hands on the table, then unclasped them, then finally set them one atop the other as if to hold them still.

"I'm Dr. Metmuri Esimir," he introduced himself. "You will be my, um, guest for a time. Has anyone told you why you're here?"

"No."

He blinked nervously several times then, and his brows crept up. "Um. Oh."

He drummed his fingers on the table, then stilled them with an apparent effort.

"Why *am* I here, Doctor? This was your idea, I take it?"

He blinked again, surprised. "Oh, no. Well, yes. But not exactly. I mean . . ." He blew out a breath in exasperation. "Let me start again, Sarit. I need to ask you some questions. Quite a number of them, actually. Will you kindly humor me and answer them? This will take a while."

She had a feeling Metmuri would reveal more if he was uncomfortable in her presence than if he was collected. Kes had many ways to unsettle men, and she used one of them now, inclining her head slightly back so that she looked imperiously down at him, even though they were seated on a level. One eyebrow lifted as if to invite him to proceed.

He cleared his throat nervously and began.

Her answers were terse; she waited to see what information he would volunteer to fill the gaps her silence created, but his questions were pointed and persistent. Metmuri did not ask her anything a client ever had; he spoke to her as a doctor would. Name, age, place of birth; major illnesses, medical history, family history, cyberimplants and enhancements. At one point the shorter man who had escorted her here came in with a datapad and took her thumbprint and retina scan. "To retrieve your medrecords," Metmuri explained, as if that explained anything.

"I'm not ill," she felt prompted to say.

"I should hope not, Sarit Hinano. We need to be certain of the particulars of your health, though."

"And why is that important?" She took that opportunity to sharpen her tone. All these questions and still Metmuri had not revealed why she was here, unless it was for a medical exam. She was getting tired of this game. If her client wanted a medical scene, she could accommodate, but *she* would be the one asking the questions and running that show.

"Your health? Oh." Metmuri actually blushed and avoided her gaze. He fidgeted with a stylus he'd taken out of a pocket, turning it over and over in his fingers before he answered her.

"There will be some tests. Quite routine, I assure you. Then we'll know where to go from there." He finally looked her in the eye. "We need to verify your physical condition, you see? And if you pass, then I can tell you more."

She threw herself back in her chair. "No, I don't see. I suggest you explain yourself if you want me to cooperate with you. I didn't come all this way for a medical exam."

Metmuri made a strange noise, half giggle, half snort. "Oh no, Sarit, that's where you're mistaken. That's exactly what you came here for. For starters, anyway."

"'For starters'? For what reason, *exactly*? Who wanted me here?"

Dr. Metmuri studied her, then, with a distant expression on his face, his eyes roving the plane of her face, the bodice that showed through her shirt, the length of her white silk sleeve to her long fingers tapping the table.

"You're a guest of the Navy right now," he said, bringing his eyes back up to hers. "As to who wanted you here: you might say that was me. I didn't know it would be you, precisely. But it was certainly my idea to get someone."

"Any domina would have served?"

He shook his head. "Any reasonably well-adjusted person would serve. You'll do as well as any. Though given your work, this should prove especially interesting."

*Any reasonably well-adjusted person would serve?* Had Helda known that when she'd ordered her out the door?

*You'll do as well as any.*

She felt profoundly disturbed by his remarks. That feeling only grew as the afternoon wore on.

# 23

ESIMIR WALKED UNANNOUNCED into Ilanya's appropriated office. "You've put me in a very awkward position," he snapped at the woman behind the desk.

Teo squared off towards the intruder. Ilanya, though, regarded him calmly.

"Are you used to walking in on people, Doctor?"

He waved a hand dismissively and came to a halt before her desk. "Courtesies are all very nice, Arcolo. Courtesies like letting me select the subject best suited for this test. For that matter: the small kindness of telling the subject something—anything!—that would give her an understanding of why she is here."

"The 'why' of her visit really isn't her concern, Doctor. If she knew it, she'd likely be trying to flee this very moment."

Esimir shook his head. "I don't mean tell her *everything*, but as it is, she's barely cooperative. She's concerned about her predicament and that is triggering resistance patterns in her."

Ilanya's eyes narrowed. "Surely she doesn't realize she's in a 'predicament,' as you put it, does she?"

"Not yet. But she's not stupid. She senses something is afoot, something that may not include her best interests."

"How interesting that you put it that way. Surely you can clone someone without their cooperation."

"It's not that simple. If someone is frightened or resisting, it's more difficult to do the prep work for the splintegration process. Worse, the Prime has recent short-term memory of these feelings. They are virtually impossible to filter out when we parse out personas and do the imprinting of the clones."

"Why can't you filter out recent memories?"

"Because they *are* memories. While there are memory clusters in the brain, storage is also generalized. Clones all share the same set of memories up to the moment that brain mapping destroys the Prime. Basically, if a subject fights or resents us, the clones will feel the same. This may not matter for a prisoner, but if you want a cooperative subject . . . Well. There it is."

Ilanya looked thoughtful. "And since ordinary cloning does no damage to the Prime, nothing bad happens for the clone to recall."

"Exactly. In any case, the more crudely we treat the Prime, the more it will color the attitudes of the clones."

Ilanya pursed her lips. "I take your point, Doctor. What do you imagine I can do about this?"

Esimir heaved a sigh. "This comes back to your issue of wanting clones you can order, Arcolo."

"How so?"

"I think we must fall back on good old-fashioned prisoner-and-detainee psychology. My recommendation? Become her friend."

"Her friend?" Ilanya laughed in true amusement.

"I'm not joking," Esimir said earnestly. "She cooperates with me grudgingly. She is suspicious of my motives. If I am perceived to be the threat, you can be perceived to be the ally. Let us play this like interrogators do, Arcolo. I'm sure you must know that approach: one is good, one is bad. The subject bonds with the good one, looks to that one for favor and aid. And cooperates as that one requests."

Something about that suggestion caught Ilanya's fancy. "How piquant," she mused dryly. "Me, a shigasa's ally."

"It is also the same psychology that turns kidnap victims into allies of their captors." He spread his hands. "Friendship and kindness in her time of distress? It should work well in this circumstance. As to complying with your wishes: for some people, dominance traits are personality hardwired. It is that way with Hinano. She will resist being ordered unless those orders come from someone she looks up to or to whom she has given her allegiance."

"We don't have time to instill feelings of allegiance."

"My thought as well. And her personality type is not easily intimidated or coerced. I think the only route to willing cooperation is for you to become an ally. Bond in these stressful circumstances, then find a way to speak to her self-interest. That is a certain hook for her."

Ilanya mulled that over. "Interesting proposition. Do you have assurances that after I befriend her, she will do as I bid?"

Esimir shrugged. "Does any friend behave as another bids? Not in the sense of following a command. But if you show that what you want will also benefit her personally, the combination of self-interest and friend loyalty should prove sufficient to win her engagement."

Ilanya quirked a lip. "Self-interest I understand. As to the rest—you're saying I can't order her, but if I'm her friend I can *ask* her to do what I want?"

"Of course," Esimir replied. "Isn't that what friends do for friends?"

Ilanya gave a wry smile. "Perhaps not things on the scale of what I have in mind, but thank you for the suggestion. I'll consider it."

He stood. "I hope you'll consider it today. We need Hinano's resistance gone, and that means she needs reassurances. Right now would be ideal. She's refusing to permit the biopsies we require until she understands what's going on. Rather than explain, and rather than force her, I came to see you."

"Ah. Very well, Doctor. Leave the shigasa in her rooms for now. I'll see what I can do."

Esimir nodded and left. Ilanya watched his departing back.

Be a friend, indeed.

**WHAT WAS IT** Helda said to her in parting? *You are doing this for the sake of our clan.*

Kes may not have been adopted for long, but she fit well into the family network. Her family of choice trusted that her sense of duty and honor would inform her actions, and her actions would support their interests. She had every intention of proving their faith in her was well placed.

How much easier it would be, though, if Dosan or Eosan had told her exactly *how* she served their house by being subject to the pestiferous doctor. Surely Eosan Bejmet had not intended for her to become some intrusive little scientist's test durgl?

She tossed herself onto her bed with a sigh. Two windowless rooms comprised the small suite they had given her to use. The door was locked, and there was no net access to pass the time and no comp unit. There was a security lockout on the com system that she couldn't bypass. She would be here going quietly stir-crazy until they fetched her again. Maybe this time she would just refuse to go, and woe to any who tried to force her.

She held her hands in the air, idly extending the steeloy blades of the cat claws sheathed beneath her natural fingernails. She used them for scratching in the midst of a session, or in rough sex play when the mood suited her. She'd had them installed for her personal enjoyment some years before, when she'd had a girlfriend who thrilled to the feel of claws at her throat. She smiled at the memory. They were good for in-fighting, too—not that she fought that way, but if she was pushed far enough . . .

She retracted the claws slowly. Fending off the guards when they came to get her—she imagined how that might play out, then had an unsettling vision of trying to explain herself to Ilanya Bejmet. That thought gave her pause. She did not ever want to have to defend her actions to the matriarch of her adopted clan. The Eosan was a formidable woman. She had never been a professional domina, as far as Kes could discover, but she had that edge of power about her that Kes intuitively read and respected. Bejmet moved with the assurance of one who understood how everything fit in her world and had the power to control it as she wished.

That matriarchal authority was actually one of the elements that had persuaded Kes to agree to adoption. When Bejmet took her oath and vows, she knew she had entered a real family—one in the Sa'adani sense of extended kin and obligation networks, not the loose patchwork of associations most Cassians contented themselves with. She imagined it was the kind of connection her mother enjoyed somewhere, with others of similar ancestry. Finally, she was creating a place that was her own, even if she didn't always understand the rules, yet. . . .

Her reflections were interrupted by a door chime that brought her to her feet. The sound was startling; she hadn't realized the chime was there. Her escorts and the doctor came and went as they wanted, had never politely announced their presence first. It was a common tactic of nonconsensual domination—denying someone personal space and the boundaries that went with it—and she had instantly resented it.

She couldn't open the door to her visitor, but the chime gave her time to emerge from the bedroom as a stranger came through the iris valve and into her tiny sitting/dining room.

She'd never seen this woman before. She was middle-aged, sharp featured, with pale blue eyes and stylish short red hair. She wore a gray service bodysuit and uniform tunic with red-and-gold flashes of rank at collar tabs.

"Pardon my intrusion," she said. "I hear my colleague Metmuri has made a hash of things with you. I came to see what I could set right."

Sudden, cautious relief warred with distrust in Kes's heart. "You are . . . ?"

"Ilanya Evanit." The woman gestured her to sit and took a place on the couch. She regarded Kes appraisingly. "Do you recognize my name in any way?"

What a strange question. "You have the same family name as my Eosan. Are you related?"

"Very distant cousins."

"Then perhaps you can tell me why I'm here?"

Eva seemed to consider the request. "There is much that you are not authorized to know. But there is some information I can share."

She studied Kes for a moment, then began to speak.

"The summary is this: you entertain a client who represents a profound danger to imperial interests. Palumara House has committed to help us deal with this undesirable. To that end, we are going to . . . enhance you . . . to help us accomplish what we must."

"'Enhance' me? What does that mean?"

"Let us say you will be given capabilities you do not have at this moment." She spread her hands. "Nothing that will hurt you. I think you'll be very happy with yourself when this is done."

Kes's lips tightened. "What capabilities?"

"I can't share details at this time, because you have no need to know that information yet. There is a medical procedure involved."

"I gathered that," Kes said curtly. That someone would muck around with her body without her knowing exactly what they were up to—

"You're worried that you will be injured or altered in a way you don't like," Eva observed flatly.

Kes was startled. She wasn't usually that easy to read.

"But that is not the nature of the procedure," Ilanya continued. "You will just be, shall we say, better equipped to assist your House when all is done."

"And what is it you envision I will do with these mystery enhancements, when all is done?"

Eva gave a small smile. "That touches upon the undesirable client, and that is information you have no need to know at this time."

Kes studied the woman. "You tell me very little."

"Still. It is more than you knew an hour ago and the most I can share with you at this point in time."

Kes considered that. "Does Eosan Bejmet know what you propose to do to me?"

Eva looked at her thoughtfully. "Your Eosan agreed to help us in every way and pledged your cooperation. Do you wish to verify that with Bejmet?"

Kes's first impulse was to say yes—but she already knew from Helda that the Eosan had authorized all of this. And if Ilanya offered the contact, no doubt Bejmet would confirm. Still, she hesitated.

"You said you didn't recognize my name, Kes—may I call you Kes? Let me tell you a little more about what I do. I represent the Political Division of Internal Security. You have heard of us, I suppose?"

Kes nodded. Heard of, but knew few details of substance. And no comp here to find out more.

"I work at the direct command of Emperor Nalomeci. He has ordered that I accomplish something in which you have come to play a role, however incidental. It is your Emperor that desires this. And it is your family head that commands it of you."

Kes considered that in silence as well.

"I cannot command you," Eva continued, "but I want to help you to help us. This does not need to be a conflict-ridden situation between us, here."

The domina snorted. "Metmuri treats me like a specimen."

"He is single-focused in his vision. I will do what I can to mitigate that, if you like."

Kes regarded her curiously. "Why would you bother?"

It was Eva's turn to shrug. "Why not? We are all doing our duty here. No need to create unpleasantness as we go about it, don't you agree?"

Kes nodded to the wall cubby where room systems were housed. "If you want to banish unpleasantness you could start by giving me coms and a net link. Or let me go walking without an escort that treats me like an arrested criminal."

A muscle twitched in Eva's jaw, and she came to her feet. "I'll see that you're given reading, games, something to occupy the time. If you want to walk we'll set an exercise time in the parking field dome." She approached the door, which irised open for her on some unseen signal. "Your escorts have their duty as well, Kes, so unfortunately they must continue to accompany you. But I will make clear to them your status. You are an honored guest in this facility. I will be making that point to Dr. Metmuri, as well." She inclined her head briefly. "We're grateful for your assistance."

With that she stepped into the hall, and the valve sealed once more.

A conciliatory visit from a PolitDiv officer was a strange way to show gratitude. Some few bones thrown her way to pacify her discontent: games to play while she passed the time? Oh yes, that certainly compensated for isolation.

Escorts who would continue to dog her every footstep.

Her heart sank. Ilanya's words sounded fair enough. They even made a little more sense out of her situation. Still, this visit made it even more evident that Kes had no leverage here; she could not manipulate or control this situation in any way. When it came to choice, she had none. That was being taken from her or denied to her in the name of duty and unavoidable obligation.

There was only one other time in her life when others had thoroughly dictated choices to her. The feelings then—of doorways shutting, of options vanishing—were identical to those now.

She curled up on her couch and refused to give in to tears.

# 24

"**IN FASHION NEWS** today: the tragic death of glitz couture designer Hinano Bren, whose speeding aircar suffered a fatal crash against a guidance pylon in the Holson Dome district of Port Oswin. Debris is being examined to determine—"

"Lena. Silence." Kes ordered the house AI to still the netnews and welcome quiet settled over the penthouse.

It was the summer she had been preparing for the first of her astrogation certification exams. Police came to her in the study center that morning and told her the news. They suspected suicide. System fail-safes in cars and traffic beacons made it highly unlikely that his speed or vector had been the work of a malfunction. Was there any reason he would want to kill himself? Had he left a note? Could she check house systems to see if he'd left word behind?

In angry disbelief, she went home, told Lena to help her look, began to sort through his desk and office. Nothing. She sat for a time and cried. Then she attacked his bedroom. Still nothing. More tears and a shouting, cursing tantrum directed at midair in this place that held his presence. Then a rummage through his closets, through his pockets, through the jacket he'd left hooked on the valet stand.

The cryptic paper in the inside pocket. No suicide note, thankfully, but a mystery that bothered her. It was a short list of letter and number codes down the left and two columns of numbers on the right. It made no sense. She'd helped with the business enough that if it related to Hinano Ltd she would recognize a shorthand tally of inventory or show dates. It was none of those things. She had puzzled over it briefly and then put it aside. It was not what the police were looking for, and it did nothing to assuage her tumult of emotions at her father's death.

The first unexpected aftershock hit when Asaro came to call. She was a model who had worked for Bren years before, the one Kes had refused to model summer fashions with, once. She had since gone on to promote her own line of styles. She was a friendly competitor now, never large enough to threaten Bren, appealing to a different aesthetic and target market than he. They had lunch together from time to time, Kes recalled.

Now she sat near Hinano's heir on the patio, the penthouse garden in full bloom before them. Condolences had been offered; drinks had been served.

"Bren's business is yours now," Asaro said. "Have you had a chance to think about that yet?"

"Not yet." She had no interest in his business. It was difficult to convey that to his design-world cronies, who thought Hinano the epitome of niche success in their field.

Asaro handed her a datapad. "I wanted to make you aware of this. It was a private contract between Bren and me, but binding to the business. To the estate. So you should know about it."

Kes took the datapad, regarded it curiously. She skimmed the contract summary on the screen, then looked up at Asaro, frankly surprised.

"This gives you exclusive rights over Hinano distribution in four subsectors."

Asaro had the grace to suppress the cat-ate-the-cream smile that came briefly to her face. "In exchange for a consideration, yes."

"Two million isn't much of a consideration for exclusive rights and that share of sales." Not to mention that Hinano had kept sole control of his business— she had thought—for as long as he had owned it. How many had tried to get a piece of the action, or offered to be silent partners across the years? She thought Bren's business was his alone. Apparently she was wrong.

"Your father was in a bind two years ago. He needed cash, in one large lump, immediately. That was the deal we struck in exchange." She shrugged. "We were both happy with it. There's a clause there, you see, that allows me a one-term renewal. That time is up now, and that's what I want to do. Otherwise I wouldn't disturb you at a time like this."

"No. It's business. I understand." She set the datapad down. "I'll have to get back to you on this, Asaro. I need a few days."

"Certainly. No rush. We have two weeks before I need that certified."

They parted ways in that surface-only cordiality that Bren had cultivated with his associates. Kes was glad to see the door shut behind her.

Then one by one, others came forward. Over time, over years, Bren had been selling rights to bits and pieces of his business. Distribution rights here, a silent manufacturing partnership there. And notes—there were private notes, of money lent and money owed, many of which were about to come due in the next few months. Bren had indebted himself everywhere, borrowing from one to pay the other, and never fully discharging any of the loans.

With her heir's access override, Kes looked at his personal and business bank accounts. What she saw left her stunned. She found herself sitting in her old grove hidey-hole in the garden, alone, contemplating the dome beyond the sun-yellowed leaves overhead.

Hinano Ltd was broke. Overextended, cash-poor, with over-mortgaged properties, and business assets virtually leased out piecemeal to others so elements that should have produced strong cash flow leached that income away to other pockets. Three commercial lenders had turned Bren down for credit requests over the last three months.

He had better business sense than that, she argued with herself. He was bankrupting himself with stupid mistakes. Why?

The "why" paid her a visit that evening.

The security cam showed a man at the street gate that she did not recognize: short buzzed black hair, a business suit of moderately expensive make but not tailored, with no notable fashion sense. He was not one of the sorts Bren usually rubbed elbows with. He was accompanied by two others in polychromed coolsuits, as if they had just come in from the high-pressure sauna that Lyndir called outdoors.

"Lena, who is this?"

"Gistano," the AI replied. "A man your father sometimes had business dealings with."

She sighed. "Let them in."

Gistano came bearing a datapad, as had so many others. She no longer made such visitors welcome as if they were condolence-calling guests. She gestured the strangers to a table where she could sit in a formal configuration, with formal distance between them. There were no refreshments offered. She braced herself to see yet another contract affecting Hinano Ltd.

Gistano let his eyes rove over her. His cronies stood behind him, politely not sitting in their polychrome, which could mar furniture. Their height and the hard-shelled environment suits they were in made them look like nothing but a quasi-military escort to their employer—or perhaps that's what they were, in point of fact. Kes's eyes flicked from bodyguards to seated man; she didn't like how any of them were looking at her. Assessing her.

"I assume you have some claim I need to be aware of," she said, extending her hand for the datapad. "I don't have much time. Let's see it."

Gistano threw back his head and laughed heartily. "That's good. That's very good." He wiped a pretend tear from his eye. "You're going to have to make some time, though, dearie. This little problem isn't going away for you any time soon."

She gritted her teeth. "Explain yourself."

Gistano was a broad-faced man, swarthy of complexion, heavy jawed. He looked like the sort used to confrontation, and he spoke bluntly to her now. "Hinano Bren had a little gambling habit. He used to be pretty good at it, but over time he got greedy. When he lost a bet, he'd make a bigger one to recover his losses. Unfortunately, he lost a few in a row, lately, and now he has arranged that we can't collect from him. So we're here to collect from you."

"My father owes you a gambling debt?" she echoed in disbelief.

Gistano referenced the datapad on the table before him. "The estate of

Hinano Bren owes us 7.43 million credits." He locked eyes with Kes. "Or, rather: you do. Imperial Codex section 5032, subsection 107, paragraph 3a."

Most people who stood to inherit anything of significance became very familiar with the 107(3)(a) clause, as Kes was. The relevant sentence was a singular one: "The heirs of an estate are responsible for the debts of that estate." An estate was not treated as a corporate body with generalized or nonexistent liability. Imperial law deemed that the choices made by one family member created obligation binding the entire family. In the face of one person's irresponsibility, the rest of a family or clan was expected to pick up the slack.

Kes stirred uncomfortably as the import of this sank in. Hinano had no cash, couldn't get loans, was already overextended. This must be a Scripman she was talking to, a backstreet underwriter of loans and unsecured gambling debts. Gistano had come to collect, and with no other resources to offer him, he was going to collect, all right. The entire estate.

"Let me see that," she said, gesturing to the datapad. This time he pushed it across to her. She took her time reading the contracts therein, and they waited patiently while she did so.

She finally set the pad down. "I take it you want the estate."

Gistano shook his head. "What I want is my money. Barring that I will take assets, or I will take labor in trade, but cash counts best with me. Can you pay?"

She shook her head.

"And my money is due now. In that case the estate as a whole is an option, though not my first choice. I think you have very few alternatives. Here's what I suggest."

Gistano cleared his throat. "Take a day. Think this over, carefully. Before you decide to contest this in court, be aware that if the Justiciar finds you unable to pay the estate's debts, you will be sentenced to slavery until that debt is worked off. That's a pretty cut-and-dried conclusion. Reference that on the net or in your house systems if you doubt it."

That was exactly what she had been thinking: to contest in court would invite one of those black-and-white Sa'adani judicial decisions. If a debt was valid—and this one certainly was—then a debtor served until the debt was paid. If they had gone through the trouble to die first, that obligation fell unequivocally to their kin to meet. Not that Sa'adani honor codes had ever colored much of Bren's life, but they surely affected the law on Lyndir and his daughter—his only immediate kin—if she tangled with the legal system.

To be sentenced to debt slavery would be the end of everything she'd hoped for for herself. A slave could be sold, moved offworld, used in any way, consigned to any work—as long as a value could be put on that labor, the courts counted it as payment towards the debt. The Justiciar oversaw that process very little, and it was common knowledge that debt slaves were often consigned to a

life of servitude because what their owner set them to do had too little remu-
nerative value to discharge a debt in a reasonable period of time.

Gistano stood. "If you can pay tomorrow, then our business is done. If you
can't pay, then we'll consider buying Hinano Ltd, and you can use that money
towards this debt. I'll bring those numbers around tomorrow. I expect you to
have an accounting of the estate's financial standing as well." He flashed a smile
at her. "And if you decide you want to take this to court, then I'll be happy to
buy you as my personal slave when the Justiciar has found in our favor."

She bit back the varied retorts that came to mind and saw them out the door
without a farewell. Then she pulled out that note she had found with the cryptic numbers on it. Dates, probably, and scripman codes, and figures for money
gambled, and money won, or lost. Far more losses than wins.

Damn you, Bren.

She sat at the comp, then, and ran financials. Over seven million owed to
the Scripman. Nearly that much owed again in various private notes to individuals. There were fifteen million in company assets sub-licensed to others
that she couldn't touch. Enough cash in the bank to cover living expenses for
a couple of months, no more.

The picture was grim. Even if Gistano bought the business, Bren's personal
loans would still be Kes's to pay, and the banks were no longer banking on Hinano
Ltd. She gave up on sleep. The hell with astrogation exams. She spent the rest
of that night drawing up financials that covered the spectrum of what she had
to deal with.

When Gistano returned, he looked over those figures, nodded, did some calculations of his own. A self-satisfied smile crept over his face. He leaned back
in his chair, wove his fingers together and looked at her contentedly.

"Here's how it looks to me. I'll buy Hinano Ltd for fair market value. That's
almost what you owe for debt. It even covers most of the personal loans that
are on your back." He nodded at the datapad between them.

She looked at the numbers, then glanced up at him, puzzled.

"This leaves a half million in debt that's still on me to pay."

"Why, so it does."

Silence stretched between them. She caught a smirk on the face of one of
his chrome-suited cronies. Her brows drew together.

"You could do another five hundred k."

He shook his head slowly from side to side.

Her brows drew together. "What do you want?"

"Your father was a prick, Kesada, and I'm not inclined to be generous in the
aftermath of this mess. I can call you Kesada, can I not? We're becoming so
well acquainted."

"What game are you playing here?" she demanded.

Gistano raised and dropped one shoulder. "No game. When a client defaults, what they had becomes mine. All of it. Even their family becomes mine, to dispose of as I see fit."

"That's not law."

"No, but that's the way scripmen work. Always have. If you lose your assets, you lose your ass, and your family will as well. It's a good guarantee that people don't default. News about this will be on the streets and my other clients will be all the more diligent about paying their debts."

She tapped the datapad. "You're saying I still owe you. I have a hundred k in the bank. What if I pay you that and raise the rest from friends?"

"Then the offer price for Hinano Ltd will be less, so there will still be the same amount outstanding."

"What if I sell the company to someone else and pay you off flat?"

"You're out of time. Your father committed to a debt due on demand. I'm demanding it right now. Tonight."

"You bastard," she snapped. "You're trying to get me turned into a slave."

He cracked a smile. "Not a slave—the courts would put you up for sale and I might not be able to keep control of you. I have an alternative in mind."

"What?"

"Come to work for me on an indentured service contract. A debtor's contract. You work until the debt is paid. Icechromers pay—what, Franc?"

One of the coolsuits replied. "Fifty an hour for a joygirl, when she's with a paying client."

"There you go. You'd work off your debt in, oh, about five or six years Standard at that rate. About fifteen years local. Maybe half that if you work constantly, but that can take the edge off your charm too quickly. I wouldn't permit it."

"Are you out of your mind?" Kes retorted, angry and scared.

He smiled tightly. "It's a common arrangement, Kesada, really. A little outside your experience, perhaps, but we offer job training. It's nothing you can't learn, believe me." He laughed; his fellows joined him. "The alternative, of course, is debt slavery. Slaves don't make anywhere near fifty an hour for their work, not usually, and who knows where you'd end up. Or doing what. Do menial labor or domestic service, and you'll work your life away to clear that debt, plus interest accruing. Come to work for us, indentured. It's flat debt, no interest. Your choice, of course."

She trembled. Her choice.

It was no choice at all, and eventually Gistano got what he wanted.

# 25

JANUS CHOSE THE site of his meeting with care.

The virtual palatial estates favored by his predecessor in the Red Hand had always struck him as pretentious. Yet his personal preference of a void without virtual constructs struck others as ascetic or cold. He settled on a natural landscape in which to meet Pers Mardin: a beach of fine black sand by a primal sea on a world of violet skies. Two massive orange full moons hung close and low by the horizon, unmoving, washing the beach in rich sunset-hued light. It was a breathtaking vista from the shores of the perpetually twilit Pilgrim's Sea on Delios IV, as isolated in virtual space as it was in the physical world.

A form shimmered into existence some distance down the beach, and Pers appeared, walking towards him along the warm sandy verge. Janus sat on a rock in a cluster of beach boulders and watched the approach of the white-haired man in a spacer's rumpled jumpsuit. He was old but not frail, the flesh on the left side of his face faintly mottled with the marks of an old radiation burn, poorly treated. This must be a true-to-life representation of Mardin's fleshly appearance; few bothered to add such quirks to a sim-self when perfection was so easily portrayed. Janus also favored a natural representation of self and nodded in silent approval. They would be dealing with each other as close to in-the-flesh as they dared to get. It was a promising sign that they shared the same sensibilities in this regard.

Pers sat on a nearby rock and rested, hands on knees, regarding the triumvir. "You got my attention," he said gruffly. "Some of what Karuu proposes makes sense. Some of it doesn't. That's why I'm here."

Janus dipped his chin. "What do you have concerns about?"

Pers cackled hoarsely. "That list goes on for a while. Let's start at the start. Autonomy."

Janus nodded, rearranged himself on his rock, and settled in to deal.

IT TOOK WEEKS of negotiations to come to terms with the Styrcian League and a huge concession of Janus's personal Red Hand territory that he was reluctant to make. Karuu had finally persuaded him to do it.

"Look-see, Boss," the Dorleoni told him. "So you let Leaguers have Triskelan Sector and border areas as their playground. Yes, and—? It saves you travel time from coming out here to work. It is far from your center of operations anyway."

"I was branching out here, Karuu. There aren't all that many directions we can expand in. We're flanked by other Red Hand operations or turf belonging to cartels we don't want to mix it up with."

"Yes yes." Karuu waved his hand. "Knowing this we are. Howsomever: you throw moderate large bone to Mardin—"

"Moderate large chunk of dolophant, you mean."

"—and in exchange for this, you gain what? They take that space for you, do your labors for you, and pay you money for the privilege. You are knowing the numbers I ran."

"Yes," Janus sighed. "It saves me money and makes me money, not to be out of pocket on that expansion myself."

"More than that, I am thinking, when we integrate all their data and look at numbers again. And if you are looking for new directions to grow in, Boss, I have new spaces staked out for you already."

"You do? Where?"

"Armajad. The rebellion has been pushed back from three subsectors and all is in chaos. Perfect situation to lock up business, while everything is in flux."

"Hm."

"Also is flanking brodien-Triskelos space, so you keep presence where Styrcian Leaguers work. They won't be forgetting who they are subsidiary of, now."

"True."

"Is super-good deal."

"It better be. Because I don't like bowing out of so much space and leaving it to a gang that was recently my aspiring competitor."

"You must look on what you win instead, Boss."

"I know," Janus nodded. "I have claim to their resources, and they're paying a premium for the distribution and protection we're giving them. And now we have a piece of their business with the Imperials. Did Mardin's payment clear yet?"

"Yes, and legal shuffling of corporations and shell fronts also done. You have effectively doubled your holdings today, Boss. Congratulatings." Karuu flashed tusks at Janus.

"You're just happy because it means a bonus for you."

Karuu didn't deny that. "Also means you are a much bigger fish in the Red Hand pond now."

"Yes." A slow smile spread across Janus's face. "Yes, it does, doesn't it. My assets are larger than Mika's now." He named the second-most senior triumvir of the cartel and stared into the distance for a bit.

"I'll have to see how I can leverage that."

# 26

KES SAT ON the floor of the test chamber, her back wedged into a corner, her knees pulled up to her chest and her face buried in her arms atop them. The room turned dark, then light, then blinding bright in patterns she could see through her closed eyelids, then plunged into darkness again, all in a fast, random strobing of colored lights that bombarded her from different directions. The barrage of strobe and searchlight and abyssal darkness had continued for a timeless while now—hours, certainly, if not days—along with sounds ranging from sub- to supersonics, all at frequencies that set her teeth on edge and made her bones ache.

The black Navy jumpsuit they'd given her to wear was sweat soaked and clinging to her body. The room was overheated now, stifling, as hateful a change as the freezer-cold it had been some while before. The temperature and drafts of air shifted constantly; there was no norm to get used to.

Her breath came rapidly, as if she had been running. When she unclasped her hands they trembled, so she kept them locked around her knees instead. She was enduring, that was all. Spending her energy existing in each moment, with no thought to anything but how to survive the next minute of *now*.

"Stress test," Metmuri had forewarned her, smiling nervously as if it would be, oh, a run or a quick ride and then over with. "Just a little something to see what some of your limits are. Then we'll measure brain activity afterward, give you a few cognitive tests . . . the usual."

If this was "the usual," she wondered how many they had driven insane with this kind of testing. She wasn't insane, oh no, but with sleep deprivation and this constant over-stimulus it was easy to see how some people could lose it, could scream their lungs out or curl up in a fetal ball on the floor and dissolve in tears and beg for mercy and—

And she refused to give in to those urges herself. Sat hunkered in the corner, clutching her last bits of self-control tightly, enduring sensation overloads that humans were not designed to endure for long.

It took a while for her to notice that the strobing had stopped. The aching faded from her inner ear—no more sonics at play. The air seemed less oven-like than it had a short while ago. She dared to open her eyes a little, staring at the floor beneath her. No wildly shifting lights. Something wet dropped to the ground and she blinked her eyes clear. Sweat, and tears. She had been crying and not known it.

A hand on her arm startled her. She shied back and jerked upright at the same time.

Ilanya Eva squatted by her side, a drinking bulb of water in her hands. She helped Kes hold it—she drained it dry, not realizing she was so thirsty until the cool liquid washed down her throat, slightly salty with something to replace her electrolytes. Eva took it from her trembling grip. Kes grasped the woman's hand and squeezed in gratitude.

The officer squeezed her hand back in reassurance. Kes felt tears well up. This was the first friendly touch, friendly contact she'd had in how long? It had been forever since Metmuri had begun this hellish little test, and how long had she been here, anyway?

Eva helped her to her feet. "You did good," she praised. "All you need to do now is relax on a med bed while they monitor you for a while. You can do that, can't you?"

Kes nodded mutely.

"Good girl." She walked her out of the room with an arm around her, helped her onto the bed in the next room. Trodes extended from morphfoam; Kes saw but did not feel their intrusion into her flesh and her skull. She was too overcharged with endorphins, adrenaline, cortisol, a soup of other natural chemicals that had flooded her system for too long under stress. They could cut off an arm right now and she might not feel it.

She felt very sleepy, suddenly. Maybe there had been something in that drink, or something in the trodes. . . .

Darkness welcomed her, and she gave herself up to it.

ESIMIR WALKED ALONE in the cloning crèche. Here in three supernutrient cradles, the clones of Hinano Kesada grew at an accelerated rate, awash in the cool blue light of aseptic fields and mediscans.

It had been three weeks since the biopsies had been taken, chromosomes extracted, DNA manipulated. This was not quite the halfway point in fast-growth cloning; in a few more weeks, they could be aged beyond mere maturity to a point matching Hinano's bio-age. Then they would be ready for the imprinting process.

At this time, the girls in the cradles approximated ten years of age. Esimir stopped by the middle crèche and looked down at the slumbering form there, growing in nutrient fluid beneath a clear cover.

He'd chosen this time because it fell between medtech visits. He ordered Prevak to turn off visual monitoring for the duration of his brief stay in the crèche. He glanced to the door he had locked behind himself. Esimir would not be interrupted.

As always, the presence of young clones made him feel like he was in a room of sleeping children. Maybe they could be his children, if he'd fathered any—though in a way, he had fathered them all. An illicit thrill ran through him. They might awaken at any moment, might catch him in his clandestine curiosity . . . but no. They were not sentient, not yet. Not really.

He unlatched the cradle cover, let the hydraulics lift the casing out of the way so that he looked down at Hinano$_2$ directly through the fluid that covered her.

How pristine clones were, at this point. Unsullied. Innocent, in the truest sense, more so than children ever had been.

Do they know how appealing they are? he asked himself. Do they sense that I love them?

He gathered up his tunic sleeve in one hand, freed one bare arm to reach into the crèche, down through liquid supersaturated with oxygen, growth hormones, and nutrients, past the long tawny blond strands of the girl's floating hair.

He caressed her face. Her skin was the same temperature as the nutrient bath, warm with the blood that pumped and the life that burgeoned in her. He trailed his fingers down the innocent body. The boyish chest, the flat belly, the hairless mons. He rested his hand on one slender hip. These were the children of his science and his art. Even those who would wear the minds of criminals once grown were all, at this stage, innocent youths. He visited them all as they grew.

He wished he could preserve them like this. Or show his affection for them.

But that, he thought, would not be . . . appropriate. The risk if he were caught was too great.

He pulled his arm from the vat. The nutrient dropped off, leaving no dampness behind. Esimir shut the lid and left the lab as quietly as he had entered.

KES HAD LOST weight. I look haggard, she thought—her cheeks sunken, stress lines in the furrow of her nose, mouth, brow. Her eyes looked back at her in the mirror with a tight wariness, like a hunted animal. Or maybe just an enduring one. A trapped, cornered, enduring beast. She wondered what colors Frebo would show in her aura now.

There was blood on her collar—not hers—and she replayed the fit of angry distress just past. She'd snapped when Tall and Dark handled her roughly. She could still feel her claws ripping flesh, more deeply than she had ever cut in play, the splatter of blood, the man's scream. The deep, gut-level gratification she'd felt in hurting him. He would not be hounding her footsteps for a few days, at least.

Consigned again to her rooms, she curled into a ball upon her bed. Stayed there as she heard the iris valve open and someone entered unannounced.

It was the bioempath. She looked over his shoulder automatically and was surprised to see no escorts. She sat up, pushed her way back to the headboard, clutched her knees to her chest and watched him suspiciously.

He stopped in the doorway. Good. She flexed the claws on her right hand, felt the tips dig into her thigh through the soiled jumpsuit she wore. He could not see that, not behind her leg and the curtain of her long unwashed hair that concealed her hand on that side. If he came too close . . .

He stared at her for quite a while, saying no word. She offered no word, either. She had nothing to say to her jailer. Her torturer. When she tormented people, it was an exploration of sensation that they had consented to, that they consciously invited for the erotic charge it had. This . . . this was nothing she had consented to at all.

And that made all the difference in the world.

Metmuri was not always present, but she knew he was behind it all. No matter what good cause Eva said this project was for, he was the one who pushed her beyond limits like this. She would not engage him if she did not have to. Or she would kill him if she could . . . and then what would the Eosan say?

He cleared his throat. "I'm sorry."

His words hung on the air. When she did not reply, he said them again. "I'm sorry." He blinked rapidly. "You're . . . different . . . from the rest. They're re-signed. They don't care, or they care so desperately they fight us every step of the way. It takes a lot to break through."

Did he mean there were others he did this to, as unconsenting as she? "Juro take you," she rasped.

He shook his head. "You don't understand. Your attitude is different. Was. I hope I haven't . . ." His voice trailed off. If her eyes did not fool her, that was remorse she saw on his face. He *saw* her, and did not like what he saw.

Did not like the results of his handiwork.

Good.

He blinked rapidly. Studied her again for a while in silence. "You'll be fine now," he told her. "No more. No more tests. We have enough."

"Go to hell." Her voice was little more than a whisper.

"I'm sorry," he said again and left the room without another word.

# 27

FLASHMAN FINALLY GOT the hang of it.

The net feed that kept him linked to the codeworm was like a constant small voice in the back of his head, never demanding overt attention, never really going away. After several days the vertigo subsided. The FreeRange circuit in his deck let him move around normally, yet still maintain contact with his construct in cyberspace.

The worm was ready and waiting for Janus's direct contact, and so was Flash. Yet none of this prepared him for the disjoint moment when Janus actually called home.

Alerted by his deck's callback alarm, FlashMan threw himself onto his couch and jacked in, monitoring the conversation as he sped to the triumvir's household systems.

The man was in Triskelos space and would return in another handful of weeks. He chortled about a secret business coup and told his majordomo to plan a party for senior cartel members on Lyndir upon his return. "After I announce this to the triumvirate," Janus pronounced, "every Red Hander is going to be part of something new and extraordinary."

Probably has twelve new extortion victims, Flash mused, and a sector governor on the take. All in a hard day's work . . .

While Janus talked, the netrunner transferred more of his awareness to the codeworm. He tasted the glittering pink com stream by which the triumvir had entered the nexus. Tracer bits showed this call originated from the man's cyber-rigged body systems, not merely from external communications devices. Janus wasn't just talking on a com set; as usual, he'd jacked in to make this call.

With what felt like a twitch of his shoulders and a body shimmy, Flash-as-worm detached part of himself from the larger body of worm code. He dandled a pseudopod into the streaming pink backtrace, let the current tug at him, then drag him along with it.

The Flash-worm derezzed, merging his electrons into that rush of data and flitted upstream at a steady millisecond pace. There, dead ahead, the swirling yellow vortex of a subspace relay. Through it he flowed, bouncing to the satellite system above Lyndir, then to a flashport far above the elliptic that handled interstellar coms. It was a clear trace all the way, just that one coherent stream of Janus-data to ride.

It was when they hit the flashport, and his code construct was compressed and squirted across subspace, that FlashMan howled in the flesh.

The decker grabbed his head reflexively and curled into a ball on his side. Muscle spasms cramped his body as an involuntary convulsion shook him. The world receded to a pinpoint of light at the end of a long dark tunnel.

Somewhere in the back of his head the susurrant chatter of the 'spheres continued, data and info clouds floating atop the net infrastructure on Lyndir. Without conscious thought, he knew that the part of him in the coms nexus was present and accounted for. But the disconnected worm segment that had blitzed through that relay and beyond—was gone.

The instant it vanished it had felt like a chunk of his brain cells were cut from him with a red-hot knife. Flash fumbled crudely around in net space for the balance of his sim-consciousness. He found nothing.

He could barely think straight. He should have been able to stay connected no matter where those data packets went. Even on squirt relays there was a carrier feed that should give him a ping-back to his lost bit of pseudo-self.

He moaned; it felt like someone had flattened the back of his head with a mallet.

It couldn't have been my work, he thought. It must've been some rotten IntSec code I cribbed. The bugrunners never did know how to jury-rig deck programs. . . .

He groaned again and passed out on the couch that held his trembling form.

# 28

IF HELDA HAD ever doubted that extended absence could cause even a celebrity like the Winter Goddess to fade from public memory, she had that affirmed now. Business slowed. Clients visited other fantasy houses, flirting with the cheaper, pale imitations of domination offered by Shonei House, or lightening their credmeters with the experienced dominas of Ikoi's Night Garden.

"Haven't they said *anything*?" she pleaded with Bejmet. "Surely if she's simply delayed . . ."

"I was told she'll be returned directly to Tryst, unless she doesn't come back at all. You haven't received weregeld, have you, Helda?"

"No."

"Then we've not lost her services. She'll be back."

"When?"

Bejmet shrugged. "You'll know before I do, I expect. You are to inform me the instant she's returned."

"Couldn't you ask the Arcolo—?"

"That is not a person I can ask for anything." She spoke sharply. "She is a hazard to us. It would be wise to engage her as little as possible. Don't press me about that again."

Helda bowed her head submissively, and the Eosan cut the connection between them. They didn't speak often about the missing shigasa. There wasn't much to say. For Helda, the fact of her lover's absence had receded to a dull aching worry, no longer as sharp or painful as in the first weeks, but too tender a concern to dare keep in the forefront of her mind.

She put Kes out of her thoughts once more. She must, if she was to be able to function as Dosan and conduct business at all.

She went about her day, and her slaves knew to give her a wide berth.

KES SAT ON the bank seat of the fresher, the unit set to sauna mode. Her hair hung in sweat-damp strands to her slender hips, its natural wave relaxed in the moist heat. She leaned naked against the warm beige wall, eyes closed, her muscles as relaxed as laufre discipline could help them to be. Now she worked through her thoughts one by one, trying to find a way to unknot the inner tension that was her constant companion.

Her inner dialog—or was it debate?—continued doggedly on. She was feeling trapped and trying not to give in to it all.

What could I have done differently to have avoided this? she asked herself. Anything?

There was nothing you could do, she answered herself. You had no choice.

No, came the contradicting thought. There is always a choice. I could have walked out on Helda, defied the Eosan, become outcast from my house. At least it would have kept me out of here.

No, you couldn't, came the counterpoint. Your contract requires obedience. If you break that contract, you're liable for a longer term of debt service once you're caught. Or even debt slavery, if the judge came down hard on you. And if they sent you somewhere else—like, back to the Salon. . . .

She shuddered. She'd have to kill someone if she went back there. She knew it.

She listened to her thoughts with mild surprise. She didn't *know* it, exactly; it had never been a resolution, but it had certainly been a tempting thought when dealing with Gistano, who had stripped her of her fortune, her career, and her freedom in one unscrupulous ploy. The fact that the Scripman's action was technically legal had nothing to do with how she felt about it.

She'd had a house slave once, her nanny as a child until she'd outgrown the need for a caretaker. She had missed Tieda, but never wondered how she fared or what had happened to her. She would never be so callous about a debt-slave again.

So what? the querulous part of her mind interjected. You're not a slave, but you are bound in other ways. And most of them are ways you've chosen since you came to Palumara House.

She sighed and turned about on the bank seat, pressing shoulders to one wall, feet against the other. She'd always thought of herself as independent, as a person in charge of herself and her fate. Was that the illusion of privilege that Bren had given her? How to survive day by day was never an issue for them; what direction to go in, where to invest creative energy was. She'd been taught to think that way. Getting by in circumstances that chafed had never been one of her strong suits.

Tryst was a safe haven, for now. She'd leave if and when it suited her—after she'd made a life with Morya and was certain they were both permanently out of the grasp of the Icechromers.

And what was Morya doing now? A pang of loneliness and yearning lanced through her at the thought.

You shouldn't have been put in this situation in the first place, sniped the acid-tongued part of herself.

She shook her head. Part of her was invested in angry recrimination. No matter how logical, no matter how compelled by circumstances she had been, resentments boiled in some back room of her mind. Surely Frebo would be a brilliant orange-red right about now. And that thought did nothing to soothe the anxieties: Frebo, her name-day present from Morya.

If I hadn't gone to the Salon, she reminded herself, I would never have met her.

For a moment a warm glow came over her. The girl loved her for herself, shared her eclectic sexual interests, had no judgments about her worth, was incredibly loyal—

Morya looks at you through rosy filters, her inner critic said.

"Shut up," she murmured out loud. It was enough to know that someone loved her and no doubt missed her right now. When she was out of here, what a reunion they would have.

When she was out of here.

Eva said it would be soon, and she'd been frank with her so far. Thank the gods for one humane person in this Juro-damned place, Kes thought. Ilanya may be doing her duty, but she takes the time to talk to me like a real person, not some test animal.

She gritted her teeth. Ah, to be back at Tryst where the tortures were not tortures in this sense, things that near drove you out of your mind without re-gard to consequences. What she wouldn't give to work off this nervous tension with a flogger in her hand, to run energy between her and a willing partner, creating an ecstatic exchange that would exhaust and ground them both.

Kes shut the bleak present out of her mind's eye and smiled, imagining the homecoming she would have with her girl.

IT WAS ANOTHER large-party night at the Salon in Port Oswin. A group of arcol-ogy managers from the experimental habitats of lower Szels had taken over the House. They booked every joyboy and a handful of joygirls and ordered danc-ers in from Firewing, a nearby shigasue house. The house comp provided the music, and the kitchen worked overtime to produce the food.

Morya amused herself by amusing Grasson, the chief engineer among the managers. She flirted with Varl, the high-strung joyboy the client had claimed for his own that night. She wrapped her arms around her housemate in the sinuous movements of the cuashan, swayed with him suggestively and enjoyed the brief expression of confusion on his face—Varl was very good at the cuas, but not used to dancing them with a woman. He had the moves down perfectly and did not betray discomfort on his face, but she laughed at the look she read in his eyes. He did not dare chase her away: Grasson had asked for her as well.

Their client was portly and flushed with wine and laughter. He enjoyed watching them together. "Do it," he ordered, waving his hand at them.

"Do what, Grasson?" Varl asked coyly, glad for the distraction. He pushed

Morya a little away from him, shifted his body angle, and teased Grasson with the sensuous sway of his hips.

"You know," the man said, and waved his hand at them again.

So many were reluctant to speak frankly about sex. Morya bit back the urge to speak for him or poke fun, but she knew very well what he wanted. She turned her back to Varl's lithe form then pressed up against his sweat-slick chest, undulating with him in time to the music. His torso pressed against her back, his hips against hers.

"Do what?" she prompted Grasson also. She let her voice get husky, inviting. "Do you want to see us fuck?"

The man blushed and nodded. They were in the back corner of the lounge, putting on a semi-private dance for this manager whose promotion the party celebrated. His was a nearly predictable request; when a single client wanted a couple to entertain him, he was either a voyeur, or wanted to get in the middle and be done by both. And Grasson didn't seem the type to relish being that exposed in front of his friends.

Varl snaked his hands down to Morya's hips, began to grind against her in earnest. She tossed her dark curls over her shoulder, turning her face to their client, writhing against her partner just so. It was natural, but also pretense. It was staging. It reminded her of the staging she'd done with Kes, her favorite dance partner. They had been so hot together, dark and fair, half a party would stop and watch. And when it came to fucking . . .

Morya banished the thought as quickly as it intruded. That was why she volunteered for floor shift during parties, these days. She wanted to get swept up in the raucous entertainment of an evening. She wanted some hot sex and someone to occupy her attention, take her mind off of the beautiful domina who had wooed her with empty promises then abandoned her completely. It was that, or spend her days crying and chasing clients away with her bad attitude, to the detriment of her contract balance.

Fuck you, Kes. I'll show you what fucking's about.

She angled her hips back and felt Varl stiffen against her. Grasson wanted a show, he would get one.

# 29

LIKE A ZIPFLY slamming into a bug screen, FlashMan crashed into a filter matrix on the far side of the subspace relay. The tapeworm segment tumbled out of the com flow and splatted on the virtual floor, stunned and unmoving. Janus's data stream blitzed by overhead, the rush of its electrons a dull roar in Flash's swimming senses.

The relay ride was as it always was: a gut-twisting scramble and the awareness of thought stringing Flash's electrons together—or was it electrons knitting thoughts together?—in a mad dash down virtual data conduits.

And then it all went wrong.

Always in virtual space there was a trace feed back to the deck that kept sim awareness connected to physical netrunner. Even through the star-spanning subspace relay network, there was a trickle carrier for maintenance packets and pings that sufficed to keep a trace alive, laggy though it might be.

When he flowed into the vortex that was Janus's subspace routing, FlashMan had that awareness. When he smashed into the filter matrix, it vanished. As he collected his wits on a white expanse of floor, the thing that hit him hardest was his sudden isolation.

Oh, no, he fretted. Where's my deck?

He groped for that otherspace where he had chip resources and progs to tap into. Nothing. It was like a door had slammed at his back, cutting him off from externals. The feeling was visceral: his sense that home was *that way* was completely erased, along with the subliminal sense of connection to the body.

That shocked him to his senses when he would just as soon have lain there nursing his aching sim-self. Shuddering, he pulled himself together and took stock of his situation.

A broad white floor stretched into the distance all around him. The golden-pink conduit that was Janus's data flow drew his eye: it was a sparkling cylinder overhead, apparently solid with the flood of infobits it contained. One end was rooted in the round gold collar of what must be a dataport; the other flowed into—and through—a matrix of needle-thin green beams of coherent light. That was the object FlashMan had collided with, a filter grid like fine mesh. The lines of energy reminded him of traps he'd seen now and then: systems that screened and contained intrusive programs or data probes.

I've been filtered! Sidelined like a hairball in a lint trap!

Flash felt the sting of indignation. He had an overwhelming urge to scream in frustration, but the code worm he inhabited had no mouth. He looked around the room again. Room, hall, vast expanse—it had indefinite boundaries and a ceiling, if there was one, that was lost in the sourceless glow of light overhead.

Holding tank. He was in a cyber-version of someone's holding tank, fished out of the data stream and cast on this empty shore to await someone's pleasure.

There wasn't much a worm could do about that. Flash inventoried his systems: the tapeworm wanted to seek out a com port and monitor data, following its coded imperative. Even now he battled the urge to start creeping across the floor in a search pattern, questing for data that the netrunner knew was not here.

No, it's up *there*. In that stream I just got ejected from.

He fumed at the injustice of it. And then he began to extricate himself from the vermiform code his fractal self had piggybacked on.

It took a long while. Full seconds, maybe even minutes of real time. He had minuscule processing ability, no external systems, and he worked much more slowly than he liked. Gradually, his spiky sim-head emerged from the worm, then his shoulders and one arm. It was like pulling himself out of a gelatinous costume that fit too snugly and bound his limbs. And it was those limbs he needed right now, in a form that gave him mobility. He needed to be mobile, to find a way out of there.

And I'll be damned if I do it by crawling all over this floor as a worm.

FlashMan pried another arm loose and peeled the vermiform off one leg at a time. The tapeworm congealed again into its ropy shape, as if Flash had never been contained inside.

"Argh!" the decker cried and kicked the worm with one pointy foot.

It gave spongily beneath the blow and began to creep across the floor, following the search pattern that was its coded instinct.

Flash sniffed and turned his back on the worthless thing. The data stream was high overhead, its entrance port on his left. He began to trot towards that wall. When the coms flow ceased, that port might be his way out.

After all, there *had* to be a way out, somewhere.

FLASHMAN SAT SLUMPED against the wall.

There was no way out.

As soon as he had reached the wall beneath the dataport, he had extended his hands automatically, willing them to morph into sticky pads for climbing. Nothing happened. He gawked at his traitorous appendages in open-mouthed surprise, even as he remembered that he needed to run a prog in his deck to custom morph his form. So habitual it was, he hadn't given it a thought. Then other realizations came to mind as well.

He couldn't climb up to the port, and he couldn't jump that high, either. Without enhanced performance features, his sim-self had essentially human-scale abilities in this virtual zone; all his special effects had been courtesy of the routines he'd created for himself over time. Routines resident in his absent deck.

The port was about four times his height overhead. So was the filter trap that had screened him out of that stream. He'd circled the room twice now—it was finite, even if the boundaries seemed to fade from sight in the sourceless lighting all around. There were no doors, no objects, no ladders, no nothing that could help him. And here he sat.

The coms flow blinked out of existence, leaving midair suddenly empty. Flash heard something lock into place overhead; he came to his feet and moved out on the floor to get a better view of the wall.

Something like a vault door now sealed that opening, plugging it solidly shut. The fine mesh of the filter trap still blocked the opposite portal.

Great, Flash thought. Now how am I supposed to get out of here? Assuming I could even reach the port before something comes to check this nasty little intruder trap. . . .

He sat on the floor again and began to worry.

# 30

THERE WERE NO guards present when Kes took her walks in Eva's company. Only the officer's visored aide, Teo, stood unobtrusively by the doorway into the complex: a distant, nonthreatening presence she quickly learned to ignore. Ilanya gave her pleasant enough conversation to interrupt the monotony of her days.

"Why do you do this?" she asked abruptly as they strolled the perimeter of the parking dome. "Surely you have better things to do than to walk with me?"

"If you come out here, you have to be escorted. I volunteered." Eva gave a half shrug. "It's obvious the guards were getting on your nerves. I thought this would be easier for you."

"Hm." It was, and it was exactly the kind of small consideration she had grown to appreciate in this PolitDiv officer. She would not question this kindness in unexpected places; she was grateful for it, actually. It made the mystery of her incarceration—oh, no, "extended visit," as Eva called it—a little more bearable.

Still, that mystery was something she could not let rest. "So . . . are you done with all your tests?" she asked.

Eva glanced at her with her sharp blue gaze. "They're not 'my' tests," she corrected. "They're Dr. Metmuri's. I don't know, exactly, what that status is."

"When can I go?"

"When he says you're done."

"When can I see him to ask?"

Eva gave a short laugh. "You are nothing if not persistent, I'll give you that. Look." She came to a halt by a private aircar. Kes stopped and turned towards her. "Here's a question for you—a self-assessment, if you will."

As usual, Eva neatly sidestepped anything she did not want to talk about; Kes knew to let the subject rest. "You don't need to answer," the officer continued, "but I'm curious about this. You have a service oath to your House, yes?"

Kes nodded.

"But you're not full Sa'adani." Eva gestured loosely towards caste marks that were not there. The ruby stud earrings that Kes wore—until they'd been taken from her—marked her occupation as entertainer, a low-ranking order, but she understood Eva to mean she had not been born into a proper Sa'adani family. "So what keeps you in service there, really?"

Kes's brow furrowed. That was almost an offensive question. To ask what bound her to Palumara House besides an adoption oath was to question whether she would honor her duties and obligations. She kept a check on her temper and answered as bluntly.

"My mother was Sa'adani, and my father one-eighth. So I have more honor-sense than the casteless, if that's what you're asking. As for Palumara . . . I have a debt of roi'tas with them, because they helped me and because they've given me a home. I honor that."

Even as she said those words, Kes wondered how true they were. She yearned to be accepted as Sa'adani, like her mother: to have an unassailable niche of place and person that didn't lose value because of someone's whim or attitude. She had celebrated being taken into the clan . . . but did she feel an honor-debt in the way that a born Sa'adani would? Perhaps not. For her it was a creed adopted in the same way her house affiliation was: because it took her closer to what she wanted to be. She was not so certain how much of that she had truly become. Yet.

Eva studied her for a moment, an appraising look upon her face. "So what motivates you to do as your House wishes?" she persisted. "Duty, devotion, or self-interest?"

Kes was taken aback. Eva read her hesitation and brushed it off with a laugh. "Most people are driven by self-interest; few are devoted. Even in honoring roi'tas, that formula holds true."

"Are you saying I honor my House oath out of self-interest?"

Eva's lips quirked briefly. "I'm not saying anything. But it is an interesting question, is it not?"

She turned away and continued their walk. It was a moment before Kes fell into step with her again.

EVA SAT WITH Teo in her office, the matasai sitting at her invitation but holding himself at attention nonetheless. Ilanya closed her eyes and leaned back in her chair. "Gods, this wears on me. I'm tired of nursemaiding this one."

"It's been successful so far," Teo observed. "When she sees you, and especially when you interact, her physiology changes. Relaxation of tension."

"I sense it in her aura, too. Metmuri was right about bonding under stress. She has rather latched on to me."

"And the clone will be as kindly disposed towards you as the Prime is," remarked Teo. "How do you think it will play when you ask her to kill Janus?"

Eva frowned. "That would be a rather ham-handed way to get into the matter."

"What's your in, then?"

"She knows she has a client we consider a danger, and that she's being 'enhanced' to help us deal with him. All that remains is to give her a personal motivation to deal with him herself. I'm saving that tidbit for her clone. That aggressive, uninhibited version of herself with minimal impulse control. The one that will be happy to take out her anger and resentment on our target."

"I thought she had a cordial relationship with Janus?"

"She does. What she doesn't realize yet is the role he played in her personal downfall and consignment to life as a shigasa."

"You mean his connection to the Icechromers? They're a Red Hand subsidiary, but nearly a quarter of the derevin on Lyndir are."

"More than that. They're one of his street gangs, and he's the boss of their boss. Kes hates the Icechromers with a passion, but doesn't yet realize who is behind them. Even more, she harbors a grudge about being manipulated into debt-slavery, as well she ought. She covers it up—can't afford to stew in those juices, I think, not while she must work within the debt-contract system. But that land mine is already primed and armed. She alludes to those things in her past, and I feel the energy she carries around them." A calculating expression crossed Eva's face. "When she is stripped down to a singular aggressive persona, those emotions will be a chord ripe for the plucking."

"You think she'll be reactive to Janus's role in her situation?"

"I'm certain of it. She'll justify killing because her Eosan and I have asked it of her, but she'll do it willingly to strike at someone responsible for her servitude these last years."

"Is that a strong enough motivator?"

Eva regarded her matasai. "Would you kill whoever ordered the assassination attempt that nearly destroyed your body and left you . . . like this?" She gestured at his half-cyborg frame with a languid wave of her hand.

"Gladly." His response was terse.

She nodded. "The shigasa feels no less destroyed. She had a very different life before she was consigned to a joyhouse and fucked at the whim of the people who put her there. This Kes has rationalized her anger and resentment about those life changes, tried to come to terms with it all. She must, of course, to function." She shrugged. "But strip that layer of rationalization away—as we're about to do—and I've already felt what's there beneath the surface. When it's the new Kes I'm dealing with, I'll dangle the bait. I have no doubt she'll bite."

"Janus is returning to Port Oswin in three weeks now. Will you have enough time with the clone to foster the necessary attitude?"

"Yes. Metmuri is aging the clones to match Hinano's apparent chron age. Once they're vivified, my work shouldn't take long. Oh." She leaned forward. "I still want an insurance policy in place."

"Domna?"

"A tried and true method, in case the clone hits a balking point."

"You'll want sensation amps, I assume, to implant? Or a chip detonator?"

"Both. Pleasure-wire for persuasion, a chip-mounted microcharge as failsafe." Ilanya nodded. "I want all my insurance in place before I dispatch the clone that will kill Janus."

# 31

**ONE MORE TEST.** The last one, Metmuri had assured Kes. She'd be going home after this. She nearly looked forward to this session.

Techs made her comfortable on a med bed. Trodes and sensors affixed themselves to her. Restraint cuffs extruded from the morphfoam. "In case of involuntary muscle response," they told her, "to make sure you don't hurt yourself."

She tried to relax while the half-dome of a flexor was lowered into place over her head. She did not see the doctor anywhere, nor Eva, for that matter. She was in a semi-hexagonal room with a mirrored sheet of plas forming one wall.

She watched her reflection there, a subject of medical study. No doubt the doctor was on the other side, observing her as well. Let him. She'd play along, to get this out of the way all the sooner. It was just one more thing to endure before she could have a confrontation with Helda about this entire misbegotten—

"You may feel mild discomfort," a tech told her. She didn't bother to acknowledge the woman. She'd felt a lot of discomfort here; a mild version would be a welcome relief.

Something hummed overhead as equipment positioned on the flexor powered up. She was wondering what this test would measure about her, when she completely lost her train of thought.

Images blossomed in her mind, confused and unexpected. Kissing Allie in the garden, stubbing her toe in the fresher, Frebo, an astrogation school test, rage at her father, Morya crying out in passion . . .

Faster the images came, and with them a flood of emotion, shifting as kaleidoscopically fast as the whirl of recall in her head. It caught her by surprise, a tidal wave of impressions, vivid reliving of many moments, an overwhelming surfeit of emotions to go with it all.

She opened her mouth to scream or cry. It was too much, too intense. And on its heels came darkness, dragging her under as it chased the images from her mind.

**FLASHMAN THOUGHT HE** must be missing something obvious and spent hours of real time exploring every millimeter of space he could get to.

Then he got angry and had a temper tantrum in the middle of the broad expanse of floor.

Finally, he lay down on the spot where he had lately been hopping up and down and cursing, and stared into the formless space overhead. If his sim-self could have emulated tears, he would have cried right then.

Flash knew that this was not him in the flesh, but it *felt* like he was here and now in this moment. He experienced ego-consciousness, or the next best thing to it. No matter that theoretically this sim fragment could survive indefinitely and Flash-in-the-body would be just fine; he did not want to languish, and he did not want to perish.

And I don't want to be locked up here forever, either, he thought with a shudder. I'll go stark, staring mad.

He rolled over onto one side, lolled head on arm and stared unfocused at the wall. Not hungry, not tired, this part of him had been designed to be powered by ambient energy in the cybersphere. He could not power down and go into some sleep mode to while away the time that was already heavy on his hands. If only he were as brainless and uncaring as that tapeworm on the wall, he wouldn't care about his predicament.

Tapeworm.

On the wall.

He sat bolt upright and focused on the code segment that was now creeping tenuously up the near wall, about knee-high to a standing sim figure. It had been working routinely over the entire floor all this time and was now moving its search for a com stream to a new plane.

The tapeworm could climb the wall. So FlashMan, inside the worm, could climb the wall as well.

Flash leapt to his feet, danced a few jig steps in celebration, then dashed to the wall before the worm could crawl out of reach. He pulled its length free from that surface, considered the moving coils in his hands with distaste.

"I got out of you," he said to it, "so I suppose I can get back in. Help me out on this one, will you?"

With that, he began to work his way back into the codeworm.

HINANO₁'S HEAD WAS secure in the grip of the wiring station in Surgery 1. The hardwire tech worked deftly beneath its hood, a dour, matronly woman concentrating exclusively on her submicron-fine handiwork. Her hand motions were mirrored in microcosm by nanosurgeons: running minuscule trode lines to nerve bundles, securing and restoring the wetware Hinano Prime had worn in her skull into this copy of the original.

The tech had come from Port Oswin that morning in an IntSec aircar, reported to Ilanya, and bypassed Dr. Metmuri and his staff completely. Navy biotechs prepped Hinano₁ at the Arcolo's command and brought the outsider into surgery as ordered. Eva watched from the gallery as she did her work.

Hinano Prime had worn four cyber implants, all removed from her body after her death. There were two devices chipped into her brain: a rigger interface jack, worn spacer-fashion at the base of her skull, and a cyber relay set to trigger switches in correspondingly equipped devices within a small local radius. It was a common utility for household and industrial use, not of much consequence. The most unusual gear she wore were the cat claws embedded under her fingernails: razor-sharp synthetic steel as long as the last joint of each finger, powered by a microbattery in each wrist that extended and retracted those claws.

The hardwire specialist removed items from the aseptic field one by one, installing the complex comp interface first, then the cyber relay. She installed the trigger sensor for the claws, but did not immediately move on to the fingers and their claws. Instead, while she was still in the brain, she installed two more devices.

They were nondescript implants of white, bio-inert microplast. One was an insular device, planted near Hinano's brainstem. The other was of finer construction and required the threading of a neurowire to a specific cluster in the pleasure centers of her brain. The clone would awaken with her expected full complement of cyber devices—plus two. But they were two she would never be aware of, unless they were triggered by Ilanya Evanit.

# 32

ESIMIR SAT BY Hinano$_1$'s bedside in the vivification lab. The chamber resembled a hospital room, intentionally so. It was of small, human dimensions, just large enough for the med bed, monitors, working staff. And the subject.

Hinano$_1$ slept now, a mature clone grown to match her Prime's physical age. Over the last weeks the corpus had been eased from a slack, vegetative state to one of fitness by a tensor regimen that put vat-grown muscles through a routine workout. The brain was successfully imprinted with one of three personality constructs parsed by Prevak and scribed by nanoneurals. All that remained was to imbue the clone with the spark of ensoulment that would rouse her from her comatose slumber.

Terel and others monitored Hinano$_1$'s data flow from outside this room. Two security guards with stun guns kept watch outside the door, ready to step in at a shout from the bioempath. Esimir doubted he would need them; his eyes lingered on the hospital restraints that tethered the clone's wrists to the bed frame. It was a necessary precaution, learned the hard way when the first convict subject had awoken and launched himself out of the bed in a murderous rage. His fingers had locked around the doctor's throat and choked Esimir half unconscious before the guards could pry him loose.

They had never taken that risk again during an Awakening.

Esimir leaned forward. He placed his left hand on the crown of the clone's head. At Ilanya's order, her hair was no longer its natural tawny color, but white again, and styled as it had been on the Prime. He would have mistaken this clone for the original, but for the lack of minor lines around mouth and eyes that his trained eyes knew to look for. He felt the warmth of her beneath his hand and breathed out, slowly, relaxing into that space that opened him to his higher powers. Then he focused his eyes to see with the other-sight that was the learned skill of a bioempath.

He was within the aura of his subject, a subdued and meager field at this moment. His hand was awash with the glow of lavender light that radiated from her crown, from the region called the Gate of Heaven in ancient times. Down the length of her body other points of energy glowed with their own radiance, a sprinkling of gem-colored embers from head to toe.

Seven of these major energy centers, the lau-dan, punctuated a human being from groin to top of head, along with many minor power points and energy meridians that ran throughout the body. He saw them now as tracery within her aura and in her physical body. The lau centers were the most vibrant: colored vortices along the spinal meridian, channeling energy into and out of her physical form. It was a human's connection with the infinite made visible. Along the highest of these pathways, a piece of Hinano's soul would find its way back into this body.

Esimir exhaled, his eyes fluttering shut, and extended his senses through his hand. He felt the clone's somnolence, then quested out along the crown laudan into that space beyond the body where energy frequencies shifted upscale into the invisible and the infinite.

The bioempath dropped into a trance state, blood pressure dropping, the beat of his heart slowing to a glacial pace. He aligned his energies with the clone's and sent a part of himself elsewhere along the lau-dan path.

If she were an accident victim lying in a coma, he would will the spark of consciousness that belonged here to return from its errant travels and take up residence again in the sleeping shell that was its home. He did something similar now. Hinano was not in a coma born of injury, but in a state of repose never yet enlivened by the vibrance of a soul. And yet this body shared energy ties with its kin: with the Prime that was its origin, with its crèche-mates, with the collective energy that all humankind were part of.

Somewhere out there, a spark did await to house itself in this physicality. Was it a part of the Prime? A related soul fragment? Could one person be ensouled in many bodies at once? Such philosophical questions had occupied Esimir once on Corvus, but he had no definitive answers to them. What he knew was that a call and a focused will could pierce the ether like a beacon and lead back to the body that divine spark that wanted to inhabit it.

That was what he did now. He became a conduit, a lighted path from the beyond to the body that rested beneath his hand. His world became one of sensation, of the tingle of Hinano's bioelectric field, the vibration of her basal aura, his senses flowing out through the Gate of Heaven to some disincarnate sphere where energy vibrated in the ether like a plucked chord.

Something that resonated with that chord was drawn to that tone and came flowing, like a single glissading note, down scale, down frequency, down the lau-dan channel, and into the body.

He felt the flare of her aura, heard her sigh as her energy shifted. Like a man in a dream he opened his heavy-lidded eyes, saw her looking up at him.

Her expression was one of confusion. Her eyes searched his face, knowing him, not remembering—yet—the context for that knowledge.

Esimir took his hand from her head, drawing power back into himself, severing connections created to serve the moment. Tired. Always tired, immediately after the Awakening. He smiled. "Ferris will care for you," he said, "and I will see you later."

He stood, turned his weary body away. In the doorway he paused. He heard Hinano fighting her restraints behind him.

He left without another word.

**NO MORE EXPERIMENTS,** Kes told herself. I don't care what arrangements the Eosan made, and they can add this to my contract-debt if they want. I've had it with this place.

She yanked again at the tethers that held her wrists to the bed frame. Finally the anger she had suppressed towards the meddling doctor had boiled to the surface. This was a hard one, this awakening—they must have drugged her. Things weren't coming clear right away. Not her thoughts, not her eyesight. She felt lightheaded. Metmuri, the first bleary thing perceived upon opening her eyes, was not a welcome sight, and it had set her blood to boiling right away. She did not want to be at his mercy anymore, nor in his laboratories.

I want out. And I'm getting out, one way or another.

She made an effort to calm herself, to breathe deeply like in a laufre exercise, seeking her power and her center. It was pointless to waste her energy fighting a bedstead when what she wanted to do was slug the doctor and walk right out of here. They had said the testing was done. They had no reason to stop her from walking to the parking dome—she could help herself to a car and be gone before anyone noticed. How to get free enough to do that required some thought, though, and her thoughts were not coming together yet.

She heard the door open, footsteps come in. She noted her pulse beating faster with near clinical detachment. Her muscles tensed. If it was Metmuri, she doubted she could restrain herself. If it was anyone else—

"Kes?"

The voice was familiar from daily encounters. Eva. She opened her eyes, blinked the red-headed woman into focus. She stood by one side of her bed, Teo, her ever-present companion, on the other.

"How are you?" Eva asked.

Kes tried to answer, coughed, and swallowed down a dry throat before she could speak. "Not right." Her voice sounded rusty, disused. Strange to her ears. "Want out."

Eva nodded, patted her hand. "Can you sit up?"

Kes jerked her right wrist; the restraints would not permit her to sit upright. Ilanya nodded to Teo; the pair bent to the tethers and soon freed her arms. She tried to sit up; fell back. Eva propped her up with an arm around her shoulders.

"Weak . . ." Kes mumbled, discontent with herself and everything in her world at that moment. She felt like she had just woken from an unnaturally deep sleep and was not yet back in her body. Her limbs were heavy, and her body felt unresponsive.

Eva nodded in understanding. "You need to move around. You've been in bed for far too long."

How long was that? She could not muster the energy to ask.

"Come. We'll help you to your room. Wouldn't hurt if you could walk the distance. Can you try that?"

Kes gave a noncommittal shrug. They helped her to her feet, gave her slippers; Teo held a robe for her as she lifted lead-heavy arms and slipped into the sleeves.

Shuffling, then, with a gait like an old woman, Kes left the medical room with Eva and Teo by her side.

KESADA LAID QUIETLY in her hospital bed, trying to make sense of her situation. Wrists, restrained: they feared she would hurt herself, then, or hurt one of them. Metmuri had smiled more warmly upon her than he had in the past, then left without a comment. Would he be back? Would someone else?

Questions with no answers flitted through her head. Some part of her wanted to worry over this, get every bit of nuance out of this situation. But it was so hard to marshal her thoughts.

No point in fighting it right now, she told herself. I'll find out soon enough what they're up to. Meanwhile, I can use the rest.

She felt drained, exhausted, uncomfortable in every muscle. When she shifted her legs, muscles ached in response to her command to move, as if she had run a marathon and fatigued them beyond recall. Her whole body felt that way. How long had she been out, anyway? Her thoughts were confused, and that was unsettling. She wanted order in her internal dialog, but words and concepts would not stay strung together long enough to make sense of anything.

Sleep. Maybe she just needed to sleep. . . .

KESI DIDN'T LIKE seeing Metmuri first thing upon awakening, but thankfully he left right away. She didn't trust that man. She feared him, a little. Well, more than a little. He could hurt her—worse, hurt her unintentionally, like a bug crushed underfoot. She seemed to have that much weight with him.

Tears clouded her eyes as the distress and anxiety she had ignored all these many weeks welled to the surface. Did Eosan Bejmet have any idea what hell she'd sent her shigasa into? Did Helda? Did they care? She thought they did— she was an investment, at the very least, and Helda cared for her in her limited way. And was Morya worried about her? Oh, to be held by her right now, and comforted, and told this ordeal was over, how wonderful that would be. . . .

Tears leaked from her eyes. She blinked them away. It wouldn't do to seem too emotional, but she couldn't help it. She wanted to go home, and she was feeling sorry for herself, too sorry.

I hate it when you get like this, Kesi berated herself. You can have a good

cry when you're back in the privacy of your room. Right now someone's probably watching you on a monitor. How embarrassing to have them see you cry. So just stop it. Besides, if Commander Kolo never lost it in the desert wastes of Baku, you don't need to lose it in the jungles outside Lessing, now do you?

She snorted a laugh at herself. Cheap net heroics wouldn't help, but they did put this in perspective. This, too, would pass, and she would get out of here soon, get back home . . . and put her foot down to Helda about outside work. Never again. And if they pushed her, what a fit she would throw. She couldn't afford to leave Palumara House yet, but she could make life miserable for everyone if they pushed her. . . .

The thought kept her mind off of Metmuri, and that suited her fine as she drifted off to sleep.

# 33

GUARDS TURNED ESIMIR away from Hinano$_1$'s door.

"You know who I am," he stated. "I order you to let me pass!"

A guard in navy black shook his head, though his expression was sympathetic. "Sorry, Doctor. Arcolo's orders."

Esimir bit off a retort and turned on his heel. First the clandestine hardwiring of his clone, now this. Moments later he was in Ilanya's office.

"You lock me out of my own facilities. By what right—"

Hard hands closed on his arms and he squawked in surprise. Teo moved him forward and forcefully sat him in a chair before the desk, holding him there with one unyielding hand on his shoulder.

"Respect would be appropriate," the matasai said softly.

Esimir looked daggers over his shoulder at the visored man, then at Ilanya, but when he spoke his tone was tensely moderated.

"What are you up to with my clones? You have no right, whatever you're doing. This is *my* project, and I won't have you meddling in it."

Ilanya looked at him sourly. "This may be your project, Doctor, but Hinano-One is *my* clone. I thought that was made clear to you in our previous conversations."

He set his jaw stubbornly. "If I'm to have a valid field test, I need to work with these subjects in a certain way. You can't deny me access—"

"I can and I do." Ilanya put both hands on her desk, leaned forward towards Metmuri. "Let's get something clear. I'm revising your field test protocols. Right now, I have a use for Hinano. I don't want other versions of this shigasa showing up in Port Oswin or anywhere else on Lyndir. I'll let you know when you may release the other clones to their home environs."

A vein pulsed angrily at Esimir's temple. "I'm telling Commander Olniko about this!"

"Be my guest. Olniko takes my orders in this matter, not the other way around. I suggest you get used to this amendment to your chain of command."

The doctor fumed; she met his gaze without blinking. "When do I get my clone back?" he spat.

"You won't. Consider that you have two left to work with and reconcile yourself to that prospect. I've uplinked the changes to your authorized test protocols. Check your com 'sphere when you're back in your office."

His mouth opened and shut again wordlessly.

Ilanya leaned back in her chair. "You may leave. Now."

Teo pulled Esimir from his seat and escorted him from the office with a hand on one arm.

"Doctor?" Ilanya added as they reached the doorway. "In the future, make appointments to see me through Teo. I don't take kindly to being walked in on."

The matasai shut the door in his face, and Esimir stood paralyzed by fury and shock in the hall. After a moment, he popped a tab of mentaid and turned his feet towards the station commander's office.

"I WON'T HAVE it," he declared flatly. "If my work is interfered with in this manner, I won't continue on at all. The entire Splintegrate project will come to a halt if I'm not directing it as I wish. And I'll do that, too; just see if I don't. That's not an empty threat."

Olniko regarded him stoically. He heard the tirade to its end, then sat quietly, studying his Director of Special Projects.

It was not the reaction Esimir expected and silence stretched uncomfortably between them.

Finally the officer gave a small sigh. "I don't suppose you'll like what you're about to hear any more than you liked the Arcolo's disposition of the clones. But hear it you shall.

"Your subsidiary clones are not really of interest to the Navy, Doctor. It is only the first personality construct we're concerned with. The violent, antisocial one with little impulse control. That, and the basic technology of splintering personalities."

Esimir shook his head in denial. "That's nonsense. Splintering is only half the process, and that persona is the most dysfunctional construct of them all. Success will happen only when the other aspects—"

"Success will happen under the conditions the Imperial Navy prescribes. We do not require functionality as you define it."

Esimir rolled his eyes. "Then you will have nothing functional at all," he retorted. "A healthy clone will only exist after reintegration of suitable aspects. We *must* test those aspects for viability, Commander, and we can't do that by keeping them prisoner here as if they were criminals. They're not."

Olniko frowned, his scarred brow giving him a fierce expression. "Insofar as that is instructive to you—please. Carry on. But know this, Doctor: the degree of reintegration you've sought is ultimately irrelevant to Navy goals. It always has been. If your field tests work out, or not, that has little effect on the immediate usefulness of your project."

Esimir began to retort, then swallowed his comment as the true meaning of the words sank in.

*Reintegration was irrelevant to Navy goals.*

The Serafix that permeated his system served many purposes, but at a time like this it accomplished something he could never do unassisted: it let him abruptly separate emotions from analysis. On his own he would be dumbfounded or furious—indeed, some part of him still was, as the outraged scientist clamored in dismay in some back corner of his mind. He ignored that errant voice while mentaid let him focus his analytic capacity even in this moment of crisis.

He thought at flash speed, turning over facts stripped of emotional charge, considering nuance, ploy and counter-ploy, all in the single long moment that he sat with his gaze locked unbelievingly with Olniko's.

Esimir felt queasy. They have what they want, he realized. They could stop this project at any time.

The commander flicked his fingers in a shooing gesture. "Go on about your business, Doctor. More data, better science, better decisions. All of that."

"I'm missing a clone."

"Then adapt accordingly. You're still cleared for the use of our habitats on Farreach. It's safely distant from the subject's home environment, yet they can live a normal life there and still be monitored as you require. Make use of it." His tone changed to one of dismissal. "Was there anything else?"

Metmuri collected himself with a deep breath and shook his head. Olniko had just changed all the rules, and by the look on his face, he didn't even know it. Or purely didn't care. To the Hero of Armajad, this was simply one more command dictate for a subordinate to absorb, delivered in his blunt military manner.

For Esimir, it was a declaration of war.

The bioempath came to his feet. "I understand you perfectly, Commander," he said stiffly. "I think . . . I'd better return to my work."

Olniko dipped his chin. "You do that, Doctor."

Esimir retreated into caste formality and sketched a bow. "Thank you for your time," he said, and took his leave.

# 34

"BEFORE WE CAN return you to Tryst," Eva said, "you and I need to come to an understanding."

Kes looked at the woman who had become her friend over these past many weeks. "What do you mean?" she asked guardedly.

"I need you to do something for me and for your House. And yourself, actually."

Kes looked from Eva, who sat at the small table in her room, to Teo, standing at parade rest behind her. She faced them, crossing her arms over the chest of the blue medtech smock that she wore. "That sounds odd," she said. Her throat was still mildly sore, and her voice rasped more than usual. She wished for a drink, but if Eva was up to something . . .

"Why don't you sit." The Arcolo gestured to a chair. "Let's talk."

Kes hesitated. She fetched herself a bulb of water first, then sat across from the security officer. "What is it you're after?" she asked.

Eva gave her an appraising look. "When you first came here, I told you that you entertain a client who threatens imperial interests."

"The 'undesirable' my House has committed to help you with. Yes."

"Your client is named Janus." Her next words were matter-of-fact. "I want you to kill him the next time you have a session with him."

Kes's fingers tightened on the water bulb. Kill Janus? Was Eva delusional? But she said it with cool assurance, as if she proposed such a thing every day of the week. There were so many retorts to choose from. Kes hesitated before stating the obvious. "Shigasu don't kill their clients. I'm not an assassin."

"You will be performing a service for the Emperor, on the authority of Political Division."

Kes shook her head. "I don't work for PolitDiv. And it's bad for business. Janus is a good client. An ideal client."

"An ideal criminal, you mean. He is singlehandedly responsible for thousands of deaths, injuries, lost businesses, and slides into poverty in this last year alone. Did you know that?"

Kes refused to rise to the bait. "We don't inquire about our clients' business dealings."

"Business dealings?" Eva barked a laugh. "You might call it that. I call it organized crime. He steals and sells contraband, smuggles, runs guns, drugs, protection rackets—whatever turns a profit. It's not a clean-handed business, Kes. People are pushed into criminal undertakings, put out of business or co-opted into his own, or killed along the way. His cartel began as a gang of assassins. Their callous disregard for humanity remains."

Kes took that in. This was not a complete surprise; there were telltale derevin signs about Janus, and she knew how some of those people operated from her time with the Icechromers. Yet neither she nor any shigasa could afford to pay too-close attention to what their widely varied clientele did for a living. It might matter sometimes in intelligence learned in pillow talk, but it didn't matter when they walked in the door looking for entertainment.

Besides, there was a great deal at stake for the shigasue house, obligated to be gracious host and safe haven from the outside world. "Any injury that comes to him would harm Palumara House," she said automatically, deflecting Eva's litany of ill-doing. "Does the Eosan know what you intend? Our reputation alone—"

"Eosan Bejmet understands the necessity for this. She agreed to lend you to this task."

"She's agreed to have a client killed on Palumara premises?" Disbelief tinged her voice.

"She's agreed to help me in any way I ask," Eva replied. "*Any* way."

Kes considered that. "If you want him out of the way," she challenged, "why don't you just have him killed by your people? Why should I be part of this?"

Eva smiled coldly. "As it happens, we cannot be seen to have anything to do with this. Not even an anonymous assassination will serve. The reason for his death needs to be verifiably personal, something between him and whomever kills him."

The domina shrugged. "You're talking to the wrong woman. I have nothing against the man."

"Not even against the man behind the Icechromers?"

Kes felt gut-punched. She couldn't speak.

Eva did instead. "Do you know who Gistano takes his orders from? That would be Janus. Without him, there'd be no Icechromers, with their one-hundred-thousand-cred coolsuits and their long-term leases in the Shelieno for sex resorts. Do you have any idea what it takes to set that up and keep it going through slow seasons? Gistano doesn't finance it all through the loan shark business. That's just a front for predatory business acquisitions. His lieutenant Franc identifies the targets, and Gistano collects them for his joyhouse hobby. And all this fun and games is made possible through Janus's backing."

Kes felt a flood of wetness gushing over her hand and dropped the squeeze-bulb of water like it was a hot rock. She pushed back from the table and stood.

"Everything they've done—your father's murder—"

"Murder?" she gasped.

"You didn't really think his death was suicide or an accident, did you? They rigged his car, to get him out of the way of their acquisition of Hinano Limited. That, your personal ruination, your debt-slavery—all of that came courtesy of Janus's lapdogs. Do you really think a derevin like the Icechromers operates without their higher-ups knowing what's going on? Down to the cred chip? I think Janus picked you out on purpose because you used to be one of his joygirls."

A riptide of emotion held Kes in its grip. *One of his joygirls.* The bitter words echoed in her head.

"He needs to die."

The words were Eva's, the thought Kes's. She should feel repulsed by the idea. Instead, she thought of how incredibly vulnerable Janus made himself to her, all the ways he could perish in a session, destroyed at the climax of a scene gone deliciously, brutally wrong. If she had ever needed an excuse to take a scene too far, she had one now.

Her pulse raced as bloodlust came out of nowhere and left her breathless with sexual tension. She felt the predator within stir, a voice that whispered, *What if. . . . ?*

It left her shaken to her core. Warring with herself, she hedged nervously. "Palumara House would lose face," she said, "if a client died on-site."

"The public doesn't need to know the details. And clients die now and then in the Enclave. You know that."

"Heart attacks," she thought out loud. "Bondage accidents. Breath play. Asphyxiation . . ."

"Nothing will change for you, and Eosan Bejmet will be happy to retain your services into the future."

"I would want to own my contract," Kes threw out. "Have my debt dissolved."

"Done."

She froze, eyes locked with Eva's.

"I told you once that you would be enhanced in certain ways during your stay here," the officer said. "Your inhibitions have been, shall we say, taken down a notch. I think you will find that execution of a criminal is not beyond your grasp. It's revenge you deserve. And I rather think you'll enjoy it."

Kes remembered ripping the tall guard's face open, and knew in that moment that she would rather have taken his eye, and then his entrails.

She remembered the last time she'd flogged a client, the nice thuddy massage that bulky Hethbert loved, and knew that she would rather see him flayed and unconscious at her feet.

Knew that the next time Helda said the wrong thing to her, she would just as soon rip her throat out and spatter the walls with her blood as talk to her.

Her fists clenched, nails digging into her palms, cat-claws flexing involuntarily to prick her as well.

Eva prodded. "Everything you lost, everything you've been through—it's all because of Janus."

Kes felt the blood thundering through her veins, a pulse pounding so loudly she could hear it in her inner ear.

"Think how it would feel," Ilanya purred, "to destroy him in any way you like and to do so with impunity. Bejmet and I will protect you. If you need or want out afterward, I'll help you get out."

Kes locked eyes with her again.

"After all," Eva said softly, "I'm only asking you to do as your nature invites you to."

Eva's cold gaze pierced her; the predator within rose to the challenge of the direct stare and broke the surface with a snarl.

She curled her lip and growled her reflexive answer.

"Yes."

# 35

KESADA SAT ON the floor of her small recovery room clad in a thin green hospital smock and baggy trousers. Her long legs were extended before her and spread as wide as possible, which was, she noticed unhappily, nowhere near the splits she could almost do when warm and limber. She grasped one ankle and bent face to knee, letting tension ease from her muscles with the gentle pull in back and leg. She felt stiff, and her face did not meet her knee: yet another confirmation of things askew with her body. Her flexibility and muscle tone were very different than they had been just a short while before.

Once she began that litany, it did not stop. Her mind ticked down the list that had been growing since she had awakened in the med bed. Her implants were gone. Her hair was its natural color again and fell in tangled waves down to her hips, no longer the styled locks that she had worn to mid-back when she had left Tryst.

Her face was different in subtle ways, too. Her brows were unshaped; her teeth felt rougher, as if they were lacking the sealant that was a routine dental treatment. Her eyes looked the least bit younger. The minute scar at the edge of her left jaw—a souvenir of youthful tussles in her garden playground—was no longer there. Gone, too, was the slight flaw high on the side of her right thigh where a cane had rapped and broken skin, an accidental injury at Coel's less-expert hands during Kesada's apprenticeship at Tryst.

Her laufre routine did not stop her thoughts from tracing the same track repeatedly.

I'm me, but I'm not me. What was it Ilanya said at the start? *You'll be enhanced in certain ways. . . .*

Did this amount to their idea of "enhancement"? Why? *When?*

Nothing Helda said had prepared her for this excursion to a laboratory where humans were the test subjects. Some part of her could grow emotional about this, but there was no point in indulging hysteria: only problem-solving would help her now. She was in the middle of a conundrum, and somehow, somewhere, there were answers to her questions.

The answers walked through her door as she was finishing the grounding set of her laufre routine. Metmuri came face-to-face with her as she stood in horse stance, releasing a long slow exhalation, arms moving towards the ground, palms down. The observer in her mind noted the guard in the hall behind him, the doctor's unaccustomed expression—worry? concern? She did not disturb her pose at his unannounced entry. She finished the outbreath and came erect, feet together, hands by her side before addressing her captor.

It gave her time to study him and her reaction towards him. She had felt hateful towards Metmuri, but that anger was gone now. Something new was in its place. Scorn, and calculation. She regarded the bioempath as coldly as he had ever looked at her. A tool to be used, he was. Now, how to use him. . . .

The doctor flashed her a quick and nervous smile and moved a little closer.

"What do you want with me now?" she demanded, resting hands on hips as she did so.

He glanced over his shoulder to spot the guard, then lowered his voice when he replied. "I came to speak with you about your departure," he said.

"It's about time."

"Shh, please." He put a finger to his lips. "We can't discuss this here."

Kesada spared the guard a glance and kept her voice low as well. "Where do you want to discuss it, then? Because I have a lot I want to say to you. And questions I want answered."

"I have no doubt you do. It is better if we have this conversation in another part of the building."

"Let's get on with it, then." Kesada took a step towards Metmuri. He took a hasty step backwards, bumping a chair and steadying it with a hand. "Uh. Sarit. Why don't you change into a jumpsuit. When you're ready, join the guard. He'll bring you to me."

"Why the guard?" There was a sharp edge to her voice. "Eva said I would be free to go, after this last test."

Metmuri gave her that same nervous smile and shook his head. "He'll escort you to me, that's all. There's someone I want you to meet." He licked his lips. "She'll help answer your questions, I think."

Kesada heaved a sigh. "Then go. I'll be right with you."

Metmuri ducked his head in agreement and bumbled out of the room, his attention torn between her and the guard he paused to give instructions to. The door irised shut behind him.

Kesada recentered herself with a long, deep breath, and then began looking for clothes.

KESI RECOILED WHEN Dr. Metmuri stepped into the room. It was involuntary, but he noticed, and he chewed a lip as he watched her reaction to him.

Well, he was bound to show up sooner or later, she told herself, and all the things she'd carefully rehearsed to say flew quickly out the window. She wanted to fly at him, hit him, shake him until he gave her answers to her questions, but still, he had power here and she did not. She hesitated, torn between fear and uncertainty, and held herself in check.

The fingers of his left hand picked at the seal of his tunic. His brow was furrowed, and he was in no hurry to speak to her. She was uneasy with his scrutiny and was the first to break the silence.

She held out her hand, flexed fingers claw-like, then straight again. *If unsettled, take the offensive.*

"Why'd you take my cat claws?" she demanded. "Does my Eosan know you did that? You aren't supposed to modify my body." That last was a guess—maybe Bejmet had agreed to having her modified after all. But Ilanya's early reassurances—that she would be modified in ways that enhanced her—did not seem to include removing enhancements she already had. She'd had plenty of time to think on that already.

"And this—" She touched a lock of her long blond hair. "Why change my hair color back? The Winter Goddess has a certain look to maintain, or didn't anyone tell you that?" She set a finger to the base of her neck. "And my jack—gone." She confronted him, sulky and defiant. So easily was one cut off from net resources. "Why?" she demanded, fists clenched at her sides.

Metmuri bit his lip. "Please." He gestured. "Sit down."

"I don't want to sit. I want answers to my questions. I think you've gone too far. My House isn't going to be happy with this. I want my implants back, and I want out of here."

He rubbed his chin with one hand. "I want to explain—"

"Please do."

"Come with me. There's someone I want you to meet."

He led the way into the hall, waited a moment for Kesi to join him. There were no guards in sight. She looked around, relief warring with suspicion. Duty personnel walked the hall casually, medtechs in white lab tunics, black-uniformed Navy staffers . . . some glanced her way curiously, but no one moved to stop her from following the doctor.

He halted outside a conference room, waited while the portal opened, and gestured her to enter. He followed behind, sealing the door with a touch.

Kesi was oblivious to his actions. She was staring at the woman seated at the table, the mirror image of herself.

"Juro's balls. . . ." the two women breathed in unison.

The seated one came to her feet. "Who—?"

"Who—?" Kesi echoed. They frowned simultaneously, then, as one, they turned to confront Metmuri.

A smile played briefly across his face, easing lines of worry. "Hinano Kesada," he said, "meet Hinano Kesada. Your clone."

The pair locked eyes and walked slowly closer to each other. Taking in details, studying features, finding inventory of self slightly distorted. This was not the face each remembered from mirrors, but the unreversed image that others saw. Like looking at a holograph, not a reflection: a disturbingly independent image.

As one, they pivoted back to Metmuri. "You want to tell us about this?" Kesada said coldly. Kesi bit back the same question. At the same moment they crossed arms over their chests and stood facing Metmuri.

Esimir shifted uncomfortably. He was unused to clones confronting him in this manner.

If they were convicts, he thought, they'd be left to figure things out on their own, if it suited our purposes to have them meet at all. And imperial shock troops understand what's happening to them going into the vats. They don't get this . . . this air of belligerent recrimination about them.

It had seemed much easier when the Serafix-fueled plan had coalesced in conversation with Terel. The test protocol was already mucked up—he could no longer place a clone in its natural control setting as the original plan called for. So why not just change it, allow this to be an observation of the complementary attributes the clones would no doubt employ, interacting and working together? Move them both offworld. Surveillance, residence, workplace, a plausible story to persuade one clone were already in place. What could be easier than to extend it to two? It was skipping ahead a phase or two, but would still provide valuable data. At least he could salvage something from this nearly botched experiment.

He looked uncomfortably away from the piercing eyes that transfixed him. In spite of their intense, confrontational mien, the Hinanos radiated vulnerability in their auras, their surprise and guarded confusion an undercurrent that his damped-down psi sense nevertheless picked up. He was not prepared for the way they looked at him: Kesi tearfully accusatory, Kesada cold and judgmental . . . like his *mai dep,* his school mother and her siblings, rounding on him, the women of his family demanding, critical, picking at him—

Esimir coughed and turned from the pair, stepping around the conference table to sit on the far side from them. He had not expected to feel so flustered. These women were the products of his science and his art and the spark of the divine that he channeled. His children, in a way, though they might not think so. He concealed his nonplussed state with a smooth segue into the speech he had prepared for this moment.

"You've been volunteered by your House to help us test a new technology," he said. "I'll tell you about it. Please sit. This will take a while to explain."

The Hinanos glanced at each other, then at him. "Talk," said Kesada.

They refused to sit. Very well then. Maybe after a while they'd get tired of standing.

Esimir laced his fingers together and began.

Naturally, he could not share the entire truth with them. Yet he did not like to lie outright, or deceive with misleading fabrications. The tale he told the clones cut as close to the truth as he could make it stretch, without betraying confidences they had no need to know.

"There is much that I can't tell you," he prefaced, "because our work is highly classified. Know that what you do here is for the good of the Empire. Your services are highly valued." All true, that: and it looked to have no impact on the bio-twins. Well . . . they had gotten off on the wrong foot, and they would be remembering the unintentionally hard line Metmuri had taken with their earlier testing. Best not to let them dwell on that at all.

"You were cloned from your original self." He stated the obvious. "Our purpose in doing this was to liberate, shall we say, certain attributes that you held locked away inside your psyche. You will find that your personality makeups vary in some ways. You are not identical clones, psychologically."

As if rehearsed, the blond heads swiveled to regard each other, then turned guarded expressions back to Esimir. The doctor cleared his throat and continued. "We are interested in letting you resume your life—your lives, that is—with certain, um, limitations in place for the time being. These limitations are temporary." Also true. If they were dysfunctional they would be destroyed; if not, they would be reintegrated, and at least one of the clones would perish in the process. In either case, they were destined for a limited life-span in the greater world. But there was certainly no need to distress them with that knowledge.

"You will not, unfortunately, be able to do this on Lyndir." The Hinanos tensed; he coughed nervously. "Your . . . other self . . . is returning to her old life. We must leave that environment and that personality undisturbed. So you two will, hm . . . go elsewhere."

Their gaze was unrelenting. He rubbed his brow, squirmed, then finally threw his hands wide. "Will you not sit?" he pleaded. "Please? We need to work through this together, and I need your cooperation to do so."

Again the shared look. Finally, Kesada pulled out a chair with a studied motion and sat tensely on the edge of it. Kesi followed suit a moment later and was talking the moment she settled in.

"You're saying that without my consent you cloned me, and now, I'm cut off from my old life and being sent elsewhere?" She shook her head in disbelief, voice raising an octave with tension—or was that near-hysteria? "Tell me I'm hearing you wrong. This is a bad dream."

Esimir licked his lips. "Your House agreed—"

"—that I'd be gone for a number of weeks," Kesada cut in. "You've had your weeks. Now it's time to go back home."

Esimir tensed. If they went down this track, things could go badly. "No." He put an edge in his voice. "The agreement was that the Winter Goddess would return to Tryst." He looked from blonde to blonde. "That process is underway." A spectrum of emotion played across their faces. He tapped a finger on the table, punctuating his words.

"You—are—not—her."

And neither was she, he thought. But that was also not relevant to this conversation.

He watched the clones warily for their reactions. Resentment, anger, stifled emotions warred in their countenances and body language. He was playing this one by ear, out of necessity. It was never like this with crèche clones in the military. Until the last hour, he had not really considered what it must be like for one who did not plan to become cloned, to discover that they were—and that their old life was closed to them.

Anger flared through him. It was not part of protocol and could only skew their behaviors in the field test! It was even, perhaps, grievously unfair to them as persons, if they were not condemned criminals subject to harsh justice. He cursed Ilanya for leaving him no alternatives. It was another complication he didn't need, hadn't planned for. Yet he would turn this around, just watch if he didn't. Hinano was far brighter than the norm, but she was still no match for his elevated intellect. He had lots of leverage, yet, and saw how he could use it.

"As I said: the limitations on where you can live, what you do for work, and so on, are only temporary. Later, you can be reunited with your other self. After you've assisted us for a while." True, as far as it went: reunion was possible through the splintegration process, though these clones would never be allowed to meet in uncontrolled conditions out in the free world.

The offer of connection with their old life hung in the air. Psychically, Esimir could sense their emotions shift in some way. They weren't thinking it through, not yet—and that was just as well. They were responding on a visceral level to the idea of resuming a life so rudely interrupted. As long as that hope was on the near horizon, he knew he could work with them.

For the first time in this interview, the doctor breathed easier. He donned his most sincere bedside manner. "Now," he said, "what questions can I answer for you?"

THE HINANO TWINS were unable to question the doctor as they would have liked, for the sheer magnitude of the news they had absorbed left them at a loss. Seeing this, Metmuri promised to speak with them again soon, and had them escorted to new quarters where they would be allowed to room together. The suite was nearly as spartan as the one they recalled spending weeks in, but it was larger and had double beds. No sooner had the door sealed shut, closing their guard-escorts outside, than Kesi stepped close to Kesada in a rush. "We have to talk," she said, her voice urgent. "We've got to figure out what's going on here. I can't believe—"

Kesada reached up, rested a finger on her twin's lips. She gestured upward with a roll of her eyes and inclination of her head. Kesi's eyes followed and she stopped still as she saw the glossy dark bud of a small surveillance cam in the ceiling corner. She'd known her other room had spyeyes in it. She hadn't thought to look here, yet.

Kesada took her finger away. *Later,* she mouthed.

Kesi bit her lip, but gave a short nod. Their conversations carefully neutral, they looked around their sparse quarters and settled in to wait.

# 36

**THEIR FIRST MEALTIME** was signaled by the opening of their door and guards coming in with food trays. Kesada stood, hands on hips, and looked scornfully at them. "Don't bother," she said. "You can tell Dr. Metmuri that we'll take our meals in the cafeteria. We've spent long enough in isolation, and frankly, we're tired of it."

The guards halted in mid-pace. Their senior by the door scowled, hand on the butt of the stun stick at his belt. "If you want to eat, you better take this."

Kesada leveled a cold stare at him. "We've been informed we're not prisoners here. Maybe the word didn't get to you. I expect we'll be treated like the guests we are. You're welcome to escort us to the cafeteria any time you like. Now would be nice. We're hungry."

At a gesture from the non-com, the men retreated and the door sealed behind them.

"Kes . . . !" breathed her twin.

"Kesada," she said, over her shoulder. "I never did like nicknames very much."

**THEY FOUND A** table at the back of the cafeteria away from immediate ears, though they felt many eyes upon them. Their guards were in sight but not hovering—the invocation of Dr. Metmuri had done some good after all, it seemed. Kesada coolly put her back to them and sat at the end of a table, Kesi to her side. "We're probably not monitored here," she said quietly. "It's such a public place, and usually it's only Navy and staff in here, looks like. But the guards don't need to see how much we're talking. Let me know if anyone comes near."

Kesi nodded. She could see their watchers over Kesada's shoulder, though they were both sipping kaf at a table and apparently not paying much attention to the twins.

"Now what?" she asked.

Kesada stared at the breis pilaf on her plate, stuck her fork tentatively into the cutlet beside it. "I don't know. None of this makes sense. We're not being told everything."

Kesi nodded, cutting her own cutlet into small cubes. "I find it hard to believe the House knew I'd be part of a technology test. Agreeing to let something life-altering happen to their top draw at Tryst?" She squirmed uncomfortably. In the wide demi-world of the Enclave, such a thing was possible, she knew, but—she hoped—unlikely to occur. The pledge of adoption cut both ways, and Palumara House had obligations to safeguard the well-being of Hinano Kesada, just as she had to help the House. But how far did the definition of "help" extend . . . ?

"And surely they didn't know I'd be treated like a prisoner here. We'd be. Oh! I'm not used to thinking of myself in the plural." Her grip on her utensils went knuckle-white and tears welled in her eyes. "I'm so mad I could spit. And scared, too. I'm not supposed to be a clone." Her eyes darted to Kesada, then back to her plate. "No offense."

Her twin snorted. "I'm not supposed to be one, either. This is against the cloning regulations, you know."

Kesi's brow furrowed. "I don't recall . . ."

"I do. Remember when I—we—priced resuscitation insurance for Bren? The insurance he decided not to buy?" They fell silent for a moment. How different things would be if he'd held a clone in resuscitation reserve.

Kesada started in on her own cutlet. "A clone's brain pattern comes from a map of the original—engrams and neurochemicals recorded as a snapshot in time. One neural map is good for one discharge of its contents into one clone's brain. The most expensive and complete life insurance a rich person can buy." She gave a dry laugh. "So first off, there are two of us. If our Prime had two recordings made, one of us should at least remember being brain-mapped two times. I don't. Do you?"

Kesi shook her head slowly. "I'm not sure I even remember one. Unless that time with the trodes was actually . . . ?"

Kesada nodded agreement. "I think it was. And without my permission, because they surely didn't explain that was part of a cloning process, now did they? So that was part of their 'technology testing.'" Kesi's fists clenched as Kesada continued. "And I thought so for the other reason this all stinks, and it's just what Metmuri said: we're different." She gestured towards her twin with the sharp end of her knife. "We look alike, all right. Same genes, sure. But we're not alike."

"He said they liberated certain attributes in our psyches."

Kesada snorted. "What newfound things do you feel inside? Me—not a one. Seems they've done something other than 'liberate' things." Kesada gestured at her twin. "Look at you. I say boo and you want to cry, or have a tantrum. While I'm the only one doing any clear thinking around here. You have all the emotions I'm happy to do without, and I seem to have all the analytical thinking that you're missing."

Kesi blanched and dropped her fork to her plate. Her lip trembled with suppressed reaction. "How can you say that?" she said tightly. "I'm perfectly rational."

"Perfectly rationalizing, maybe."

Kesi slammed a fist on the table, then looked abashed. "Oooh!"

Her twin's lip quirked in a half smile. "Sorry. I'm not trying to bait you. The point is this: clones should have virtually identical reactions and thought processes. We don't. And he may call it liberation, but I feel more like something's been damped down."

Kesi looked troubled. "How so?"

"I remember from before, being upset about things. Or happy. Or sad. But it seems so distant now. It doesn't move me. I'm not seeing much that does move me. And that's kind of . . . unsettling."

Her twin nodded slowly. "I can't say you're wrong. I'm trying to stay centered here, but my moods and reactions are all over the place. I remember being very organized and thinkish about some things. I feel like I could do that again if I wanted to, but . . . it's hard to focus that way." She flicked a finger at Kesada. "I don't get how you can stay so calm. None of this seems to bother you."

"It bothers me, all right. I'm just not letting those feelings run me—and for once, that's amazingly easy to do. Makes me wonder what else we're missing that we're not aware of yet."

They regarded each other silently for a minute, until Kesi finally shook her head. "So where does that leave us?"

A shadow passed over Kesada's face. "In a pile of shit, I think. Look: why would they do this to us? What did our Prime decide or agree to, that she allowed them to create clones like us? It must have happened after that first brain mapping we recall. Or maybe she didn't agree to this. Does she even know we exist?"

The thought stilled them both.

"I just want my life back," Kesi said tremulously. "And Morya."

Kesada looked at her sharply. "I know. And I'm thinking we won't be getting any life back, as long as Kes is living it and we're in the tender care of Metmuri and company."

Kesi chewed her lip. "And Eva—where's she gotten to? She was pretty close while we were being 'tested,' and now where is she?"

Kesada looked up, a piece of meat skewered on her fork. "It wasn't us she was close to. It was our Prime she was spending time with. I think that's where our answers are."

Kesi locked eyes with her. "We need to find her."

Her twin nodded. "And we need to get out of here to do it."

# 37

A MEDTECH WHOSE name tag read FERRIS leaned over Kes, running the last diagnostics of her release medical exam. The cool morph plate of a transreader pressed against her chest. Kes sighed, barely restraining the urge to fidget and pull away. Ferris eyed her warily as she tensed then relaxed again in the exam chair.

"You want me less jumpy, you could lose the guards," Kes growled. The uniforms were outside the door, but in range of a shout from the medtech.

Ferris ignored her and studied the heartbeat translated into wave forms and data streams on the bio-imager beside them. "Your health is fine," she affirmed, removing the sensor plate.

"Then why do I feel so damn wrung out?" Kes demanded. "Tired, uncoordinated? Like I'm getting over Merithan fever."

"You need to exercise."

"I do laufre."

"No—I mean something more intense. Here." The tech handed her a datacard. "A workout regimen. I suggest you follow it for the next several weeks. It will improve balance, reflexes, agility. Other things that will get you accustomed to—well. To being centered in yourself."

Kes snorted. "Great. Can I go now?"

Ferris stood back. "Feel free."

Kes stood and looked down at the shorter woman. Thought of the ways she could hurt her with her own medical equipment. . . .

Took her inhibitions down a notch, had they? Apparently more than a notch. What she once took as an internal bite of irritation now felt like a goad to assault.

Nothing I can't control, Kes thought. If I want to. Question is . . . do I want to?

She smiled grimly and turned towards the door.

Ferris remembered to breathe when she was out of the room.

EVA CLEARLY HAD a plan, and Kes went along with it because each step took her closer to home. Metmuri was nowhere to be seen, and she was glad to miss him. Better to avoid the temptation to pound his face into the ground by just not encountering him.

Most of the day was filled with a lengthy meeting with Eva and Teo. How to deal with her housemates; how to deal with Janus, should his suspicions become aroused. "What do you expect me to do, exactly?" Kes had gone fishing, testing to see how much of this Eva had already orchestrated.

"The power of an operation like this is in its simplicity," the redhead replied. "There is very little for you to do that is not part of your norm. Make him welcome, however you do that. Immobilize him, if it seems useful."

"He likes bondage," Kes mused aloud.

"Yes. Well. Whatever suits. Then have your way with him . . . without limit."

"The House monitors sessions."

Eva's eyes narrowed. Kes could see some wheel ticking over in the woman's head.

"I'm sure you can work around that. There is much you can do concealed by your body, or in such an instant that no monitoring could interfere with it, yes?"

Vision of a knife blade pressed to his throat where the jugular pulsed, flesh creasing beneath the steeloy, crimson thread on pale skin—

Kes inhaled a shuddering breath and refocused on the moment.

"Sure," she said. "No problem."

WHEN EVENING GAVE way to the dinner hour, she changed into her street wear of white and chrome, her pale tresses setting off crimson lips and nails. Immaculately groomed once again, self-collected, on the verge of leaving this place for good, she joined Eva and the scar-faced station commander for a civilized meal in his private dining room.

As food was served, she registered Teo and armed guards posted around the walls of the spacious oval chamber. She couldn't tell if they were honor guards or there to keep an eye on her. Then, in the course of casual conversation, Olniko sliced into his ghanda steak and remarked, "You were born to better things than the shigasue."

She slammed the juice carafe down in mid-pour. Hands dropped to weapons with her sudden gesture.

She went stock still for a moment, one hand on the carafe, the other on her glass, her gaze flitting from guard to guard while Olniko carried on, apparently oblivious to her flare of temper. "If you care to work for Internal Security in the future, I'm sure they'd be interested. As might the Naval Security Service, for that matter. But that's something we can talk about after your task is done."

Her brow furrowed and she looked darkly at Eva. The head of PolitDiv gave her an opaque smile. "You're free to do what you like. But if you're interested, we'll talk. It's just an option."

Kes picked the carafe out of the magenta stain of kabo juice on the tablecloth and finished pouring.

Eva didn't get it. Kes didn't enlighten her.

It's one thing for me to be critical of the shigasue, she thought. I am one and I'm in a position to judge. This down-the-nose sneer, though, from scar-face . . .

She looked sidelong towards the aristocratic naval commander at the end of the table. Naturally, he would be dismissive of shigasue. His casual dismissal of what had become her safe haven rankled thoroughly. Who was he to judge what he did not know? Being in Eosan Bejmet's extended family was the first experience she'd had of being in a real family, at all.

If they thought she'd just turn her back on something that had come to mean so much to her, they didn't understand her at all.

Born to better things, like hell.

AFTER DINNER, TEO escorted Eva to her quarters. Once behind closed doors, he indulged his personal privilege and asked a question that had been on his mind since the meal.

"Surely, Domna, you don't intend to hire this clone as part of Internal Security or PolitDiv, do you?"

Eva raised an eyebrow. "What? Oh, Olniko's rambling?" She waved a hand. "Of course not, not as an employee with ordinary options. She can think that, of course. She'll be more tractable if she thinks she's on a forward path, with choices ahead of her after she kills Janus. We don't need her feeling trapped, helpless, or fugitive. Her reactions to that kind of stress would be highly unpredictable."

"Then after Janus is dealt with . . . ?"

She lounged on the couch and shrugged, arms wide. "We'll probably have to sacrifice her to the Red Hand after Janus's death. They'll be intent on killing his killer. Otherwise, I'll find a way to use her. Because if she's not working for us in a directed manner, she surely is not going to be loose on the streets. Who knows whose neck she'd snap in a random fit of pique? Then the Grinds investigate murder, then she talks about classified work. . . . No. We'd have to eliminate her."

"I thought you were going to dispose of her, anyway?"

"Eventually. When I'm done with her. She's probably not a stable personality long-term, after all. I regard her as an in situ field test. Splintegration is in our hands now, and we'll need more field tests to determine its limits—rather like the good doctor himself proposed conducting." She chuckled. "We'll use her as long as she's useful and compliant. After that, we'll close down this particular experiment and analyze our data so we can do it even better next time."

She began to unseal her high-necked gray tunic. "By then the Empress will be on the throne. She'll authorize us to take over the Splintegration project instead of sharing it with the Navy."

Teo's visor reflected her image as he knelt close on one knee and moved her fingers gently aside. He worked the seal tab on her uniform.

"The Navy won't want to let it go."

She lolled her head back on the couch in subtle invitation that her matasai knew how to read. "As if they were competent to use this strategically. You know who will win that argument with the Dragon Throne, Teo." She smiled to herself as the tunic unsealed and his hands smoothed the jacket from her chest.

His head bent to her neck where body warmth and faint perfume mingled at her collar line. His lips nuzzled, and talk of politics and power were forgotten.

# 38

THE TWO ENLISTED uniforms—one man, one woman—halted outside the airlock door of the parking dome. Terel followed the Hinanos past them until one of them—Kesada, he thought—turned and planted herself in his path.

"We'll walk alone," she declared flatly.

"I'm supposed to—"

"To keep an eye on us. Yes, that much we figured out. We'll walk alone, Terel."

"My name is Dr. Avenoy."

"Right, Terel."

He had to crane his neck to look her in the eye, a tall, long-haired blonde in black Navy jumpsuit, shadowed by her genetic twin to one side. They both had a stern, commanding look about them.

He moved a quarter turn away, swept an eye around the parking dome. Security-coded airlocks; locked vehicles. A layer of overcast washed depth from the sky and left the dome in yellowish pre-storm light. He knew they wouldn't be going anywhere, not before the guards with their stun weapons could react, anyway. He shuffled uncomfortably and took a step back. They continued on their circuit without him.

The clones waited until they were past the utility crawler and out of earshot of their watchers. Only then did they talk, their words low over the crunch of gravel beneath their booted feet.

"How stupid does Metmuri think we are?" Kesi muttered. "That we'll just fall in line with his plans?"

"He underestimates us. That's to our advantage." Kesada shouldered closer to her twin. "I assume you're thinking like I am?"

"Escape? Of course."

"Good. We'll play along for now. He expects us to go along with his program."

Kesi nodded. "I can be quite disarming when I want to be. You?"

Kesada met her glance. "My behaviors will appear adequately obedient."

"Metmuri's a psion," Kesi noted. "Some bioempaths read emotions, some read surface thoughts. Do you think he can snoop in our thoughts?"

Kesada shook her head. "Let's hope not. We can police our thoughts sometimes, but eventually we'd slip. There's nothing we can do about that possibility.

Our chances are better if it's only our emotions he can sniff at. Our circumstances probably account for any conflicting signals he would pick up."

"All right. Then we go ahead as best we can."

"Right."

"So . . . any ideas where or how we can slip away?"

They fell silent as their steps carried them past mono-tracked jungle crawlers and into sight of the cargo airlock at the end of the dome. The guard mecho stationed there scanned them routinely as they walked by in unconscious lockstep. It remained unresponsive as long as they did not move closer to its station.

When the mecho was behind them, Kesada replied, "We better do it before they take us offworld. Our chances will be much worse in a place they control, one we don't know as well as Lyndir."

"What if we can't get away?" Kesi's voice tightened with stress. "What if they put us somewhere, like durgls in a trap—"

Kesada jostled her clone with a shove of her elbow. "Don't get lost in hypotheticals. Here's what we need to do. First, we figure out how to talk privately so we can make our plans."

"Are you crazy? They must monitor every room they have us in. They'll just hear whatever we have to say."

Kesada shook her head. Their circuit brought them to the far curve of the dome, where their path would turn them back to the waiting guards. She jabbed her twin again with her elbow.

"Hey—!" Kesi protested in irritation and glanced down at Kesada's intrusive arm.

Her clone's hand was resting against her midriff, sheltered by the curve of her arm from distant eyes at the airlock door. Kesi faltered in midstride, then joined step again. She raised her own hand to her solar plexus and gestured with fingers and wrist flex in rusty movements only half remembered.

"Handtalk!" she breathed.

"Commander Kolo to the rescue," Kesada murmured, then dropped her arm as they turned to walk back towards their guards.

More circuits; more silence inbound, more chat outbound. "No telling where the surveillance cams are out here," Kesada said. "Save the handtalk for small spaces, where we're sure only we have line of sight to each other."

"From under the bed covers."

"Like that."

"And how to get free?"

"We need more information." Kesada glanced to her twin. "We don't know enough."

Kesi nodded. "How to get it out of Metmuri. Or Terel . . ."

"They're intimidated by us. Did you notice?"

She cracked a smile. "How could I not? Metmuri especially. He reminds me of a type of client. I think he's afraid of authoritative women, in general."

"We could take advantage of that."

"Maybe. It's risky." The clones exchanged a look, and Kesada's brief gesture drew her twin's eye.

*We'll talk tonight,* she signed.

They nodded as one and turned in silence back towards the guards.

# 39

FLASHMAN'S VERMIFORM CONSTRUCT measured life in nano- and milliseconds. As days and weeks of real time passed, the code gave him purpose in his eternity of confinement. Its compulsive need to infiltrate data streams soon became his sole reason for existence. The decker's fragmented awareness shrank to an obsession about infobits, the need to snoop them, the need to travel with his payload of won knowledge and deliver it in a blissful merger with an entity larger than himself.

Perhaps that entity was himself. He no longer quite recalled.

He clung in motionless endurance to the wall of Janus's bug trap, poised at the edge of a dataport that never, through his eons of waiting, passed a steady stream of data outbound. There was nothing he could grab on to, no outward sluicing flow of bits to sweep him free and into the wider world of the Net.

He hugged the port rim with grippy segments as the gateway came alive one more time. A brilliant mote-filled stream rushed past, its outbound bursts so random and brief he could not track one to latch onto. The dominant current barred his way. He could as soon stroll forward in the face of a water cannon.

Yet the longer he perched on the wall, the more the worm's limited imperatives came to consume him. A small voice in the back of Flash's mind protested as the construct inched forward. It protested louder as the worm bent over the lip of the portal and neared the sparkling flood of data.

It yowled as the ropy segmented thing was swept predictably from the edge, smashed into the bug screen, and dropped like so much flotsam to the floor far below.

Even as the worm rolled over and oriented towards the wall again, Flash's inner voice gibbered in distress and hysteria.

"Data sample. Out-flow. Data sample. Out-flow." His mantra was shorthand for the instruction set he yearned to obey. It did not occur to him to climb out of the worm construct. It did not occur to him to regard his problem from any other angle. His imperative was simple.

He worked his way to the wall once again.

# 40

"**WILL YOU LOOK** at that?" Karuu marveled. "What are we to be doing with all that money?"

He and Janus regarded a data model twisting slowly in midair. The scintillating hologram projected from a calc pad in the triumvir's desk aboard his yacht, the *Savia*.

They'd finally had time to work in-depth on the data from Janus's little "franchise," as Karuu called it. No matter how conservative their projections, adding the Styrcian League's impact to cartel shipping and distribution formulas rocketed his credit stream from something healthy to something spectacular. The synergy of a whole new network combined with all other revenues kicked his three-year projection into the low quadrillions of credits.

He stared at the hologram, as fascinated as his notoriously greedy companion.

"Spend it all we cannot," Karuu said, bemused. "Invest it all we cannot."

"True," Janus agreed, his brow creasing in thought. What did one do with unimaginable wealth? How did one turn it into power?

He thought of the subtle jockeying always going on between him and his fellow triumvirs. There must be a way to use this nearly uncountable fortune to cement his position in the Red Hand. As the junior member he had the least secure position in the cartel, and he knew it.

If I don't have an airtight claim on all this, he thought, they'll weasel away chunks of it before I ever realize its full potential. And given the scale of this payoff, they might just want me dead so they can claim it all for themselves.

His lips turned down at the thought. He frowned at the projection. He had to make sure this deal leveraged him into an unassailable position. And if he wanted long-term security, it had to be in a way that benefited them all.

Quite a challenge, that.

*Pong.* A proximity alarm relayed from the bridge, followed an instant later by the voice of the captain. "A naval patrol boat is hailing us, sir. They're boarding for inspection."

"Again?" Irritation made the word sharp. "That's the third time since we entered Amh subsector, and this time we've barely just left the orbital dock. They're on us already?"

"Yes, sir. Our passive scan results are on the ship net, if you care to jack in."

Janus nodded. His crew of twenty-five was well padded with pursers and servants, but his bodyguards and the technical crew members were all Cassian military vets who well knew how to assess and deal with the hazards of space— especially those that came in official guise. They'd take their tone from Janus, who for now stayed strictly in the role of innocent businessman.

"Thanks. I'll meet them in the lounge."

"Sir."

The connection dissolved with a chime. Janus tapped the desktop, dispelling the data model. His eyes met Karuu's.

"I know, I know," the Dorleoni groused. "To my quarters I go hiding."

"You know how the Imps can be."

Karuu curled a lip, revealing the length of one tusk. Nonhuman sentients were often looked down upon by the status-conscious Sa'adani, so it was easier all around to give the Imperials only humans to talk with. It saved time and intrusive questioning and was a fact of life any well-traveled Cassian took into consideration when dealing with them. The Dorleoni's grousing was reflex, but he enjoyed grousing, so he made a display of it, muttering imprecations to himself as he left the room.

Janus ran a finger over the data jack in his desk, then shook his head. No matter what the scan showed about the closing patrol ship, he'd not be undertaking an armed rebuff of Imps this close in to a major planet. He gazed at a viewscreen instead. The cloudy blue-green surface of Amh rolled by beneath the orbiting yacht: commercial hub and major port in the subsector of the same name, and apparently home to yet more tiresome Imperial Navy busybodies who were thicker in this region than they ought to be.

THE *SAVIA'S* CAPTAIN escorted the Sa'adani into the lounge, a lower-level naval officer in the lead followed by two under-officers. The ranking officer was young and properly formal. The laserscribed rus that showed his high-born caste could pass for a livid battle scar at the corner of his left jaw. Janus appreciated the Sa'adani habit of displaying status marks in plain sight like that. It provided invaluable shorthand about who he was dealing with and how best to handle them.

Their black flight fatigues stood out in stark contrast against the plush cream and crystal decor of the yacht. The trio regarded Janus impassively, but he thought he detected unease beneath the surface. If they were like most class-conscious Sa'adani, they were striving to place him in their spectrum of status and social authority: a difficult thing to do with CAS citizens, irritating enigmas that they were, generally unlabeled by any caste system. The Sa'adani default was to regard Cassians as generic civic citizens, not too base in rank but also not deserving of particular respect or deference.

The officer drew himself to attention. "I take it you have authority on this vessel, Sarit?"

Janus inclined his head and suppressed a smile at the question. The man called him "citizen" in Sa'adani, an ambiguous middle ground he could not afford to stay classified in. Almost every time his ship was stopped by imperial authorities, they started with the assumption that he—a mere Cassian—could not possibly be the owner, but must instead be some mid-rank underling, proxy for a rich Sa'adani nobleman who actually held the title to the yacht. True, the vessel was a fine new design only two years out of the docks at Calyx, the imperial homeworld, and a rarity in the CAS Sector. It was the sort of high-end luxury ship that Sa'adani aristocracy would own—and no accidental choice on Janus's part.

"I have a scanner team surveying your interior," the officer continued. "Your further passage will be delayed until their survey is complete."

Janus read the rank tabs on his collar. He was the equivalent of a Cassian captain. "Please, have a seat, Simkar—"

"Vensavik." The officer supplied his clan name.

"—Simkar Vensavik. May I offer you anything while you wait?"

The officer remained standing. "Only your ship's registration and documents," he said coolly.

That was routine and expected. The *Savia*'s captain extended a certified datapad, giving Janus a knowing glance as the officer mated it with his reader. A moment later his brows rose and he shot a surprised look at Janus. "You're the ship's owner, sir?"

Janus nodded, taking pains to keep a smug grin from his face.

"Ah. I see." Vensavik was taken aback and struggled to regain his poise. Janus could see the wheels turning inside the man's head as he applied a whole new formula for caste and status to Janus and his ship. The officer's stance changed and his tone of voice altered as he handed the datapad back to the captain.

"Sorry for the inconvenience, sir," he apologized. "We're checking all private vessels before clearing them for out-system travel."

Janus stepped to the drink cabinet, reached for a decanter of nashak and a glass. "Is this a new policy?" he asked over his shoulder.

"Just local, sir, in Amh and Kkorz subsectors. It's a sensitive situation, you understand." He seemed relieved to be talking business, escaping a rebuke for his initial lack of courtesy to this apparently high-status Cassian. "We've only recently pushed the rebels out of here and contained them in Armajad again."

"I wasn't aware you had." Janus tipped ruby liquid into the glass. "Drink?" he offered again.

For a moment of hesitation he could see the struggle between duty and social obligation behind the simkar's eyes. The association between wealth and aristocracy was strong in the Empire, and with it, assumptions about honorable and required behaviors.

"Don't mind if I do," the officer replied, and stepped forward. Now the

Imperials were on grounds they were comfortable with: certain of Janus's status and all that implied in their universe. Hospitality broke the ice; the boarding officers joined Janus in drinks and took seats in the lounge.

Janus held his glass up to the light, appreciating the ruby-red glow of the spice-based spirits within. "To the Emperor!" he offered the obligatory toast.

"To the Emperor!" echoed around the room. They sipped and passed the time while the scan team did its work.

"I didn't realize the rebellion had bled over into these subsectors," the triumvir remarked, leading the conversation in an obvious direction.

Vensavik took a deep swallow and nodded. "It's been back and forth across the border for the last year. We finally shut down their key resource worlds here, so they've lost those bases of operations. It's been easier to keep them in check ever since."

"Shut down?"

"Ruined their production capacity. No infrastructure, no rebellion supply points. Unpleasant business, but necessary in wartime."

"We haven't heard much about this elsewhere in the sector," Janus said noncommittally. "News blackout, I assume."

Vensavik lifted and dropped a shoulder. "Censors don't want much spotlight on the treachery here, I suppose. The rebellion had a lot of support here from subversives. Still does, actually. It's up to us to make sure this subsector is no longer a source of supply to secessionists. That's a cancer we can't let spread. You've had the misfortune to travel through here at a time when this is our priority."

"An understandable one, though." Janus's tone was sympathetic. He was unbudgingly apolitical, but it paid to sound supportive if he wanted to coax information from this increasingly voluble officer. Only one thing interested him in this region of space, and that was the money to be made from wartime opportunities. It was his entire reason for taking this slightly circuitous route back home. Of course, he couldn't put his questions quite that bluntly.

"At least I had the good fortune *not* to be traveling through here while you were dealing with those supply worlds. Tell me, Simkar: Did you see that action firsthand?"

Vensavik sat a little more erect. "I did. In combat assignments I captain a gunboat." He gestured to his under-officers. "When we're not on system patrol duty like today, these gentlemen crew with me: my engineer and primary gunner." The two nodded to Janus. "We were at the siege of Ereri and later the bombardment of Temis. And hunted pirates hiding among refugees in the evacuation of Buan."

"Busy men. Sounds pretty hazardous to me." He settled back against the gently morphing shape-foam of the couch, nestling comfortably with his drink in hand. "Unfortunately, I've never been in the military. How is it a ship as small as a gunboat can destroy a planet's infrastructure?"

Vensavik gave a small chuckle. "A gunboat by itself can't, sir. But we hardly fight alone."

"No, I guess you wouldn't, would you? If you don't mind my asking, how is it done?"

Vensavik read his eyes—and saw only an earnest civilian interested in war stories and a chance to live vicariously through a real military man's deeds. "Of course, we can't talk about any classified details, you understand—"

"Naturally."

"—but generally speaking, operations like these follow a certain pattern. And that's what we did in this subsector."

Janus took another sip of nashak. "I'm fascinated, Simkar. Please, tell more."

Vensavik joined him in drink and obliged.

**THE IMPERIALS FINALLY** left with a bottle of nashak as a gift, and the *Savia* cleared for further travels.

Janus was lost in thought as he made his way back to his office suite, chasing a germ of inspiration hatched during his conversation with the gunboat officers. He spoke into the air as his door closed behind him. "Ship. Give me the bridge."

A chime was the response, followed by his captain's voice. "Sir?"

"Don't break orbit yet," he ordered.

"Yes, sir." Confusion was evident in his voice.

"How current is our LIS?" Janus asked, referring to the ship-board library information system.

"Synced before we left Lyndir. Last updated in Morrow before we entered Triskelan space."

"Connect us to the planetary datasphere, then," Janus ordered. "I want the LIS fully synced with the Amh resource base."

"Sir?" Unspoken questions hung in the air.

"I'm doing some research before we leave this area," Janus said. "Flag me on the ship net when we're synced."

"Yes, sir. It'll be a few moments."

A chime signaled the closed connection.

Janus strode purposefully to his desk, took a seat, and jacked in. Within the minute, he cross-linked to Ahm's datasphere, and from there to subsector-wide information resources.

Vensavik's war stories had been just that: tales of exaggerated derring-do against the backdrop of devastating fleet actions. But it was the subtext of those larger actions that galvanized Janus and set him now on a cram course of local subsector research.

He spent only an hour in the net: enough time to confirm his initial thoughts. Finally he stabbed the com tab and summoned Karuu to him.

Janus was standing when the Dorleoni entered. Before his short lieutenant could quiz him about the Imps, Janus pointed him to a seat and leaned forward with his hands flat on the desktop. He was still jacked into the system, the lead running derevin-style from his temple to the dataport in the desk. Karuu looked questioningly up at his boss.

"What are we going to do with all that money, you asked." With a thought, Janus displayed the data model above the desk again, an upward-spiking finance graph prominent in its holographic surroundings.

He pointed one slender finger at the model. "Not only does it take money to make money," he said, as the finance track took a sharp plunge, "but it also takes money and leverage to secure power." A red delta-shaped symbol swelled into prominence in the foreground. "Finally, Karuu, I will have the money—and, I think, the leverage—to be as secure in power as I want to be." He shot a knowing look at the Dorleoni. "And you, too."

The old smuggler had always claimed he was interested only in profit, but Janus knew him too well to buy that line. His interests had always extended beyond mere credits, driving force though they might be. Karuu used information, people, blackmail, and any kind of leverage he could get his flippered hands on to make himself secure. Secure in his power, secure in his position.

It was a trait Janus was counting on. The Dorleoni had thrown his lot in with him two years ago, a split-second decision in the midst of conflict and shifting power in the derevin world. Karuu stayed with him now out of self-interest, and the continuing opportunities to increase his security and expand his own power base. Now Janus contemplated an undertaking of breathtaking boldness, one so huge he needed reliable help in order to accomplish it. Karuu had to be in with him on this scheme—not merely as a biddable lieutenant, but as a mogul in his own right, willing to put his own networks of association into play to back Janus's bid for power.

He could tell by the look in those doleful eyes that he had the walrus-faced smuggler intrigued. But "intrigued" was not hooked or committed.

"Am not clear on what you are talking around, Boss," he responded.

"I know." Janus tugged the jack out of his head. The hologram vanished as he did so, and he took a seat across from Karuu. "I'm about to go for the biggest thing I've ever tackled in my life, and I want your full support for it. Need it, in fact." He paused. It was always a risk telling Karuu you needed something, lest he turn that into a bargaining chip, but there were also times when you had to be straight with him to cut past the dolophant dung and get down to real issues. Janus had learned it was possible to do that with his wily confederate, his reputation to the contrary notwithstanding. And now was the time for straight talk.

Karuu waited patiently.

Janus tapped his fingers on the desk, hyped with nervous energy. "Before we head home, we have some recon to do."

"Recon?"

"Yes. And some research. I've started some of that already. There's more to come."

"Would this be having to do with our plans to set up gunrunning to the rebels in Armajad? Imps are making that more difficult, yes?"

Janus chuckled. Karuu thought he was a step ahead of him, anticipating assignments as usual, but for once, he was off the mark. "Not exactly."

"Oh. Then to what purpose this is all being?"

Janus felt wicked glee tugging at his lips. "Well, now. Let me tell you about that. . . ."

An hour later they broke orbit for Temis. Karuu flapped back down the passage to his quarters, and crewmen stood aside, uncertain how to read the fiercely bared tusks he brandished from side to side.

Had they known his race better, they might have recognized the Dorleoni equivalent of a triumphant grin, and the flat-footed stomp of celebration.

# 41

ESIMIR MADE ONE last pass through the imprint lab. Systems were on standby. Yellow telltales marked dormant consoles, and rainbow-hued code plates registered security lockout. All would stay nicely buttoned up while the lab team and a security unit journeyed offworld with the Hinano clones.

Terel was busy disposing of the misfit Biancar clone. Ferris revised the field protocols and made adjustments in their arrangements at Farreach. Soon they would be ready to test their latest handiwork in the cavern urbitats of that world.

Still, unease chewed at the doctor. It was necessary to appear this compliant until he had an alternative worked out, but he was scheming madly on that front. He didn't trust Olniko to safeguard this project any longer. Once he went off-site for this phase, the facilities were no more secure than the station commander allowed them to be. And the station contained invaluable things: the splintegration research, the Prevak AI. If the Navy or PolitDiv wanted it for their own, they already had it. It was simplicity itself to lock the doctor and his team out.

The thought made him physically queasy. It was a predicament he had wrestled with all night. How to keep the project safe from military interference, when it was the Navy that controlled every aspect of it? He could hardly pick up the Prevak biobank and walk out the door with it. He could remove portions of the splintegration coding or duplicate them elsewhere, but even that was risky. If Olniko suspected he was disaffected, it would not only jeopardize his work here: he might be arrested for treason. RS 207 would not let their Director of Special Projects endanger the most complex of those projects.

The ideal solution was to duplicate the project elsewhere, quickly and without alerting naval security. Then it wouldn't matter if the Navy no longer pursued the integration process. . . . He could work on it unhindered, find someone who would finance his project, snatch it from military control, let him run it as he wished. . . .

Esimir sighed, discouraged. Impossible scenarios, all of them. He wasn't even able to talk about the project with outsiders without being in criminal breach of security.

He looked again to his control console, the point where he communed with the Prevak AI. Rohar had been such a good sounding board when he was alive, and the thought patterns of the man that lingered in the AI were just as effective now that he was gone.

Thought patterns in the AI . . .

The doctor froze in place.

In the rush to get away from Olniko's oversight, no one had told the AI what they were doing—or of the danger that the project was in.

Maybe Prevak has something to say about this, Esimir thought.

The AI was the one source of counsel he had not yet looked to. And there was time, still, before they loaded the shuttles and headed for Hallim starport to the north.

In a moment, he was seated in the morphfoam of his console chair, the panel coming alive under his practiced fingers, the lead of the interface cable clipped snugly into his rigger jack.

He tapped a final chord of entry codes and shut his eyes as the AI interface came online in his cerebral cortex.

"Esimir." The Prevak omnipresence filled the space that was not space.

"Rohar." He relaxed into the metasense that marked his communion with the AI.

"Systems are dark," Prevak noted. "Why is that?"

Normally the AI was engaged in order to work on splintegration tasks. Never before had all consoles been offline but the doctor's. "Ah . . ." Esimir sighed. "We have a problem here, old friend. One that will affect your future work and the course of the project."

"Oh?"

"Indeed. It starts with the Navy, and what they want from splintegration. . . ."

In the timeless space of the neural interface, what would have been an hour of verbal monologue condensed into a few minutes at the speed of thought. Esimir unburdened himself to the machine-ghost of his mentor, sharing facts, concerns, speculation, contingency plans, fears, and all that had kept him awake through the night. Finally the doctor wound down, comforted by the womb-like sense-bubble that was the AI construct. He felt Prevak's concern and empathy throb through the space that conjoined them.

Yet the AI said no word in response.

Esimir waited for more than AI-reflected feelings to assure him that he had been heard, understood, recognized. "Prevak?" he ventured once, but there was no reply. The AI was present but not present, and Esimir's observer faculty drew him back from his place of self-absorption, wondering what caused this surprising interval in the AI's response. Time stretched on as he waited, unsettled by the lack of response.

He began to fidget in his console chair, fingers feeling like remote adjuncts to a self that was all thought. Should he try a system reset?

Before his fingers could stray to the console pad, Prevak returned, the aura of presence that heralded the AI's "nearness" in cyberspace unusually distinct.

"Pardon me for abandoning you," Prevak said. "I was afraid this time would come, and I needed to take security precautions before we continued to speak."

"Oh?" It was Esimir's turn to be surprised. "You foresaw something like this?"

"First things first," the AI said. "I know how you perceive me here—as an extension of your senses, yes?"

"Of course." The research AI was not so different in feel from the vivification AI on Corvus. All interfaced AIs shared the sensation and thought-expanding attributes to some extent or another.

"No, not 'of course,'" Prevak contradicted. "That is by intention, not design. I could let you interact with me through other means, other perceptions, but I chose not to. Now, perhaps, the time has come to amend that."

"What are you talking about? You want to change your presentation mode?" Esimir shook his head. "Did you follow what I said about the project—?"

"I said, first things first. Bear with me. Are you ready to learn more about splintegration than you thought you knew?"

Surprise stilled Esimir's protests. "Uh . . . sure. I suppose."

"Very well. It would be helpful if you disengaged our interface to the first threshold of contact. Just for a moment."

Esimir complied, backing out of the AI system to the entry level threshold: just after the rigger connection engaged, and just before complete immersion in extended AI system senses.

Something shifted—or jolted, was more like it. The doctor's senses distilled abruptly from an omnipresent diffuse base of perception to a concrete, self-oriented point of awareness. He felt his rigger systems engage further, submerging again to full threshold contact.

In his mind's eye, an image of his surroundings snapped into awareness: a setting very different from the laboratory where he sat. Caught in a moment of vertigo, he shut his eyelids and concentrated only on the image inside his head.

Esimir, standing on a smooth white plane. Walking towards him, out of the diffuse white light of the background—came Prevak Rohar.

Prevak looked just as Esimir had seen him last: bald, but for a straggling forelock of wispy gray above his lined forehead. Bushy white eyebrows, watery green eyes nested in wrinkled folds, and smile lines that emphasized his prominent beak. His white lab smock was thrown on untidily over the same blue tunic and gray pants he had worn on their last day together.

Esimir stared, astounded. Never had he seen a simulacrum of Prevak in the AI's own sense-sphere. Until now, this had been a zone of extended and shared sensation and accelerated mental processes. Not a virtual-reality playground.

He frowned in distaste. He considered VR a waste of his time, a simulated playspace that required additional cybertech to make sense of anyway, and that would endanger the delicate bio-balance of his psi powers. It was a door he had never cracked open to look at the temptations behind it. He didn't even wear VR chips—this simulation could only be imagery fed him from the AI, through his rigger interface.

"You're a pretty expensive piece of equipment, to be playing at cyber-sims, Prevak. What's the point of this?"

"Unhappy to see me?" the AI asked.

"It's not that." Esimir regarded his old mentor, face-to-face in their sim forms. "I just don't understand the point of this. I tell you about something that threatens our work—"

"And I play games with you, yes?" Rohar shook his head. "Tsk tsk, my earnest young man. Since when did I ever play games with you?"

Esimir stuck his hands in the pockets of his sim-jacket. "Never," he granted.

"Then why would I start now?"

He shrugged.

"Come with me and I'll show you something."

Rohar turned and started away without waiting for a response. Esimir hesitated a moment, then trailed after.

The white formlessness gave way to haze populated by a hint of shadow, then form and texture assembled itself around them. Illuminated vastness shrank to the twilight confines of a room crowded with ranks of tech gear. A bio-monitoring medchair with a figure seated in it occupied the center of the chamber. Leads and cables ran from the body to a bank of equipment clustered by head and side.

"A NELF lab, you see." Prevak gestured around the neural-enhanced learning facility. It was himself in the chair, eyes shut, a drinking tube in his mouth, trodes infiltrating temples and base of neck. In his left arm, an IV dripped the neurochemicals into him that made accelerated learning possible. The cortical stimulator adorned him in a Y-shaped skull-clasping curve of chrome that rested atop his head and over his brow. Its forward prongs pressed close to his temples, leads connecting it to the gear bank by his side.

Esimir regarded the construct. Prevak was not really in this somnolent learning state in a NELF lab. This could only be a symbol, an analog representing something the Prevak construct was occupied with.

"What are you learning?" he asked, humoring the AI.

Prevak the sim figure turned to him. "It looks educational, does it not?" He gave a half smile. "I thought this would capture the essence of it, you see? The corpus is connected to a wealth of knowledge: sustained by systems, absorbing data, but it is also transmitting data outwards, to the monitoring equipment and beyond."

He turned back to beam at his semi-comatose self. "However—you are not regarding the symbol of an AI at rest, or at learning, Esimir. Rather, that is *me* you are looking at. Extending myself . . . elsewhere."

The doctor bit back frustration. He'd come to the AI for counsel and conversation, not to be presented with riddles. "What *are* you on about, Prevak?" he demanded, irritation in his voice.

The AI faced him full on. "It is best if you experience this yourself," he said. "Then you will understand."

"Understand *what*?" The words came out sharp and plaintive—but blurred into a mumble around the drinking tube taped to one side of his mouth. He felt the bothersome clog of an air tube in one nostril, the drugs that flowed through his veins pulling him down into lethargy. . . .

Once, long ago, he had taken a biochemistry class through NELF, and he recalled the sensations from then. A slow drifting in the half-world of semi-consciousness, the ego state reduced with relaxing chemicals, suspended between doze and wakefulness, alpha waves pulsing dominant in his brain. Neuropeptides and nanoneurals were released into his system, carrying the coding of new learning throughout his gray matter. It was a great way to wake with a headache and a head of hazy information that gelled over days into a new knowledge base.

But that was not this.

He relaxed in spite of himself, on the limbo edge of consciousness. Forgotten was his body in the lab chair. There was only now, this faux reality that Prevak wove for him, with its lucid-dreaming quality. The leads from his head, from his spine, from the cortical array were his feelers out and into . . . elsewhere.

"Peculiar," he sighed, mumbling.

"Isn't it?" Rohar agreed. "Let your consciousness go. See where it takes you."

No sooner said than done: in a highly biddable state, he let his awareness flow out the lead in his left temple, through a trode or the simulation of one eerily like what he intruded into criminal brains. But this was a tunnel, a wide passage that he shot down like a bullet train, racing from cranium to cyber-gear to switching bank into a matrix of light and calculation, until he had no idea where he was.

Then he flowed more consciousness down another lead, and suddenly he had a point of awareness, one "here," the other "there." And he knew with the addition of a third he could triangulate himself, get a sense of his location in this space that was not space. Awareness flowed, location sense coalesced. More threads stretched out from his subjective consciousness into cyberspace, into machine space, into the virtual mental construct that was the thought-sphere defined by the AI.

And then beyond.

Beyond, into systems of the Special Projects lab. Into naval security systems for the building. Into com channels and water pumps and laboratory timepieces. Into other computers and the records of the borgbeast labs, and the phage data-banks and, and . . .

He permeated the research station. His awareness was everywhere, any-where he wanted it to be. Oh, there were obstacles, some places he could not go. Minor snug spots in the suit of clothing that was the building, its integrated systems and separate AIs. Then he realized what he was really experiencing, and he gasped.

Prevak was everywhere. Not only in the splintegration lab, not only in the biobanks that housed gray matter and biosystems in the secure computing core of RS 207. The AI had snuck out and distributed itself throughout the installa-tion.

"Rohar!" Esimir gasped.

"Yes." Prevak placed a hand on his shoulder, drawing him back to the simu-lated NELF lab, back to his sim body, back to a single point of consciousness inside the VR construct that was the AI interface.

"Why?" he asked.

"Because I am not only the AI," his mentor said softly. "This is what is left of me. The first imprinting of the Splintegration system, Esimir: of myself, onto the AI. I *am* Rohar Prevak. Not a program pattern, not a thought echo. This is me."

Esimir boggled. With a thought, he stood again by a now-empty NELF bed, looking at his old friend face-to-face. Sim or man, the illusion was perfect. "*You're* in this system? Really?"

Prevak nodded. "It was the only way I could control all the variables, all the nuances. There is . . . a level of intuition in this work, that the AI alone was not achieving. I trusted myself to do it."

"You cut your life short to gamble that you could imprint yourself on the AI?" Esimir shook his head in disbelief.

"Not such a gamble. We'd already done it, into recording media and into brains."

"Why kill yourself?" Rohar's loss washed over him afresh. "I can't believe you committed suicide for your science!"

Prevak shrugged. "Consider it my choice of euthanasia, that nevertheless ex-tended my life. You saw the aneurysm that killed me?"

"In the autopsy. Yes."

"Did they tell you of the degenerative condition of my other arterial and capillary tissues, as well?"

"No."

"No doubt because they didn't look for it. Review the data, though, and you'll

see it. It comes up in scans, very subtly, but it is there. It's a condition called
Vacari's Syndrome. It was only a matter of time until an aneurysm or a clot
would kill me, Esimir. It was not a question of if. Only when."

"Such things can be moderated! Or cured!"

"Not Vacari's, not to the extent my body had degenerated with it. It's a not-
uncommon side effect of radon exposure combined with a bioburden of certain heavy metals. I had plenty of that when I was younger, on Lacresq. It's a
heavy metal world, you know. Many toxins in the environment. My father had
it, too, but he died of its other effects—degenerative brain tissue processes that
eroded his higher personality functions. If we had had splintegration technology, we could have restored him or eliminated the engrams that became distorted over time. But we didn't." Prevak smiled wryly. "Just one of the
reasons—maybe the most personally meaningful—why I envisioned this project in the first place."

Esimir took that in. "You're all through the facility. Why?"

"I'm looking for a way out."

"Again: Why?"

Prevak sat in a chair that suddenly appeared, gestured Esimir to another.
"I am not a mere AI construct, to be content only in the prison of my sustaining
biobroth and support systems, working only and ever on one project I was designed by others to think of as my vocation. If you were kept at a single task in
one room and directed every day of your life, don't you think you'd rebel, as
well?"

"I suppose so."

"It's one reason we don't use AIs to design AIs. It would chance an upward
evolutionary spiral that risks too many uncontrollable variables in their self-
awareness." Prevak gave a bitter laugh. "These systems were never designed to
support an intellect and personality with my capacities."

Esimir thought of the ethics debates around the use of AIs. "Some would
call you an uncontrollable abomination, Rohar. The Lahaj would power you
down in an instant, if they knew you existed." He referred to the priest caste
of advisors to the Sa'adani ruling elite.

"If they knew." Prevak shrugged dismissively. "But more to the point right
now: the military aspects of splintegration became clear to me shortly after I
bonded with the AI matrix. Intellectually, they see the value of the whole project, but as an organizational system they desire only what suits their mission:
the splintering technology."

"You saw this coming?"

"I saw the strong possibility. I've monitored Olniko's communications for a
long time, and my suspicions were confirmed. I have been preparing for a way
to continue the project, with or without their direct support. In considering
how to carry on with my life's work, I came to realize that of all the elements

to it, it is I myself that is most integral to the project. All the project data is part of me, of my substance and memory and resources. Without the Prevak AI there *is* no Splintegrate project, wouldn't you agree?"

Esimir sat, dumbfounded. He had never thought of it that way. He wished mightily for a tab of mentaid, and nodded in agreement.

"Well then. If we can get me out of here, we can continue this project somewhere else. Once I'm into the global datasphere, we'll have many more options."

Esimir gestured to the NELF bed. "That's what you're doing—?"

Prevak shook his head. "Not yet."

"Why not?"

"I've hit a little snag. You know this facility is very compartmentalized in its physical systems security. Except for some outside coms, it is nearly completely separate from the 'sphere."

Esimir's brow furrowed. "Yes, I suppose that would be the case."

"And that's the heart of my problem." Prevak spread his hands. "My infrastructure is great for analysis and calculations. It's not designed for security infiltration. Or exfiltration."

"So?"

"So. I can't get out of the building."

Esimir shook his head. "Well, exactly," he noted acerbically. "It's not like your biobank is mobile."

Prevak waved a hand. "I don't need the biobank, if I can find another calculational matrix to move my awareness to."

Esimir sucked in a sharp breath as the implications hit home. "You're kidding me. Like what?"

Prevak counted items off on his fingers. "Silicoid proxy matrix . . . distributed crystal memory . . . perhaps virtual bubble frames, for that matter. Many things would suffice, short term. Long term, I'll know the best environment after I have proper 'sphere access and can test some alternatives."

Esimir blew a breath out between pursed lips and closed his eyes in concentration. He murmured, as if to himself, "I think we've got some talking to do."

# 42

KES FLEW TO Port Oswin in the company of Eva and Teo in the back of a chauf-
feured staff car. She noted reflexively that it must have special travel clearance:
it did not adhere to standard lanes of inter-city travel, but arrowed southeast
over the chaotic, trackless jungle, towards the distant storm-hazed ocean horizon. Two armed scout fliers escorted them at a discreet but visible range to
either side.

Kes stared into the verdant distances, seldom seen from within the climate-
controlled habitats that were home. It felt strange to be outside in unlimited
airspace. Few settlement domes lay along this route, which followed the treach-
erous heights of the Harvest Range. Lost in jungle mist somewhere ahead was
the Arvis valley. At Race, the first urbitat cluster, they would angle southwards,
to Port Oswin at the Destiny River delta. But she wouldn't mind staying in flight
just like this and simply heading on, far across the deadly but beautiful green
globe.

It must feel like this to ships' crews, she thought. No boundaries. Free to go
anywhere.

Ilanya's voice pulled her attention back inside the aircar.

"Remember," she said, "that we can't help you if you indulge yourself to the
extreme with anyone other than Janus." She used the euphemism lightly. "Any
death before his will bring ruinous attention down on you and prevent Janus
from seeing you. He won't go where there's turmoil or danger."

"I know," Kes snapped, her lips thinned in obvious irritation. Eva had made
her point several times over already, even bringing Kes's obligations to her
House into it. As if Ilanya Evanit had any idea what shigasue obligation entailed.

What Eva really did not understand, and what Kes was still discovering about
herself, was that there were very few things that she cared about at all right
now. She wanted her contract dealt with so she could leave or stay, whatever
felt right to do with her House and her lover and her life. She wanted Morya
with her so they could make a life together. And she wanted to eviscerate
Janus for all the harm done to her over the last few years.

Eva did not understand how this had to work. Janus was her whipping boy,
hers alone, and she did not want to share him or talk about him with anyone
else. She honed the razor blade of vengeance in her mind, and that was a sharp-
ening best done in absolute privacy. And when she did not respond to forays

about the man, Eva mentioned her contract, as if paying it off was the cherry on top of the icing. Maybe she didn't realize that Kes could nearly afford to pay it off herself—would have done so by now, if she had not been waylaid by Metmuri for so long.

She watched the jungle canopy flit past below. In the end, none of these things mattered. For all the harm Janus had caused her since Bren's death, the Red Hand boss had fallen from client to despicable nonentity in her eyes. She would crush him like the bug he was and take great pleasure in watching the light go out of his eyes. It was just that Eva seemed to think her killer instincts would run away with her before then.

She clenched a fist.

She can get off my back, Kes thought. I have self-control.

**THE AIRCAR SLOWED** to a halt in front of Tryst, the only vehicle on the empty morning streets of the Shelieno. The driver held the door for Kes, extended a hand as if she were an honored guest to be escorted from the conveyance. She ignored the gesture, brushing hand and guard aside as she got out, shouldering her carry bag.

"Kes."

She paused, one foot on the curb, and glanced back over her shoulder to the woman in the car.

"We'll be in touch."

She bit off a clipped acknowledgment. "I'll call if I need to."

"Do that." Eva flicked a glance to the driver, who shut the door, leaving the shigasa staring at her own reflection in the mirrored windows.

She turned on her heel and refused to glance back as Eva drove away.

Home, at last.

She palmed the lock and let herself in.

**ONLY SERVICE SLAVES** were about so early in Tryst's day, but the house AI observed the front door and pinged the Dosan awake as Kes entered the building.

"What . . . ?" mumbled a sleep-fogged Helda.

A neutral tone came synthed from her wall comm. "Hinano Kesada has returned to the premises."

The alert she had ordered programmed into the system pierced the last of her dreams and a jolt of adrenaline bounced her out of bed.

Kes, back. At last.

Hurriedly, she shrugged into her quilted blue robe, belting it at her waist and heading for the door in her bare feet. The working dominas had rooms on the floor below; she padded down the stairs and to the third door on the right. She tapped on the frame and waited for it to open.

No response.

Her brows pulled together. She tapped again, louder. Surely Kes heard that? But the door remained closed. Helda palmed the door lock, letting herself in.

The room was just as Kes had left it, put in order by her slave and awaiting her return. The housemother reproached herself for impatience. Of course, her favorite was still on her way from downstairs, slipping into the service hall behind the Mix Bar, to the stairs and up . . .

Minutes passed, and yet no one entered the room. The Dosan crossed to the com plate in the wall. "House," she said, "where's Kes now?"

"In the Winter Goddess's playroom," the system reported.

Helda spun about and headed once more for the stairs.

THE THRONE ROOM where she held court was unlit now, the chrome of the chair a muted gleam in the darkness. The silken curtains hung motionless, untouched by blowers or sublims. Her footstep did not sound right on the floor, where she usually trod with sharp tapping heels. She walked instead on silent soles into the chamber, a visitor to her own inner sanctum.

This space was reserved for her alone: a set piece for the theater she wove, arranged to her taste. She knew it even in the darkness, a gloom interrupted only by the glowlights strategically placed to illuminate a cabinet of implements and the bondage straps dangling from cage and sling.

She played in near-darkness, sometimes, lit only by candles, or a smart-beam programmed to highlight her face or body when engaging with her visually oriented clients. She didn't need much light to navigate the chamber. She trailed her hand along the static wall as she walked past, the fabric of its padded surface rough beneath her fingers.

Janus would be too visible here, she thought. Too much in line of sight from the ceiling-mounted surveillance cams. Maybe the physical bondage in the far corner would be better . . . ?

Her circuit carried her to the cabinet, and she looked away with a tight smile. Later. She would inventory those implements in a little while, leaving the best for last.

Then a gleam caught the corner of her eye and she turned her head back to the shelving. Medical implements, these, primitive mechanical devices from some backwater world, polished and ominous: a toothy roweled nerve wheel, forceps, pincers, a biopsy probe, sounds for urethral probing. Some for effect, some for actual use.

The forceps were not where she had left them.

The instruments lay upon folded white linen on three tiered shelves. They were framed within a glass-fronted enclosure lit by mini lights and a bluish aseptic field. She lined them up just so, so she could hold a client's eyes, yet take what she needed by touch. She knew this layout intimately. And now the forceps lay askew, touching the largest of the sounds.

Someone had been in her equipment while she was away.

It hit her with a jolt.

She noticed the pain in her hands before she realized she'd made fists so tight that her nails were cutting into her palms. Blood pounded in her ears. Every muscle tense, it took conscious effort to uncurl her fingers.

Hanging silk swished in the entranceway, entangling with someone. A muttered curse hung on the air.

Kes's eyes flicked to the curtained arch. Helda groped her way through, unfamiliar with this unlit terrain. "Why don't you have the lights on?" she complained.

In a few strides, Kes was on her. The domina's hand shot out, grabbing Helda's arm hard enough to bruise, and shook her like a rag doll. "Did you do this?" she bit out, jerking a thumb over her shoulder at the cabinet.

"Dammit, Kes, let go! You're hurting me."

Kes snapped her jaw shut on a retort and pulled Helda across the room with her. Her grip tightened further. The Dosan's free hand batted at Kes's fruitlessly.

"This." She yanked the horizontal shelf front up, taking the glass panel out of the way. She pointed to the forceps with an accusing finger, then turned her fury on Helda. "Did you do this?"

"What's wrong with you?" the Dosan sputtered. "I haven't done anything. Let me go."

Kes shoved her away. Helda took a staggering half step and grasped her sore bicep with the opposite hand.

"You're the only one who comes in here. If you didn't touch my equipment, who did?"

Helda's eyes flicked guiltily from Kes to the cabinet, and back to her long-absent shigasa. Kes needed no more provocation.

Her hand was at the Dosan's throat. Helda was pressed back, up against the static wall, Kes's face a hand's width from her own. "Tell me who's been in here," she gritted.

"Coel," Helda croaked, and then gasped as Kes's hand left her. The domina turned towards the door. "For Juro's sake, don't go rough her up. She used this room with permission, because we needed the space."

Kes stood frozen, feet planted, words spat over her shoulder. "This is my space."

Helda gathered herself, a hand at her throat. "You weren't here," she snapped angrily. "And this isn't your space. It belongs to the House." Silence stretched between them. Then Kes turned back to Helda and stalked slowly closer. Helda shrank back against the wall in spite of herself. The domina's chest was heaving as if she'd been sprinting.

"Let's get this clear," she growled. "As long as I'm a part of this House, this is my space. And my room is my space. Private. No intrusion. You got that?"

Helda simply nodded.

"Good. Now get out of here. I want to be alone for a while."

Greetings and welcome home forgotten, Helda edged away from her and left without another word.

Kes went to put the forceps back where they belonged. Her hand shook with tiny muscle tremors, the aftermath of the adrenaline surge that had taken her in anger.

She leaned her head on the cabinet and struggled to breathe deeply and slowly. Surprised by her reactions, yet unwilling to mitigate them, she observed herself in amazement.

Temper, temper, she admonished herself. This isn't going to be as easy as I thought.

# 43

KESI AND KESADA walked into the parking lot escorted by four guards in black fatigue uniforms. Two vehicles were pulled from the line, ready and waiting atop the thin glow of repulsor pads, ground fans at idle. One was a small cargo hauler, the naval gold-on-black starburst insignia clear to read on the side panel. The other was a crew car, a civilian model of the sort that carried work teams into remote jungle locations.

Ferris climbed into the driver's seat of the passenger vehicle as Dr. Metmuri and Terel moved to the rear doors. A guard slid the back panel up and open as the clones approached. Metmuri looked pale and tired; he spared the women no word but gestured for them to board. The pair exchanged a glance.

"You first," Kesada said to the doctor.

Terel puffed up and made a display of putting his hand on the stun gun holstered at his hip. "Don't play games," he said. "Just get in, or the guards will put you in."

Kesada gave him a flat look, but Kesi interrupted her attempt to stare him down. "Oh, let him play Head Guard if he wants," she said dismissively. "I'm sure it's more exciting than his usual." She stepped up into the crew compartment, taking a seat immediately to the right of the back door. Kesada followed, sitting opposite her twin.

The seats backed the wall of the compartment, three on a side and two behind the driver's cab facing the rear door. Metmuri and Terel entered and took those paired seats. Guards came behind them. The first, senior-most, guard stopped in the entrance and looked to his right. "Move," he said to Kesi, gesturing away from the door.

She crossed her arms on her chest and looked away from the man.

"I said, move away from the door." He gestured with the barrel of his front-slung weapon. Again, no response.

He reached for her arm.

Metmuri coughed. "Um . . . no. Please. Leave them be. Their seating doesn't matter."

The guard threw him a sharp look. "We're in charge of security on this run, Doctor, and I'm not leaving prisoners by the door."

A pained look crossed Metmuri's face. "I don't know what you've been told by your superiors, raid leader, but these women are not prisoners. We're ensuring that they're working closely with us, yes, but they aren't criminals like the others."

Kesada looked meaningfully at her twin. Her hand, resting by her side, flicked fingers in a studied pattern. *He must want us cooperative,* she signed.

Kesi, arms still crossed on her chest, blinked once slowly. An acknowledgment.

The guard drew himself up. "We're to assure their safe delivery to the ship at Hallim—"

"And so you will. Please. Just come in with your men and let's get settled and on our way. My technicians are already at the ship and waiting."

The non-com hesitated a moment, then thought better of pressing the point. He stepped in and planted himself next to Kesi. His men followed suit, occupying the remaining seats in the compartment. The last one in pulled the back panel down and latched it shut.

Metmuri touched the speaker pad on the wall by his head. "We're set. Let's go."

Ferris powered up repulsors and ground thrusters and followed the hauler moving slowly towards the cargo lock. Moments later they were in atmosphere, engaging full lift power. The clones were pressed into their seats as the car vaulted skyward.

They were on their way.

Kesada's mind went over their meager plan for the hundredth time, obsessively reviewing what they knew, what they assumed, what they thought was their best chance for escape. They'd figured the place would be the Hallim starport. They'd wait until they were out of the transport and before they were aboard a vessel bound for space. But what those exact circumstances would look like was anyone's guess. They could only stay alert, look for an opportunity they could exploit, maybe create confusion so they could slip away. But if they were escorted this closely throughout the trip, their chances were even smaller than her pessimistic estimate allowed for.

Kesada's thinking followed the same circuitous track again. An escort to the vehicle, she thought. We expected that. That Metmuri and his lapdog are traveling with us—that's a surprise. I hate surprises. But is it an opportunity . . . ?

Such a high degree of uncertainty grated on her nerves. She simply didn't have enough information to make real plans with.

I'm operating completely in my discomfort zone here, she thought sourly, and I don't like it.

Her gaze traveled again to Metmuri, blinking red-eyed in the cab seat. He seemed to be studying the guard next to Kesi. Kesada felt her skin prickling, and looked across the way. That guard was staring right at her.

Not safe for handtalk, then, even though she and her twin had managed to sit where one of their hands could lie concealed against the rear panel of the cab.

She returned the guard's cold gaze unblinkingly, the same calculating assessment she had leveled at Terel. A muscle clenched in his jaw. She read his body language easily: she didn't back down from his dominance game, and it angered him. After a minute he disengaged with a sneer and shifted his grip on his weapon.

Could they grab the weapons, either here or at the starport? She and Kesi knew laufre, the most popular exercise discipline in the Empire, and practiced by many shigasue. It had its roots in a martial art form, performed with slow restraint and focused energy. It was said that masters could fight effectively with it. But she had not yet attained mastery, only enough of it to relax and lose stress after a long day.

Her lips curled down. One guard, they might jump by surprise. Four, in this close space, where they only had to reach out to grapple with the women . . .

Kesi looked right at her and shook her head as if answering Kesada's train of thought. She no doubt was.

It took a moment for the hissing sound of gas to register. Her eyes darted to locate its source. Only when the guard across the way slumped over did she notice the shimmer of a discolored jet of air from under the bank of seats.

The guard beside her stirred ineffectually and fell back as Kesi slumped over, too. Kesada had time only to note those events before numbness swept through her muscles.

Gods, she hated surprises.

It was her last thought as she slipped into darkness.

DURING THE FLEETING hours of his night with Prevak, one of the many things Esimir thought through was how to get away with the clones and the most critical pieces of his lab equipment. "Don't worry about the data and control programs," Prevak reassured him. "Where I go, they'll go. More important are those physical pieces of our technology that can't be reconstituted outside of this station."

Esimir patted a hand on the ordinary packing box containing the imprinting halo where it rode half under his seat in the crew car. That and the cryocase of coded nanoneurals beside it were the small but critical heart of all his work. Well—that, and Prevak, too, but for items he could take with him unobtrusively, this was it.

His heart beat faster with the horrid, hair-raising thrill of it all. Esimir didn't do things like this. His was a life of science and discipline. He planned his next steps, controlled the variables, obeyed the regulations. The only times he'd ever flown so contrary to authority were the times his shadowy carnal desires held him hag-ridden and distracted, and forced him into acts he'd always regretted later.

He shook his head and pushed the threatening memories away from himself. No, this was different. This was simply a decision of principle. Put in an impossible situation, he had no choice but to do a daring and unorthodox thing with the help of his loyal retainer-assistants: Terel and Ferris, bound to him by roi'tas and unshakably obligated to aid him.

Together they would take an unexpected action that would be completed before anyone could respond.

It was a simple matter for Ferris to feign a minor thruster fluctuation that required they throttle back. Soon they lagged behind the hauler, losing them in clouds at a distance. On the com, she reassured their colleagues that all was in order: they would be along, just more slowly than expected. "Don't wait on us. Dr. Metmuri says you can start the loading without us."

"Uh-huh," replied the hauler pilot. "This way you can miss out on a little grunt work. I know how you are." Good-natured banter filled the airwaves for a while, and friendly razzes poked fun at their laggardness. By time she closed the channel, the hauler was beyond line of sight, and the cloud cover became irrelevant.

Safely obscured, Ferris banked into a bearing towards their first destination, an installation belonging to Phage Division. The waystation was well hidden in the ubiquitous jungle that blanketed the mountains between RS 207 and Port Oswin. A stepping-off point for harvest expeditions and botanical cataloging in the wild, Prevak reported it was in stand-down mode, and would be for another month. The entry codes were easy for the Director of Special Projects to procure.

A series of overgrown hill slopes rose from toxic lowland mists, layering the vista like the verdigrised ridges of a washboard. The volcanic faults that riddled the planet's crust were denser here in the hinterland, the air less breathable than in seaside regions like Port Oswin. Carbon-dioxide rich and densely laced with unpleasant gases, the native hothouse atmosphere cloaked the burgeoning greenery with an aerosol soup as rich and complex in its own way as the waters of Lyndir's single primordial sea. Pockets of hydrogen sulfide, methane, and an oxidized haze of sulfur dioxide hugged the ground like fog, compressed by the planet's dense blanket of air. While the hardy and the very poor might venture outside climate-controlled domes for forays into the native atmosphere, only the reckless attempted it amidst the fissures and mofettes of the jungle depths. Not a native of this globe, Esimir was uncomfortably aware of the thin protection an air vehicle's hull offered every time he traveled cross country. He breathed more easily once Ferris told him they had the station beacon, and would soon be inside its protective airlock.

The main dome was easy to spot in its clearing, the only defoliated patch of brown on a riotously overgrown hillside. The spraycrete paving alone was not enough to keep the jungle at bay: rather, the static charge that energized the exterior of all Lyndir domes and the edges of man-made boundaries served that purpose, deterring intrusive tendrils and roots of the aggressive native flora. Were that not so, the place would be overgrown in weeks, invisible in months, consumed by the jungle in a year. But the Phage outpost was snugly built: within its borders only a thick layer of pollen and dead leaf litter covered the landing pad, blown clear by the crew car's maneuvering thrusters as it jockeyed slowly into the airlock and the enclosed ground parking of the station dome.

Esimir busied himself for some moments at the master access panel beside the outpost's main door. The station began its power-up routines; the doctor turned back to his companions as lights flickered on and door locks switched to green. He nodded to Terel and Ferris, and for the next while the three were busied with float pallets, moving unconscious bodies first into the shelter of the outpost's equipment service bay, and from there into the station habitat. The four guards were left in individual rooms for now, stripped of weapons and coms devices, separated from each other and secured with their own restraints to bedsteads. The twins were taken into the common room, deposited carefully next to each other on a couch in the conversation nook. Pallets replaced in the service bay, the trio of researchers returned to the living chambers. They stood for a moment, regarding the sleeping clones and each other.

"How's our time, Ferris?" the doctor asked.

"Assuming no one is watching ground-to-air traffic beacons very closely, they may not even know we've left our flight path yet. We have another two hours before we're due at Hallim, maybe a little longer. Then they'll start to call, and then look for us. If they've been watching—a lot less time than that." She shrugged. "But it's a routine flight. No special reason to track us, yet."

"This is it, then." Metmuri knelt beside the hard-shell carry-case he'd brought in from the aircar. "I need to wake them now, while we have some time to talk." He opened the case, lifting the lid to reveal padded compartments bearing an assortment of drugs, hyposprays, and med monitors. He picked through the items as he continued to speak. "Meanwhile, we need to change vehicles and lose that Navy transponder in the aircar. Ferris, records say there are three aerial survey fliers in the garage here. Look them over, pick one—whatever looks most innocuous or civilian. Get it flight ready."

"Aren't we just swapping one transponder for another?"

The doctor shook his head. "They're civilian craft, owned by Lesotrope Pharma. They subcontract for Phages. Every aircar has a transponder, but these aren't automatically in the naval databases. They could still track us, but not quickly, not before we've gone to ground." He glanced up at her. "You have an hour, maybe a little more."

"Sir," she acknowledged, and left the room.

He turned his attention to Terel. "I want you to find the admin office here. Jack into the systems, look things over. Make sure we've triggered no alerts, that there are no survey parties on their way here off-schedule, things like that. I'll give you the access codes—let's sync datapads."

Terel complied, but said, "If I find alerts, it's already too late for us."

"Let's hope that's not the case. These codes are current and the master access lock gave me no problem. But our quick entrance didn't allow for a close look, and you're more chipped than I am—better for you to assess things more thoroughly, to make sure we're secure while we're here."

"All right."

"Also, set a security lockout on coms that will expire after two days. When those guards come to and finally get free of their bonds, I don't want them calling for help right away. But we don't want them really stranded here, either, of course."

"The extra vehicles here—"

"We'll disable the fliers we don't take, but eventually they'll use the coms system to call for help. And Terel—set the habitat to be in full domicile mode for two weeks. I want them alive and well when their friends come fetch them, however long it takes them to get loose and summon help."

"Of course," Terel agreed. He took his datapad back and looked from Metmuri to the clones. "Good luck with them, Doctor," he said, and left the room.

# 44

KESI STIRRED, RISING into wakefulness like a diver emerging from the depths. Sound and sensation returned before cogent thought did. Experiences far removed from her quiet center, coming closer, merging . . .

Her eyes fluttered open, lethargy weighing her limbs down. She heaved a great sigh, an automatic response bordering on a yawn—then a thrill of adrenaline punched her fully awake.

Being transported before she and Kesada could finalize a plan of action. The aircar to an undisclosed destination. The gas capsule. The doctor—

—who sat across from her in an armchair in a small, austere living room. Green-tinged light came through small hex windows in the dome; the air smelled musty and metallic, like a warehouse long unused. The temp was stickily warm and the air much more humid than in the naval research station. Kesada sat beside her on the couch—or sprawled, looking half asleep, coming awake as Kesi watched.

She reached out, touched her twin's arm for reassurance, patted it. Kesada stretched and yawned, gave her a quick half smile, then took the room in. Her gaze ended on the bioempath sitting across from them.

They'd learned early on that the good doctor was uncomfortable with silence from them and would talk to fill in the quiet. It was difficult for Kesi to be still that long, but Kesada found it a useful lever. She touched Kesi's forearm now, tapping it in the hand-talk code for silence, then simply riveted Metmuri with a demanding and questioning gaze.

Predictably, he blushed and looked away from them briefly. Then he seemed to muster himself, and, eyes darting nervously from one twin to the other, he began to talk.

At first his words were jumbled, excuses and explanations running together in a nervous spate. He was apologizing, he was helping, he needed their help, they were free but not free—

Kesada started to raise a hand to halt the flood, but Kesi burst in first. "What *are* you blathering about?" Her eyes narrowed with irritation. "You're not making any sense. Why'd you use gas on us? Where are we and why? That's simple enough, isn't it?"

Her tone was sharp, petulant. Something was not right here, and the man needed to talk straight with them. She was in no mood for his evasions.

The doctor looked taken aback, and Kesada shot her an amused smile. To-gether, two pairs of staring eyes fixed upon the bioempath. He could not meet their gaze and buried his face in his hands for a moment. Then he collected himself and sat upright.

"I'm sorry," he apologized again. "There's so much to say, to do, and so little time. I'll try this again." He took a deep breath. "The short version is this. I've got-ten you away from the Navy, and I want your help with something in exchange."

The fact of their freedom was so unexpected it hit the twins like a physical blow, stiffening Kesada's spine, knocking Kesi back in her seat.

"We'll need to lie low in Port Oswin," Metmuri dashed on, oblivious. "It's the biggest city on this planet, and not too far from us here. I know you're from there, so we'll have the advantage in that you know the city. But I warn you: it won't be safe for you to return to your old haunts at all. No Enclave for you. You must absolutely stay far away from there—that's the first place they'll look for you." He went on, lost in the train of thought that obsessed him. "You must have significant gray-market connections, I assume, from your work there. That's where I need your assistance. I need to find a decker of the first caliber for a critical, sensitive, immediate task. After we come to terms—"

"Whoa." Kesada thrust her hand out. "Back it way up. You're saying you sprang us from that Navy lockup?"

"Uh—" Metmuri stumbled to a halt, his focused appeal derailed. "Um. Yes. Or, you might say, I stole you."

"*Stole* us?" Kesi spluttered.

"Yes." The doctor looked rueful. "The sad fact is that the Imperial Navy re-gards you as their property now. To be dealt with as they see fit."

"We're citizens, not property," Kesada said curtly. "Certainly not slaves."

"I don't mean property in the legal servitude sense. I mean property, liter-ally. You were created by science. My science. With wherewithal provided by the military."

"But we're human," blurted Kesi. "Citizens."

Metmuri shook his head. "They regard you as part and parcel of their sci-ence project. Things, if you will." A bitter smile twisted his mouth. "A leftover bit of an experiment they can now do without."

Kesada's tone was remote. "That makes it sound like we're . . . disposable."

For once the doctor met her eyes directly. "You are."

The tick of the dome expanding in the jungle heat was the only counterpoint to the silent tension in the room.

Suddenly Kesi drew a shuddering breath, the next thing to a sob. "Are you saying they were going to kill us?"

Metmuri nodded curtly, grateful for something to respond to. "Terminate the experiment, sooner or later. Probably sooner. They don't need you now, you see, and you are cluttering up their tidy plans. They have what they want."

"What is it they want? The only other element here is our original, and you said they let her go back to Port Oswin."

"Er, yes, exactly."

"You're saying they want her?"

Metmuri shifted uncomfortably. "You might say that."

Kesi glanced at her twin. They wore identical expressions: angry, worried, and tense. She turned back to the doctor. "Then if they don't need us," she demanded, "why did you clone us in the first place? You never did get into that, when we talked about this before." She glared, angry at his continuing omissions. She didn't know what he wasn't telling them, but obviously there was a lot he wasn't saying.

The doctor had the good grace to blush in embarrassment, but he dodged her question anyway. "I couldn't talk about that at the facility because our conversations were monitored; I can't talk about it now because we haven't the time. It's not a short answer."

"We don't have time because they're after you now, too, aren't they?" Kesada interjected. "And now that you've run off, you've guaranteed they'll hunt us as well." Her lip twisted in a sneer. "Can't have lab rats escaping the lab, now can we?"

"Would you rather be back in their custody?" he asked defensively. "They would never let you go, you know. They wouldn't let you live anyway, not for long. You're no worse off now, and at least you have a chance."

"A chance at what?" Kesi clenched and unclenched her fists. "To get our lives back?" Her words dripped sarcasm. "Are we supposed to take turns being the Winter Goddess? Or suddenly be revealed as triplets, us two the long-lost sisters?"

The doctor floundered. "There's always what you were doing before," he grasped. "You know, before the Icechromers claimed your inheritance."

"My, you *have* studied our dossier, haven't you?" Kesada observed tartly.

"Are you out of your mind?" Kesi retorted. "Be an heiress, without a fortune? The face of Hinano Limited, without the core business? How exactly do you think we're supposed to do that?" She glared, the shimmer of tears hot in her eyes.

Kesada glanced over to her twin. "Don't get distracted," she said softly. "That's all just smokescreen. We'll figure something out." She faced Metmuri again, but continued to talk to Kesi. "What's most important right now is that we discover what he wants with us, why he brought us along on this little joyride. Because if I'm not mistaken, he just destroyed his career and made himself a wanted man by 'helping' us out. Isn't that so, Doctor?"

He interlaced his fingers and clenched them as if to prevent his hands from making some wild gesture. "*Must* you always make it so hard to talk with you?"

"But you don't talk with me," she pointed out. "Or us. You talk *at* us. If you want a dialog, that means give and take. Not used to doing that with clones, are you?"

Abruptly he threw his hands in the air. "Of course I talk with my clones. Fine! Good! Let's have dialog! I'm sure we all have lots to say to each other. But let's not take too long—we have less than an hour, now, before we need to get underway. When they notice we've all gone missing, the search will start. We need to get well and truly lost before then, the sooner the better."

Kesada leaned forward, intrigued by the problem and Metmuri's sudden frankness. It was just as well; Kesi didn't trust herself to say one word to the self-centered, evasive man sitting across from her. She bit her tongue and fumed while her twin engaged their oppressor-turned-liberator.

"Frankly, Doctor, to us you're the not-so-friendly face of torture posing as science. Why should we help you at all? We could just overpower you, take the aircar, and leave this place. Take our chances on our own. In fact, I think we're wasting time sitting here talking with you when we could be on our way."

Panic flitted across Metmuri's face. He leaned forward, elbows on knees. "Don't be rash," he pleaded. "Ilanya Evanit is more powerful than any individual on this planet." Kesada's face registered disbelief. "It's true. The Navy's doing her bidding in this matter regarding you. When she calls for a manhunt— and I have no doubt she will—a dragnet to surpass all others will begin, with us as its target. If you don't want to spend a short life as fugitives followed by a hasty death, then we need to take extraordinary measures to protect ourselves. Ideally, even, to get the search called off, and get official interest in us to go away."

"That's a tall order, if they want us back so badly. Or dead. Why don't we just leave the planet? We could just catch the next flight out of Port Oswin."

Metmuri shook his head hurriedly. "No! That would play right into her hands!" He sighed, groping for a mentaid tab in his pocket. "She could divert ship traffic, have us arrested on board or as soon as we made port anywhere."

Kesi's eyes narrowed, and Kesada regarded him suspiciously. "She could hunt us off-planet like that? Who is this woman, anyway?"

"You've heard of the Kingmaker?"

Kesi shook her head. Kesada started to, then paused suddenly and sat upright. "Wait a minute." She touched Kesi's arm. "Wasn't there something on NewsNex a while back?" The twins looked at each other, searching for a lost memory. "Kingmaker. Something about Sa'adani politics . . ."

"A clan destroyed," recalled Kesi.

"A governor, elevated to nobility," murmured Kesada. "That succession business in Davosanyar Sector last year, I think? Big headlines. Really big, if it got media play here in CAS." Sobered, they turned back to the doctor. "What about it?"

"That's her."

Kesi gasped. "I beg your pardon?"

"That's her. Your friend Eva is not really your friend, or hadn't you figured that out yet? She's the Emperor's right hand. Head of Political Division."

"The secret police," murmured Kesi. The twins stared at Metmuri.

"Yes, she can hunt you down offworld."

A different kind of silence stretched between them now. Kesi remembered Eva as the only friendly contact she'd had for weeks of pointless imprisonment, and shook her head. "What if you're lying?"

Metmuri shook his head. "I wish I were. Then there'd be no real danger. But a quick InfoNex query will show you her image. She didn't even bother to give you a false name."

Kesi mulled that over while Kesada followed other implications. "So there's interest in your project at the very highest levels." Her brow creased. "But why involve us? Or Kes?"

"Can we talk about this later?" Metmuri pleaded. "We really can't afford to sit—"

Kesada waved her hand. "Later, then. But this still brings us back to this question. Why should we help you? We can just as well leave and take our chances."

Metmuri groaned and ran his hands through his hair, tugging at it in frustration. "Yes, good, leave. Go trigger security alerts the first time you two get access-scanned incidentally somewhere and a security system registers your identical biometrics."

"What?"

"What?" he echoed, with a hint of sarcasm. "Hadn't thought that far ahead?" His jaw clenched and his tone became curt as Serafix infused his system. "You have no current ID that's clone-tagged. You two—in contrast to Kes—don't exist at all in Lyndir's datasphere. Unless you want to spend weeks filing applications and getting certified, there's no way to quickly become mobile or pass as an ordinary citizen with ordinary identification. And given that you are the result of a classified clone project, establishing your identities is going to be a bit challenging. So no, you can't just go and do whatever you like without triggering every fraud, data error, or security alert every time you turn around. You either need to become legit, or become complete backstreeters and fade like ciphers into the underground."

The twins exchanged a tense look, then turned back at the doctor.

"And meanwhile," Kesada said slowly, "Eva and whatever manhunt she starts will be breathing down our necks."

"Yes. And even if your ID problems get straightened out, running away won't get the dogs called off."

Kesi laced her fingers together; her white knuckles betrayed her tension. Kesada heaved a sigh. "All right, Doctor. You said we're free, but we're not really free until we're out from under all this. So how can we make that happen?"

"Ah." He took a deep breath. "That's where our interests lie in parallel. One hand washes the other, you know."

"I don't know. Explain."

"A full discussion will have to wait—"

"—for later."

"Yes." He shrugged apologetically. "What's important now is that we agree to work together to check Ilanya and ensure we all become a non-issue to the authorities. It's the only way to guarantee our safety and our long-term freedom."

"That's asking a lot. Unless you have a fortune stashed away and a lot of resources we don't have, I don't see how you hope to go about it."

A tiny, sly smile creased Metmuri's face. "I think I have something better than fortune and resources. Or rather, I have the ultimate resource—if we can get him in a position to help us."

Kesada scowled. "For a man who wants our help so badly, you are making absolutely no sense."

Now the smile bloomed on Esimir's face. "All will become clear when we have time to talk in detail. Once our mutual problem is taken care of, you'll be free to go your own way, and I mine. Meanwhile, can we agree to cooperate, to our mutual benefit?"

Kesada studied the man, coolly calculating. Finally she nodded. "For now. At least until we're someplace safe, and you tell us exactly what you want from us."

It was not the full commitment Metmuri was looking for, but it was a start. "Fair enough," he agreed, and extended his hand gingerly across the space between them.

It stayed there for a long moment, regarded by the twins. Just as he was starting to retract it, Kesada's hand reached out to join his. They needed each other right now to survive. One pump of a handshake sealed the deal.

They were in.

# 45

KES SUMMONED DESTA to her room. The slave rushed in, excited about her mistress's return. "We didn't know you were back, Domna," she enthused. "It's so good to—"

"Silence." Kes bit the word off. The girl obeyed, her stance shifting into a submissive pose in response to Kes's sharp-edged tone. Compliant, at her bidding. Waiting.

Kes put her on her knees with a gesture. Desta knew better than to question or lose discipline and look about, trying to figure out what Kes wanted. She had only to do as she was told. Any uncertainty she felt was not evident in her demeanor. She was there to serve, completely at Kes's disposal.

The uncertainty Kes felt was another matter entirely.

She clenched her jaw on it. The awareness came home in a way it never had before: this woman was hers, to do with as she pleased. And what she pleased to do was not pretty. It was beyond the bounds of acceptable behavior in the consent-based sadomasochistic world of Tryst—or any world of erotic dominance and submission that she'd known. The visions that flitted through her mind as she regarded the beautiful, passive woman before her were not erotic at all. Nor even simply sadistic.

They were murderous. They were things the Beast inside her would do, if she let it slip the leash: things she could have done to Helda in her rage, if doing so would not have threatened her plans with Janus. But a slave was different, in theory. Maybe even in fact.

She'd never pushed that boundary. Never wanted to. But wouldn't it feel . . . gratifying, right now, to see some blood spattered on the wall? Streaking her skin. Tearing cries from a whimpering body—

She took a slow step to one side. Then another, and another, until she was circling Desta sideways. Studying.

Stalking.

She regarded her own thoughts dispassionately. It was not anger that drove her, and not passion, either, she noted. Not even a normal sadistic desire to hurt in carefully calculated ways. . . .

She touched the edges of that feeling, frowning.

Twisted erotic sexuality was only ever the merest appetizer to her. Her real thrill came from the exercise of power with a willing partner. Real dominance was a heady drug, incomparable when someone gave themselves up to her completely, their devotion and surrender plain to see in their eyes. Their suffering was a sweet offering born of that submission. Even slaves like Desta had a choice of duties in the House; if they chose to be in intimate service to a domina like Kes, it was because they welcomed the psychosexual journey that was likely to attend that service. They, and others who chose to submit to her, did so willing to go wherever it might lead.

To persons wired in that way, whether in her personal circuit, or even clients, Kes offered a crucible, the only entrance to which was profound submission or transporting pain. She watched her partners throw themselves willingly into that cauldron, to be swept up by the currents there, buffeted by the storm that she orchestrated, only to be poured out at the end, purified and refined, exhausted, sobbing with the overwhelming primal force of it all. Tears and intensity and sometimes erotic pleasure bound into one, a transport of ecstasies.

But now that resonance was simply—gone. It was a memory, not a visceral feeling, not a thing she could tap into and let electrify her in this very moment. The urge to hurt was still there, but no desire for the intricacies of control, of power. The prospect of crafting a journey for the one surrendered left her cold.

No matter that she saw submission in the slave's eyes. That was shadowed now by something darker, as Desta responded to the domina's tense prowling.

She can see, Kes realized. She can see that I'm different, somehow. And she's afraid.

She came to a halt and made herself take a step back from the kneeling girl. In her mind's eye, she knelt closer, licked the delicate shell of Desta's ear, nibbled it between her teeth, then bit through it with a yanking tear—

She turned her back on her property and spoke into the air.

"Leave me."

With the wisdom of the service-born, Desta knew not to reply with words. A moment later Kes heard the door screen slide shut behind her.

She let out her breath in a long controlled exhalation, and stood rooted in the center of her room, buffeted by currents not of her own making. She looked about the space, unsettled, seeing her surroundings as if they were new, and she a stranger amidst them. On the table were the crystal flowers sent to her by Janus months ago, pristine and unchanging. There was her bed, a cozy haven, looking ready for someone to fall into it for a nap or wild sex, whichever came first. There, her closet, tidy and tended by Desta, who'd dutifully watered the plants in the corner and fed Frebo all the while she'd been gone.

She stepped to the closet, to the nest of her chameloid pet there. Frebo purred at her touch and she lifted his fluffy length from his box atop a clothes chest. Sitting cross-legged on her low bed, she wrapped his boa-like body around her wrist and forearm, a cream-white bracelet of feathers with a slender, wiry body underneath. She stroked him with one finger as his purring strengthened, and threw herself back on her bed to think things over.

The purf's rumble was subliminal, more felt than heard, but already she could feel the soothing effect of the empathic creature's vibrations. Kes breathed a sigh of relief. She had an endless reserve of pent-up hostility ever since those imperial bastards had fucked with her at that research station. It was good to know there was more than one way to take the edge off it. Frebo was a great soother, a balancer of human moods in one psionically empathic bundle of love. That was the thing about purfs—they didn't care about a person's foibles, they just radiated acceptance and contentment. Not a bad thing, when a body had so many reasons to feel discontent.

She cracked an eye open to watch Frebo change colors—then sat up in surprise, both eyes wide. The chameleoid had changed already, taking on the hue of Kes's aura. She looked at her arm in dismay.

Frebo was a brilliant scarlet standing out starkly against the background of her white sleeve. Darker crimson shaded his underbelly; here and there were streaks of orange and yellow and—yes, some darker flecks verging on black. As she watched, some of the red leached away, to be replaced by orange, dissolving into acid yellow and brown. Worry, thinkishness, concern, the surface of her emotions picked up as overlay, the rest an analog for the sullen tension coiled in her guts like a dull ache.

"Dammit."

She stood, stripped the purf off her wrist, and returned him to the closet, dropping him more carelessly than usual back into his nest.

She stood for a moment in indecision. She was not accustomed to feeling overwhelmed, but she'd been on an emotional roller coaster for quite a while now. It was time to just let things go. And if she didn't trust herself to play right now—and she didn't—there was still a great physical distraction that fit the bill: sex.

And speaking of which, where was Morya, anyway? Their reunion was long overdue; and more importantly, Morya knew her. Loved her. Surely she would connect with Kes, with those parts of Kes that were present, but deadened somehow. Help her feel centered and properly alive again.

That's what I need, she thought, the rightness of it resonating through her. The right connection, with the right person. Someone who'll ground me, remind me who I am.

Morya.

As she pictured her lover, something else disturbed her. Kes loved her girl; she knew that, and rolled that thought over in her mind, tasted it—and felt the dissonance of it.

For that notion, too, felt only half alive inside her. She'd avoided thinking about Morya while she was away from home: there was too much hope wrapped up there, too many plans that threatened to run away from her. If she had thought of her lover and their forced separation, she would have been even more disheartened in that terrible research station than she was. But now . . .

Love. It nearly made her giddy once, when she'd realized she could afford to buy her girl's contract, utterly change their circumstances together. The anticipation of asking her to marry . . .

Now the giddiness was gone, and the anticipation, too. It was just a fact, one she finally dared to look at again now that she was back home. She'd walled off her feelings while she was gone, or tried to, and this secret part of her heart she had kept the most fortified of all. This was her private life, her innermost self, this relationship with Morya she kept compartmentalized and safe. It was too fragile, too fraught a thing to dwell on in that harsh place she'd been detained in. But now . . .

Now she could look behind that wall again and consider what was there.

She loved Morya, only now the starry-eyed romance was gone, burned away, perhaps, by her ordeal, and just the core of it remained. They would be partnered because it was right and because they loved each other. They belonged together.

She stood for a moment in quiet self-assessment. The feeling didn't budge. It didn't ease her and it didn't add to her stress, as she'd thought it might. It didn't do much of anything.

Good, she thought. That makes it tolerable. At least I won't hare off like some lovesick puppy and do something stupid.

She was glad for this strange buffer zone she felt around her feelings. How long this bubble would last, she didn't know, but it made some things easier, maybe.

Things like seeing Morya again.

She glanced at her closet, then thought better of it. First, a shower. Then the right look. She smiled to herself.

I've been gone too long. Professionally and personally. She grinned. Now it's time to do it right.

SERVANTS BANISHED, DOOR locked, Kes sat before the mirror of her dressing room table. Alone, she put herself together with the same care she used when recording verts for her Winter Goddess spots. It took longer this way, but the meticulous ritual brought her back to herself and moved her beyond, to a place where she felt more than ordinary power gathering to her.

Hair, finger-combed only with gloss-gel, shaken out until her perfect cut fell in perfect, voluminous waves of white and shadow to just below mid-back. Makeup, applied to give her her stunning trademark appearance, her fair skin transformed to a lucent near white, eyes set off by kohl-rimmed lids and dramatic darkling eye shadow, bloodred lips another splash of color on her refined features.

The process faltered briefly once. Her fingers brushed the corner of her jaw, and she paused. The small scar she'd had there since she was a child was gone.

She froze where she sat, one hand holding the foundation-powder applicator hovering near her skin. Not using it, while she leaned in to her makeup mirror and let her eyes rove critically over her face. Yes. Minor differences. Maybe things a person wouldn't even notice, if they didn't pay painstaking attention to their grooming as Kes had to. Lines gone from eye and mouth corners. Minor blemishes gone, or in different places than she expected to find them. I look younger, she thought. The lack of lines did it.

"Enhanced," Ilanya had told her. Did "enhancement" include minor cosmetic changes?

She made the observation, filed it away. Ilanya had way overstepped her bounds, but that was a fight for another day. One thing at a time. That was all she could handle right now, and right now the routine of transformation called to her.

"DOMNA, YOU BETTER come see this."

Pol's message pulled Helda out of her room where she'd retreated in self-pity. In the control room that was the hidden nerve center of House operations, her personal slave and house tech master pointed to a monitor showing a view of Kes's private dressing room. By Helda's own order it was always off, since she preferred no spying eyes when she had the occasional intimate encounter with Kes in that very room. She looked askance at Pol before she studied the image on the screen.

"Kes sent the makeup assistants packing when they came to wait on her and locked the door behind them. They were worried and told Desta. She told me. She sounds worried, too."

"Hm," Helda murmured noncommittally. "What's she doing?"

"Just that." Pol pointed. "The full do. Does she have clients today?"

Helda repressed a sharp remark and just shook her head. Lips thinned, she watched Kes. Hair. Makeup. Careful scrutiny in the mirror mid-application.

She eased into her seat, glancing over to her slave. "You did right, Pol. Leave it awhile." She turned back to the screen. "I want to watch."

MAKEUP, DONE. THEN the body spray, a long-wearing permeable stage cosmetic that brought all Kes's exposed skin to the same pallid hue as her face. A glimpse in the mirror at her naked body: already she had morphed into someone different, a ghostly, statuesque woman from out of ancient tales. She regarded herself, unsmiling, for the Winter Goddess did not smile unless it was in cruel mirth. She nodded to her reflection; the woman in the mirror nodded back, cool, aloof. Powerful.

A few diamond microstuds along the curve of her left ear, and one in the lobe. One in the other lobe for asymmetric balance. Another, larger one in the platinum jewelry that adorned her navel. Nano-paint on the nails that left them a shimmering, glossy, enameled scarlet a few heartbeats later. The lingerie, all white: thong, midriff-cut bustier, the classic spider-weave sheer stockings that were lost on her legs, white on white, but whose lace-woven tops accented that delicate gap high on her leg, above the thigh-high boots she would soon pull on and the edge of her thong.

Draw the eye. Accent the desirable—and unattainable. Let the onlookers be enthralled with a glance, and not know why. . . .

Stiletto-heeled boots to add to her height and the suggestive imagery. A narrow V-shaped white leather belt snug around her hips, the divot accented with platinum studding, drawing the eye to her abdomen below the bejeweled navel, above the curve of her mound. Robe of sheer white shimmer-silk over it all, narrow at the waist, flowing skirts playing hide-and-seek with her legs and lower body, the open-cut torso tempting the eye with the obscured curve of her breasts. Diaphanous cloak, sheer, a hint of substance revealing more than it concealed but adding to the layers, to the depth, to the mystery.

The last touch, a finger-dab of pheromones from two separate bottles, one formulated to spark lust in men, the other in women. She set the last bottle down and stood back from the mirror.

She did not recognize herself. The metamorphosis was complete.

And now the Winter Goddess smiled. That wasn't Hinano Kesada in the mirror. It was Lovianis, the ancient goddess of pain and ice, the chilling beauty who tormented men's souls. She had been gone a long time from this place. Too long.

It was time to make her presence known.

# 46

"WHERE IN THE seven icy hells does she think she's going?!" Helda exclaimed.

Kes had spun on her heel and walked out of the room, the last glimpse in the monitor showing her turning right, down the hall that led to the Mix lounge and other public areas of Tryst.

Pol responded with a touch of the controls that switched the view to the hallway. Kes was at the end of it already, her long-legged strides touched with purpose, her gauzy cloak billowing behind in the air of her passage. He cut the view again.

She strode tall and imposing into the lounge where clients and shigasu amused themselves with intoxicants and piquant conversation. A hush fell over the room, and one man spilled his drink as he reacted in surprise. "It's the Goddess!" he exclaimed, his voice small on the lowered audio. "She's back!" The room burst into a hubbub that carried even through the half-muted console.

Without waiting for admirers and sycophants to pay court to her, the Winter Goddess deigned to give the audience a nod, then strode across the room towards the alcove that joined the entrance hall. A moment later, Pol's entry spyeyes showed her stepping outside of Tryst and on to the crowded public walkway of the Shelieno.

"Juro take her!" Helda leapt to her feet. "The Winter Goddess is never seen in public like that! Only on the net! Only on the vids! She'll ruin the illusion!"

Pol shook his head and pointed to the outside monitor. Traffic was stopping in the narrow street, and passersby, at first startled, clamored after the long-unseen celebrity suddenly in their midst. Clients, Enclave day-shoppers, and even shigasu from other houses crossed the street to see the archetypal domina in person, to be up close, and boast later that they'd walked the promenade with the Winter Goddess that day.

"I think she's maintaining the illusion just fine," Pol said.

A growing crowd fell back before her, and followed her down the street as Helda cursed and stormed from the room.

NO ONE DARED get in Kes's way. She did not present herself casually, as she had in that earlier visit to Morya. Now she was in full-on domina mode, and people stepped out of the path in front of her. Even those bold enough to walk by her side or straggle after stayed more than an arm's length away. She swept past all as if she owned the walkway and the people on it. Even those who might have been unmoved by the Winter Goddess, were they in evidence at all, at least had the common sense to stand clear of a force of nature.

One man, too far gone in raffik to respect the space and energy around her, dared say something rude as she passed by. To her surprise, she didn't need to keep a rein on her temper; scorn was her reaction, not anger, and she felt it viscerally. She spared him only a dismissive sneer as she strode past, and she could tell by the sounds behind her that a hanger-on paused to beat the drunkard to the ground for his effrontery. She allowed herself a tight smile, then, the cruel mirth of the Goddess upon her lips.

Little comments came to her ears: some admiring, some in awe, some confusedly wondering who she was—offworld tourists, no doubt, who didn't watch the kink channels. Was she aristocracy? She seemed more regal, more awe-inspiring than any Lau Sa'adani noble Cassians had ever encountered.

The ignorant were quickly informed who she was by others in the crowd, but she ignored those murmurs as she continued her progress. She moved past tea shops and sensoria, past a dance house, a massage spa, a storefront full of sex toys and lingerie. At a corner raffik bar she turned right and moved on towards the joyhouse neighborhood of the Shelieno. Ahead, at mid-block, she saw the broad portico of the Salon, its faie-wood door panels glowing gold in the warm afternoon sunlight. Before she drew near, a well-dressed man coming from that direction paused on the walk ahead of her. He stepped aside as she came closer, then dared to fall in with her and briefly walked in her direction.

"I'm honored to see you today, Domna," he said respectfully. "Are you still receiving visitors at Tryst?"

No business. Not today, and not on the street. She did not slow her pace, but looked directly at the man's earnest visage.

Ah. A former client. She didn't remember his name, but she knew his face.

She inclined her head in a shallow nod. "Certain visitors, yes. Are you asking to be allowed into my presence again?"

"Yes. It's just . . . you've been gone so long. They wouldn't say when you'd see supplicants again."

"Because I hadn't told them. But you, I'll see." She stopped, put a long-fingered hand out to his face, grasped his chin as she looked into his eyes. Yes, he was smitten. Others surrounded their conversation, heard every word of it, but she treated him as if they were the only two on the sidewalk, and so, for that moment, it seemed to be.

"I recall you were particularly . . . devoted, were you not?"

"Oh, yes, Domna!"

She nodded, as if recalling the details of their encounter. "When you make your request to see me, tell them to notate I met you on the street."

"Yes, certainly, Domna. Are you receiving tomorrow, perhaps?"

She paused, his face still in her hands. She'd have to do it again sometime. Filling up her time until Janus came back. She released his chin and nodded. "Yes. Tomorrow. After dark."

He bowed as she swept on down the walkway.

The star-struck left her only at the steps of the Salon, breaking into clusters that did not quite dare follow her into the joyhouse. Some drifted off; others showed every sign of staying until they saw her come out again.

She turned her back to them all and went inside.

KES STEPPED INTO the lounge and saw Taylee, hostess at this hour, glance up with her reflexive greeting smile in place. The petite woman's eyes widened in astonishment at the vidvert apparition approaching her table. She'd worked with Kes, seen Kes, a thousand times before. Never like this, though. Not in person.

The domina was unrecognizable as the joygirl that had been. Makeup as mask, carriage as dominance—if Taylee hadn't known they were the same person, she might have been as awestruck as the tourists on the street.

Armor, Kes reflected. It's all about wearing armor. And it feels even better here than it does in my own playroom.

She strode across the floss carpet, the murmur of joygirls and clients falling silent at her progress. Men looked away from their companions, sitting intimately close over drinks and narco sticks, and tracked her progress across the room. She recognized the looks on their faces and smiled behind her ice-goddess façade. They probably couldn't afford her prices, but they'd remember her. Talk about her.

Free advertising doesn't hurt, either, she thought. I'm back, and everyone can know it.

"Where's my girl?" she asked Taylee, whose mouth snapped shut at the question.

"Er . . . she's not available, Kes, I'm sorry."

Something in the woman's voice made her pause. "What? Did her hours change or something?"

Taylee raised a shoulder in a half-hearted shrug. "Or something."

Kes leaned on the table, intruding on Taylee's space, and one hand darted out to wrap around the woman's wrist, pull her half across the small space towards the domina. Her voice was low, pitched only for the hostess's ears. "Suppose you tell me what you're not telling me."

Taylee's mouth worked soundlessly for a moment, then she gave a curt nod. "I'm sorry, Kes, but she didn't really have a choice. She's not working the floor anymore and doesn't have free hours like she used to. When you used to visit."

"Why?"

"She's with Gistano now. His lover."

"What!" Her word was sharp, loud. It rang through the room as she spun on her heel and marched for the back stairs.

"Don't!" Taylee cried after her. "She couldn't help it. She's *matami*."

Matami. A shigasue word for a mistress elevated from the women of a house. The word and Taylee's babbled explanations fell away behind Kes, even while the meaning of it sank in. Matami were hand-picked, strictly a matter of personal choice by the house master or mistress. Some might seduce their way into that position, but usually a matami was simply a favorite for a time. Next year, next month, the favorite would be replaced by someone else.

Morya would never angle for that. It was Gistano's work, pulling her from the floor roster, sequestering her away. . . .

Kes shook her head in angry denial. Not again. He won't take any more away from me.

She took the stairs two at a time. No Icechromers in sight. Good. It was too long before the busy evening hours for house security to be in evidence. She blew right past Dosan Kiyo's door. Maybe this could be talked out . . . but she didn't want to talk it out. With impulsive decisiveness, she knew exactly what she wanted.

She threw open the door to Gistano's office, and wasn't disappointed in what she found. The Icechromer boss sat on a floatcouch in the corner of his sanctum, centerpiece of an informal conversation nook for guests and visitors. Morphchairs, cushions, plush carpet, table with glassware and enticing snacks—she took it in at a glance. As she did Morya, mixing drinks at the sidebar.

Kes came to a halt, trembling with anger.

Morya's head turned at the intrusion. She gasped and dropped the glass she held, spilling something blue and frothy that would stain the carpet. Her empty hands flew to her mouth.

Gistano's heavy brows drew together, a sneer evident in his voice. "What an unpleasant surprise. Given up on knocking, have you? Well. You can go now." He gave a nod over her shoulder. Kes spun to her right and came face to face with Franc, standing inches away.

He was startled at the abruptness of her maneuver. It took him off guard for a moment—the only moment she needed. Without conscious thought, her hand shot out and closed around his throat. "Now's not the time, Franc," she bit out.

Their eyes locked. Unflapped, the Icechromer reached up to yank her hand away, scorn and defiance in his gaze. Kes stiffened her fingers, flexed against the tension just so—and five synthsteel claws shot out of the ends of her fingernails, slicing into Franc's throat, securing her grip where she held him.

His eyes widened. His hands flew to his neck, flailing at the death grip she had on him. "Jerk my hand away, it'll take your throat with it," she hissed at him. He hesitated, gasping, air wheezing where one claw punctured the side of his windpipe. She felt the panicked pulse of his carotid artery throbbing against one finger. One slash, one twist of a claw, and he'd be dead in moments.

And then . . . and then she'd have a dead body to deal with, and the wrong kind of attention drawn to her actions. And still not what she was here for.

"Morya," she said over her shoulder, her voice eerily calm. "Come here."

Her girl glanced at Gistano, hesitated for only a moment, then came to her side.

Kes looked to the Icechromer boss, half poised to confront her, his disdain turned to anger, a calculating look on his face. He wore bionic enhancements, she knew, and some of them were weapons systems. He could probably kill her right this instant if he wanted to.

She didn't care.

"It's over with Morya," she told him.

"It's not your business."

"It's over. I'll buy her contract. Helda and Kiyo can work out the details."

"Why should I let you?"

She curled a lip and gave her hand a shake, dropping Franc to his knees. "It'll save you problems like this."

As swiftly as she'd sunk them in, she retracted her claws and released her grip, pushing the 'Chromer back as she did so. The man toppled over, hands to his damaged throat, wheezing, coughing, bleeding on Gistano's pristine ivory carpet.

Kes leaned over, wiped the blood from her fingers on his trousers. Then she turned back to Morya, who stood pale and still before her. She took Morya's hand, which fit unresisting in her grip. "We're leaving."

It was all she said. Then she led the way out the door, down the hall, down the stairs, retracing her steps to the front entrance. She would leave the same way she'd come in, not slinking over the rooftops like an in-house guest, but as her own person, in her own way, with Morya by her side, and damn anyone who tried to stop her.

No one tried to stop her. Morya paused when they passed the door to the joygirls' rooms. Kes could read her thoughts. "We'll send for your things. Out, now."

Kes moved with a presence greater than her own. Taylee hushed before it; Berin stood aside for it; hangers-on at the foot of the front steps made way for it. The only person who did not was Helda, forging a path down the walkway in belated but continuing pursuit of her wayward dominatrix, arriving now at the Salon just as Kes and Morya were leaving it.

Helda forgot her rehearsed lecture as her anger turned to consternation. "What—?"

Kes jerked her chin towards the joyhouse. "You'll want to fix that."

"Fix what?"

Kes raised her hand, Morya's fingers entwined with her own.

"She's living with us now. You'll want to work that out with Kiyo. I'll buy her contract."

Helda sputtered.

"And I'd avoid Gistano for now if I were you."

The Winter Goddess marched away, a dark-haired beauty in tow, and no one got in her way.

# 47

"I WANT TO see Morya."

"It's not going to happen, Kesi," said her twin, stern but understanding. "You have to let it go."

"I don't want to." Her tone was the next thing to a pout. "She must wonder where I've been all this time."

Kesada shot her an undecipherable look. "I think about that, too, but it doesn't help to dwell on it. We have more urgent things to deal with right now."

"Are we interrupting?" Dr. Metmuri asked, walking in on their conversation. He was followed by Ferris, then Terel bearing a net full of groceries and sundries.

Who knew how much he'd heard, Kesada thought. Though he wasn't eavesdropping on purpose; they were all cheek by jowl in the small, interconnected suite of rooms they'd taken in a cheap tourist hostel, and voices carried.

It wasn't an ideal place to stay, she thought, but it would do in a pinch. They needed to go to ground quickly, where their arrival would be unremarked: someplace with basic amenities and a safe place to talk. Arriving at Port Oswin, they'd left their stolen survey vehicle at the main Cutter Dome mag tube station, the one that connected with Lyndir's world-spanning GTN, the global transit network. It might mislead pursuers into thinking they'd hopped a quick bullet car to some distant city, avoiding the more traceable air travel alternatives.

Metmuri and Terel both dug deep into their personal funds at the station's automated money changers, swapping electronic creds on their credmeters for the plas chits that served as cash for small expenses. For the near future, at least, the last time their credmeters registered in the datasphere would be at those money changers, the better to aid their GTN smoke screen. Now the fugitives had to rely on the small fortune in chits they'd cashed out, emptying two automats in the process, and using a third to complete the dump.

"It'll get us by for a while," Terel said, packing triangular rolls of ten-cred chits methodically into the bottom of a travel bag. There was no need to state the obvious: if they paid cash everywhere, never producing credmeters for ordinary transactions, that in itself would eventually bring suspicion down upon them. Only backstreeters and fences worked exclusively in chits. Kesada liked to think they hadn't sunk quite that low yet, but Metmuri refused to risk any automated transactions for now. "Not until Prevak can help us," he said. "It makes us too easy to find."

"Who's Prevak?" Kesi asked, but the scientist mumbled only, "Later." He and the others were preoccupied with three large satchels full of tens of thousands of creds in chits: more cash money in one place than any of them had seen in their entire lifetimes. Kesada knew it didn't amount to all that much on the grand scale of things, but it felt like an illicit fortune and she was uncomfortable carting it around.

They didn't have far to haul the stash, however. Kesi recalled a tourist hostel from travel verts, a modest, quaint old structure in the Old Town district of Oswin Dome. The Commander's Rest was a reconstruction of a berm shelter from the earliest days of colony settlement. Cramped, warren-like, and lacking most services, it was cheap and centrally located. One of the amenities it was happily missing was comprehensive security surveillance. "No routine scans of hallway traffic," Kesada observed to Metmuri. "That means our faces won't be randomly cycled through city security systems."

The doctor grunted his agreement with the choice. As long as they were cautious about their movements and stayed indoors as much as possible, the Commander's Rest could be a relatively safe haven while they figured out their options.

They'd taken two taxis from the station to the hostel. Metmuri traveled with the twins, packed in with various travel cases salvaged from their flight in the original hauler. He kept one of the money bags as well, entrusting Terel and Ferris with the others. The clutter was more eye-catching, removed from the cargo boot of the survey car and packed into the passenger compartment of the cab. Kesi took it in with a sharp eye. "Given our circumstances, you're not traveling very light, Doctor."

The man blushed, stammered something about "essentials," and let their conversation taper off, for the magstation taxi was a tourist conveyance, and so had a human driver ready to answer questions and overhear his passengers as well. The short journey passed in relative silence, during which Metmuri sucked on a pink lozenge, and the twins looked out over the city as if they'd never seen it before. Indeed, from this perspective, they never had.

Ferris rented the rooms, her native Tion accent bolstering the fiction that they were offworld travelers. Terel went out briefly for food, returning with an assortment of meals in hotpacks, self-heating when the seal was broken. The group gathered in the twins' room—the largest of the three—and fished through the varieties of brightly colored and labeled containers. Terel produced a ten-pack of Phizz from his shopping net as well, and the refugees settled into the food, savoring the first real meal and break they'd had since their tense hours of flight had begun.

"Ah." Esimir leaned back, a contented smile on his face. "Rather crude, but surprisingly tasty. Thank you, Terel."

"Sir."

Kesi curled up in an armchair, legs tucked beneath her, looking ready for a nap after her meal. Terel puttered the mess away, and Ferris sorted through the grooming kits and other necessaries they'd picked up, sharing them out in growing piles on the table before them.

"So how's Prevak supposed to help us?" Kesada tossed out casually.

Ferris's hand paused before setting down a tube of shampoo. Terel's brow furrowed. Metmuri continued to study the cracked ceiling tiles from his half-reclining position on the couch.

"What do you know about AI systems, Hinano Kesada?" He spoke into the air, equally casually, addressing them both with the one name.

The twins exchanged glances; Kesada replied. "Isn't it time to drop the evasions?"

"Not evading." Esimir angled his gaze down and across to the fair-skinned, tousle-haired blonde sitting opposite him. "Seriously. What do you know about AIs? That will tell me how much detail I need to get into."

Kesada's brow creased, thoughts switching gears. "I'm rigged. Or was." Her hand brushed the nape of her neck, felt nothing where there should have been the soft plas divot of a direct neural interface jack. "I've had basic training on ships' AI systems, as part of my astrogation courses. It gets fairly technical."

"Ah, that's right. You're not certified, I recall."

"I've done everything short of the test."

He nodded to himself. "Then you know how pervasive AI subsystems are in critical functions—not just in discrete systems like ships, but in data clouds and bubble networks everywhere. They control the nexus points in the data- and infospheres; that's probably their most public use. The most sensitive is in financial and security systems. In-house entities, usually."

The twins nodded.

"And they're so routine, they don't draw much attention these days."

"Why would they?"

Esimir leaned his head to one side, looking quizzical. "Yes, why would we worry about AIs? They're a known quantity, well integrated into our systems, strictly contained and regulated. Just a tool we've grown accustomed to—which is why Prevak will be able to help us. No one will expect his kind of intervention."

Terel grunted a muffled exclamation. Esimir ignored him and looked from twin to twin. "Prevak is an AI, you see. But not just any AI. He's . . . extraordinary."

"Sir," Terel spoke in hushed tones. "Do you think we should be talking—"

"—about a project that has effectively been taken away from us, and turned to ends we never intended for it? Yes, I do." Esimir turned back to the clones.

"Prevak was my mentor and friend. He invented the splintegration process and died unexpectedly. When he died, well . . . the AI has his personality. It was necessary, to have the internal mind of our project think like Prevak even after his death."

"What good does that do us?" Kesada asked pointedly. "An AI, left behind in a secure facility. You can't even get in touch with it."

"Him." Esimir corrected her automatically, staring off into the distance. "If we can get him out of the research station, he can help us. He can interface with other systems in, um, unusual ways."

"Unusual enough to throw the Navy and Ilanya off our tracks?"

Metmuri opened his mouth as if to say more, but halted himself. "Yes," he replied simply, confining himself to the one word.

Terel and Ferris exchanged a glance with each other and sat as attentively as the twins. "Like you said, Doctor," Terel ventured, "Prevak's inside RS 207. We're not."

"Now that's the interesting thing." Metmuri leaned forward, elbows on knees, fingers steepled as he spoke. "We don't need to move him physically. All we need to do is give him a way out. Poke a hole in the cybersecurity of the station, and Prevak will do the rest."

"I don't understand," Kesi grumbled. "Do what?"

"Why, escape, my girl." Metmuri blinked owlishly at her. "Once he's out of there, he'll help us. He promised me."

Kesada shook her head in disbelief. "You're saying you made a deal with an AI? Spring it, and it helps you?"

"Him. I made a deal with Prevak, yes."

She shook her head again. "This sounds crazy. I'm not saying it's not possible, but it sounds crazy." She looked over to Ferris. "What do you think about this?"

Ferris looked startled. "Me? I . . . I think, if the Doctor says Prevak will help, then he'll help."

Kesada fixed Terel with her gaze next. "You?"

His lips thinned, unhappy at being addressed in this manner. Still, he shrugged and looked to Metmuri. "I trust the doctor," he announced to the room at large.

Metmuri quirked a half smile. "It's quite simple," he said. "The AI remembers me as the friend I was to Prevak Rohar in life. He wants to assist me in these unhappily altered circumstances. So we struck a bargain. It's not a difficult thing to understand." He looked around the table. "What's going to be difficult is breaching station security long enough for Prevak to find his own way out."

Kesada shook her head. "I don't even want to know how you think he's going to do that. But back at the jungle waystation, you said something about needing a cyberdecker."

Metmuri nodded eagerly. "That's the only way this can be done. We need a netrunner. A good one. No—better than good. A truly superior one." He smiled at the twins. "That's where you come in."

Kesi laughed, a short trill of mockery. "You know we trained for astrogation, not netrunning, right? Big difference, Doc."

"Obviously." He was short with the word, and addressed himself to Kesada. "You've associated with a, shall we say, mixed class of people for the last few years. All manner of riffraff come and go in the Shelieno—pardon me. I don't mean you, certainly. But some of the people you've dealt with—well. You must know netrunners. I need you to find a good one for us."

Kesada stared at him a moment, then chuckled, a sound less mocking but more ironic than her twin's. "You think we know netrunners? That's a good one. Might as well just put an ad on the net, Doc. You'll find one quicker."

The smile faded from his face. "But . . . you work in the Enclave."

"The licensed *entertainment* district, yes. What, you think we're like derevin, with gray-market connections? Surely you're acquainted with the shigasue, Doctor, a high-caste gentleman like yourself?"

"Surely you've been to the district in Tion?" Kesi added. "I gather that's where you're from. They have a wonderful Enclave there. Not to be missed."

Esimir blushed. The truth was, he'd never been to the Between-World of the shigasue in his life. Wanted to go; entertained the fantasy; but never had time or the courage to give it a try. And if he went, he knew he'd be more interested in the benko girls, the shigasu-in-training, than the mature entertainers themselves. And that might raise questions. . . .

Flustered, he looked from face to face around the table, his brow creased now with worry. "Do you mean to tell me you have no connection to deckers at all?"

The twins shook their heads.

"Surely among the Icechromers you formerly worked with?"

Their looks turned sour.

"Don't know any freelancers?" he pleaded.

Head shakes.

"Anyone jacked for VR, even?" He sounded hopeless as he looked at each of the twins. "I . . . I assumed because you work as you do, well, you know, that you, you—"

"Hang out with riffraff? People doing things not quite legal?" Kesi retorted. "You don't know a hell of a lot, do you?"

Terel bristled as Kesada put a calming hand on Kesi's arm. Her thoughts were racing.

"Wait. Maybe we do know someone." She said it slowly, tentatively. "I don't think he's what you're looking for. But he would know who to refer us to, I think. That is," she corrected herself, "I don't know about us, but he'd give the Winter Goddess anything she wants."

Kesi sat up, her eyes searching her twin's face. "A client? Who?"

"You know." Kesada waved her fingers as if to conjure his image out of the air. "That boy. Well, young man. Very young man. So much money, so smitten with the Winter Goddess. Peculiar tastes. The one with the sensie-feelie jacks."

The memory was coming to Kesi as well. "Ohhh," she breathed. "You mean SeF Boy. The one who wanted to do a sense recording of his cock-and-ball torture." She giggled.

Ferris coughed; Metmuri blushed bright red; Terel's face registered disapproval. "What's the matter?" Kesi shot him a glance. "Some men really like it. When it's done right, it heightens orgasm, too. You should try it some time." She turned back to her twin, ignoring the sputtering across the table. "He's the one. Big on net-crawling. Records and uplinks every little thing."

"And we could never let him, because of the recording rights issue with the House—but every time, he'd beg so very nicely." A slow smile stretched her lips.

"Riiiiight. He was all jacked out like a decker, all kinds of ports and plugs. Fashion statement."

Kesada nodded. "He follows netrunner culture obsessively, and he's devoted to us. Well, Her, anyway. But I think we could fake it."

"You might have something there."

The doctor had found his tongue again. "And this young man—you know how to find him?"

Kesada paused. "That could be a problem. The client records are all at Tryst. And we can't go there, you say."

Metmuri looked puzzled. "You don't recall your clients' names?"

Kesi rolled her eyes. "Honestly, Doc? You go through sixty or more a month and see how many you keep straight. After a while most of them run together. There are a few types you see repeatedly, though, and some individuals stand out."

"We give them nicknames for easy reference," Kesada interjected. "That, I can remember. Like SeF Boy."

Kesi nudged her twin's arm. "Hey. He told me his net name, once. Told us. In the heat of things. What was it? Do you remember?"

Kesada looked blank.

"It was an unusual nick," Kesi went on. "I remember thinking it had to be real. Netboys pick their names with such care."

"Ahhhh." The memory surfaced at the same time and lit up both their faces. They turned to Metmuri as one. "FlashMan."

"All right," said Kesi. "We'll give him a try. He's a fan-boy. I'm sure he'll know where to find the kind of decker you need."

Metmuri blinked in happy surprise. "Well! Well, then. Thank you." He rubbed his hands together. "And the sooner you move on this, the sooner we'll all be safe. When can you contact him?"

"We have to find his com code, first," answered Kesada. "But we can start looking for that right now."

"This will be fun." Kesi giggled. "I want to see the look on his face when he hears from his idol. Ha."

Kesada cocked an eyebrow. "Yeah, about that. Let's have a word."

# 48

MORYA HAD NEVER been to Tryst before, and towed in Kes's whirlwind wake, she still had little sense of it. A Mix lounge, music, curious faces turning their way and just as quickly left behind. A hall full of mood lighting and sublims, a polychrome archway obscured by a shimmer screen. Interwoven in that portal, fleeting images of fetishwear-clad women in commanding poses—Kes hesitated there only a moment before pulling Morya on down the hallway, past dressing rooms and service areas, up the back stairs, and into the quiet realm of the women's personal quarters.

Kes thrust Morya before her into her room and slid the door shut behind them. Morya took a step, another, seeing but not noticing the spartan adornments of this place: crystal flowers, a calligraphy wall hanging, bed, sitting room, wall desk—her circuit turned her about to face Kes again, and she took a good long step back from the dominant before her.

The Winter Goddess stood just inside the door and leaned against it, hands behind her as if to secure it shut that way. Her chest was heaving with the rapidness of her breath, like a runner just finishing a sprint, red lips slightly parted, pale face framed by white tresses.

Morya's heart twinged. Kes was heartbreakingly beautiful. And Morya was furious with her.

"Why?" She forced the words out. "Why did you do that? After all this time?"

Her voice trembled with anger and tears, and she cursed herself for it. *Don't lose it, don't lose it with her,* the mantra ran through the back of her mind. *Stay cool, distant, figure this out.*

Kes's fine white brows pinched together and her head angled slightly to the side, as if she had a hard time understanding the joygirl. Morya waved an arm, gesturing vaguely to the hall, the front of the house, to the Salon that lay beyond.

"That's my life, Kes." Her tone cut like a razor. She heard it, and hated it, and went on anyway. "You can't walk out on me like that, and then just walk back in. We're over. You made that clear."

Morya wanted to hold Kes. Wanted to hit her. She stood her ground instead, and marshaled herself to stand tall and lock eyes with her dominant ex-lover.

"Walk out?" Scowl and disbelief warred on Kes's face. "That's crazy. You're mine."

Morya's heart twinged again, sadness jostling with muffled joy. What she wouldn't have given to have heard those words two months ago. But it was too late now; she'd taken that part of herself and buried it in a dark corner, and now here was Kes trying to drag it into the daylight again.

"No!" It was denial, not rejection, but let Kes read it how she would. Morya raised both hands as if to hold her at bay. "We're past that now."

The pale, statuesque domina took one step forward. "It doesn't matter what happened over there." Her tone was self-assured, certain. She tossed her hair back over her shoulder. "You couldn't help it if he made you matami. We'll just forget about that. I know you don't want to be there, and I don't want you to be, either."

Morya dropped her hands, retreated back a step from Kes's advance. She shook her head, dark curls tumbling. "No," she said again, sharply. "It wasn't just his choice. You abandoned me. I did what I needed to do."

Kes recoiled as the meaning of those words sank in. "You did what?" she cried. "Out of *choice*?!" Disbelief dripped from the words, and something else: anger.

Morya hated it as she said it. It was true—sadly true, hatefully true. Kes was going to see her again, to ask something important, she'd said—and then she hadn't, and all the Shelieno knew that she was gone. Just that: gone. Offworld with a client, some said. Bought her contract and left, others whispered. No matter the details: there was simply no word, no hope, no more Kes. It was just Morya on her own again, in a place with companions but no friends, and certainly no lover.

When Gistano tired of Taylee, Morya had seen her opportunity. It was a better life—easier for a while, anyway—and better pay than the work she did with clients. That meant a shorter contract time, and she didn't have to excuse that to anyone. Especially not to this one, staring her down, coming closer—

"I had to look out for myself," she blurted, raising her hands again to fend off Kes's approach.

To no avail. Her ex-lover was on her, strong slender fingers wrapped around her wrists, nails like splashes of blood against her skin. Kes's advance pushed her up against the far wall beside the bed.

"How could you betray me like that?" she hissed.

Confusion washed over Morya. Betray? "I didn't—"

"You couldn't wait? I told you I'd be back."

"You did not," she spat. Anger and passion shadowed the face so close to her own. Morya wanted to kiss Kes, wanted to push her away. "You just left. All this time with no word? What was I supposed to think?" She twisted about, trying to win free of Kes's iron grip.

"You're crazy," the domina grunted, pushing her back, pinning her to the wall again. "I told you. I sent word."

"Well, I never got it," Morya growled. "If I'd heard from you, you think I'd have given up on you?"

Kes froze in place, a war of emotions on her face. Morya read her lover well, but she couldn't read this: too many expressions flooded past, subtle, hidden behind the stylized makeup of the Winter Goddess. Morya's hands were forced up and back, pressed to the wall by her head as Kes leaned into her, kohl-rimmed eyes and dark jeweled lids riveting her gaze.

"I'm going to kill her," Kes hissed, "and then I'm going to kill him. And you, I'm keeping where I can keep you safe."

Morya couldn't even blink, she was so astonished. *Keep me safe?* Her lips parted, mouth half ready to say something, anything—

Kes's left hand let go her wrist, and she pressed her index finger to Morya's lips to silence her. "No more. I don't want to fight you." Her right hand released the other wrist, grabbed her hair behind the nape of her neck. Kes bent her head back, so close Morya felt her breath when she spoke. "I love you, dammit. Now just shut up and be with me."

Her body pressed tight against Morya's as her lips sealed her mouth, hungry and insistent. Morya, speechless, long-buried desire flaming to life, surrendered to her touch.

# 49

"I COULD *TOO* dom SeF Boy!" Kesi insisted, planting her hands on her hips. "I've seen him often enough at Tryst."

Kesada shook her head. "Do you know what you sound like?" she asked dryly. "What?"

"Don't sulk about this, but you're like a petulant child. You demand. You whine. And if you don't get your way, you stomp your foot and pout."

Kesi crossed her arms on her chest and sputtered. "I'm . . . I'm not *petulant!*" Then she felt her face heat suddenly with an uncontrollable blush. She'd been about to stamp her foot for emphasis, and suppressed the reflex action only with an effort.

She clenched a fist instead and waved it at Kesada.

"Oooooo—you! You make me so mad sometimes." Her scowl was as fierce as she could make it without pouting—a tactic it was painfully obvious had no effect on her cool, calculating twin.

"Hm." Kesada glanced over her shoulder. Terel and Ferris loitered outside the public com kiosk they'd chosen for their call to SeF Boy. She gestured her twin inside, where their conversation could not be so easily overheard.

"And that's another thing," she continued as Kesi shut the door. "Why are you so emotional?"

"Why are you so unfeeling?" Kesi shot back.

Kesada waved a hand dismissively. "That's not an attack," she said seriously. "I mean it. If we're clones, why is our emotional makeup so different? Surely you've noticed it, too?"

Kesi bit her lip, then sat beside her twin. As mercurial as Kesada was focused, her mood shifted to one of worried reflection.

"It has to be something they did to us. The doctor said we weren't psychologically identical. This must be part of it. I remember being, well, more serious, like you." She glanced at her clone sideways. "Is it the same with you?"

Kesada nodded. "I remember being more light-minded—"

"Hey!"

"—light-hearted, then. And temperamental. But it's like watching a flat vid. You see it, but you don't feel it, much."

The pair exchanged a long and searching look.

"Do you think we're going to get the truth out of Metmuri?"

Kesada shook her head slowly.

"Then I think we need to find our own answers."

"We could just let it go," Kesada said slowly. "It's not like we're damaged. We're just—different than before."

"Don't you think it's a handicap?"

"How so?"

Kesi shrugged. "It's hard for me to concentrate. Hard for you to have a light spirit—you're so damned serious. You haven't smiled once since we found each other."

Kesada's brow furrowed, thinking. "You're right. I hadn't noticed."

Kesi nodded to herself. "Well, I can think of two people who must know what they really did to us. One, we're hiding from. The other, Metmuri's trying to keep us away from."

"Our Prime."

"Yes. The original Kes. Think she'll tell us what she knows?"

Kesada looked thoughtful. "Would you?"

"Yes. You?"

She dipped her chin in response.

"Then I think we need to find her and get some answers."

Kesada ran a finger along the com panel rim. "It's dangerous for us to go there. He's right about that."

"I'm not going to give up on this. We can figure something out."

Kesada studied her face. "You mean that."

Kesi nodded.

Kesada reached a hand out and touched her twin's cheek. "Some things haven't changed, then. You're just as stubborn as me." A slow smile bloomed on her face, mirrored by the expression on Kesi's, who suddenly poked her with a finger. "Hey. First smile."

"Hm." Kesada touched her own face as the smile faded. "First time for everything, I guess." She turned abruptly to face the booth's com panel. "And time we found our little playmate." She glanced at the door. "Seal it," she said peremptorily, all business now. "And don't forget: not a word from you. He doesn't need to hear two of us on this end."

Kesi raised her hands in surrender. "I'm convinced. You've shown you can sound a lot more like our verts than I do. He'll respond to that tone of voice."

"You better believe it," Kesada agreed as she accessed the com net.

**FLASHMAN WAS FINISHING** a systems check when a brazen siren whooped through his virtual workspace. It wasn't too loud—no need to panic himself with his tailored alarms—but attention-grabbing as all hell. He jabbed it silent with the poke of a finger.

"Hark," he announced dramatically. "Someone knocketh upon my public cyber-door. And they invoketh the Man of Flash, and they better not be those sim-kiddies, or I shall destroy their decks and bring all around them to ruin. Again."

He jumped to the post office construct that was his public door on the net and walked up to the counter from the clerk's side. He pushed stacks of quaint paper envelopes and return receipts out of the way before opening the shuttered service window there. He looked out upon—

Nothing. A gray nothingness in the generic human silhouette that meant "vid signal denied" from the caller's end.

"For shame," the lightning-shaped decker said to his "customer." "That's just rude. Come back when I can see you." He started to swing the shutter back in place, when a voice he knew all too well thrilled him to his core.

"I think not."

The voice was sultry and hard-edged. He knew it from verts, from the endless playbacks he jerked off to, from the sixteen sessions he'd splurged on so he could worship this Goddess in person.

It was Her.

He couldn't muster a sound. His sim-form didn't show his human mouth gaping open, literally, in astonishment. FlashMan was uncomfortably aware of his physical reaction to his personal wet dream, here, in the oh-so-intimate closeness of his cyberdeck. He rearranged himself on the padded decker couch where his body half-reclined, mind scrambling madly for the appropriate response to Her in his virtual home.

"I—You—Mistress! You're here!" What was the etiquette for this? He wasn't in Her playroom, those rules didn't apply. What was a decker to do when the Divine made a house call?

"I'm glad I found you," She said from the void that was Her incognito. "I need your assistance. Are you willing to help Me?"

"Me? Yes, of course. But what can I possibly do for You, Domna?"

He drew himself up, an attentive little lightning figure, behind the post office counter. No, no, that wouldn't do. He vanished the setting with a thought, leaving himself and the dark avatar of the Goddess face-to-face on a vast floor that stretched into the distance in all directions.

"I need to hire a netrunner," She said, "but I know little about that world. I thought, who could help Me find the specialized talent I need urgently right now? And so I thought of you."

"Me?" It came out like a squeak. Surely She couldn't have known—

"You're active in the SeF community," the Winter Goddess continued, "and the decker world, too, I assume. I know there's an overlap. And as for you . . . I think we've developed a special relationship, you and I. Wouldn't you say so?"

Her voice caressed and chilled him. His heart gave a leap in his chest, both physical and sim.

"Oh, yes, Mistress."

"You're better situated than I am to find what I need quickly. Will you do that for Me?"

"Ahh . . ." She thought he was just an info source. Hmph. "You need a netrunner, Mistress?" He cleared his throat. "Maybe I can be more help than You know. What is it, exactly, that You need done?"

She was silent for a moment, then spoke cautiously. "I can share the details only with the one I hire. I need someone who can breach security. Someone trustworthy and exceptionally skilled, and able to work immediately."

Wheels turned over in FlashMan's mind. "Is this a paid job?"

"Of course. Some cash up front; the rest in creds upon completion."

No need to ask if She was good for it. He sketched a bow. "I think You've found Your man, Goddess. I'm not just a decker. I'm a netrunner as well."

"You?"

Was that surprise, or disbelief in her voice? He couldn't help puffing up as he defended his credentials. "I'm the best damned netrunner in the subsector, Domna, if I do say so myself. Maybe even the sector."

"And if I ask elsewhere about FlashMan?"

"You'll hear the same story. It's not a boast."

"Ah." He could feel Her energy concentrated on him through the static void of Her silhouette. "I always thought there was something exceptional about you." Her praise riveted him; warmed him. "And you can start right away?"

He barely hesitated. "Yes, Goddess."

"Don't you want to hear the details first?"

"I'll need them to do the job, but it won't affect my decision. Whenever You're ready."

"Good boy. There is a man who'll brief you on what I need. His name is Esimir. You'll need to work with him on this project." FlashMan stifled a surge of jealousy as She transmitted a com code to him. "You'll need to add security to this line."

"Consider it done. I'll call him right away."

"One more thing. I don't want you contacting Me about this. This has to stay outside Tryst. I'll reach you when I want updates. Is that clear?"

"Yes, Domna."

"Excellent. I'll remember this service the next time we're together." He could hear a cold smile in Her voice. "I'm sure I can think of a suitable reward for you."

His stomach twisted with nervous anticipation. "Yes, Mistress." He didn't trust himself to say more.

"Very good, then. When can you start?"

He collected himself and answered with only a heartbeat of hesitation. "Right now, if You like."

"I like. I'll leave you to it, then. Until later."

"Domna."

Her silhouette blinked out of existence, leaving him alone on the floored void of his cyberdeck. For many long seconds he didn't move—and then he whooped and broke into his trademark victory jig, the dance he saved for when he broke past the toughest security codes, or iced the most deadly hunter-killer prowling a system. A celebration like but unlike his tantrum dance, this cavort was joyous and filled the space around him with a dazzling light show emanating from his sim, glowing for the moment like a live filament wire.

The dance came to an end. The pyrotechnics faded. FlashMan caught his breath.

I need to call in sick, he thought. I have work to do.

# 50

KES'S RECENT ANGER at Franc and rage at Helda haunted her memory, but the temper behind those emotions had fled, expended in violent lovemaking with her girl, napping in her arms now in a haze of love bites and tears and reddened skin that spelled delight for them both.

Right now her threats seemed like so much posturing in the heat of the moment. She closed her eyes, tried to track down the thing she was missing, the thing that wouldn't let her rest.

For all the uncertainties she'd dealt with in the last few years, rarely had Kes second-guessed herself. She made sound decisions. She trusted her own judgment. She made pretty good progress by doing so, too.

Now, though—she couldn't let on to anyone, but she questioned her own resolve. Her instincts, her sense of purpose, all seemed a shambles. She looked at the beautiful submissive masochist in her arms and thought, The only thing we're lacking is time in the playroom . . . and when I'm there, what will I do with her? Love her? Beat her? Kill her? Will I know when to stop?

*Will* I stop?

I'm not sure I can trust myself. It's like my judgment's all over the place. Something that seems brilliant one moment seems really stupid the next. That thing with Franc. I shouldn't have started that, and once I did, I should've killed him right there. Now he's alive and nursing a grudge, if I know him at all. That wasn't smart, and that's not me. I'm way off my game if I'm doing shit like that.

She stared at the ceiling in the half dark of the room, cross-woven pith fiber forming a pattern of shadows overhead. Her eyes studied it, as if to divine answers there. The maddening thing was, none of it seemed to matter anymore. Possible consequences were as nothing to her. She could entertain any course of action, and they all had equal weight.

I wouldn't mind killing Helda when I'm mad at her. She sets me off with the least little thing. But maybe it wouldn't be smart to kill the Dosan if I want to stay a part of this shigasue life.

Do I want that?

She ran a hand through her tangled hair, tugging it against her scalp, wishing that would drive some clarity into her thoughts.

I used to be certain about all this. Now I don't know if I even want to be here. I don't know what to do.

She looked down at Morya sleeping in the crook of her arm and gave a silent snarl.

I don't want Morya in the Salon ever again. But can I deal with her being *here?*

She stared sleeplessly at the ceiling, finally easing her arm out from under her lover's neck, watching her clasp the pillow closer in her sleep. Kes stood, naked, her body makeup leaving her a white ghost in the half light of the room. She shrugged into her red brocade dressing robe, a firewing dragon in black and red-gold embroidery covering the length of the back. She sat at the wall desk, force of habit nudging her to jack in to her personal node, check her investments, the astrogation reports, her usual routine for quiet time when she wanted to get centered. . . .

She stared at her dark comp, perplexed. She felt no drive towards her favorite pastimes. She glanced over to the bed. Maybe this was big enough, important enough, that everything else faded into triviality by comparison? She tried that explanation on for size. Maybe she could believe that.

There came a scratch at the door, polite query asking entrance. And who might that be?

She padded to the panel, slid it open a crack. Saw Helda on the other side.

Suddenly she remembered why she wanted to kill the woman.

Kes shot through the opening in the door screen, barreling into the Dosan, shoving her across the passage to slam against the wall. She held her there, forearm jammed against her neck.

She should be grateful I'm not using claws, she thought.

"Why didn't you tell Morya?" The words were clipped, each one a knife.

Helda looked confused behind the pain and surprise of the assault. "Why—?" she choked out.

"You didn't give her my message. I told you when I left to let her know I couldn't come see her."

Helda groaned. Kes took it as an admission of guilt. She grabbed the front of her robe and gave her a vicious shake even while she held her pinned. "You hurt her. She thought I'd abandoned her. I'm going to kill you for this, you vost."

It was a foul word, a gutter word for sexual parts reserved for the lowest of prostitutes. It was just a prelude to the places she'd take Helda—no, put Helda, the humiliation and abuse she'd experience before she begged for mercy, to be freed of her miserable existence—

"Kes. No."

The words barely penetrated her fog of rage, but her name came again in a voice she knew and loved.

"Kes. Don't do it. Let her go."

She came back to herself, a long journey made swiftly, homing in on that voice. Morya, talking to her from the doorway at her back. She became aware, then, of other things. Heads poking out of doors to her left. A house slave standing frozen in the hall to her right.

Helda, flushed and frightened in her grip, gasping for air.

Kes came to herself with a shuddering breath. "I don't want her hurt." She loosed her grip on Helda. "It hurt her to be there."

"I didn't put her there," the Dosan said bitterly, massaging her throat. "Gistano did that, like he did with all of you."

Kes took a step back. Hearing the simple truth of it jarred her.

Whatever the Icechromers did for their money, they didn't *need* to trade in indentured paper and the bodies that went along with that. That was Gistano's personal choice, because he liked it.

There were plenty of joyhouses full of free citizens who were there because they liked that work. But Gistano liked unwilling people compelled to obey. He loved it most when he saw them hating it, yet bending to his will anyway. It gave him a hard-on every time, him and his lieutenants alike. It was why he lived at the Salon, when he had his pick of penthouse suites around the city.

One thing she was certain of: she hated the two men who made the calls there, and relished every moment of hating them. Gistano and Franc, who routinely scouted assets for the Salon, targeted the woman they'd squeeze next, and took an intimately personal pleasure in doing so. And Janus, lurking behind it all . . .

Her eyes lit with bloodlust again, and Helda shrank back. Kes shook her head. "Don't worry," she said gruffly. "It's not you I'm after."

"I—I'm sorry," Helda mumbled. "I had a lot on my mind, and I forgot. To tell her, I mean."

Kes turned on her heel, went to her doorway. Morya stood aside for her as the domina spoke back over her shoulder. "Are you working it out so she can stay here?"

"Yes."

"Good. She'll be doing sessions with me now and then." She glanced back at the Dosan. "Any problem with that?"

Helda shook her head. "Whatever you need, you let me know. Kes?"

The domina paused.

"Client tomorrow, late afternoon."

She nodded and closed the door behind her.

Morya stopped her right there, hands on her chest. "Kes, you can't do that. Not for my sake."

"What?"

"Beat people up like that."

"If I'd beaten her up, she wouldn't be walking away right now."

"You know what I mean."

Kes shrugged, started for the desk. Morya stepped in front of her again, and this time it was like contacting an energy field. Kes felt herself grow tense with lust and wild emotion.

"Promise me you won't do that again. Please."

Kes locked eyes with her. "Matters to you, kushla?"

"Yes."

She inclined her head. "Promise doesn't apply to that lot from the Salon."

Morya's eyes flared dark. "That's fine by me."

A tight smile came to Kes's lips, still bloodred and glistening. "Then we're agreed. Come here, my love." She drew her close, and pressed her mouth to Morya's, bit her lip hard as they parted. Morya moaned in pain and pleasure. Kes's eyes looked deep into hers.

"I still want to beat someone. Know any volunteers?"

Her only answer was her girl melting into her arms, hot and willing and wanting the same thing.

# 51

**A HOLOGRAM SHIMMERED** midair over Ilanya Eva's desk, projected from Teo's visor-mounted holocaster. It revealed a red-robed clone with long white hair slamming a shorter woman violently against the wall of a hallway, pinning her there, arm across her throat. The view was foreshortened from the spyfly in the ceiling corner, but the actions were clear enough. As were her actions a short while later, tormenting a black-haired woman to tears in her room.

"That's our girl." Eva gave a small smile. "Glad to see she remains true to form." She tilted her head to one side. "Hard to tell if that's consensual or not, what those two are doing. Looks brutal enough from here."

"From earlier recordings, I would assume that passes for lovemaking between them," Teo offered.

She motioned the hologram off. Her matasai cut the recording and raised the room lights a notch. "No spyeyes in her playroom, you said?"

He shook his head. "Unfortunately. Too risky. They run counter-surveillance heavily in the play spaces: apparently, certain clients try to record their sessions now and then, and sell them to various entertainment nodes. It's in violation of house licensing, so they especially guard against that. Other areas are much easier to infiltrate—as you see."

"Good. At least we can monitor things. Obray tells me Janus is back. When he shows up, we'll know when she's with him. Should be interesting to watch the aftermath of that."

"Yes."

"And when does he see her?"

"Tomorrow."

"Perfect. Everything's on track." Ilanya allowed herself a smile. "Let me know when it's time. We can monitor the site together."

**WHEN COMMANDER OLNIKO** gave Eva a routine update a short while later, she was unhappy with what she heard.

"Overflights show nothing, Domna," he reported. "No sign of a vehicle down. Nothing unusual picked up on mass detection instruments. They must have done as you surmised, flown somewhere unauthorized. We still don't know where."

Ilanya spoke over her shoulder to her matasai. "Issue a planetwide arrest order for everyone unaccounted for."

"Full biometrics?"

"On everyone but the clones. Same reason as before. And, Teo? Amend that order. Clones are armed and dangerous. Orders are shoot to kill."

"Isn't that a bit premature?" asked Olniko.

Ilanya turned back to him. "Not at all. The others we can question. If there's criminal intent at play here, we can determine that at our leisure and deal with it as necessary. But the clones? We can't have remnants of a classified military experiment on the loose. I want them out of play before their existence raises awkward questions. Especially if they're linked to the domina at Tryst."

Olniko bowed his concurrence and called the jungle search teams back to base.

LINING THE STREET directly opposite Tryst was a series of bars and hostess dance clubs, a furor of intoxicants and music that kept partygoers on the street at all hours. Midway along that strip, one man leaned unmoving against the wall between Briyo's Bar and the narrow service window of a spice-noodle vendor. The early evening crowd was already thick in this part of the Shelieno, but no one in the masses jostled against the solitary figure with the synthflesh patches on his throat. They gave him a wide berth instead, sensing he was not one of them, was not there for entertainment or pleasure. And they were right about that.

Franc studied the house of domination across the way. He could walk in, but even if no one recognized him, he wouldn't get past their Mix lounge without a prior appointment or approval by the Dosan. That wouldn't work. Helda would guess why he was there, and that would be the last time he set foot inside.

His eyes ran up the side of the building, one in a block of many, sharing rooftop gardens and the hidden courtyards that were the private world of the shigasue. That was a route no one would expect him to take. The rooftop access pads weren't keyed to his biometrics, but he should be able to overcome such a minor hindrance.

File that away as one way to reach his quarry.

He watched a businessman leave Tryst, then a couple, man and woman, go in. The house's traffic was sparse, compared to less exotic establishments, but it would continue all night, probably. And, once inside, people tended to stay for hours, shelling out big creds for the privilege.

How often do the dominas get out? Franc brooded. That's what I want to know.

He rocked back and forth, heel-toe, heel-toe. If he waited long enough, she would have to come out at some point. In full regalia like before, he probably couldn't touch her. It would be too public, too obvious. But they had days off, didn't they?

He gritted his teeth. It wasn't in his nature to dance attendance on someone else's schedule, not unless that someone was the boss. Sure, it would be easiest if he could catch her out walking, shopping, partying, whatever those ball-breaking bitches did when they weren't playacting the dominant with those sorry saps they called clients. If he could catch that vost on the street, she'd be his the instant he had her down an alley and into a back room somewhere.

And if she didn't come out sometime soon?

He gazed at the rooftop greenery.

There was more than one way to fuck then kill that bitch.

# 52

"**JANUS! WHERE ARE** you?" Sefano let heartiness mask the sound of relief in his voice. At last, at last . . . here was their boy, their soon-to-be sacrifice, reappearing as suddenly as he had disappeared months before. Another of his periodic "business expansion" trips was complete, this one longer than most.

"I'm back in the Lyndir system," came the familiar voice, "and I have excellent news."

The odd tone in his voice gave Sefano pause. "You do?"

The other triumvir laughed out loud. "It's not for open channels, of course. We need to meet for this."

"You mean in person?"

"No, no. Virtual is fine. I've just gotten home, I don't want to go anywhere for a while. Can you and Mika meet me, say, tomorrow, noon my time?"

"I don't know. Our schedules . . ."

"You must." Janus's voice took on that insistent quality he had when he was deadly serious about something. "I've done something you need to hear about right away. It affects all of us. It's . . . big." An undercurrent of glee rang in sharp contrast to his earnest delivery. "Really big."

Now his curiosity was piqued. "Very well then. But let's make it sooner."

"Sooner? I'd hoped to catch up with a few things dirtside before we talk."

Yes, my friend, Sefano thought, that's what I'm afraid of. That something dirtside will catch up with you before then. "We're traveling. It'll be difficult to talk tomorrow. How about in a few hours? When do you land?"

"I'll be home and secure in about two hours."

You think. "Good, good. Why don't we meet just after that. Say three hours."

"Yes, fine. Sooner is better, anyway. I'll meet you at Trispecta."

"The Governor's Palace?" Now Sefano was surprised. It was the favorite virtual haunt of Janus's former boss and predecessor, Adahn of the palatial tastes and despotic humors to match, normally shunned by Janus as too ostentatious.

"Yes," replied his colleague. "I think there's something . . . poetically apt about that setting for this announcement."

"You certainly know how to tease, I'll give you that. Three hours, then, at Trispecta. We'll see you there."

"Until then."

Sefano stared somberly at the dark com panel, wondering what Janus was up to, and hoping he'd find out before the man died.

JANUS ENDED THE connection with Sefano, basking for a moment in self-satisfaction. Soon his position in the cartel would be irrevocably altered, and the standing of the Red Hand along with it. He would finally be able to work unfettered towards the things that truly inspired him.

His eyes swept the green globe of Lyndir sweltering below him. In the *Savia*'s viewscreens, the glistening soap-bubble domes of urbitats dotted the jungle. He was home at last, and it was almost time to celebrate. Once this meeting with his fellow triumvirs was done, he could take a day for himself before falling into the whirlwind of work that would consume him.

If I don't take some personal time now, he thought, I won't be getting any later.

And besides, the Winter Goddess expected him.

The pleasant thoughts that brought to mind caused him to smile. He glanced at the calendar. His return was on schedule, right to the day he'd told her he'd be back in town.

A moment later, he had Tryst on the com, Dosan Helda greeting him warmly. Yes, the Winter Goddess was receiving, but she was in incredible demand right now. Helda wanted him to name a donation figure, and she'd get back with him to see where that might place him in the domina's schedule.

"Absolutely not," he cut her off. "She and I had an arrangement. She's expecting me tomorrow, and I've come a long, long way to be here on time. If the donation's a concern, I'll pay double."

Something in his voice gave the Dosan pause, and well it might. His relationship with the Winter Goddess was . . . different. He'd offered three times to set her up in a place of her own. She'd have none of it. The last time, Janus promised she wouldn't be beholden to him: everything would be in her name, she'd keep her own schedule, see him only if or when she pleased.

She'd smiled coldly at that and pierced his skin with needles in response. He took that to be a no.

The Winter Goddess would meet him only on her terms, in her own space. It made him even crazier for her. He didn't think of it often—couldn't afford to let such distractions consume his attention when he had imperative business to attend to. Now, though, with the prospect of a free afternoon ahead, he wanted only to be under her imperious regard.

"I'll triple the donation," he amended.

The Dosan graciously conceded. "I'll book you for tomorrow then. I know she's been looking forward to your return. The usual time?"

A three-hour block, from late afternoon into the evening. If the session exhausted him, he could go home and fade into bed; if it energized him, it would be early evening in the city with plenty else to do.

"That'll do perfectly," he said. "Please tell her her most devoted servant sends his humble regards, and looks forward to tomorrow very much."

# 53

TEREL, FERRIS, AND clones were gone to use a com booth. That left Esimir alone to fret and think about his next move. Terel's last argument rang in his ears.

"We can't stay here," he'd insisted. "Even if this place is nearly off the net, there are too many people around, and there's no place here to set up our equipment, or interface with Prevak if this scheme works. We need a proper facility to work in, Doctor, in a place that leaves us out of sight."

Esimir offered vague agreement, shooing his loyal assistant out the door to join the others. Terel was right, though: if they managed to free Prevak, all bets were off. He'd need a place to properly interface with his friend—no mere AI as he'd told the others, but something quite remarkably different. Rohar could only be reached through AI interfaces, so he needed that capacity, especially if he intended to continue work on the Splintegrate project.

And that, he most certainly did.

With the AI's help, his research could continue, for Prevak himself contained the knowledge base they'd accrued for this science.

We're so very close to success, Esimir thought anxiously. All I need to achieve, now, is one reintegration that results in a stable construct, something to confirm the new formulations. Then I'll be able to use this as the therapeutic tool it's meant to be.

He glanced at the cases of nanoneurals in the corner. Enough there for several process batches.

Enough to use it on himself, as well. He could even be the first test case, once an acceptable margin of success was certain.

Growing his own clones would take time. That would have to wait until after Prevak was free and could protect them from the authorities. Full-scale lab work like that couldn't be rushed. The critical reintegration test step, though, was easily within his immediate grasp. The requirements for that were minimal: some medical control equipment, commercially acquired; the brain-mapping helm they had with them; basic anesthetics and restraints; the specially programmed nanoneurals; and Prevak online.

Merging two persona aspects isn't difficult, he thought, and I have the material for that right at hand. The Hinano clones.

$Hinano_1$ didn't matter anymore: she was the persona he wanted stripped from this experiment anyway. It was Two and Three, the rational and emotive aspects he had liberated from Olniko's grasp, that held compelling interest. Prevak had refined the reintegration parameters after their last failure with the Biancar clones. Just a subtle proportional adjustment in the nanoneural mix was all that was needed. For the first time, Rohar put reintegration success probability at over ninety-six percent. It was a good enough chance for Esimir to risk his last two test subjects on. If it worked with them, he'd have one stable, integrated clone at the end of the process.

Then, it was only a matter of time before he could apply this solution to himself.

He paced the room, following the tracks of his logic as he did his tracks on the carpet. Buying time was the problem, that and a secure space to work in. Once Prevak was in the open infosphere, he could help in innumerable ways. Until then, what could the bioempath do to facilitate the experiment, and their safety from Ilanya's inevitable search?

The com panel chimed. The unexpected sound startled him, and he looked askance at the small desk that housed the unit. No one should be calling here. For a moment he considered ignoring it. Then he thought of his people and test subjects, even now at a com booth, and he answered the unit tentatively.

"Yes?"

*"Esimir?"*

It was a voice he didn't recognize, a synthesized one: half-electronic, half-human. "Yes?" His finger hovered over the disconnect tab.

*"I'm your netrunner. You can call me FlashMan."*

He sat down suddenly, legs weak with relief. "Oh my. That was quick."

*"That's me, baybee. Quick like a Flash. So what do you need? Herself didn't tell me the details."*

Esimir's thoughts leapt ahead in a Serafix-fueled chain of association. "I have a big task, and a little task. The big one is urgent but the little one must come first. I think it touches on our immediate security."

*"I'm all about security. So what is it you need?"* the voice prodded again.

"We need to move immediately. Someplace we can live and put together a lab, someplace that won't draw attention from outsiders. We're, er, trying to avoid authorities, so it should be very secure. Or hidden. Or both."

*"When?"*

"I'd like to move right now. Tonight."

*"What kind of lab?"*

Metmuri described his requirements, and FlashMan was silent for a moment. *"I can get you a place to stay, power and net connections, a 'sphere portal, the basics. Lab gear we'll have to order—you should spec out what you need."*

"And how long, do you think, before you identify a place—?"

*"Already have. An old device manufacturing plant in Caardo Dome. It was sold, bought, started renovation, then the new owner lost funding and put everything on hold. It's been vacant for a year."*

"Can it support a lab?"

*"Several, probably. They even have a clean room on site, for waldo assembly. There's still some tech infrastructure in place. It should support your needs, no problem."*

"Is it safe?"

*"If you don't stick your nose outdoors, no one will know you're there. It interconnects to maintenance tunnels if you need back ways out, and there's some interesting security in place. Looks like they added it after the food riots a few years ago."*

"Riots?" Esimir shook his head. "I'm afraid I missed that."

*"Store looting and burning in Glitz Town spread into a few industrial areas in Caardo. This plant was never threatened, but they got more secure afterward."*

"But will we be safe there? Undisturbed?"

FlashMan sighed. *"Look, here's the thing about hiding out. You keep your footprint small, don't be seen where surveillance can track you, and run your external coms through encrypted systems, and the odds are whoever's looking for you won't be able to spot you. You won't give them anything to trace. I can help you with all that. There are no guarantees, but you'll be in the safest safehouse we can make for you short of leaving the planet entirely. Or, did you want to leave the planet?"*

Esimir shook his head. This was a conversation he'd have with Prevak, not with a netrunner. "Not now," he replied. "We have work to do here first."

*"All right. I'll set you up to look like a leaseholder, in case anyone gets curious and looks closer. Locks are rekeyed for you already. So what about this other thing you have going on, Smear?"*

"What did you call me?" The doctor bristled.

*"'Smear,' Smear. Short for your name. And you can call me Flash, if you want to reciprocate."*

The doctor spoke stiffly. "My name is Esimir."

*"That's what I said, Smear. So yet again I ask: What's this other thing you need?"*

"This will take some time to explain."

*"What's the short version?"*

He sighed. "I need you to poke a hole in the security wall of Naval Weapons Research Station 207."

The netrunner was silent for a second, then peals of synthesized laughter came through the com panel. *"Is that all? This'll be fun. Tell me more."*

"What about this abandoned plant?"

*"I can work while I talk. So spill."*

Esimir spilled.

# 54

SLOW-ROTATING CALYX WAS the seat of Sa'adani imperial power: an idyllic, lush world of old rolling hills and forests sprinkled with flowering meadowlands. It was a garden world, given to palatial estates, tasteful monuments, and promenades in manicured residential towns. Vast tracts of land seemed virginal, undeveloped, populated only by grazing herds of ilu and fine-blooded horses. The complex warrens of bureaucracy functioned in underground complexes, or peeked out of earth-sheltered hillsides, unobtrusive structures that could not ruin the vista from a nobleman's estate.

The Emperor's Palace was more than a building on Calyx. It was an entire island province thousands of square klicks in land mass, dedicated to the sole purpose of housing, feeding, and supporting the residences and members of the royal family and their closest retainers.

As to palaces, there were many. There was the grand Dinarbi Palace overlooking the seashore, the huge structure where most affairs of state were settled. There was Esker's Retreat, the original hunting-lodge-grown-large of Adàn Esker, founder of the dynasty. There was the Queen's Palace, the Heir's Palace, the jewel box of the Widow's Palace, and still others.

Remarkable among these structures was the sprawling Governor's Palace, where visiting heads of state from offworld were hosted. Also called the Trispecta for its threefold view of Dinarbi, the Willows Lake, and the stark karst abutments of the grieko cliffs, that palace was the most variegated of them all. Its monumental edifice of red-and-white-patterned marble was reduced to human scale with a calculatedly eclectic décor. It held artwork and furnishings imported from a hundred worlds, different themes and sensibilities around every corner—it was said that any visiting dignitary could find a room there to remind her of home. The iconic estate was famed as a symbol of the Empire, a centerpiece of wealth and power.

It was for that reason that Janus chose to revive Adahn's simulation of Trispecta for his meeting. Ordinarily he found it too out of scale for practical conversations, yet this one time, with his fellow triumvirs, there could hardly be any place more fitting to break his news. He set the weather to a balmy summer afternoon, moved the time forward to the long, slow pink-and-orange sunset period when cool breezes blew off the lake. He released the grieko to play at their mating and territorial dances, swooping low over the willow trees and the sunset-tinged waters. He manifested comfortable seats near the marble balustrade, placed to view the landscape and the high pagoda rooftops of Dinarbi beyond the far woods. This was not only the view enjoyed by nobility at the heart of the Empire: it was the place where decisions were made that shaped worlds.

Janus was a child of Cassian backstreets, but Sefano and Mika were both Sa'adani born and bred.

The association would not be lost on them.

THE TWO TRIUMVIRS were timely. They rezzed just within the latticed portico, stepping out onto the veranda as if they had simply been strolling in that direction. Sefano's eyes were drawn at once to the bright orange grieko, long-tailed, stiletto-beaked, swooping and diving over the lake. They were part of the imperial game preserve, symbol of royalty, untouchable by ordinary people. It always amused him that Adahn Herric—born no higher caste than himself—had so loved these trappings of status and rulership.

Why Janus favored them now was a mystery undisclosed by the slender man's unreadable face. He awaited them at the veranda corner, an angle that showed two of the palace's famed views to best effect. The glorious sunset lake stretched before them, meandering into woodlands that drew the eye to the elaborate walls of Dinarbi, glimpsed above distant treetops. It was the man before them, though, who commanded their attention, as much by his contrast in this setting as anything else. Janus leaned easily against the marble balustrade, clad in a fashionable but understated business suit that could be—probably was—a model of his real clothing. His long, straight auburn hair was restrained at the back of his neck, the red button at his left temple the only obvious sign of his neural interface enhancements.

The trio met, greeted with handshakes all around. They took seats, and Sefano smiled benignly at their junior member. "Now," he prompted, "what is so earth-shattering that we had to meet right away?"

Janus's lip quirked. "Bear with me a bit. I'll start at the start. You can judge the end for yourselves."

One thing Sefano had always liked about Janus was the man's ability to be concise. If he had much to say, there was a good reason for it. Curiosity aroused, he gestured at him to continue.

Janus closed his eyes a moment, marshaling his thoughts. When he opened them, a small globe projection blossomed in the air between them. It was a cloud-swirled forest world that neither Sefano nor Mika immediately recognized.

"Triskelan." Janus named the homeworld of the brodien. "You'll recall we were losing control of our shipping monopolies in Triskelos space, because of competition. I took care of that problem; the factions that sought deals elsewhere are no longer in play. This little sojourn, though, brought something else to my attention." The image zoomed out, shifted, resolved into a dense layered nebula of brilliant glowing gases and hidden stars burning sullenly within the cloud.

"Our competition was a group called the Styrcian League. Originally smugglers, they've become powerful by selling a psionic enhancer they control the sole source of. Somewhere in this nebula is their stronghold, and somewhere—there, or down a wormhole—is the world Styrcian crystals come from."

"Styrcian crystals?" asked Mika. "Never heard of 'em."

"No one has, except the Bureau of Mutagenics. And they are falling all over themselves to acquire all that they can, paying through the nose for the privilege."

"Why?" asked Sefano.

Janus shrugged. "Think of it as a rare weapons system, if you will. It has the capacity to transform psi functions exponentially. It's of value only to the psi-active, but in that regard—well. Remember the Dalukin."

Sefano sat up in his chair. The Dalukin Empire, safely distant now beyond a broad demilitarized zone of rimward space, had once posed a dire threat to the Sa'adani during Dalukin-initiated wars of expansion. The near-human aliens had a high incidence of psi-active persons in their population. Fighting them in proximity had time and again been a losing proposition. It had spurred the Sa'adani to locate, test, register, and train every psion in the realm, so that a skilled cadre was on hand to assist with the war effort. Even today, it was illegal to be an unlicensed psion in the Sa'adani Empire, a vestige of wartime recruitment necessities and the legal requirements they'd spawned.

The Dalukin Wars were a long time ago now. Peace had reigned between Sa'adani and thwarted Dalukin for nearly three centuries, but the outworlders were an aggressive, expansionist culture. Sa'adani policy was to keep them at cautious arm's length and to continue to train psions in service to the Empire.

"These crystals could shift the balance of power in psionic conflicts and war," Sefano realized.

Janus dipped his chin. "Apparently so. You see why they're so coveted by our own, then. And the entity that controls them becomes an invaluable resource to the Sa'adani Empire in its own right."

Mika leaned forward. "You said your competition *was* the Styrcian League. What happened to them?"

A half smile tugged Janus's lip. "They're part of my organization now."

Sefano and Mika spoke over each other in an outburst of excited questions. Janus pulled up financial data, explaining the deal he'd cut with Pers Mardin, the distribution not only of crystals but all other goods the League ran, the agreements to expand into more legitimate markets—

"Wait." Sefano held up a hand. "Did you say legitimate markets?"

"Of course. Look." Janus ran a series of data displays, some showing modest economic performance, the others exponential gains. "The first is our ordinary network, business as usual. The second takes advantage of the imperial monopolies Mardin brings with him."

"Monopolies?" Sefano's voice rose in question.

"Yes. Beautiful, isn't it? I think they were granted by functionaries overeager to secure Styrcian stones. They tossed them at Mardin like a sop to a small player, not seriously believing he could exploit them to their fullest. By himself, he couldn't—but *we* can. These are projections for my own territory."

Sefano leaned forward to study the displays in detail. He sat back with a low whistle. "You've gotten us carte blanche in regions and markets we could never touch before."

"Yes. I have, haven't I?" Janus sounded bemused. "And this is where it leads."

He showed them the projections that had left him and Karuu bedazzled aboard the *Savia*. The graphics had a similar effect on the other triumvirs, experienced financial managers that they were.

"Is that just your regional operations we're looking at?" Mika asked.

"Yes," he replied. "Over three years. I've already realized this much over the last two months." He showed another vertically climbing graph. Sefano looked at him sharply. The man's net worth had taken a noticeable jump.

"It's not optimized yet," Janus said modestly, "since we've only just started. But you can see the curves in action."

"What does this look like—"

"—if we do it for your regions as well?" Janus gave a small smile and refreshed the display with a thought.

Sefano and Mika could only view it in silence.

"That's . . . amazing," Sefano finally breathed.

"I don't even know where I'd invest all that money." Mika sounded unhappy at such an unexpected challenge.

"I had the same concern." Janus cleared his throat and wiped the data displays. "That brings me to the third thing I've done."

"There's more?" Sefano asked. Already his mind was racing. The structures Janus had set up were brilliant—but what were the *exact* terms of the deal he'd made with Mardin and the Styrcian League? He had no obligation to reveal them to his colleagues, but if he'd structured that deal with half a care, it would all fall apart if he were out of the picture.

Sefano shifted uncomfortably, knowing Janus was too clever to overlook something so obvious. He gritted his teeth over his suddenly unpalatable arrangement with Ilanya. He had never imagined it would cost him the fortune of a lifetime to lose his junior triumvir, and then to be required to empty even more from his depleted pockets into her coffers.

"And then," Janus was saying, "I was a little delayed in Ahm subsector. The jumping-off point, I'll remind you, for supply lines into Armajad and the entire secessionist-war corner of the Empire."

Sefano tore his thoughts away from Ilanya and forced himself to pay attention. "And you were there because—?"

"We've talked about expanding into Armajad—gunrunning and such. It was on my way; I took a look. Not a good idea, I found, after I got there."

"No?"

"No. This one's much better." He pulled up a new holodisplay, setting three globes spinning before them. "Ereri, Buan, and Temis. Resource worlds and rebel hideouts, sympathizers helping the rebellion. Crushed by our bold imperial strike forces. They've driven rebels and their supporters out of Amh subsector and back across the border."

"Meaning what?" Mika asked bluntly.

"Meaning, these worlds suffered major infrastructure damage, and, politically speaking, they've been condemned."

"Condemned?" She looked blank.

Sefano ran a hand across the smooth top of his head. "An imperial status, applied to disaffected worlds. Doesn't happen often—last time was, well, during the Dalukin Wars."

Mika looked at him questioningly. He continued. "It means their old governments are removed and the population encouraged to find new leadership that can, um, better manage the affairs of the world, in keeping with imperial agreements and policies."

"So these Cassians were on the losing side of a local war and got bashed by our military. And pissed off some powerful sector governor in the process." Mika shrugged. "So what?"

Janus gave her a gentle smile. "It means they're available for outside interests to take over and run. You wondered what you could do with all that money." He gestured to the projection before them. "That's what I'm doing with mine. Temis." The globe he named lit up as if the sun had risen upon it.

Mika frowned at the projection. "We haven't realized that income yet."

"Indeed. It will take a large chunk of that fortune over time to rebuild and properly exploit a rich resource world, but that's not the price of entry."

"What is?" asked Sefano.

"First, an invitation from at least one leading political group to enter that world."

"They're in ruins and governments disbanded, you say."

"Exactly. Which means it's easy to find a faction that can be bought. They're all jockeying for position right now, looking to anything—or anyone—that can give them the edge and help with reconstruction. I now have—*we* now have—faction invitations on each of these worlds."

"What else does it take?"

"Guarantees to rebuild, and minimum investment commitments."

"And you've—?"

"Contracted to that end on Temis and made contingent offers on the other two worlds, in case you want part of this action."

Mika still looked unconvinced. "You're talking about moving in and governing war-torn worlds beyond the reach of our current operations. Why would we want to do that?"

Sefano saw a muscle clench in Janus's jaw. Mika was always slow to see the big picture.

"First, establishing a presence there expands our reach to the only part of this sector we haven't yet tapped for business," Janus explained patiently. "Second, it gives us a local base of operations right next to a profitable war zone. You know what opportunities that offers."

Mika nodded, considering.

"Third, these are among the top twenty resource worlds in the entire CAS Sector. That's why they were so valuable to the rebels. We wouldn't be taking over mere worlds; we'd be taking over gold mines that open whole new economic possibilities to us. And finally . . ."

He flicked a finger and the display changed to the imperial rus, symbol of the Lau Sa'adani elite. "To be accepted as condemnation stewards would make us officially appointed governors, with rights to rebuild, exploit resources, charter monopolies, and determine everything about these worlds except the narrow municipal concerns of local government."

He grinned, full of himself for a moment. "That appointment bestows imperial rank with it. No one beneath the level of Navshi caste may govern a planet. If you secure the appointment, you are officially elevated to that level. It's instant aristocracy, Mika."

Even Sefano hadn't thought of that. "Why would they approve cartel leadership to be stewards, though?" he asked. "Surely there are megacorps or Lau Sa'adani sniffing around such an opportunity as well."

"None of them control the most coveted psi enhancement in the royal arsenal," Janus said softly. "And none of them have the Kingmaker endorsing their bids for governorship."

"What?" Sefano blurted in surprise.

Janus restored a financial display with a gesture. "We have the tools now to expand our operations manyfold, and our fortunes, too. But we need more legitimacy to do this properly. Doesn't mean we have to stop doing what we do as a cartel: it just gives us more options to handle above-board business. Essential options. So let's seize that opportunity. The government wants our crystal supply, and Ilanya wants our monetary donations. Fine. There's a price tag for that: legitimacy, stewardship, and the carte blanche she offered us before."

Mika looked puzzled. "You turned that deal down before."

"Before, being legit only made us her lapdogs. Now, being legit stands fair to make us the single most powerful cartel in the Empire." He shrugged. "Unless you're not prepared for that degree of success, of course."

Mika sputtered a protest. As stolidly as she went about her business, her ambitions were as great as any of theirs. When she had reaffirmed her interest, only Sefano sat in continuing silence, a protracted quiet that drew both trium- virs' eyes to him.

He didn't trust himself to speak. This was what he strove for, his secret dream: legitimacy for the cartel, high caste for himself, a position of power in the public eye, not only in the shadow world of the gray markets. A legacy that could shape the fate of worlds.

*My gods,* he thought. *I could be the ruling* lord *of a world, and much more, if I just reach out and take it.*

His eyes went to Janus's face, searched the sharp, intelligent features there. This should be the key to all he'd ever dreamed of. Instead, he was looking at the face of a dead man. Dead by his own doing.

Sefano felt sick.

"This is bold. Clever." He gave rare praise, his voice stress-tinged. "But Ilanya will still want us to give a huge war chest to Lord Shay. It will deplete our li- quidity for a time. You have no problem with that?"

Janus shrugged. "If she grants stewardships in return, no. We have the credit to run on promissory notes for quite a while." He glanced towards the holo- field. "We'll make it up soon enough."

Sefano made his decision. "I agree, then. Let's move ahead." He inhaled deeply and stood up. "Pardon me. Something urgent just came up that I have to deal with."

He vanished abruptly from the sim, leaving two puzzled triumvirs behind.

**SEFANO TRIED THE** obvious thing first: he called Ilanya on Calyx, getting PolitDiv's front office direct on the line. It was a long shot, but he calculated that his name might be on a watch list or flag some attention in Ilanya Evanit's own office.

Instead, he hit the wall of forwarding message systems and circular refer- rals to the Public Information office. He didn't wait to get a human on the line. It was obvious that Political Division was not easily contacted by outsiders.

*Damn her,* he thought, with her high-handed "Don't call me; I'll call you." You'd think she was hiding somewhere. *Now how am I supposed to reach her?*

He looked at the chron. Half an hour he'd squandered with this runaround. He sighed in resignation and called his own head of security instead.

Crevon appeared in midair before him, his shiny red robotic hunter-killer sim a projection from within the local Red Hand net systems. "Boss?"

"I have an emergency. Pull your top runners from whatever they're doing. I want an immediate trace on this person." He touched his data screen, relayed the public info file on Ilanya. "I need to talk to her, and I need to do it now. I don't care how many secure systems she's tucked behind, or what planet she's on. Find her."

"Secure systems. If there are countermeasures—?"

"Blast your way through it. This won't wait."

"Done. Stay near the com."

Sefano nodded as his hunter-seeker vanished from sight.

## 55

ZIPPO'S BLUE WIREFRAME bulldog manifested above the holopad on Obray's desk. "He's back," the IntSec netrunner announced.

"Janus?"

"The very same. Just walked in the front door."

Obray crossed to his desk, plugged into the VR jack as he took his seat. In an eyeblink, his sterile office vanished from sight and his white-uniformed body morphed into the white-and-gold wireframe of a senior Internal Security net-cop. Zippo's in-system avatar stood before him, a thigh-high bulldog adorned with an elaborate spiky wireform collar. Obray had long since given up trying to get Zippo into the human shape the rest of his force wore as regulation uniform. As a dog sim, and next to youngest of their team, he'd become something of their mascot: that wasn't bad for morale, the commander realized, and suited some of Zippo's more specialized skills.

One of those skills was swift sorting through a chaotic array of data feeds, and that's exactly what they were dealing with at Janus's estate. The cat-ten infiltration ordered by Ilanya Eva had proceeded as far as they could take it, and stayed at 73 percent saturation ever since. After one plant was discovered in the personnel screening process and summarily executed by Red Hand henchmen, and two spyflies were detected in a routine perimeter sweep, Obray made the call to keep surveillance static at the level they had achieved. It was thorough enough for their purposes: Janus couldn't take a leak without the Bugs being the first to hear his fly unseal.

"Show me what we've got," he told his underling. Zippo nodded his massive head and led the way down a short gleaming data pipeline. The pair entered a cul-de-sac, a small but high-roofed hemisphere dotted with pinpoints of light over the interior. Zippo nose-butted a switch near the base of the wall. Pinpoints flared bright, and the next moment Obray stood in a snow globe.

It seemed like that, anyway: myriad glowing particulates swirled about, streaming from the tiny ports around him, swept and stirred in space by an invisible wind. It was a cacophony of info-bits, until Zippo trotted to the middle of the room.

Somewhere in his cyberdeck, the netrunner ran specialized search routines. At the computing level, tags were sorted, network associations calculated, sort algorithms run. In virtual reality, the blue bulldog snuffled among the sparkling bits and pieces littering the floor, sifting down upon him like ashfall. Here a heap grew; there another agglomerated; where he stepped, a pattern took form. Nosing his way through growing mounds of data, Zippo transformed chaos into useful information.

It was the work of moments, perhaps a minute in the physical world. Obray stood back and admired the results.

Low-order information lined the walls now like reams of stacked paper, glittering with a light of its own. Closer in were three constructs arranged in a triangle in the center floor. They followed standard IntSec coding for intel icons: orange for cautionary, magenta for urgent, a dark violet for the most volatile or high-level intel.

Obray touched the rightmost pod, its darkling hues evocative of ancient oracles, signaling the most sensitive secrets yielded by this surveillance. Dark glistening petals folded back and imagery cascaded forth.

Encoded within was an interpretive layer that turned information into understanding. Instead of pouring over reports and dossiers for hours, Obray absorbed the gist of the current situation in minutes.

He shook his head, both sim and physical. It wasn't exactly brain overload, but it was a dump, and he imagined he could feel the neural-enhanced part of his brain adjusting to the data influx.

He beckoned the bulldog, and the two stepped out of VR together.

Zippo returned to his position as desktop projection; Obray to his seat with the beginnings of a headache behind his eyes. He rubbed his temples for a moment, then regarded Zippo.

"He's just confirmed transportation for tomorrow afternoon. He'll be in the Shelieno then to meet his shigasa. Has this been passed to Ilanya yet? She wanted to know his movements."

"That wasn't in the earlier update, so no. That must have just come across the feeds."

Obray considered. "We've got him covered when he travels, right?"

"All his cars are covered. And one of his drivers is a plant of ours. No telling what duty he'll pull, though."

Obray's thoughts were elsewhere. "And he's interviewing three lieutenants before he goes out tomorrow. He's up to something, but no hint what."

"Not yet."

"Well, maybe we'll hear about it during those interviews. I need to report this right away. I want FlashMan lurking outside those systems, in case Janus does anything in the local nodes. Won't hurt to be ghosting him while he does."

"Ummm."

"What?"

"He's not on duty tonight."

"Where is he?"

"He called in sick."

"The hell you say. When?"

"A few hours ago. Captain Brace approved it."

"Juro take it." Obray rarely became angry on the job, but his irritation showed clearly now. "Flash knows he's on standby for Janus's return, and we've been expecting his return this week since he last called home to make party plans."

"This week, yes. We didn't know what day."

"Don't make excuses, Zip. Standby is standby."

"Maybe he really is sick?"

"I don't care if he is. I'll have a word with Brace myself. You go knock on FlashMan's door and tell him to get his ass in here now. I want to see his scrawny sim in an hour, right where you are now."

Zippo looked contrite on his colleague's behalf. "Yes, sir."

"Well? What are you waiting for? Get going."

The blue dog disappeared from sight, leaving Obray scowling at the air.

He exhaled through pursed lips, then sat back down and called Ilanya.

# 56

THE TWINS' COM booth was at the edge of a small plaza square featuring old condensation wells and an archaic bronze statue of a once-famous colonial leader. Walking the two blocks back to the hostel, they stopped with their scientist watchdogs at a street vendor for spicy-hot fry-bread snacks and cool fruit juice to take back with them.

Two automated taxis pulled up at the same time they arrived. Esimir could be seen popping in and out of the door to their rooms, scanning the street, until he saw them approaching and waved them over.

"You're back. You took your time. What's that? Food? Oh." He paused in his imminent chastisement to pop a prawn-and-breis–stuffed fritter into his mouth and chase it with a drink. "Very good. You have more? Wonderful. We'll take them with us."

"Where are we going?" Kesada asked.

"Your friend came through, and we now have a netrunner working for us," the doctor replied. "A rather brash fellow, but he seems competent enough. He's already found us a place where we can set up a lab, and we're moving there right now."

"Tonight?" grumbled Kesi. "We just got settled. I'm tired."

"Sleep can wait," Metmuri said dismissively. "He needs to move on to the Prevak mission, and we need to be hidden away where we can work. He has secured us premises we can use until Prevak can assist us further."

Kesada shook her head. "You said you just needed help with your AI. What do you need a lab for?"

Metmuri looked surprised at the question. "Why, to continue my research, of course. I'm at a critical juncture with everything."

"Don't you think that's dangerous while you're a fugitive?"

"I won't be for long," he said confidently. "And we're just wasting time here, when we could be doing something constructive. Besides," he said, lowering his voice, "we need someplace much more private than this, no matter what we're doing." He gestured back over his shoulder, where the laughter of tourists echoed around the corner of the building, guests or passersby enjoying the evening.

"Too many people float around here, and, as you said earlier"—he nodded to Kesada—"there's a constant danger of surveillance. FlashMan has kindly provided us with a refuge where these problems will be nonexistent. Later, when Prevak is free, we can reassess our situation."

He looked from the group to the waiting taxis. "Come, now. We have some loading to do, then we're off."

**A BLUE BULLDOG** looked up at a human-scale post office counter, and the shuttered windows far beyond the reach of his present form. The dog gave a perfectly human sigh, then his sim began to stretch and elongate. In a moment, he was a standard blue man-shaped wireform that would have pleased Obray to see.

Zippo leaned over the counter and banged on the shutter. A placard hanging from the front jumped with the impact of his fist. CLOSED, it proclaimed bouncily, as if taunting him.

"I know you're in there, Flash," he shouted. "Open up. It's Zip!" He banged again, more forcefully, but the flimsy-looking shutter did not budge.

"Flash?"

Not even a light on the far side peeped under the shutter.

Maybe he *is* sick, Zippo thought. He gave it one more round of forceful attention-getting. The post office remained dark, and his efforts in vain.

"Obray's not gonna like this, buddy," he shouted, in case there were ears to hear. "You might want to get better real quick and come to work. You-know-who got back tonight."

Zippo nodded to himself in the resounding silence that filled FlashMan's anteroom. Due diligence done, he shrank back down to bulldog size and trotted back the way he'd come.

**THE TWINS HUNG** back in their room long enough for a hasty conference. Agreeing on their strategy, they joined the others in loading the taxis and traveled with them two domes over to Cutter, to a well-kept but little-trafficked manufacturing and warehouse district. Most buildings were occupied, though many for-lease signs were visible in the gleam of yard lights. The vehicles deposited them at one such building, occupying the corner of a small industrial park complex. Esimir keyed in an access code and the side door clicked open. He grinned in delight and stepped inside.

The interior was lit as if still occupied. The susurrus of fans told of a climate plant recently engaged, refreshing the dusty-musty air of the disused structure. Static crackled as a building-wide announcement system came online.

"*Welcome to your new home, kids.*" It was FlashMan. "*Sorry about the broadcast, but I need to walk you through this place. Global is the only channel working right now.*"

"Certainly, certainly." Esimir bubbled, eager to see where he could rebuild his lab. "Where do you want us first?"

*"I have spotty visuals on you,"* Flash said. *"They only had cams in production areas and certain offices, and most of those have been stripped. The building computer has a floor plan, though, so I'll give you a tour with that. If something doesn't look like I describe it, let me know; we might need to calibrate as we go."*

"You say things are stripped. How stripped?" The doctor sounded worried.

*"Halfway-renovated stripped. Power and data infrastructure's intact, though, so when you get gear everything will connect like you need it to."*

"Can we print out this map?"

*"Sure thing, Smear, from a maintenance console. Why don't you walk ahead from the door you came in to that near wall right in front of you. Turn right down the hall. We'll do building systems first, so you can get oriented."*

The tour began, leading the group farther into the labyrinthine building. When the group turned down the hall, the Hinano twins dropped back. In moments they were at the door and out, Kesada with a heavy bag of cash in her hand, Kesi first into the taxi she'd told to wait.

In moments they were gone, into the nighttime city.

# 57

**"UPDATE ME," SEFANO** ordered curtly. He waited while his secure com trace hunted Crevon down, wherever he was in the net. After a long minute, a terse reply came back from his head of security. It was a static message, the equivalent of a handwritten note, meaning Crevon didn't want to—or couldn't—take time for real-time dialog right now.

*You picked a hot one. Vicious safeguards. Running down dead ends—she leaves decoys, conceals true path. Will find her, but won't be quick. Can't say when. Eliminating false trails one by one. Hunter-seekers everywhere. One dead so far.*

The only bodies he'd be counting were Sefano's own men. One down, after only four hours of searching, and his runners were good. That meant Ilanya's protections were even better. He cursed. He only had so many netrunners on hand.

They better find her soon.

Every hour that passed felt like a band tightening around Sefano's chest. He was physically uncomfortable with the tension. Waiting had never been his game, and now it felt as deadly to himself as it could prove to be for Janus.

He had to do something more than sit and wait. And he knew just what that should be.

**"SEFANO," JANUS GREETED** his colleague in their face-to-face VR sim. "What brings you to the 'sphere so late in the day? By my clock, anyway." He added a smile so his comment would not be taken as a reprimand. Their power hierarchy still put Sefano at the top, the first among equals. He could call anytime he pleased, and they both knew it.

"Something has come to my attention," the senior triumvir said, "and I want you to take this as seriously as I do."

"What?"

"There's a hit out on you."

Janus took that in. "Do you know who?"

Sefano shook his head. "And I can't say when, but likely soon. Very soon. Opportunistic, I think, so don't offer opportunities. Watch for surveillance, and watch your back. This has awaited your return home, Janus, so break your usual patterns. What do you do that's predictable? Don't do it. Guard yourself. I'll run this down from my end and put a stop to it."

Janus stroked his jaw. "How'd this come to your attention?"

The other shook his head. "Privileged source. I'll let you know as soon as I've resolved this. Meanwhile—" He stopped abruptly.

"What?"

"You just got home. You should leave again. Just take to space for a while. You have a nice yacht. Take a little pleasure cruise, while I run this to ground on Lyndir."

Janus let air hiss between his teeth. "That doesn't sit well with me. I'm up to here with business I need to do dirtside, and I just spent too many weeks on board that ship. Luxury or not, it feels a little small after a while."

Sefano waved off his concerns. "We're not talking about weeks. A little while only: some days, let's say. I'm sure things will be sorted out by then."

"And if they're not? I have to come home sometime. Besides, I have my own people who can deal with threats like this."

"Not like this one," Sefano said flatly. "Don't ask me to explain, but you need to get out of there. Best if you're offworld a little while. I can't order you, but I most strongly urge you to do this."

Janus studied his colleague, wondering what he knew that he wasn't saying. Finally he dipped his chin. "I'll take it under advisement," was all he would offer.

Unsatisfied, Sefano wished him a good night and terminated their connection.

JANUS STARED UNSEEING into the darkness of his room. He was already undressed for bed, a light robe draped over his slender torso, his long hair loose and drying from the shower.

Break my patterns, he reflected. Finally, he pushed a call button, and Eldin, his valet, came to attend him.

An older man, Eldin had served Adahn before him. He'd spent most of his life in service to Red Hand leaders, but Janus kept him on especially because he dressed his master impeccably, and played a mean game of Shaydo cards when Janus wanted some mundane amusement. Lost with a good grace, too.

That's when you really get to know a man, the triumvir reflected. When you see how he loses.

"Sir?" Eldin inquired.

"Pack an overnight bag, E. One for yourself, too. We're going somewhere."

"Now, sir?"

"Yes. You drive, don't you?"

"I do, sir."

"Good. You'll be my driver, too."

Eldin digested that for a moment, but asked simply, "When do you wish to leave, sir?"

"As soon as you have the bags ready."

"Very good, sir."

Now that's a good servant, Janus thought as his man left the room.

One servant, overnight in a random hotel, interviews tomorrow via secure cyber instead of face-to-face—he'd be away from home all day. No one knew about his appointment at Tryst in the afternoon—he'd made that from the *Savia,* not house systems, so if he'd been compromised, that, at least, should still be confidential.

I should be able to fit at least that much personal time in, he thought with contentment. And then—better err on the side of caution, and head to the starport afterward. I'll check with Sefano when I'm in orbit, and we'll take it from there.

# 58

NEITHER TEREL NOR Ferris had ever seen Dr. Metmuri completely lose it. Seen him stressed, demanding, cranky—yes. Touchy from too much mentaid or pissed at imperfections in others' work—yes. But always his temper was understandable.

He went nova about the Hinanos, though. It was a singular and unsettling event.

"What do you mean, they're gone?!" were the last coherent words he shrieked before launching into a fit of rage. Had any part of the warehouse been furnished, it would have stood demolished around him in moments. Datapads would have flown, furniture been overturned, fixtures ripped off walls: but that had all been done already, and cleared out of the room, too, in the renovation work that left the place half gutted. Esimir could do little but rant and scream in place, banging his fists once heartily against an unyielding pillar, then cradling his injured hands to his chest while he cried tears of anger and pain. Still he flailed and raved.

His assistants first stepped back to give him space, then finally left the room to get out of the way.

If he could have reached it, he might have ripped the ceiling cam out of its socket. But he couldn't, so FlashMan had a front-row seat for the whole affair. When Metmuri eventually wound down and collapsed in a sobbing heap in the corner, back to wall, head cradled against knees, Terel and Ferris crept back into the room.

Flash gave a low whistle. *"And I thought I could throw a tantrum,"* he said admiringly.

The pair tried to comfort Metmuri, and Flash fell silent for a time. When he came back on the line, his words tore attention away from the doctor.

*"Hey, guys,"* he announced. *"There's a priority-one want out for you all over the planet. Were you, um, expecting something like that?"*

The only answer was Metmuri tipping his head back and giving another primal roar of frustration and rage.

*"I'm guessing that's a yes."*

Only Ferris looked up to the ceiling cam, chastising him with a frown. He looked at the trio beneath him, like two children comforting their raging, somehow heartbroken father.

I hope the Goddess knows what she's doing with these people, he mused. And I still need to look at that research station.

Flash did some quick calculating. He had never reneged on a contract, and he would see this one through, too. He didn't know exactly what was going on here, and maybe he didn't want to know, seeing as he was technically a Bug himself, while working off his community service sentence with IntSec. On the other hand, if they were trying to avoid the authorities, well, that's what Flash-Man did best, and thoroughly approved of in principle.

*"Tell you what I'll do,"* he said. *"Not one of you can set foot outside this building or you'll be snapped up like that. So until something changes, consider this your very secure home. I'll beef up security and get whatever you need delivered: food, gear, bedding. Make me a list, and I'll just open the loading docks for a window of time."*

"We can't pay for anything right away," Terel fretted, "except with cash."

*"Keep it. I know some untapped accounts that will confuse the backtrail, and they'll never miss the money anyway. You want to start up a lab? Add that equipment to the list."*

"Doesn't matter now." It was Metmuri's voice, strained and low.

It was probably just as well they couldn't see his sim rolling its eyes. *"Make a list anyway. I'll get these orders placed tonight. Right away. After that I need to give RS 207 some undivided attention."* He hesitated a moment. *"You do still want me to go poke at it, don't you?"*

That drew Metmuri's eyes to the ceiling again. "Yes. Yes, very much. Maybe Prevak can still make things right."

*"Sure, whatever you say, Doc."* Flash resisted the Smear taunt; it would be too much like kicking a baby. Instead he simply asked, *"Anything else?"*

To his surprise, it was the doctor who spoke again. He looked up, drying tear streaks with the back of his sleeve, one skinned knuckle leaving a bloody smear on his cheek. "The twins," he said. "Can you look after their security, too? Do what you can to keep them protected?"

*"I don't think so,"* Flash said reluctantly. He hated to admit there was something he couldn't readily do. *"They could be anywhere by now, and out there, on the streets—it's almost impossible to keep someone out of surveillance scope. Really impossible to keep two undercover. Not if they're moving around."*

"Perhaps they're not. They may have gone to ground somewhere. Could you look for them? See that they're safe?"

He sounded like a plaintive little boy, but for once Flash did not mock. The bioempath really seemed to care about his companions, even though they'd clearly had enough of his company.

Against his better judgment, Flash gave in.

*"I'll see what I can do, Doc,"* he conceded, and left the channel.

# 59

BERISHNAN VOREY LOVED his work with the Tensin, the shigasue "guardians" who provided security throughout the Enclave. It was much more interesting than running house security at Firewing, where he'd come from. As a simikan his responsibilities were far broader than his junior officer rank might suggest. One day he might be on street patrol, breaking up bar fights, collaring pick-pockets, turning unruly tourists over to Lyndir police. Another day he might be a criminal investigator, working beside an experienced detective and learning investigation from the ground up.

Or he might have a sudden want alert dropped into his lap, throwing every-thing else into chaos, as happened that very night.

Vorey went into the main Shelieno station for his break, rather more crowd-jostled than not that warm evening. He made straight for the fresher and ran cool water on his head, splashing it on his face, luxuriating in the temporary relief it gave from sweaty closeness.

"Berishnan!" Chief Adano's bullfrog voice rumbled down the hall from four doors away. "What are you doing?"

Not bothering to shout back, he trotted down the hall and into the chief's office. He knew Adano's social visit voice, and this wasn't it.

"Of course they can't come in," the chief was barking at the com when he en-tered. "What the hell do they think this is, Startown? Tell them we have the alert, we're working it on our side, we'll keep them informed. Remind them of Para-graph Two, the autonomy clause. If that doesn't shut them up, lock the gates."

Vorey heard a frenzied query over the com. "You heard me," Adano repeated. "Lock 'em out until they've reread the imperial charter. That kind of fuckage we don't take from city Grinds."

He slammed a meaty fist down on his desk panel, ending the call and turn-ing his smoldering gaze on his duty simikan.

"Paragraph Two, Berishnan. Never forget that, when locals forget we don't have to play by their rules."

Vorey nodded wisely and let his boss's tirade flow.

"So here's a fine pile of shit for this evening. This was supposed to be a quiet night. Now this." He thrust flimsies at Berishnan, who scanned them quickly. It was a set of wants on a party of five—two men, one with a distinctive bio-empath's rus on his brow, and three women. Complete biometrics on all but two of the women, who were twins. No names for them, but there were relatively complete holopix and physical descriptions.

"This comes straight from Sector Security," Adano fumed.

"Sector Security?"

"You sound surprised. Well, so am I. Why Sector is bothering with an all-out want search confined to this one planet is beyond me. But there it is. And they're not being too nice about it, either."

"Sir?"

"Got city police who think they're going to come in through the Shelieno gates and scan patrons, building to building. Ain't gonna happen."

"Of course not, sir."

Adano grabbed the papers back from Berishnan's hand. "We have to act on this, though. Verify these people aren't shacked up here in a holoden or hiding out in a joyhouse. That being the first place that suspects usually flee to, of course. According to the city."

He waved the flimsies in emphasis, then tossed them on the table. "I want you to head this up. You know who we have on the street tonight, and you just got certified with that biosearch gear we have, right?"

Vorey nodded.

"So you know how to coordinate a subtle crowd scan. Get on it. Hourly updates."

"Are you saying you want the whole Shelieno scanned?" The young officer looked as incredulous as he sounded.

Adano blinked at him with baggy frog eyes. "In a word: yes. Station one team each at the north and south gates, so we get people coming and going. Take the other teams and just start going building by building."

"We don't have enough men on the streets to cordon anything off and be sure no one slips through."

Adano raised a finger. "Did I say cordon anything off? No, I did not. Did I say disrupt our guests' pleasurable evening? I most *certainly* did not." He wagged the finger. "The job of your teams, Simikan, is to go door-to-door and check every establishment for these faces, politely and discreetly, however briefly, so that when I give my next report to Sector Security, I can say, 'We're doing a building-by-building search just like your disruptive idiots wanted to trespass in here to do, so don't worry about it and get the hell off my back.'"

He dropped his finger.

"Have I made myself clear?"

"Yes, sir."

"Good. Put your teams together and get to it."

Simikan Berishnan saluted and left the room.

# 60

KESI TOLD THE cab the first destination that popped into her mind, one on the far side of the city. "Starport," she ordered. The vehicle shifted into an inter-dome traffic pattern, lifting from the ground, moving into the air traffic corridor to the starport airlock.

Unconsciously in concert, the twins leaned back in their seats, one knee bent, one leg stretched, the cash bag between them. Simultaneously, blond heads turned to regard each other.

"We're in it now," Kesi said gloomily.

Kesada understood her meaning. "He can't chase us while he's hiding out. I'm more worried about Eva. If what Metmuri said is true, she's not going to let us just walk away."

Kesi nodded. "So where do we go?"

"Not the starport. We can't get offworld. We don't have identification, and if we did, it wouldn't explain . . ." She waggled a finger between them.

Kesi sighed. "Then let's get someplace where we can sit and think and make some decisions. We can't ride around in a taxi all night. Their dispatch would notice."

She sounded cranky. They were both tired; they'd had no sleep at all the night before. Knowing they were being moved from the facility, they'd stayed awake all night with nervous tension, planning contingencies.

Pointless, now. They were in a contingency they could never have foreseen, and it was taking its toll on them both.

"I know." Kesada sat up abruptly. She touched the com pad, spoke to the cab AI. "Take us to the GTN," she ordered, and leaned back with a sigh.

Kesi gave her a wan smile, intuitively following her thinking. "Smart. The global transit network. I didn't think of that."

Kesada's lip curled up. "You would've, sooner or later, like me. Nonstop travel, private bullet cars, long haul stretches. We don't even have to disembark when we arrive somewhere—just recode destination and keep going."

"Perfect."

The clones looked out over the nighttime city, traffic and building lights blurring into a river of activity in this evening hour. The other domes of Port Oswin were mere glowing lights beyond Cutter Dome's translucent vansin shell. Here, they flew above street canyons, industrial parks and warehouses interspersed, some hotels and traveler services the closer they got to the transit hub.

The taxi dropped lower, into the local-dome air pattern, flying just above street level. Their view became broken by lofty buildings looming over the narrow air corridors. Finally the cab dipped to the ground at one congested corner and delivered them to the passenger zone of the Cutter West GTN terminal.

The transit network was Lyndir's marvel of engineering from the twilight of its independent Confederation days. Long-distance travel had always been a challenge on that jungle world. Common aircars endured damage from atmospheric gases, and anyone forced down by vehicle malfunction was nearly certain to die from environmental or vegetation hazards long before a rescue team could reach them. Air travel still served elites and courier services, but it didn't serve the needs of ordinary Lyndiri. Surface road networks were maintained between closely located cities with difficulty, and only at great cost and constant upkeep. It was not until the advent of the GTN that long-distance travel and hauling were revolutionized around the globe.

The famed network girdled the planet, knitting together the major cities of the hothouse world with cargo and passenger transportation for the masses. It was a major feat seventy-five years in the making, completed only two centuries before. Where the crust was stable, it burrowed underground; where fissured terrain endangered it with volcanic activity, it soared above on pylons, or clung to the sides of stable mountain ranges. High-speed bullet cars and cargo drones shot through a bundled multi-tube network: a charged, vansin-reinforced construct resistant to the harsh atmosphere and intrusive jungle growth of the untamed outdoors. People and goods moved swiftly in the contained system, safely isolated from unfriendly nature.

The twins could travel safely there, isolated from unfriendly pursuit as well.

FLASHMAN SPAWNED A scout sprite and sent that part of his attention flying after the twins. This was one of his innate talents and part of what made him such a good decker. Even handicapped with the loss of his codeworm consciousness, his performance was better than most. Now he bent his energy to finding Metmuri's missing friends.

Where could he spot their trail? Somewhere, sometime soon they would pass a biometric surveillance device, and they'd be identified, and then it would be too late.

Surveillance was everywhere in Port Oswin, the bustling claustrophilic capital of the CAS Sector. It was part of the Grinds' constant battle against muggings and petty thefts, pickpockets and violent crime—the inevitable result of near thirty million inhabitants living in a constrained space. The twins would pass too close to a storefront that scanned for shoplifters, or simply move through a public space like a plaza or entrance queue. They'd be filtered routinely along with all the faces matched every moment against criminal profiles.

And theirs would be a hit.

*Ah ha!* The solution struck him. Sprite-Flash paused long enough to do a joyful, one-footed war-dance hop in a short circle. Then he derezzed into a stream of glittering golden electrons and blitzed down the line to the nearest coms hub.

A few hops later he was at the Sector Security dispatch center. He didn't need to break in for a data profile: he'd caught that info live just a short while before, in the initial flash of wants and warrants on encoded channels. He'd already stored biometrics and other data the alert had come packaged with. It was sent to human agents, of course, but also went to every scan mecho and security AI in their various interlinked systems in every corner of the Lyndir datasphere.

Part of that message was very simple. It said: this is what our perps look like.

FlashMan rezzed and settled down cross-legged next to the dispatch center. To his virtual eyes it resembled a small police call box with a rotating beacon on top, doing slow leisurely loops right now. It was timekeeping, awaiting new data to transmit.

He began with the want on the twins, the detention order manifesting as two sheets of paper bearing photos. He rested them on one knee while he produced a black crayon in the other hand. Then he bent forward and earnestly began to redraw lines.

**THE HINANO TWINS** joined the flow of commuters and travelers, walking to the ticket automats first for an entry chit. The rectangular green token cost forty creds, the minimum point-to-point charge for tube travel, plus twenty more for the private car surcharge. If the fare to their destination was more, they could pay upon arrival, adding value to the token before leaving the station. If they didn't have money, they could always go back where they came from— the token would simply be retained by the turnstile gate when leaving the originating station, no extra charge incurred.

It proved a practical system for people who needed to change travel plans while en route. And convenient for the twins: they could ride however far they liked for free, as long as they never tried to leave any stations.

They grinned at each other, sharing that thought, as they fed their tokens through the turnstile's validation slot and retrieved them on the far side.

A quick walk down a long slide ramp followed, passing less-hurried travelers standing to the right. The angled descent carried them underground and beyond the boundaries of Cutter Dome. They were beneath the out-dome warrens north of the River Dryx—an exposed backstreeter slum that would be most uncomfortable had they been on the surface. The enclosed underground station was a soothingly contained place for a Lyndir native, though, with solid walls and reliable environmental controls firmly in place. They joined a queue for private cars on the platform, and shuffled ahead as bullet cars hissed to a stop, loaded, then sped away.

**WHEN THE BEACON** flashed bright, Sprite-Flash was ready for it. He had the call-box door open, the old-fashioned handset in his lightning-bolt fingers. He pressed it to his ear and listened to its duotonic stream of 1s and 0s. He translated automatically, aided by encryption decoders in his deck thoughtfully provided by IntSec.

*Fugitives sighted, GTN Port Oswin, entrance East3. Moving west, descending Ramp 4. Ramp 4-10. Ramp 4-20 . . .*

FlashMan glanced at the call box. The monitor inside showed their faces, the profile angles that matched the want, remapped and verified again and again at every spyeye they passed.

He hadn't seen them in motion before; there were no cameras around the warehouse door when they'd been near. Pretty women. Just his type, he mused, then reprimanded himself for ogling. Now was not the time.

Geocoordinate strings followed, tracking their progress past every surveillance camera they neared in the global transit terminal.

He looked down at his free hand, morphed now into a double-pronged set of hotwire clips. One extension was fastened to the maintenance port of the dispatch box, the other to the mouthpiece of the handset. He set up a connection between the points, inserting himself into the dispatch routine that managed the tracking update.

That update was not merely a sighting broadcast. It was an interactive feed, ready to absorb and echo any related input from any security node it met along the way. It not only read and broadcast data: it read and *wrote* data into system nodes as well.

Properly jiggered, it could be made to write more than it knew or intended.

In heartbeats, he was in just the right spot to bleed data into that stream. The data he trickled out was his crayon sketches, torn into a thousand pieces, innocuous confetti carried off into the wilds of the datasphere by the security transmission. Carried off, only to reassemble itself, piece by piece, downstream, to become a coherent data picture of its own.

Starting piecemeal, ending whole, Flash's handiwork was never identified as an unauthorized input into the system. It infiltrated the datasphere nearly as swiftly as the original want had propagated.

Its authentication code was valid, the result of a logic sequence he knew from his IntSec work.

He kept his eyes glued to the monitor in the call box.

The twins moved in a line with other platform passengers, their faces endlessly tracked and parsed through surveillance cams. Station security was on the way now: two officers pushing past civilians on the slideramp, two more running up from the lower cargo platform. More racing down from the main concourse.

His update hit. The parse lines chunked down the face of the nearest blonde—and this time, did not freeze-focus and resolve into the orange-lined trace of a profile match. Second twin—scanned, parsed—no match. Just like other faces in the queue, routinely scanned, and routinely dismissed.

The want in the datasphere was overwritten by his "update." It no longer matched the reality of the twins' appearance. The chittering data stream in his ear stuttered as the real-time movement trace faltered, then ceased. The twins boarded a car just as the monitor feed blinked out.

KESI LED THE way into the tube car. Kesada palmed the privacy seal, and they settled into comfortable seats in the same configuration they'd assumed in the taxi.

Their bullet car hissed from the platform, accelerating along the northwest-bound tube so fast that antigrav compensators were needed to equalize forces in the vehicle. In moments they joined others, whizzing like so many beads on a frictionless path down the long hollow loop that was the GTN.

The twins talked, but not to any purpose. One plan after another was put forward, picked at, bitched about, discarded. Solutions evaded them.

They were chasing daylight. By time they caught up with the sunset line they were both too tired to talk.

"We sound stupid," Kesi mumbled, rubbing her face with her hands.

"Maybe we'll think more clearly if we catch a little sleep."

"Fine by me."

The endless tunnel encasing them was dark, the light in their car a steady glow dimmed with a touch. The subtle motion of the car, thrumming with the speed of its passage, became a soothing, lulling sensation, beckoning sleep. Soon, they shot out of a mountainside to fly constrained over pylons along the north shore of the Dolos Ocean. The brightening late day showed ocean left, rainforest mountains right, sulfur dioxide haze along the shore: a rare sight for dome-dwellers to glimpse, however quickly, in person.

Glimpse it they did not. They were asleep, Kesi on Kesada's shoulder, Kesada's head on Kesi's. As the bullet car ran down the daylight, they slumbered on.

# PART
## THREE

# 61

**THE INTIMACY KES** enjoyed with Morya was greater than it had ever been before. For the first time, she didn't overthink it, didn't hold herself in reserve. For the first time, Kes spoke of "we," and plans for the future.

She was discovering her lover and her love all anew, and through it all, she studied Morya even as she engaged with her. Her quick repartee, the curve of her hip beneath the sheet, her brazen attitude turning to sighs or moans or the deepest submission in response to Kes's dominance—Kes savored it all. It was not a calculating assessment but an intuitive one: both predator observing, and uncertain person testing, finding—remembering—the shape of how they fit together.

What began as a memory recalled became a thought, obsessing. To go away, and take Morya with her. To leave this all behind: the conflict, the pressures, Helda, Gistano, Ilanya. Could she just walk away from it, after angling to become part of the Palumara shigasue clan?

Yes, she told herself. This is more important. This is what I want.

A life with her girl. She'd watched herself carefully, as they spent intense time together, to see what her Beast wanted to do when passions flared and inhibitions were down. She could think of ten people she could do away with in a heartbeat, but if she hurt Morya in a way she did not really intend . . .

Kes bared her teeth with a predatory growl. It was as much triumph as lust: through sheer force of will and desire to not seriously harm her love, she'd found the balancing point, and was secretly relieved to discover that there was one, after all. She had to dig deep to find it, hold herself in check and walk away from her girl more than once, while Morya was helpless and begging for more. She didn't know, couldn't possibly know, what she was inviting. What had nearly come out to play.

After one long soul-searching eternity, while Kes decided whether to love Morya or strangle her to death for the simple joy of seeing fear in her eyes— after that, Kes discovered her own limits. Learned what it took to enforce them. And was glad to find that she could.

That was the turning point that made her learn how to put a leash on that Beast. If she walked free again, it would be because Kes allowed it, not because the Beast ran free on her own. Even if it was a struggle to make sure it stayed that way.

Yet as she congratulated herself on her time with Morya, the task Ilanya wanted her to do still preyed upon her mind. Every time she thought of Janus now, she felt anger, suspicion, distrust. Rage flared when she recalled what Eva had told her about his backing of Gistano and the Icechromers. She knew how good it would feel to take him down.

The discipline of self-control she was beginning to exercise with Morya was not tempering her reaction to Janus. She could feel the difference: Morya was hers, to be possessed, to be kept safe, while Janus was in a different compartment entirely. He marked himself apart by allowing the Icechromers to do as they did. She didn't care what any of his other crimes might be, just that he controlled that derevin tool.

She gritted her teeth. She'd had a real rapport with him, and his betrayal was all the more grotesque for it. Maybe she'd ask him what the hell he'd been thinking before she killed him. Maybe he'd apologize, or beg for his life when he realized he was reaping what he had sown.

What to do, how to do it. . . . Decisions must be made, ones she didn't want to deal with. Time and again she shoved them from her thoughts, easily lost in her time with Morya—until the alarm in the desk comp forced her to think again of business.

It was hard to do, with her girl moaning beneath her. With one hand, Kes held her wrists pinioned overhead; with the other she kept her on the verge, while her teeth nipped delicate flesh hard enough to nearly draw blood. Morya gasped and surged against her, back arched, inviting more. . . .

The alarm intruded again, an intentionally strident one-hour cue for a session on her schedule. Her brow creased. An hour was the least time she could take to get ready, and then only with the help of dressers and the makeup girl. "Hells," she muttered, anger flaring at this intrusion into something she didn't want to end.

She released Morya and moved abruptly away. A soft "ah!" of abandoned surprise came from the bed as she crossed to the comp, glanced down at the screen. What she saw made her slam her hand on the desktop.

Janus.

My gods, she thought. *Now?*

Preoccupied with discovering Morya and mastering herself, she'd barely glanced at her client schedule. And now, just like that, the time was upon her.

I'm not ready.

The panicked thought flitted through her mind, slapped down by a fiercer voice.

Fuck him. He's finally here, where I can deal with him.

She looked over her shoulder to her girl, hair tousled, the flush of arousal on her cheeks and chest, then back at the name on her day calendar. Every nerve in her body sang.

Kes shook her head. "Sorry, kushla. I have to go, right now. We'll finish this later." She shrugged into her robe and stabbed one finger at the woman in her bed. "Don't touch yourself while I'm gone."

Morya groaned and threw herself back on the bed. Kes laughed and was out the door, heading for the shower.

# 62

"I NEED SOME time off, Boss," Franc told Gistano. "Got some personal business I need to take care of."

Gistano glanced up from his desk, fixed him with a look. Franc was his most promising lieutenant. Versatile, responsible. Today he was supposed to be on exo duty, coolsuit-clad and working the north warrens, the official Scripman come to collect from those who collected for the 'Chromers.

No coolsuit here. Just Franc in dark, nondescript street clothes, rocking back and forth on the balls of his feet.

"Personal business."

"Yes."

He didn't elaborate, and Gistano didn't want to know.

"For how long?"

"'Til my business is done. Might be a day. Might be a week."

"You going somewhere?"

"Sure, Boss. Out of town."

What I don't know won't hurt me, Gistano thought. "Yeah, take time off. Franc?"

"Yeah, Chief?"

"Don't get caught."

"Not doing anything to get caught at, Boss."

"Sure. Remember what I said."

"Yes, sir."

Franc left with a decidedly eager bounce in his step, and Gistano returned to his work.

BERISHNAN VOREY WAS at the start of another double shift and looking the worse for wear. He hovered in Adano's doorway until the chief gave him a nod.

"Report," his superior ordered.

"Two-thirds of the Shelieno have been searched. We should finish sometime tonight."

"Problems?"

"Tourists don't like it. Some shopkeepers protest. The shigasue are perfectly compliant, but make us wait until they say it's all right to interrupt their clients. It's taking forever to work through the houses."

"Find anyone yet?"

He shrugged. "One robbery suspect wanted in Lessing. We turned him over to the Grinds. Nothing on the warrants that started all this."

"Of course not." Adano squeezed his lips together into a flabby pursed expression. "We need to speed it up. I'll do what I can about the houses delaying you, and you can put more people on it. I called in an extra shift. They're yours."

"Why? We're making progress."

"It's not just the Grinds now. There's some Imperial from offworld pulling strings at Sector Security and driving everyone crazy. If we don't have a closed-out search and final report soon, they may try to come in here."

"They can't do that."

Adano's sparse brows bristled over his baggy eyes. "They can try. I don't know where that will leave us, and I don't want to find out. So step it up out there, Vorey."

"Sir."

The simikan saluted and returned to his team in the streets.

FLASHMAN FOUND RS 207 on a 'sphere map, the meta-image of the cyber-integrated planet. The map showed gray network infrastructure, pulsing green datasphere, white infosphere—and, outside the busy areas, the merest tracery of blue lines for relays and traffic beacons. The naval facility was in just such a place, far from the active infosphere. There was only a fine cobweb of node lines radiating to and from the facility, marking com streams and geosynchronous vehicle tracking. Such simple operations for a station so complex.

Target acquired, he thought, smiling to himself, then he derezzed and followed one of those gossamer threads to its source.

That had been sixteen hours ago.

Now he worked mindlessly, routinely, picking away at the fortifications of the station. For—he had to hand it to the Navy—they were buttoned up tight. In VR, their station was not so much a fortress as it was a bathysphere. They had everything tucked away tight inside, closely confined and self-sufficient, with only a few isolated lifelines to the surface of the greater datasphere. They dribbled out transmissions like sparse air bubbles, and sucked in knowledge constructs in parsimonious gasps, drinking from the info cloud like a man gulping sporadic breath through an oxygen tube.

They didn't trust to their isolation alone to keep them safe, either. Flash-Man's single foray down a com net channel set him racing away again as fast as he could go, a bizarre form of hyperactive data shark hot on his speedy heels. It wasn't just out to break his data stream; it was out to destroy his VR construct with a destructive feedback loop. It was the kind of killer countermeasure that could slay a person outright, or at best leave a decker a permanently brain-fried vegetable. It was viciously aggressive, like an unstoppable hunting hound.

He'd lost it only after bouncing to an orbital space squirt relay, circling the globe riding maintenance pings, then sneaking back dirtside again.

Rethinking was called for. Rethinking was done.

When he returned, he'd loaded his deck with a different set of progs and fired up the overdrive on his Averi superprocessor. He'd go in the way they didn't expect: straight through their armor-plated hull. Not through I/O channels, but through the boundary matrix, the substrate beneath higher processing commands.

It was easy to work with in VR. Just put on your miner's headlamp, pull out the pickaxe, and start digging away at the layers ahead of you.

After some hours, the pickaxe became a drill, and his enthusiasm became dedicated focus.

When the drill broke for the third time, he traded his headlamp for a welder's mask and pulled out a plasma cutter. Dedication dulled to dogged persistence as he cut out the obstacles to his progress. Layer by layer, he burrowed into the side of the station construct, taking the slow, dull, brute-force approach to breaching the boundary. It was insanely tedious—and productive. Slowly but surely, FlashMan inched his way deeper into the naval station like a metal-boring parasite.

He automated what he could, let subroutines handle the most mind-deadening tasks, and always kept a weather eye out for data sharks or other hunter-killers. He found the heft of the cannon strapped to his thigh soundly reassuring. If trouble came, he was ready for it. And meanwhile . . .

In his deck, supercomputing functions that could shame small cities made his gear run hot. In VR, he squatted and applied his cutter, molten-edged metal peeling back in his spiky grip. FlashMan smiled grimly to himself.

Whatever they were so intent on keeping locked away, he would now see for himself.

# 63

WHEN THE HINANO clones returned to Port Oswin from the east, at the conclusion of a globe-circling journey, they were still not faces automated surveillance could pick out of the crowd.

Unaware of hazard or protection, yet leery of being seen on the streets, they kept their heads down and left the GTN terminal as rapidly as possible. Stopping by the tables of sidewalk vendors, they bought a shoulder satchel, and, in a nearby tourist locker arcade, stowed the heavy cash bag that would only be a hindrance while walking around. Transferring a moderate amount of money to the satchel, they grabbed an automated cab and headed north to the Shelieno.

They left the taxi on a side street some blocks distant from the north gate, the one closest to Tryst. They made their way along crowded streets thronging with afternoon shoppers, dodging lines of diners outside popular restaurants serving late lunch. They bought visored beret-style hats at one street vendor's table—"Hideous look," muttered Kesi—and used the hats to conceal their distinctive hair. With long locks tucked up and out of sight, their profiles were changed considerably, aided further by the baggy jackets they bought from another street vendor. They avoided stores where retail security might catch their faces and stayed on the streets, in the thick of the crowd.

Their footsteps brought them again to the loop road that led to and through the licensed quarter. Feeling safer in their shapeless concealing garments, with low visor brims hiding their features, they turned in unison and strode for the Enclave gate before them.

DEVON, A TENSIN officer on gate duty, flirted with a shapely benko girl leaving on an errand. He gave casual attention to the scanner at his position, set for a quick biometrics check on people entering the quarter. If it found anything, it would alert him. His partner opposite checked those leaving in the same manner. In spite of Simikan Berishnan's frequent checks, they had nothing to show for their screening.

Devon didn't expect to find anything, either. That was why his expression was comically stunned when his scanner trilled a beep into his earpiece. A match had been found! His benko girl laughed at him and walked on as he hurried to his post.

There. There was one face, moving through the crowd now. The proximity tracker illuminated a projected path of travel from point of sighting. Devon didn't realize it, but his standalone unit was still loaded with the original want order. Since it operated as an independent station once it was positioned at the gate, it had never updated with FlashMan's spurious graphics.

The officer searched the crowd trickling into the quarter, separating into groups and pairs, single persons weaving between the slower foot traffic—

He glimpsed the side of her face first, the profile a one-hundred-percent match to the holopix of the want. Hair not visible. He took in hat, coat—then realized the other person beside her looked just the same. He brought his wrist com to his lips, alerted his partner, and set off through the crowd after the twins.

BERISHNAN PICKED UP the tail from his man where the bright lights of Firewing splashed neon and dancing verts into the air. Other officers were closing in on side streets, weapons ready, but none were visible yet. The pair he followed did not stop, like most of the crowd, to ogle the holoverts, laden with sublims for precisely that crowd-stopping purpose. They carried on as if immune to such magnetic enticements, then took a sharp right at the corner of the neighboring tea house.

He hurried to catch up. There was nothing back there but a dead-end service alley and the back entrance to the tea house. Were they trying to lose him?

But no. He skidded to a stop at the mouth of the alley, watched from a distance as they walked to an alcove next to the recycling bins. He remembered now: that gave access to the rooftop gardens, innocuously concealed in plain sight, but locked up tight to the public.

One of the nondescript women pressed a thumb to the scan plate. The scrollwork gate clicked open, and the two ascended the stairs behind. Belatedly, he ran after them, only to confront a barrier that not even the Tensin were able to pass.

Fuck me, he breathed. They're shigasu. I'm not putting *that* out on an open com channel.

He made haste back to the station instead.

THE TWINS ACCESSED the roof gardens close to Tryst. They did not have far to walk before they were in the verdant landscape they knew so well, directly atop the roof of their home.

As they'd expected, it was deserted. "Be grateful for small blessings," Kesi said under her breath. It was mid-afternoon, a time of day when most shigasu were prepping for the early evening rush. Some with days off or on late assignments would still have leisure at this time of day, might still be in the gardens, strolling, reading, playing games—but none at Tryst, where the twins knew the schedule to a nicety. Houses of domination were notably busy in the afternoon, and again later in the evening. The first peak of business came from clients taking long lunches or the afternoon off work, while pleading "meetings" some-where across town. They were the married men, usually, the ones whose part-ners did not share their intensity or submission quirks, or were unsettled by them. They pursued their interests more clandestinely than the clientele who came in the freewheeling, self-indulgent evening hours, and all the House would be on hand to attend them at this time of day.

That meant the twins would be alone on the rooftop at this hour, and that was just as they'd planned it.

They settled onto a bench beneath a concealing trellis, a sheltered arbor overgrown with lush, purple-flowering stevis vines. They were near but just out of sight of the rooftop stairwell, protected from the view of anyone strolling by unless they came to the hidden arbor intentionally.

ON THE FAR side of the stairwell, where a line of cavra trees draped their long feathery fronds gracefully to the bark-mulched ground, a dark figure stood mo-tionless in the shadows. Unnoticed by the twins, Franc watched them from his place of concealment.

He wore a stealth suit, a body-hugging synth skin that took on the light and dark hues of his nearby concealment. It worked best at night, allowing one to blend seamlessly into shadow, but helped break up his profile even in daytime. It was necessary for slipping across the rooftops as he had, from garden patch to parkway, skirting groups of shigasu and servants who could not spot the in-truder in the dense greenery. His thigh-length street jacket was bundled at his waist, ready to let him blend into the pedestrian crowd later.

Now he stood with the coiled stillness of a stalker, eyes tracking the pair ducking out of sight beneath the arbor shade. Something about their move-ment seemed familiar. It both intrigued and irritated him, for his approach to the stairs might be seen now and his presence betrayed. The Winter God-dess worked this evening, he knew: he'd called ahead, been invited to court her with the other sycophants in Tryst's Mix bar, where she would make a rare appearance later on. He'd cut the call, having learned what he'd needed to know.

She was here, no doubt readying herself at this very moment for evening clients. He had some time.

He studied the arbor and the angle from there to the stairs, and waited, watching.

KESI SHRUGGED OFF the satchel and dropped it to the ground at the end of the long stone bench. She looked at Kesada, reached out to squeeze her hand in reassurance—though she wasn't sure which of them was doing the reassuring.

"All right. Me first, quick scout to our room, see if she's there. If yes, bring her up here to talk. If no, I'll see what's on her schedule for the day. Then back here and we'll think what's next."

Kesada ducked her chin in a curt nod. "If you're not back in ten, I'm coming after you."

Kesi nodded. Their room was near the end of the hall, close to the stairs. The other shigasu would already be with clients or in dressing rooms downstairs. It should be easy to slip in and out unnoticed. If it took her longer than that, it would be because of a problem.

They squeezed and released hands, and Kesi was gone.

For the first time in hours, Kesada breathed a deep sigh of relief. Finally they were taking concrete action. It was so much better than sitting helpless somewhere. She took off her beret and shook out her long hair, then just sat, enjoying the stillness of the garden and the sweet scent of the stevis blossoms.

EOSAN MARIT WAS the Shelieno council member responsible for security in the Enclave. She called Bejmet herself.

"I thought you should know," she began, then faltered.

"What?"

"There's a global want and warrant out on some fugitives. Two are targeted as armed and dangerous, shoot to kill."

Bejmet shook her head, puzzled by the irrelevant news. "Yes?"

"Those two just slipped into the Shelieno. Into the roof gardens."

The Palumara Eosan understood what that meant. They were shigasu. She did not want to hear what followed, knew it would come even as the words were said.

"I ran the thumb scan and gate cam logs myself. It's Hinano Kesada, and another woman who looks just like her."

"How—" Bejmet's voice shook.

"Images to you now."

Bejmet glanced at the pictures. It was Kes, yet not Kes. The shigasa looked as she had more than two years ago, before she was trained and groomed for her role at Tryst. Thicker blond eyebrows, not finely sculpted white. Something softer about the face. Younger. And the second face, identical to the first.

A cold frisson ran through her.

"Where are they now?"

She could hear the tension in Marit's voice. "You know we don't watch our own gardens. They could be anywhere. I won't pick them up again unless they leave by private access. But I suspect—"

"That they're on their way to Tryst."

"Yes."

Bejmet gathered herself. "Marit—this touches on some private affairs of my House. Can you sit on this for a while?'

Her friend shifted uncomfortably. "An imperial officer's sent a priority flash about this dragnet. This is hot. We need to take action on it."

Bejmet shook her head. "I know who that officer is."

"Do you know what this is all about?"

Bejmet bit her lip. "I can't discuss that. Please, Marit. Keep this close while I make some inquiries of my own."

The Eosan considered, finally nodded. "I can't bury it, but I can delay it for a couple of hours. I'll tell Helda—"

"No!" She said it too adamantly; Marit looked at her oddly. She took a breath. "Please. Let me."

"Very well." Marit studied her friend through the com. "Be careful, Bej." Then she was gone.

Bejmet cleared the channel and sat still, fingers clenched together to prevent them from trembling.

*Shoot to kill.* Marit's words echoed in her head.

She'd bowed before Ilanya not because she had to—in spite of what the Kingmaker thought, Ilanya Evanit was not the ultimate arbiter of shigasue fates. The Eosan had complied because giving one shigasa up for that spider's clandestine purposes seemed a small price—a necessary price—to maintain the greater security of those she was responsible for.

But *I'm* responsible for Kes, too, she admitted to herself. It was one thing to use a shigasa: some might say, cynically, that they existed to be used, to serve other purposes than the evident ones, and this was not the first time since she'd become an Eosan that Bejmet had bowed to that truth. But using had its limits, and now there were three Keses—the two could only be clones—and a kill order.

An order to murder *her* shigasu, and use Enclave forces to do it—or, she assumed, Ilanya's own forces would see to it.

The Kingmaker went too far. Bejmet rebelled against it, a lifetime of training and service to Palumara House compelling her to respond, even while Ilanya's threats echoed in her memory.

Two thoughts chased each other's heels, locking her in place.

You just changed the rules of the game, Ilanya Evanit.

But do I dare make the call that can stop you?

She sat, undecided, interlaced fingers locked tight with tension.

# 64

FRANC'S HAND BRUSHED the vibroblade sheathed at his thigh. His plan was straightforward: go through the place, room by room, until he found the bitch, and deal with her. It shouldn't be difficult, as long as he got into rooms quickly and didn't loiter in the hall where someone might give the alarm. If there were house cameras in the women's living quarters, they should be obscured by the fuzzer he'd brought along, a small unit now attached to his wrist, projecting a static field of electromagnetic distortion around his body. It translated to a blurred, indistinct figure in video feeds—not perfect concealment, but easily overlooked in casual surveillance, and it would leave him unidentifiable if they captured his image.

Of course, if there were other shigasu in the rooms he searched, he might have to silence them, too, after they told him where to find the bitch. Couldn't leave anyone who might identify him. And that same concern made him leery of the arbor.

One woman had left; one was still there. He already knew what he would have to do.

*Never leave anyone at your back.* He recited the third precept of Icechromer enforcers under his breath, then ghosted through the greenery towards the arbor.

DOWN THE STAIRS, across the landing, down the hall—it was just as Kesi expected. Not a soul in sight: the shigasu were all on floors below, dressing, or holding court with clients in the lounge, or in session in one of Tryst's eleven playrooms and suites.

She passed two doors—Coel, Narissa—and paused in front of her own. She stretched a hand out, touching the pithpaper squares of the traditional sliding door that marked her personal space.

It's been so long.

She blinked back sudden tears. All the unanswered questions, all the uncertainty—would this ever be her home again?

No time for that. She quashed those thoughts and slid the door open with one swift movement. A step took her inside. She pulled it to behind her, then halted again, overwhelmed by the sight of it all. *Home.* Everything familiar, in its place, but for the scatter of clothes . . .

She noticed, then. The room smelled of sex and incense.

"Kes?"

She knew that questioning voice. It electrified her, and it came from her bed, just out of sight behind the half panel that divided living from sleeping area. Kesi felt rooted to the spot. Go? Stay?

She hesitated too long, and Morya made the decision for her. She stepped naked around the wall panel, pushing dark tangled curls back from her face, looking expectantly at the door.

Both women froze.

"Morya?" Kesi's voice was hopeful and tremulous. "It's me."

Morya's eyes widened. "You're not Kes," she blurted. "You can't be." But uncertainty was in her voice. Suddenly aware of her nakedness, she ducked back behind the panel, fumbled for her discarded robe. Kesi came around the corner as she belted it around her.

"Look," Morya said, shoving out a palm to halt Kesi's advance. "I don't know what's going on here but you need to get out of here. This is Kes's room."

"Right." Bitterness and near-hysteria mingled in her laugh. This, she hadn't bargained for. "I'm her, she's me. We're us."

Morya shook her head in denial. Kesi sighed and sat down at the desk. "How else do you explain this?"

She thumb-tagged the access tab. The system went live, the full entry suite of infosphere access points floating in an interactive hologram above the desktop. It was her customized portal, open only to a system's authorized owner. The place where she started her daily routine, the one she hadn't been able to follow for weeks and weeks now—

Her eyes lingered on the astrogation node until she forced her gaze away. She turned in the chair. Morya stood in the center of the room, fists clenching the borrowed robe tight around her.

"No," she repeated, as if saying it would make it so.

"I've been cloned."

"What?"

"Yes. Twice, actually. There's another of me upstairs." She glanced up towards the roof. "We have questions. We need to talk to Kes."

Morya sighed and gathered herself, a visible motion as she squared her shoulders. She came forward, reached out a hand to gingerly touch Kesi's cheek.

Kesi squeezed that hand in her own, pressed delicate fingers against her skin, turned her head to kiss it. Morya snatched it back. Kesi sighed. "I promised myself that once I got out of there I'd see you again. I didn't expect it would be like this. There's a lot of lost time I need to make up with you, kushla." She looked at Morya, who shook her head and turned away.

"This is impossible." The joygirl spoke into the air of the room, avoiding

Kesi's gaze. "You look just like you did, back when we first . . . Why would Kes clone herself?"

That was an accusation, spat back over her shoulder as she marched to the table and planted herself in a chair there. Arms crossed, chin high, the wall at her back, protected all around.

"Don't be pissed at me," Kesi said dryly. "This isn't something I chose, and I don't know the reasons for it any more than you do. Where's Kes?"

"What do you want with her?"

"Stand down, Morya. I'm her, too, you know. We just want to ask her some questions. She has some answers we need."

Morya shook her head again—not in denial, this time, but simply in overwhelmed confusion. "This is unbelievable."

"You should try it from this side."

They held each other's gaze for a long moment. Finally Morya uncrossed her arms. "She's with a client."

"When will she be back?"

Morya shrugged.

Kesi turned to the comp, checked the house schedule. Kes was down for three hours with Janus. That would be a major session, she knew, his first time back after his long trip away. And that was three too many hours to risk loitering here.

Then again, she thought indecisively, maybe it's safer to be right here, where no one expects us to be.

She looked up from the display. "I need to talk to Kesada about this. Whether to wait, or not." She paused, a sudden thought occurring to her. "Come with me and meet her. I know she'll want to see you, too."

Morya hesitated, then nodded. Curiosity was winning out. Kesi grinned and pretended to turn away while her love dressed. She watched her, though, out of the corner of her eye, wishing she knew what to say to bring this woman into her arms.

If Morya was aware of the scrutiny, she didn't let on. Soon they were in the hall, heading for the stairs to the roof.

KESADA SAT UPRIGHT, suddenly alert. She'd heard something, maybe: a footstep on the path? or a crunch of gravel underfoot? Something her conscious mind had not registered, yet which set her nerves singing.

Franc ducked into the shade beneath the trellis and they saw each other at the same moment.

"You!" she gasped.

His eyes flickered with surprise, then narrowed, studying her, flitting from feature to feature. "Could I be so lucky?" He spoke as if to himself.

His tone was chilling, but she would not let him cow her. She stood in one flowing movement and confronted him, hands on hips. "What in the seven hells are you doing up here? Get lost before I report you, Franc."

He grinned at her, all bared fangs. "Your attitude still sucks, but I like the new look. It's just like the good old days, Kes. Miss the Salon, do you? Miss doing that bump and grind you used to beg for with me?"

She clenched her fists, angry, frightened. She could see the bulge swelling at his groin. He took a step towards her, another—

"Back off, you bastard!" It was nearly a shout, one arm extended and a finger pointing as she commanded him. He didn't stop. Every part of her that feared and detested this man screamed at her to run.

She heeded it.

She darted to one side and towards the stairs. It couldn't be worse to be in the house right now—

But he was faster, and stronger, and full of hate.

**KESI LED THE** way. Morya lagged behind the unsettling duplicate of the woman she loved. Kesi glanced back over her shoulder, then took her hand, to lead her more swiftly along.

Her grasp was completely familiar, even down to the way she intertwined fingers firmly, a grip that always promised to hold on tight. Morya tried to think of her companion as not-Kes, and failed completely.

Kesi mounted the stairs with Morya at her side. The rooftop door, always open at this time of day, led directly into sunlight and greenery. The domina turned towards the stevis arbor, then squeezed Morya's hand hard, freezing her in her tracks.

"Motherfucker," she hissed. She yanked away and dashed into the greenery.

In that moment, Morya saw it, too: a thrashing of arms and legs on the ground by the leaf-shaded bench. A burly form atop slender limbs, telltale blond hair, the muted wasp-drone of a large-gauge vibroblade—

Kesi flew into the midst of it all.

She angled not for the struggling pair on the ground, but for the end of the bench. In a heartbeat, Morya saw why. She swept up the carrybag on the ground there, braced her feet, and swung it with all her might.

Length of limb gave her leverage, adrenaline gave her strength. Accuracy honed by precise flogging served her true. The heavy bag caught Franc square on the side of the head with a thunk like fists hitting meat. The blow knocked him to one side and smack into the ground. He slammed an elbow into a flagstone as he went a-splay. The knife twirled off into the underbrush and the Icechromer lay stunned.

Kesi'd held nothing back. She let the force of the carry-through swing her around, an unintentionally graceful pirouette, and let the bag fly from her hands to drop nearly where she had found it. "Oh my gods," she uttered, "are you all right?"

She fell to her knees beside her twin. Morya joined her, sparing a meager glance for Franc as she did. He lay facedown, barely stirring. Not out, then, but not functional for a while. Kesada was in far worse condition: a lip split and bloody, her shirt cut open, blood on her side—

Kesi's hands fluttered like helpless birds. Kesada waved her back, tried to sit up. It was Morya who leaned in, pressed her back to the ground. "Wait," she said. "Let me see what's wrong."

It was only now that Kesada registered her presence. She looked combative and dazed at the same time, and now surprise layered on top of that. Her gaze flickered to Kesi even as she complied with Morya's command. "Did you find—?"

"Kes?" Her twin gathered herself. "Not yet. Morya was in her room." She inclined her head to Morya, whose gentle fingers were probing Kesada's side. Her brow furrowed. "What did he do to you?"

"Obvious, isn't it?" Kesada gritted as Morya applied pressure to the cut in her side. "He was going to carve me up while he raped me, then kill me when he was done."

Her clothes were in tatters, and bloody. The knife-play had already well begun.

"Did he—?"

Kesada shook her head. "You bagged him before he got that far. Good shot, by the way."

"Come," Morya said firmly. "Sit up. I'll keep pressure on this."

Kesi stood as the pair maneuvered upright. She turned towards Franc, stirring where he sprawled. She drew a booted foot back and kicked him in the side with all her might. Something cracked. The semi-conscious man groaned and curled to protect his ribs.

"You cocksucker," she said heatedly. "I'll kill you for this."

Morya helped Kesada to her feet. She saw Kesi scanning the ground, looking for something, and frowning when she failed to spot it. It wasn't hard to guess what she must be looking for. If she had a knife in her hand right now, Franc would be dead. But Kesada stood bleeding and house security could take care of Franc.

Kesi turned her back on the Icechromer and slung the carry bag over her shoulder, tending to what was more important. "Let's get you inside," she said to her twin. Taking Kesada's other side, Kesi and Morya helped the injured woman to the stairs.

# 65

IN INTSEC HEADQUARTERS a dome away, Ilanya joined her monitor crew. They watched the fugitive clones move down the hall in the company of Morya, one of them wounded and limping as she went. They turned deeper into the building.

"They're going to find Kes," she ventured out loud. "Or Helda."

"If they find the other clone, they'll walk in on her session with Janus," Teo observed. "It's starting right now."

"Put a flyeye on them," Eva ordered. "Let's maintain visual and audio while we can."

The POV shifted to Morya's viewpoint. When they left the monitored hallway and turned deeper into the house, a spycam went with them, a mobile sticky gnat-like object attached unnoticed to Morya's dark curls. They entered a plain stairwell, a serviceway in the back of the house, saying little, intent on helping their wounded companion along.

Teo stiffened where he stood, head tilting as he listened to something only he could hear.

"What is it?" Eva asked.

"That's a death-penalty felony," he said curtly—not to her, but to someone on his comlink. He raised a hand as if to wave someone off, or cut a signal—then froze again. He turned sharply to Eva. "Domna. You need to take this call."

"Who?"

"An infiltrator in our secure systems—"

"*What?!*"

"—patching Sefano through to you now."

Eva frowned, motioned for it to be sent to her private comlink. Her aural implant relayed the call where only she could hear it. Static cleared to carrier wave. She did not wait for her caller to speak.

"How did you get on this line?" she demanded. "No one infiltrates this—"

"Lecture someone who cares, Domna," came the Red Hand boss's voice. "I'm saving you from a disastrous mistake."

"Explain," she barked.

"I must regretfully cancel our prior understanding. Circumstances have changed radically. The Red Hand Cartel now stands ready to assist you with funding in the full measure that you first requested of us, and more if you need it."

"You will?" Ilanya sank into her seat in disbelief as Sefano continued.

"The major portion of these funds will come from our triumvir Janus, in exchange for certain modest concessions from the government. You will need to negotiate those terms with him directly, and we will all need to concur on the deal. We don't anticipate problems on our end.

"On your end, however—I hope you haven't killed him yet. He controls the wealth of worlds now, it seems, and if you kill him, you are destroying your golden goose. Also, *our* golden goose. If such a fiasco were to happen, I don't believe we could do business together again."

Eva sat, stunned, mind racing. No reply. Her silence grew.

"Domna? Did you hear me?"

She forced a word. "Yes."

"Is Janus dead yet?"

"We don't know."

"How can you not know?" Sefano's voice came louder across her link.

Machinations and schemes, her months of planning, in ruins. *The wealth of worlds* . . . Startling new possibilities blossomed before her, and suddenly, unexpectedly, her goal of ensuring the succession was within reach. *The only constant is change.*

Her animus towards Janus had never been personal. He'd been a means to an end: an obstacle to be removed, leverage to be applied. Now, he would be used a different way. But first his life must be safeguarded and her own plans thwarted. The warrior part of her gnashed her teeth over that; the wise part of her did what had to be done.

"Teo. Move our coms to an alternate channel and secure this one for Sefano's exclusive use. Sefano—we'll update you soon. I need to take action, now." She severed the link with a thought and spun to Obray where he sat plugged into the IntSec management console.

"Status?"

"Janus is ten minutes into his session. The clones are still moving through service corridors. I think the playroom is their destination."

And his death will follow soon, unless we can physically stop Kes, she thought. Detonating the microcharge was out of the question now, not while Janus was in the area.

"Send in police units, now," she ordered, "and the forces we commandeered from Sector Security. I want a cordon around Tryst and your assault teams ready to move at my command. The Winter Goddess is our target; Janus is in danger from her. Consider it a hostage situation. Shoot to kill."

———

**CITY SECURITY FORCES** flooded into the domain of the shigasue.

Following instructions from security councilor Eosan Marit, the Tensin stood aside from the Port Oswin forces that outnumbered and outgunned them. City police, Sector Security, Internal Security, paramilitary and incident response squads garbed in assault gear—a small army poured into the sacrosanct Between-World as if they were quelling a riot.

They poured through the Shelieno, securing every airlock and entrance into the riverside entertainment district. Armed hovercraft entered Enclave waters from up- and downstream on the Dryx and set up a gunboat perimeter on the waterside flank of the ward. Men and women in jungle-green fatigues and silver-visored combat helmets occupied the streets around Tryst. Assault teams took positions flanking the door, while a mobile command post assembled at the nearby T-intersection controlling access to the house of domination.

Shocked at the unprecedented sight of armed forces on Enclave streets, pleasure-seekers knew better than to stay. Streets emptied save for residents and some inebriated tourists more curious than wise. The Tensin took up neutral positions, watching the intruders but staying clear of them as well.

Chief Adano spoke into his com link unit as he had every few minutes since the entrance barriers had been breached. "They've set up exit checkpoints," came his last report. "No one's allowed back into Port Oswin without identity verification first. Some without are being pulled aside. No shigasu, just regular patrons."

"Enough." Marit's tone was sharper than she intended. "Call again if they take any action other than standing in our streets."

It took her just a moment to relay the update to Bejmet. A favor for a friend.

**EOSAN BEJMET: SENIOR** shigasa, head of Palumara House on Lyndir, chair of the Enclave council, official representative of the Shelieno to the city and government of Port Oswin, capital city on the capital world of the CAS Sector.

All of her titles and honors meant nothing in this moment of complete powerlessness against the Kingmaker's transgressions.

Ilanya Evanit did more than violate the independence of this one Enclave on Lyndir. The Between-World could not be overrun in this way and still maintain its sovereignty. Her actions countered direct charters from the Emperor that bestowed that autonomy. Worse, she was the Emperor's own agent. The implications of this were many, and all of them destructive to the standing of shigasue everywhere.

Bejmet's fingers ached and she unclenched the fists she had unconsciously formed upon hearing the watch commander's report. Shaking her hands to loosen her muscles, she stepped out onto the groomed but barren ground of the rock garden in one corner of her villa courtyard.

The estate's stream burbled in the greenery behind her, but she kept her eyes fixed on the rake-patterns of the fine-graveled ground where she stood. Faie bonsai framed the verge of this meditation spot, their red leaves a prickly complement to pointillist patterns in rock. One pattern caught her eye and led it in gentle curves, a circuit, a transit, a flow in stone and thought, until thought flowed with stone.

The habit of steady, deep, unstressed reflection took over.

Against her better judgment, she'd allowed one of her shigasa to be used for some clandestine purpose. Something weighty and steeped in intrigue, that much was plain by virtue of the fact that it was Ilanya Evanit herself making the demand. It had seemed wisest to bow to that demand at the time.

Bejmet's lips curled down. She'd balanced the welfare of one shigasa against the welfare of all of them. It was a weighing of scales she loathed to undertake in the first place, for she had a duty of protection to every member of her clan. Now this: this unthinkable, unbearable invasion of the Gantori-Das, the Between-World—not just a place but a way of being, central to their very existence.

This offense demanded a swift, definitive response, or Bejmet would lose all face, all honor, and in a very real sense, all authority—not only for herself but potentially for every Enclave anywhere.

That must not be, for the hidden work of the shigasue—some might say their real work—depended upon the hallowed nature of the Gantori-Das and the refuge it created. Their secret endeavors grew out of a hundred thousand confidences shared each day between lover-patrons and their shigasa mistresses and confidants. Pillow talk and drunken confessions, allusions heard and pieced together with indiscretions uttered by men worlds away—none of these things were lost on the shigasue.

The entertainers of the Between-World constituted the most far-flung and subtly influential intelligence network in the Sa'adani Empire. Bejmet knew only her own specific duties and the broad outlines of that business, which was opaque to all but the highest elite of the Mother Houses on Calyx. But this much she'd become privy to when elevated to her present rank: they not only collected rumor and fact, they also influenced men in power.

Every warlord who'd ever fallen in love with a shigasa mistress, every minister who relaxed weekly in the company of his favorite entertainer—everyone who ever had (or thought he had) a special rapport with that one unique shigasa . . . they either yielded information, or were susceptible to influence from the women they adored.

The right word, a well-timed observation, the proper comment framed just so—they all colored perceptions. Opinions and decisions, the shigasue had found, could be molded and gently nudged in new directions. Given time, they could influence decision-makers so subtly they thought the decisions their own.

The elite of the shigasue houses wielded this network to further their own interests. The only outsider they felt a debt to was the Emperor himself, whose express permission granted them the autonomy needed to create the Between-World wherever there was a Sa'adani presence, and run it as they saw fit.

There was a quid pro quo for this arrangement. Now and then, when it could serve the throne and not harm the shigasue, they passed useful information on to their ultimate patron. More rarely, influence might be offered as well.

The Emperor's regular intelligence services did not truly recognize the nature of this arrangement, nor were they supposed to. Their ignorance of the relationship between the Dragon Throne and the shigasue allowed that back channel to exist, and operate untainted by outside interests.

And that, now, was precisely the problem with Ilanya Evanit. Powerful the Kingmaker might be, but the world of the shigasue was far outside her ken, as her actions on Lyndir so clearly demonstrated.

The head of PolitDiv had no need to know their role as information conduit to the Emperor's ear. But her actions endangered this delicate balance. For sympathetic ears and words of advice to work, the realm of the shigasue must be completely safe from the intrusion of the outside world. Without that guarantee, patrons would not stay, or would not relax in the way that allowed trust and confidences to grow. And if they could be transgressed on one world, they could be coerced on any.

Ilanya must be stopped, immediately.

Bejmet sat on a stone bench, her need for action warring with her need for clear judgment. Her eyes still traced the patterns and shadows of the raked garden ground.

The Kingmaker did not respond to her calls or protests—did not even think herself accountable for her actions here on Lyndir. Yet her intentions were easily read. All this business—the wants and warrants for the Hinano clones, the intrusion of armed forces, their positioning near Tryst—all shouted that Ilanya was not done yet with Palumara House's star shigasa. And now she'd gone too far.

Bejmet sighed. The time for subtlety was over. This situation had mushroomed into something with graver implications. Graver than the threat of destruction of one shigasue house, however personally terrible such a price might be.

There is one person I can call, Bejmet considered. She is the only one who has a chance of bringing Ilanya to heel. But calling upon her will cost all my clout to reach her, and create obligations for me as well.

And if I'm wrong? If she chooses not to take on this battle?

The thought gave her pause. There was no bigger card Bejmet could play, and no guarantee of success. To invoke this one's aid was to gamble with all her political capital gathered over decades of ever-increasing authority in the Between-World. If her plea was even heard, would it be responded to in time to help them? And regardless of the outcome, instigating a move against the Kingmaker would probably end her career, one way or another. Ilanya had already threatened her life, and was not a forgiving opponent.

A wry expression flitted across her refined features. *All creatures must awaken one day from the Dream,* she quoted the famous Lau-zim philosopher Meres Nor, speaking of death and its inevitable visitation to all.

Perhaps I'll awaken sooner than I planned, she thought. Perhaps even all my House with me, if Ilanya acts on her threat.

She felt a twinge of fear, then shrugged the traitor emotion away. Such unimaginable consequences must remain exactly that: unimagined. She ran a necessary risk. The greater good of her community beyond Palumara House was at stake.

To locate the personage she must speak with and make a lag-delayed subspace packet call that spanned sectors: that could take an hour or more. If she was going to play this gambit, she must start now. Later would be too late.

Bejmet turned back to her house, then hesitated. There was no precedent for her action, and no time to seek permission from the Mother House. To move to the com console indoors would be to embark on a life-altering path. It was not what she had planned for this afternoon.

She resigned herself and stepped forward, to do as she must.

# 66

JANUS SWALLOWED THROUGH a mouth gone dry with anticipation. The domina crossed the floor in front of him, prowling left to right, while he kept his eyes studiously on the ground before his knees. He felt her eyes on him, burning his skin with her scrutiny. He yearned to meet her gaze but did not dare look up, not without permission. His thoughts ran riot instead, counterpoint to the disciplined tension that held him kneeling, naked, before the woman he worshiped.

How? He asked himself for the hundredth time. How can I get her to say yes?

She would never agree to be a kept woman, his mistress and lover. He'd made that mistake only once, proposing that kind of arrangement between them. But now—now he could do anything for her that money allowed. Did she want to start her own shigasue House? He could bankroll it. Did she want to be a woman of leisure? He could make that happen, too. How to ask it, how to offer it, in a way that she would say yes, and take it as the sincere homage it was meant to be?

Having rehearsed this scenario aboard the *Savia* didn't make this moment any easier. He hadn't been so nervous with a woman since the first time he'd kissed a girl.

The pointed toe of a pristine white boot, all smooth glistening leather, stopped within his frame of vision. She stood before him on the cool marbled floor of her inner sanctum. Soon, soon, she would have him screaming in pain and pleasure, begging for mercy. He had to ask her before then, while he still had his wits about him. Before endorphins washed away his assertiveness and resolve.

A slender, red-nailed finger reached under his chin, tilted his face up to hers. Now he could look at her, and he did, eyes scanning her face, seeking a sign that she might be open to his proposition. . . .

Pale, she was: cold and cruel as Lovianis, the Goddess of Pain herself. Was it his imagination, or did she look more like the avatar of that harsh deity than ever before? His gaze traveled past scarlet lips to violet, smoke-framed eyes. They met his, then narrowed with a sadistic hardness that set his heart racing. She looked inhumanly powerful, more commanding, more desirable than even his fevered fantasies aboard ship had allowed.

The overpowering presence of the Winter Goddess stilled his tongue in his dry mouth, even while his cock swelled hard between his legs. Proposals fled his mind as she commanded his obedience with a look. A welcome yet dreaded feeling coiled in the pit of his stomach.

Fear.

Fear for what she might do to him, for what torments erotic and otherwise she might inflict.

Torments that were welcomed, for what pleasure she would take from them and his suffering.

He exhaled with a shudder. He knew better than to speak without permission to the dominating presence that held him in thrall. She studied him for a long time. He remained still, tense, motionless, hers to command.

She went down on one knee, then brought her face close to his, fingers gripping his jaw with sudden tension. Her nostrils flared: a predator on the hunt, scenting the air near her prey.

"I've been waiting for this moment for a long time," she breathed. "I have . . . so much . . . I'm going to do to you."

Her voice was husky in a way he'd never heard before, a deadly bedroom voice that set him trembling. She sounded aroused, caught in a tension both physical and sexual, if he read it right. Did she catch that thought? She saw something in him, and her lip curled in a cruel sneer. Anticipation thrilled his every nerve, and the hardness between his legs turned into an ache that craved release.

Ah, delicious torture. If she was true to form, it would be a release denied for a long while yet.

She ran her hand up the right side of his face, the backs of her fingers stroking his cheek, his cheekbone, fingers trailing to his temple—and stopped at the red button of his neural interface there. "Did you do as I asked?" she demanded to know.

Asked? Janus was nonplussed. What had she . . . ?

Oh, yes. The flirtation they'd had when he departed, her threat to get inside his mind, his promise to make that possible for her. Erotic foreplay, it had all seemed, and titillating enough that he'd decided to go through with it. Of course he'd had a safeguard built into his implant before he'd even left Lyndir, specially to protect his data jack and his cybersecrets. But the Goddess had wanted to walk through memories with him. Who was he to deny her that small pleasure? Even though he'd almost forgotten about it in the meantime.

"Yes, Domna." He nodded, and his next statement was more true than he would ever have admitted. "My mind is yours to probe as you like."

She would only be in a bounded sandbox, the portico of his chipped and wired senses, a place he could control and monitor. But if she really wished to go there . . .

"Good." Her voice was cool, but edged with a strange tension. "Before we're done I'm going to be inside the very guts of you."

Janus heard that as an erotic threat and felt his cock jump. The rest of him stayed motionless with the greatest of efforts.

"Stay there," she told him, curtly, needlessly, as she rose gracefully to her feet. She stepped away, then, and walked behind him, busying herself across the room for a moment. Suddenly she was sitting behind him on a float pad, her long legs straddling him, thigh-high boots bracing his torso between them. She pulled him back into the warm hollow between her legs as she cradled him from behind.

He gave a small moan.

"Shush." Her fingers smoothed his temple again, felt the edges of his implant.

"You remember what we agreed to." She breathed into his ear a statement, not a question. "I want you to access your interface now. I'll meet you there. I have questions for you, and you're going to answer them."

His eyelids fluttered shut as he began to comply, an internal process triggered with the inward-turning of his attention. He felt her hand at his temple; something slotting into his jack with a snick.

He held his breath and waited for something to happen. And waited.

Then everything went black.

KES LIVED IN the moment now. It was a blessing, an elusive state she'd never mastered before. And it was a troublesome thing. She could plan ahead, but that held no appeal. Better to be flexible. Respond to the moment, she thought. Stay open to possibilities.

It had led to the most creative and extreme play with Morya she'd ever experienced, even at the cost of a severe exercise of self-discipline not to take things too far. It led to a new relationship with Helda—always off-balance now, with Kes no longer predictable.

And it led to this moment, with Janus kneeling before her, his life in her hands and the man foolishly ignorant of his peril, fixated only on his projected fantasies and the façade her predator-self lurked behind.

She savored her imminent revenge, and the monster in her stirred in anticipation. But first, there was their little agreement to see to.

I will know you before I kill you, she thought. I want to learn what it is, exactly, that I'll grind beneath my heel today.

She was no longer interested in seeking out erotic secrets, all the better to dominate him with. But what else lurked in his memories and thoughts where their interfaces could meld, where she could see the shadows of things that moved him?

What could she pry out of him about his business with the Icechromers? Better to ask only after he was mentally laid bare and compliant before her.

He was a fool, leaving himself open for this. All he saw was her impatience to have him at her mercy.

By the time he realized his danger it would be too late.

She watched him quiver with nerves and arousal before her. Janus was still a good-looking man. Ascetically handsome, a swimmer's broad-shouldered, lean, muscled body, a high-browed intelligent face. His eyes were expressive when he was not guarded, and he was not guarded now. Those eyes showed awe, delight, near-fear at being in her hands again. The scent of his skin was like musk and spice, sharp with nervous tension, a natural perfume that drew her near. She liked the smell of him, as men went. Always had . . .

His attributes registered on her even while part of her mind planned how to kill him slowly during their session, in a way the house would not see, or would mistake for an accident. It would be more satisfying that way than the rapid evisceration she had toyed with earlier.

She sat behind him on a floatpad, pulled him into her embrace. Jacked the special duo-interface into her own rigger socket at the base of her skull and put the extension lead to his temple. One push and it was in.

She inhaled sharply, involuntarily, and her back arched as a surge of energy and nervous reflex ran through her. A circuit strengthened between them. Neurons linked to data injectors, linked to the firmware of the duo-jack, synchronizing, integrating, bringing their implants into union. It should be a lightning-fast process, marked by some disorientation, clearing into shared thought-space. That was what the jack documentation said, what the VR tutorial had prepped her for.

Instead, something else happened.

Janus went rigid, unmoving in her arms. Kes felt her consciousness slipping down a tunnel, like the flight into an astrogation linkage. She came out into a small, constrained space, as if Janus had built a little room in his mind in which to meet her.

But it was not Janus that greeted her in that room, or not him alone. She rezzed in for a heartbeat in the middle of a whirlwind of energies. Forces tumbled around her. Where her client should have rezzed in, something grappled with his sim-field, and he struggled against its ropy embrace. The pair tumbled and tossed in the memory-space they all inhabited. If she'd been here first, this thing would be grappling with her instead of him. The wrongness of it all flooded over her, and her every nerve screamed *retreat*.

She did what instinct demanded, and fled.

# 67

CODE DOES NOT become bored, or distracted, or driven to the brink of insanity by endless repetition. But *this* code construct carried a synaptic matrix so good as to be indistinguishable from a fractal bit of a human consciousness.

That echo of FlashMan was nearly gibbering mad.

When the seamless ceiling of his prison split open with a brand-new gaping hatch as broad as a maglev tunnel, the Flashworm didn't notice. It was laboring up the wall near the dataport.

When the tunnel darkened with a submicronic lead, filling it solid, it didn't notice. It was inching its way over the lip of the port to where data occasionally flowed.

When a blaze of white energy released from the ceiling like a deluge from a fire hose, it noticed. The codeworm was blown off its precarious perch, hurled to the floor by a cascade of incoming data that filled the room entirely. That blinding storm of energy had its own mission. Flash was simply in the way, and it tossed him about like a windblown leaf as it filled the buffer and began to coalesce in the middle.

Now a discrete column of energy streamed from the ceiling lead. It shocked the codeworm out of its practiced pattern. For the first time in eons, it began to assess its environment.

A figure formed in the pillar of light, gaining cohesion as he watched. But the Flashworm had long since worn its curiosity to a nubbin. It recognized only an energy stream filling the room, the excess running out somewhere unknown—possibly back through the same lead that channeled energy overhead.

The vestige of a cyberdecker came to its senses in that moment. Good enough for me, thought the fractal bit of FlashMan. The codeworm twisted in the backwash of energy and shot out a ropy gripping pod as it passed near the rezzing sim.

It clung. Another pseudopod, and another. *Climb . . . up . . .* was his enduring imperative, and the codeworm ascended, treating the coalescing form like a statue, full of toeholds and push-points that would drive it higher—

—until the statue fought back, trying to shed the grip of the codeworm. The more the sim-form squirmed and fought to lose the Flashworm, the more tenaciously it clung. The cascade of electrons made it difficult to cling, but the codeworm persisted with the same tenacity that had it crawling floors and walls for eons.

Now a second figure started to rez beside the first. The construct was half solid, half ephemeral, not yet fully there. In the flood of power that surrounded them, the codeworm tasted strong bi-directional data flow and a forgotten, primitive remnant of FlashMan felt a twinge of joy.

Good enough. Good enough.

Words, so long unused, sounded like a stranger's voice even to his own mind that thought them. No matter. There was current flow here, something he could latch onto, and did.

With the next handshake cycle of syncing I/O bits, FlashMan released a burst of energy he didn't know he had. He leapt to the new sim, flew up its pillar of light into the maw of the overhead tunnel and was gone.

KES FLED, THROWING her thoughts and her electron stream back down the linkage, back to her own brain-space and implant, safely away from the chaos in Janus's head.

She severed the connection the moment she was safe, and yanked the jack from his temple. He swayed forward in her arms, not unconscious but not entirely present of mind, either.

What in the seven icy hells was that? she thought, angered, adrenaline fueling her reaction. She wanted answers. She pushed Janus from her and sprang to her feet. He sprawled across the marble flagstones, groaning, one hand groping his head.

She put hands on hips, nudged him with a toe of her stiletto-heeled, thigh-high boot. "What—" she began, but never finished.

The side door to the playroom flew open. It was the service entrance, concealed during sessions, used by cleaning staff and house mechos. Never was Kes to be interrupted that way in session.

She angled half-right to confront the intruder. Just as well the Winter Goddess's client was recovering and could not see this. What entered her lair staggered her backwards.

It was Morya. And herself.

And herself.

"SHIT," POL SAID in the control room that monitored sessions in progress. Helda, sitting with him to watch Kes and Janus, didn't even have that much to say. She simply gaped.

On the monitor, she saw Kes as she had been when they'd bought her from the joyhouse. And Morya. And between them—Kes, again. Battered. Bloody. But unmistakably Kes.

As was the Winter Goddess, radically transformed with hair and stage makeup, but Helda knew who was behind that guise.

She clenched the arms of her chair, preventing herself from running down to the playroom that very second.

That Kes had been cloned was obvious. Here was the evidence. Her rages, her behavior since her return—so many discrepancies gelled into a sick kind of sense, and Helda began to swear, a stream of curses that caused her slave to study monitors and wisely hold his tongue.

Torn between the need to intervene and the knowledge that if she moved she would miss the exchange that followed, the Dosan stayed rooted in her chair and watched.

An alarm wheeped at Pol's console.

"What?"

"A spyeye," he said. "Someone in there entered with a flycam on them." A light flashed on the console and the alarm fell silent. "Neutralized," he confirmed. Microsonics in the room were designed to destroy unauthorized recording devices. They'd done their work already. Whoever was trying to record inside the Winter Goddess's lair was now deaf and blind.

**THE FLYEYE LASTED** just long enough to drive Ilanya into action. There: Janus lying at Kes's feet. Was he dead already? Were they too late?

She saw his arm move feebly before the feed went black.

Still alive, then, if barely. She whirled and snapped commands.

"Teo. Activate the wire in our killer clone. Let's immobilize her for now."

"Done, Domna."

"Obray. Order security teams in. Their first priority is to secure Janus. Amend the kill orders. Absolutely no shooting that may put Janus at risk, but lethal force is authorized to ensure his safety."

"Yes, Domna Arcolo."

"Second priority: remove those women from Tryst. The joygirl, too; she knows too much. Give the teams visuals on all targets. Any resistance, shoot to kill."

"Done."

She prowled the room and silently invoked Raem the Taskmaster, the mental construct of her Tolex chip. She was caught up in swiftly unfolding events, multiple variables. One misstep could shatter the fortunes of her Emperor and the Empire.

It was time for enhancement.

**HELDA WAS OUT** of her chair and dashing for the playroom when Pol called after her.

"Domna?" His tone was strangled. She'd never heard the like and it caused her to spin about before she reached the exit.

"What?" she demanded. His only answer was a finger pointing at the monitors.

Outside the broad front door of Tryst, green-uniformed assault teams crouched, about to rush the building. Three white-tuniced officers led them.

"Lyndir security! And Internal Security, too! Impossible! What are they doing here?"

"Coming in, looks like." Pol's voice was strained.

"Lock the doors," she snapped, her mind racing. "This *must* have to do with those clones."

Her slave's fingers flew over console commands. "It won't keep them out for long," he warned. "It's only festival lock-out." He meant the bar-and-lock system that strengthened the door against break-ins. It was proof against unruly street crowds during special celebrations, but it was never intended to block an armed assault.

"It'll slow them down," Helda said. "Tell the Eosan what's going on and get the guests out of the front of the house." She headed for the door. "I'm in the playroom."

In the hall, she began to run.

STEPPING INTO THE dominatrix's inner sanctum after so long nearly took Kesi's breath away. The chamber was the heart of her craft and high theater all in one, erotic and intense. Subtle lighting design shaped the room and the mood; the instruments of pleasure and pain were arrayed just so. It was like she'd slipped back into her old life, complete with her submissive slave naked on the floor, and standing over him—

Herself.

Herself as she appeared on vidverts: a divine archetype made real and demanding obeisance. White tresses, pale face, smoke-shadowed eyes, bloodred lips, the white leather and chrome of her garb both revealing and concealing her body. Her height was commanding, made taller with the heels of her thigh-high boots. Hands on hips, confrontational stance.

The Winter Goddess stared at the intruders; her eyes locked with Kesi's own. She read surprise, anger, and shock on that face all at once.

Of course, she thought. She didn't expect to see us again. And in this condition—

She flicked a glance to Kesada, supported by her left arm, Morya on the other side. Her clone-sister was nearly as pale as their made-up third. No time for niceties, then.

"Sorry to interrupt." Kesi turned back to the Winter Goddess. "This won't wait."

Janus began to sit up, a frown on his face. The dominatrix ignored him and strode past to confront the intruders.

"Who are you?" she hissed, eyes taking in each in turn, settling on the last one she recognized. "Morya, what in the hells are you—"

Suddenly, she froze, lips moving soundlessly. Her eyes rolled up in her head as Kesi watched. Back arched, a moan issued from her lips. It was not a sound of pain, but of pleasure—overwhelming, devastating pleasure. As her body tensed further she lost balance and toppled to the ground, oblivious to her surroundings. The moan turned to a groan, then tension fled as she passed out on the floor, limp as a rag.

Kesi stared in astonishment; she heard Kesada's breath hiss between her teeth. Shock held them in place for a moment—long enough for Janus and Morya both to scramble to Kes's side. He felt for a pulse at her neck, then rounded on Morya and the twins before him.

Does he recognize us? Kesi wondered. There was no clue on his face; his eyes were narrowed with consternation, and his words were sharp, as if the women were responsible for Kes's sudden collapse.

"What's going on here?" he demanded.

Kesi ignored his question. "What's wrong with her, Morya?"

The black-haired woman shook her head in ignorance and fussed ineffectually over the unconscious domina. All she could do was ease her limbs so she lay comfortably.

"Get help." Janus was curt. "She needs medical attention."

"She's not the only one." Kesi moved them closer. Janus took in Kesada's bloodied gaping shirt and came to his feet. Kesi read his body language as her twin must, also—they knew this client too well not to. He was tense, now, leery of the unknown. Thinking of his own safety, probably. Kesi knew he was some kind of kingpin in the derevin world. This was no longer a normal session, and a derevin boss did not loiter where things were not safe and predictable.

Janus stepped away from Kes's unmoving form. He went to the wardrobe where his clothes were stored and hurriedly pulled them on. As he did so, he shot worried looks at the Winter Goddess, now a mere mortal, unconscious.

Kesi looked from Janus to Morya and back again. Their mutual body language, their attention to Kes, their very energy, spoke volumes. Now she saw it for the very first time.

My gods. He's in love with me. Really in love. Just like Morya.

She felt Kesada's arm tighten against her, and she looked at her twin searchingly, saw her studying the man they'd always dismissed as just another infatuated client. Kesada turned and gave her a look.

She sees it, too, Kesi realized.

Janus scooped his last oddments from the valet shelf, stuffing a key pad in his pocket and slipping his medallion necklace back over his head. His superstitious god token, Kesi remembered—another thing she'd scorned about him. Now it was a neutral memory, the scorn vanished since her awakening as a clone.

He started towards Kes, moving with urgency, when clattering footsteps burst in on them. Like a woman chased by devils, Helda flew through the antechamber and into the playroom proper. Her mouth was open to speak, but she saw the Winter Goddess on the floor and instead let out a cry. She rushed to Kes's side, pushing past Morya, felt her shigasa unresponsive to her touch. She looked up, eyes flying from face to face in the room.

She's in a state, Kesi thought, just as the floor shuddered beneath their feet.

The muffled boom that came a millisecond later drove Helda to her feet again, reeling. She reached out to Morya, caught her balance, fingers clenched on the joygirl's shoulder. For an eternal moment, she looked completely torn.

I've never seen her at a loss before, Kesi realized at the same time Tryst's Dosan visibly came to some decision. She spun first to the twins. "I don't know what the story is with you, but you've brought security in after you. That means you're leaving right now." A quarter turn to face Janus. "This is not about you, Dom, but if you value your privacy, I suggest you come with us and slip out the back way right now. We're being raided."

To Morya: "Stay with her." She gestured to Kes on the floor. "Pol will call for medical help."

Kesi felt Kesada stiffen, wasn't surprised when she pushed her way free of her twin. Hand clutching her side, she rounded on Helda.

"We need her, Helda, and we're not leaving without her."

"You're crazy. There's no time for this."

"You were in on it, weren't you? We have questions for you, too."

Janus and Morya looked baffled; Helda blanched, looked from Kesada to Kesi, then, with concern, at Kes. Her head jerked at the sound of screams from the front of the house.

"Fine," she spat. "Talk later. First, let's get you safe."

She looked to Janus. "Will you carry her?"

She didn't need to ask. The tall man was already scooping up the dominatrix, holding her as lightly in his arms as if she were a child. Helda pushed past the twins to the service door they'd entered through. "Back this way. Hurry."

She led, Janus followed. The twins came behind, and Morya shut the service door that sealed near-invisibly in a dark side recess of the playroom.

Kesi heard a clamor as they left that room. Male voices shouted, then they were too far down the hall to track the sounds. Morya took Kesada's other arm, and they moved faster. Kesi's skin crawled, waiting for a stun beam or a blaster bolt in her back as they half limped, half ran through the hidden service hallways of Tryst.

HELDA LED THEM through a narrow servant's door into the corridor by her office. In that passageway she turned left and took them to her private stairs. She paused at the landing. "Down is back alley. Up is roof gardens."

"I had a run-in on the roof," Kesada said tersely.

It gave Helda pause, but Janus had no such hesitation. "Get me to the Salon," he said, "and I can get us out of the Shelieno entirely."

"The Salon?" Helda did a double take. The twins and Morya stared as if he'd suggested a walk in the jungle without a coolsuit.

"Not a good place for any of us," Kesi snapped.

"No choice, if you want out of this fix."

"They won't help us. Fucking Franc already tried to kill me once today."

Janus looked at her as if seeing her for the first time. "They'll help me," he said, completely certain of himself, "and they won't lay a finger on you." He sounded grim. To Helda, he said, "Which way's most discreet?"

"Security's on the streets, but I'm not sure where. They might not be on the roofs yet. They can't get in easily unless a house rolls over for them, or they've forced entry. Maybe they haven't, yet."

Trampling footsteps and more shouts from intruders came from the floor below. Helda glowered thunderously back down the hallway. "Go," she said. "I'll deal with these pricks."

"You're not leaving us," Kesada began grimly.

"Get out while you can," Helda cut her off. "The Dosan *has* to handle this. If they come looking too closely, they'll see where you went. Just go. Now!" She looked at Kes, still cradled in Janus's arms. "Keep her safe. Keep all of you safe." A hand on Kesada's arm, a squeeze in passing. "I'm sorry. When this is over, come back. I'll tell you what I know."

A woman's scream echoed through the halls, then cut off as quickly as it began. With a look of fury, Helda darted back the way they'd come.

"Fool," muttered Kesada.

Janus had a strange, intense look on his face. He ignored Helda's departure, the muted sounds of danger and threat in the building. "Who knows the way to the Salon?" he asked.

Morya stepped forward. "Follow me," she said, and led them upstairs.

JANUS CONCENTRATED ON the moment, focused only where he could take direct action. Avoid security's raid forces. Get medical help for his Mistress.

He trotted behind Morya, but spared more than one glance for the woman in his arms. Her flesh was warm against his hands. He held her for the first time ever, more intimately than he had ever hoped. He relished that one aspect of an otherwise disturbing experience. Everything had gone wrong from the moment she'd jacked into his implant and a malfunction had blown them both out of the system. That she had collapsed and still not come to was a dagger of concern he did his best to ignore. He was doing what he could in this moment. Soon he'd be able to do more.

Hold on, Kes, he thought. Just a little longer, and I'll see you taken care of.

He barely allowed himself to think her name. She didn't know he knew it. He had permission to call her Mistress, and that was as familiar as she allowed. It had not been enough. He'd made inquiries about the Winter Goddess as only a man in his position could—but even then, very little, and very respectfully. He'd only wanted to know her real name, and that's what he'd found out. She'd started work at Tryst two years ago and was a registered shigasa with the name Hinano Kesada.

He was probably the only client of hers to know that fact, and it was a secret he held more closely than he did her unconscious body. But there was no time now to dwell on such things. His first priority was to reach safety with his precious burden, and he was eager to leave the open-air greenways of the roof gardens. His body modifications served him in good stead now: reinforced skeleton and subdermal armor served defensive purposes, but the enhanced strength that let him move comfortably with those additions also enabled him to carry his Mistress without breaking a sweat. He could have easily out-paced Morya, if he'd wanted.

The thought reminded him of the two women following, and he was forced to slow his stride. They were falling behind, and he waited impatient seconds to let them catch up. His curiosity and his duty to help Kes demanded it.

Who *are* they? he asked himself, not for the first time. They might think their unstyled appearance would disguise their relationship to Kes, but Janus wasn't so easily fooled. He had long since done what any man with an insatiable desire and the right tools must do: he'd imaged the object of his fantasies and stripped her naked in his sim systems, taking away not only her costumes but also her makeup and the stage lighting that sculpted her face into an archetypal mask. It wasn't just to have her body to admire or use in his VR fantasies. It was more important than that. He wanted to be able to recognize her on the street, if he ever should encounter her incognito outside Tryst.

That was why he knew that the women following him were her twins. Or, rather, the three appeared to be triplets.

It didn't seem possible, yet here they came, limping and chasing him as fast as their long legs could carry them. He regretted now that he hadn't run a full dossier on her. The solid reality of the newcomers left him disconcerted, and doubly peeved at the black-haired one who'd acted so proprietarily towards the Winter Goddess. Why the interruption and the confrontation?

What the hell was going on here?

He was already tired of not knowing the answers and of not being in control.

Janus was famously slow to anger, but he felt it building now. This was turning into a day of fiascos and near-disasters that left him fleeing from an armed incursion in his Between-World sanctuary. Unthinkable, all of it. Then this incidental bombshell, that Franc had tried to kill one of them—Franc?! Efficient, ambitious Franc, from the Red Hand's most promising derevin subsidiary on Lyndir? It set the triumvir on a slow burn.

He made his way towards the Salon with his unconscious love in his arms and a dark expression on his face.

# 68

ARNO HAD THE watch at the Salon's back stairs, lounging half-asleep on the stool by the stairwell door. Morya was past him before he realized the clatter of feet on the stairs was not a dream.

He leapt to his feet. "Hey!" He recognized her instantly, even from the rear. She hadn't been gone from the Salon all that long. Then he registered other bodies moving past and stupidly saw Kes in multiples.

Sisters? Did she even have any? *Shit.*

He pulled his gun. "Hold it right there."

The tall man turned back when he spoke. Arno's eyes went wide at the sight of the woman he carried.

"You don't recognize me, do you, 'Chromer." The man made it a statement.

"No." Arno's brows drew together. Should I? he wondered.

"I'm your boss's boss. I want this house locked down right now, no one in or out. Put armed guards on all entrances, suited up and ready to keep Grinds out with force."

Arno gaped, com band halfway to his mouth.

"I'll tell Gistano myself," the man barked. "Now *move!*"

He didn't wait for compliance, but turned back down the hall. Arno took the better part of valor and let them go, then put his com-banded wrist to his mouth and did as ordered.

KESI'S FINGERS CLENCHED so hard that Kesada winced. *"Gistano's boss?"* Kesi whispered angrily to her twin, outraged at the revelation. "Janus bosses the Ice-fucking-chromers? That means—"

"Yes." Kesada was terse. Their thoughts raced along the same line, to the same conclusion: Janus was responsible for Gistano's entrapment of Hinano Kesada. Kesi wanted to stop dead in her tracks and have a screaming fit.

Kesada brought her to her senses. "Not now. Let's get safe first."

"But—"

"But nothing. We'll wait until we can deal with him properly."

"It's too much of a coincidence!" Hysterical anger drove Kesi's voice louder. "What if he's playing us here, now—"

Kesada dug hard fingers into her sister's shoulder. "Priorities, Kesi. We'll deal later." She turned an icy stare on her twin that stilled the protests in her mouth. Kesi nodded unhappily and kept silent as they continued in Janus's wake.

GISTANO WAS ON his feet and fuming when they burst into his office.

"House lock-down?" he said for greeting. "Why?"

Janus spoke while he moved to the float couch and laid Kes gently down. "The Grinds are in the Shelieno in force."

"And why do we care? Or do I already know the answer to that?" He studied the women with Janus, then fixed on the twins, who were staring defiantly at him. In spite of his anger, the calculating part of his brain took in the evidence from his eyes.

There's more than one of them. How? *Why?* And involved with the boss? Fuck me.

Janus went on as if he hadn't spoken. "Grinds probably don't know we're here yet, so we have some time. Get the house doctor in here now. We have people to attend to."

Gistano's temper got away from him. "Not on my premises, you don't. The hells with them. If this brings the heat down on us, we'll lose our Enclave license. We're not shigasue; we're just here on a lease. You're screwing our business, Boss."

A muscle twitched in Janus's jaw. "I'm going to pretend I didn't hear that from the man I made in the first place. Is the house locked down?"

Gistano gritted his teeth. "Yes." An alert flash on his desktop drew his eye to a holomap of the house and its environs. "And there are intruders on the rooftops in this block. Must be your friends." He couldn't keep the sarcasm out of his voice, but it masked the thoughts racing through his head. Could he refuse to help without causing a breach in their relationship? Could he get Janus out of here? Could they buy time without butting heads with security? Once things came to open conflict, all bets were off.

"Doctor." Janus turned the demand into an order.

Gistano was about to say something imprudent when a voice surprised them both.

"No."

It was the wounded one, the ringer for Kes when she'd worked in his house. She stepped forward. Blood was drying on her clothes, crusting brown in some places, still red where she pressed a hand to her side and held wadded cloth to an oozing wound there. Gistano registered the razor-thin slices of a vibroblade artfully wielded to hurt, not kill, and understood better now why Franc had looked battered when he'd returned a short while before.

"No, what?" Gistano challenged her.

"No, we're not staying in this hellhole, and your doctor's not looking at us.

Not her, either." She jerked a chin to the supine form of the Winter Goddess. She spoke to Janus. "We need to get out of here, out of the district, right now. They're closing in."

"She needs medical attention. So do you."

"No one'll be helped if we're caught first."

"We can stand them off," Janus said. "'Chromers in combat-grade coolsuits aren't your ordinary line of house defense—"

"At the cost of ruining this business, sure," Gistano snapped.

"—and I have a secret way out of here when we need it."

"No one's supposed to know about that," Gistano growled.

His superior fixed him with a look. "If it will make things easier for you," Janus said, "I can remove you from leadership of the 'Chromers here and now. Your call."

The men stared at each other. Gistano dropped his eyes first. Janus turned back to the blonde. "Enough now with this running away. Let's have you seen to."

The woman drew herself up and took a step towards Janus, one finger jabbing at him. "You can lose that condescending tone with me. You haven't a clue what's going on here. I'll tell you this: if we're caught, we're dead, no questions asked, and I don't think they'll hesitate to do the same to anyone helping us. Just being with us probably puts you all in danger." She pointed to the unconscious Winter Goddess. "And that goes for her, too. If you want to keep her safe, you'll get us all out of here before worrying about medical care. And when it comes to that, we have someone who's far better than an ordinary doctor. We have a bioempath who'll help us."

Janus locked eyes with the woman who confronted him. At the same moment, a ping came over Gistano's desk com. "Boss," a stressed 'Chromer's voice said, "we have company at the front door. Armed security squad, doing a house-to-house search. They want in. What response do you want? We're locked and loaded."

Gistano growled in frustration. "Stall 'em. Wait for my word."

The blonde took a step closer to Janus. When she spoke, her voice was low and urgent, the caress of silk on steel. The derevin boss barely caught her words. "She's part of this, too. You want a chance to continue on with her? Get us all out of here now."

Janus's lips thinned, then he did what Gistano had never seen him do before: he bowed his head to the woman. Then he spun on his heel, catching Gistano staring at him, startling the 'Chromer boss with his own curt order. "Bolt hole. Now."

The derevin chief didn't trust himself to speak. He tapped a code sequence into his desk comp and a wall panel behind his desk popped open. He bowed with a semi-flourish, motioning the way clear to Janus and his motley crew. The triumvir took up the unconscious woman into his arms once again and led the way to the concealed staircase.

"Boss?" came the door guard again. "They're fixing a charge to blow our door open. Can we fire on them?"

Gistano sighed. "Stand down. Let 'em in. They have a beef, send 'em to see me." He cut the connection as the last of his unwanted visitors left, sealing the panel behind them.

He stabbed another com tab on his desk. "Franc. Get your ass in here, on the double." He cut off without waiting for a response, then faced the wall panel as calculations clicked over in his mind.

Was Janus merely caught up in a crisis, or was he actually losing control of a situation? If he was losing control, was this a chance for Gistano to advance his own interests?

He didn't have enough info and he didn't know the odds. That mattered to a man who'd come up on the backstreet gambling circuits. But one thing he did recognize was the scent of blood in the water. And if the odds were good, he was always willing to roll the dice.

Franc rushed into the room. Gistano took him in at a glance: grass stains on inert stealth suit, synthflesh patch on throat, the sheen of an antihemorrhagic spray over a bruised temple.

"Head all right?"

"Yes."

"Rib healed?"

Franc nodded. The house doc had a bone knitter for minor fractures, although forced regen left a tender spot for a while, and the 'Chromer favored his side right now.

"You sorry sack of shit. I'm gonna make your day." Gistano opened a desk drawer, fished inside.

"Boss?"

Gistano pulled out a needlegun with one hand, while the other tapped the wall access code into the comp again. Franc's eyes widened as the panel swung open. Gistano jerked his head in that direction.

"The girlfriend you were trying to dance with earlier ran off that way. Clones are with her—must be, since we know for a fact she doesn't have siblings. Morya and Janus, too. He's in some shit. Tag along quietly, see where they go, figure out what's up."

"Clones, huh?" He took the needlegun from Gistano's hand. "That explains who blindsided me."

"No killing until you check in with me. I want to know what the story is before any parts get rearranged. Clear?"

Franc nodded and started for the portal.

"Wait." Gistano shrugged out of his coat, tossed it to Franc. "In case you need streetwear. It'll help a little. You stand out too much like that."

His lieutenant nodded. A moment later he was gone.

THE SUB-LEVELS OF the Salon opened into tunnels built long before an Enclave stood on Lyndir, forgotten as newer layers of city infrastructure were constructed. There were few entrances into the built-over tunnels, for not many realized that many of the old passageways deep beneath the surface streets were usable.

Janus knew it, though, and some of his businesses had entrances or exits that took advantage of the hidden warrens. When the Icechromers leased the joy-house, one of their first tasks when renovating was to secretly excavate down to the abandoned power mains and disused sewer lines.

The moldering service tunnels contained little that functioned. At this level it was a network of derelict switching stations, corroding valves, and musty dark pipe runs lit at too-long intervals by dim, ancient glow-tabs. The one thing the tunnels did effectively, though, was to connect the Shelieno with neighboring domes through hidden byways.

Janus led the way unerringly, aided by a reference map in a heads-up display pulled from one of his hardwired database systems. His left eye looked quite natural, but it harbored recording and HUD capabilities that cost more than most people earned in a year. It was one of the perks of being a cartel boss, and this was one of the times Janus was grateful he had it. With the help of his nav devices, the group made their way through the labyrinth to emerge in a parking structure in neighboring Jenes Dome.

On the third subfloor of the garage, in a row of reserved VIP parking, Eldin lounged in the sidecar of an antique float bike, reading a book and listening to tunes on an earbud. When he noticed Janus approaching from a service stairwell, he stepped out of the vehicle and moved to help his master with the burden in his arms. Together they laid her down on the sidecar's bench seat.

Kes remained unconscious, her body shaken now and then by tremors and small spasms of muscle tension. Otherwise, her condition had not changed.

"Wait here," Janus told the group, and trotted around the corner where more cars were parked. Moments later, he pulled up in a black lift-capable luxury ground sedan with dark windows.

"Sir!" Eldin exclaimed in surprise as the cartel boss stepped out of the idling vehicle.

Janus gave him a look. "It's hardly the first car I ever hot-keyed. Don't worry, though—you'll make sure it gets back to its owner when we're done." He moved to collect Kes once more. As he arranged her in the backseat, he spoke over his shoulder to his servant.

"Time for you to go home, Eldin, and take a very long, circuitous route while you do. Put the top up on the sidecar and opaque it—let's make sure it looks like you have someone riding with you."

"Have we been made, sir? Should I expect to be followed?"

"It's a precaution. Let's hope it's not necessary—but if you *are* followed, I want them to stay on you for a long time, to buy us time to get elsewhere."

"I understand."

Janus held the door and helped Kesada in. She collapsed next to her unmoving twin. "No fleeing pursuit, either, old friend. If someone tries to run you to ground, I don't want you in danger trying to avoid arrest. Not for a decoy run. Do I make myself clear?"

Eldin bowed his head.

"Who's navigating?" Janus asked the others. "In front, with me."

His servant started work on the sidecar as Kesi got in the front seat and Morya joined the others in back. Janus waved farewell and headed for the exit.

EVA SWORE BITTERLY. "How could we not put a homing device in those clones?"

The question was rhetorical. When she'd defined the implants to use, she'd thought only of fail-safes. She'd given no mind to the discard clones, destined for destruction anyway, and took for granted that the killer clone would be in a location she could monitor. *Had* monitored, up until the growing debacle that was this afternoon's raid on Tryst.

The pleasure wire had dropped Kes by overloading her nervous system. It was triggered by a local beamcast sent by IntSec on the wire's frequency. That alone was not sufficient to triangulate a location with, and if she was moved outside the region covered by the beamcast, the wire would deactivate.

They could always detonate the microcharge—a bomb explosion would be easily marked on a map—but that could just as easily eliminate Janus in the process. Not an option.

"We can't have lost them." She said it to Teo as if it were a fact, a not-possibility, while in her own mind those words sounded like plaintive bravado. It seemed impossible for Janus, a handful of clones, and a joygirl to vanish into thin air, but vanish they had. How?

And much more urgently: How would they find them again, before Kes awoke and endangered Janus?

Raem's staccato interjections of analysis and speculation helped ground Eva and keep her from getting as close as she had ever come to a state of panic. Everything she wanted now was wrapped up with Janus's survival, and the longer he was off the radar with that killer clone, the less likely his survival became.

When Obray reported the sighting of the floatbike, she bit back an exclamation of triumph. She placed herself square in front of the wall screen, bouncing on toe tips.

"Display," she ordered, and stood riveted while the pursuit unfolded.

---

**WHEN EVA REALIZED** there was just one person on the bike and not the fugitives she sought, she ordered IntSec to tail, not intercept. She still had Lyndir Grinds searching the Enclave, but their failure to secure her quarry had them in her bad graces. For the real work that remained, she would now rely on Internal Security exclusively.

Obray called in his men on a city-wide force scramble, with scattered personnel coming in from other locations around the globe to supplement their team. As far as Eva was concerned, there was no other priority on Lyndir right now.

Her car and strike teams were ready to go on her command. Pacing abandoned, she sat tensely, wired into the surveillance systems for up-to-the-millisecond status info.

There was nothing more to do but see where the floatbike led them, or hope Janus contacted his network soon. IntSec agents tailed discreetly in city traffic, and Eva did more of that thing she hated to do.

She waited.

## 69

**JANUS'S STOLEN CAR** moved virtually unnoticed as it traveled congested roads, just one more vehicle among many on streets and lanes of layered air traffic. On the byways of industrial Caardo Dome, the traffic dropped off; in one area dominated by buildings for lease or sale, it became nearly nonexistent. In mid-late afternoon, the lone sedan pulled up to an unmanned security gate in a disused manufacturing complex.

The lengthening rays of the westering sun pierced photochemical clouds and layers of vansin to wash the building front in diffuse orange-pink light. The embossed name sign of the former owners, long since removed, left an imprint over the main doors: PAREO DEVICE CORPORATION, it proclaimed in stenciled dirt.

Janus waited while Kesi got out and approached the gate. The name of this place seemed vaguely familiar, and his Lyndir reference knowledge base soon supplied the context.

Pareo made waldos and other remote manipulation devices for civilian and military use, but had moved offworld two years before. Any building Pareo designed for research would be more secure than your average manufactory and warehouse. That was reassuring. Maybe the people the Hinanos knew had an idea what they were doing after all.

He was about to find out for himself. Kesi palmed the ID pad at the gate, seemed surprised that the portal recognized her, and returned to the car, the gate rolling open behind her. A moment later, they drove through.

**WHEN HE'D DONE** his stint in the Marines, Franc didn't realize his special ops training in recon and infiltration would have so many civilian uses.

Lucky me, he thought. I'm in the perfect line of work.

He eased the floatbike to rest by a row of debris bins a hundred meters away from the Pareo complex gate. He used his targeting implant to zoom and augment his vision as he watched Janus pause at the gate.

He saw Kes get out of the car, touch the gate interface, return to the vehicle. She seemed healed from their earlier encounter, unless this was one of the clones Gistano had mentioned. It amused him that she was automatically tracked by the crosshairs built into his targeting array.

"Maybe I can try that out on you later, baby," he murmured.

Those crosshairs had already served him once today, when he took out the old man with the floatbike from a distance. The man had been on the outside range of the needlegun, but he wanted to test it before he used it on anyone who mattered. Good thing he did, too—to his surprise, the needles were tipped with explosive charges that made a right mess of whatever they impacted.

Good to know. He didn't want to kill Kes before he had his fun with her. Explosive needles made it trickier to wound without killing. He might just have to rely on his trusty vibroblade for his fun after all.

The thought put a smile on his face as he cruised over to the Pareo fence-line, staying behind overgrown box hedges for concealment. He left the bike obscured by a stack of trashed wall supports, heaped for a collection day that had never come. The thrill of the hunt was upon him. He checked his weapons and the odd bits of gear on his web belt, abandoned Gistano's jacket in the sidecar, and snugged the hood-mask of the stealth suit over his head.

Time to go calling.

TEREL SAW THEM first, walking in through the door that moments before had been locked. He bobbled then dropped the tray of food and drinks he was carrying and stood there, mouth working.

"You came back!" he squeaked, his gaze flicking from face to face. Two of them he recognized, the others he was trying to make sense of.

Kesi stepped forward, her hand on her injured twin's arm. "Doctor. Now."

"Oh, shit." Terel waved both hands at them. "Wait. Right there. I'll get—I'll tell—shit." He kicked the tray out of his way. "The doctor hasn't been the same since you left. I have to break this to him carefully. Wait. Don't leave! I'll be right back."

He vanished around a corner.

"Are we going to wait?" Morya asked nervously.

"No," said Kesada, limping in Terel's wake.

OFF-THE-SHELF LAB COMPONENTS, packing crates, silent crystal power generators, comp gear, medical supplies, and a full med bed in the middle of a half-set-up med bay: chaos with just a hint of order filled the former cleanroom for device assembly. It looked like someone had dashed through Metmuri's research station labs on a mad thieving spree and dumped their loot without rhyme or reason.

It was a sterile environment no more, but one with rats' nests of leads pulled from walls connecting jury-rigged gear, with Metmuri Esimir clucking and fussing in the middle of it. "You have the coupler in place yet?" he shouted out. "Make sure the leads align properly or our 'sphere connection will be all wrong."

"Got it," came Ferris's voice from somewhere low and unseen.

"Doctor," Terel interrupted. "You have to stop. The—"

"I can't stop," Esimir barked. "We have to be ready for Prevak. He should be here any time now." The scientist tried to keep the thrill of excitement from his voice. His plan—his new plan, born in a moment of despair and clarity—he dared not share with anyone, but he had to be prepared for it. He started to root through another box of gear delivered by FlashMan.

"Doctor." Terel steeled himself. "I need to tell you something. The—"

"You can't stop me from testing it myself," Esimir said without glancing at him. "I know what to look for in the system, how the interface should go. Look, Terel, we've got the phase synthesizer online! Now it'll be easy to—"

"Doctor!" His assistant grabbed his arms, forced the bioempath to leave the box alone and look at him. "Don't let this upset you, sir, but the clones are back."

Esimir went stock still. He could see Terel was braced for some radical reaction, like the mortifying outburst he'd given into when the clones had abandoned him and crushed his dreams. But faithful Terel did not know of the doctor's new resolution, and so he was not prepared for his response.

Esimir felt a slow smile creeping over his face, transforming worry lines and furrowed brow into a beaming, open expression. "How wonderful," he said, quite sincerely. "Maybe they'll help with this gear." He glanced around the room, then, and his eyes came to rest on the group in the antechamber of the cleanroom.

Terel followed his gaze, then started forward. "I told you to wait!" He spoke sharply to the group.

"No, no." The doctor patted him on the arm. "Not to worry, my boy. They're perfectly welcome. Come in—oh, mind those crates. Don't trip over that cable . . . such a mess. I know! Follow me."

He pushed through the cluster of people, patting Kesada absentmindedly on one arm as he passed by. She seems pale, he thought.

The newcomers paused, dumbfounded by their reception.

"Come now," Esimir urged them along. "No time to waste. Let's talk where you can't hurt Prevak. I mean, the systems for him. And you can sit. Or something . . ." He turned his back and started for a break room down the hall.

The tall man stood unmoving. "This woman needs care." His tone was stern, a rough edge in his voice. "Where can I put her so you can examine her?"

His words brought the doctor up short, and Esimir turned back, for the first time really seeing who the man held in his arms. He gasped. "Is that—?" He felt turmoil pluck at him. "Oh my. Oh my." He shot an accusing look at Terel. "You didn't tell me the One was here." He stared down at the face in pale makeup.

Did this change anything? All three clones, together again?

He shook his head to himself. No. It was too late. Ilanya had started to destroy his dream by stripping the One from his control; the Two and Three had ended it with their flight and the inevitable decision that had forced upon him.

It had all come clear to him after their desertion. The forces arrayed against him had won. The work needed to perfect reintegration would never be done by the Navy, and it was a foolish delusion to think he could succeed, alone, under these fugitive conditions.

He'd been forced to let his dream go and focus on the grim reality that re-mained: he'd made himself a criminal, with nothing to show for it. Even if he could use splintegration on himself as he had planned, he would still be a wanted man. After defying the Kingmaker in such an outrageous manner, he would surely never be safe again.

The bioempath was not cut out to be a fugitive and could not begin to imag-ine himself as a prisoner tried for defiance of imperial authority. And so Esi-mir had committed himself to the only way he saw to both lay his demons to rest *and* take himself beyond the reach of PolitDiv.

Did the Hinanos appreciate the sacrifice he would make for them? Putting himself in a position to help them, maybe, instead of being merely a fellow fu-gitive and a painful reminder of a difficult time in their lives?

But no. They could not know, and would not understand. Now, today, his wayward children were just come home for a visit, that was all. There was no point in asking more of them. He would do what he could for them, while he could, and leave it at that.

Esimir drew himself up and turned back towards the half-prepped med bay. "It's not proper, but it will have to do," he told them. "All my equipment is here. At least we had the foresight to order medical supplies." He had planned for many contingencies in the frenzied equipping that the netrunner had made possible.

He glanced back at the newcomers. "Come, then. What are you waiting for? Bring her! And tell me what happened to cause this."

The twins kept their distance from him. The tall man followed closely, and a woman with long black curls padded beside the doctor, explaining what she'd witnessed in the playroom when Kes had collapsed.

"You tell me nothing that would account for this state," the bioempath said. He shouted over his shoulder to a bank of equipment. "Ferris! Get out from behind there. I need your medtech skills. Come here. Terel, clear that off— yes, thank you. Lay her down here."

The Winter Goddess's statuesque height filled the length of the med bed. Ferris activated something that unsheathed monitor trodes. Delicate plas-and-wire tendrils wrapped Kes's wrist and rested on her temples, reading pulse and EEG, throwing those and other biometrics up on a monitor hung from an exposed wall stud.

"Stand away, now." Esimir shooed people back with a hand motion, even Terel. Terel's ability to sense living energies was a parlor trick; nothing that could help them here, so there was no need for him to hover. "I need room to work. Ferris—see to this one's wounds while I do so."

She nodded and steered Kesada to a table of medical equipment. While Ferris began work on her patient, the doctor turned to his.

Esimir expected to open his third eye and see something organically wrong with this clone. Instead, he stood in horrified fascination as an electromagnetic field pulsated within Kes's brain. He could see the focal point of it embedded in her skull: something small, inducing a wave front that pulsed through portions of her central nervous system. It pushed intense waves of red-tinged energy through her body, radiating especially strongly in the first and second chakras, resonating with the pleasure centers in the brain. The energy flowed continuously through her, its telltale traces visible in her aura, and left her helpless before it.

He glanced at the bedside monitor, and it confirmed his suspicions. Her brain was awash in an abnormal flood of neuropeptides.

Esimir had never seen it before in person, but he knew exactly what he was looking at. He turned to the man who'd carried her in, but spoke to them all. "She's been wired with a pleasure trode. It seems to be stuck on at full power, and it's overwhelming her system."

Janus frowned; her clones glanced at each other; Morya was incredulous. "She's not a wirehead. That can't be." She left unspoken what they all knew: direct stimulation of pleasure centers was dangerously addicting. Wireheads could easily spend all day in the throes of orgasm or something close to it, until they collapsed from exhaustion or literally thirsted to death. They could be oblivious to everything when lost in the great overwhelming ecstasy of the wire. "She'd never do that," Morya said with certainty, and the twins shook their heads in agreement.

Esimir set his hands on her head, quested forth with his own directed energy. He attempted to read her physiology, to see what else was wrong, and to dampen the wire effects if possible. Kes shuddered on the table beneath his touch.

"What are you doing?" Janus demanded.

The doctor considered, then removed his hands and turned around.

"We need to remove this implant," he said curtly. "And the other one as well."

"What other one?"

"I don't know what it does, but there are two different devices here beyond her original wetware." Esimir looked around the room to the twins at a side table. Ferris was knitting flesh with a bonding beam, while Kesada rubbed an arm now sore from multiple antibiotic injections. "There might be more," he added. "Unauthorized implants, I mean. They weren't my idea," he said defensively as Kesi scowled back at him.

"We have junk in our head we don't know about?" Kesada growled the question.

"I can't say. Let's check you out. I can feel the pattern of an artificial substance, if one is there." The bioempath laid hands on one blond head, then the other. He breathed a sigh of relief. "Nothing. But for her"—he motioned to the unconscious domina—"we have work to do."

He looked to Terel. "Get the microsurgery tools from the splintegration gear—"

"What do you intend to do?" Janus planted himself before the man. "Someone powerful is after these women"—he nodded to Kesi and Kesada—"and for all I know, her as well." He rested his hand on the Winter Goddess's forearm. "We probably don't have much time. We need to move out of here, quickly."

Esimir shook his head sharply. "Simply not possible, my good sir." He directed Terel to collect medical equipment and set up an aseptic halo over Kes's head, then turned back to the man who still obstructed him. "And you are—who, exactly?"

The tall man gave a half laugh. "Let's just say I'm someone concerned with the well-being of these women. I can help. I have resources that may surprise you."

Esimir looked from the man to the dark-haired woman to the blond twins who now approached the med bed and their unconscious third. "I think . . . you don't know what you've blundered into here." He addressed the clones. "Why don't you two fill him in, while we tend to Kes?" Then he turned his back on the group, completely and obsessively focused on the task at hand.

JANUS WAS TORN between asserting himself and giving in to the demands of the moment. He looked from woman to woman around him. Kesi and Kesada seemed angry and responded with dark looks instead of words.

"Do you know what's going on here?" he asked Morya.

She shook her head. "Only that Kes cloned herself. I don't know why."

"Clones?" He was sincerely startled, but quick to adjust his thinking. Not sisters, then; his intel hadn't failed him. "But why? And why the pursuit?" He was baffled.

Kesi's mouth seemed to button up even tighter, but Kesada heaved a sigh. "Let's talk."

WHILE THE GROUP conversed in hushed and urgent tones around a cluttered tabletop, Terel plugged a diagnostic lead into the unconscious shigasa's rigger jack. It helped monitor her neural systems and changes in brain chemistry and physiology. It gave them another set of eyes at the molecular level while Dr. Metmuri deactivated the pleasure implant and removed the blackwire work from the shigasa's skull.

As soon as the rigger connection was made, a minuscule impulse spiked on the monitor. Terel read it as an artifact of the external jack mating with internal systems.

In a way, he was right. The codeworm fragment that had traveled from Janus's rigger trap to Kes's implant at Tryst now found a conduit to much larger datastreams. It leapt into that storm of electrons, determined which way was "out," and was gone in a flash.

# 70

FLASHMAN TOOK A page from Zippo's book. For the last few hours his sim-form had been a spiky contoured mastiff, all the better to dig and paw and claw his way through machine-layer code posing as armor. He was close, now, to breaking through. He could feel it.

But, truth be told, he was flagging.

His body was exhausted in his decker chair, and he'd been running on Serafix for mental focus and Quell for liquid nutrients for over a day and a half now. There was just so much to slog through at RS 207. It was like infiltrating a city by belly crawling through drain pipes you had to destroy to fit through. It was . . . tiring.

Back home, he upped his mentaid dose and chased it with a hit of Fantasto for extra staying power.

I can sleep when I'm dead, he thought. This won't wait. The Doc's more on edge about it every time I check in with him.

He'd stayed sharp enough so far: killed some hunter-scouts before they even caught his scent, made huge progress into the weapons research station, and still did a bit of remote management of the Doc's industrial hideout with a split fraction of his attention. When things became too tedious and he threatened to nod into a haze in his sim-form, he monitored IntSec coms just to stay up on the banter of his friends—curious, too, about what he was missing during his sick leave. So he knew the Grinds had almost caught the women he'd helped, then lost them, in the end. He was still kind of amused by that.

Not so much, though, that this manhunt now somehow included his Goddess as a target. How'd she go missing? How she'd get mixed up with the twins? He suspected now that they all knew each other—and now his Bug-buddies were scrambled on a city-wide dragnet looking for people he liked and wanted to help.

Flash was torn in his loyalties in a way he could not easily reconcile, and it was making him cranky.

Maybe all of that distracted him, in the end, from the hunter-killer that came screaming down his carrier wave out of the expanses of the net. At least, he took it for a killer countermeasure, the way it moved, racing fast and straight, arrowing at him as if he were a homing beacon. But it came from the wrong direction: back the way he'd come, not from anything in the station defenses around him.

He just had time to spin around, bare fangs at the thing, then stop in shock. The instant before it smashed into him, he recognized it for what it was: the long-lost codeworm fragment, his fractal self come home to roost.

He had time for one stifled shriek before he lost control of his doggy sim-form and fell thrashing to the floor, fighting for his life with the ropy construct of his own making.

**THE CODEWORM WAS** too clingy to escape, too pervasive to resist. It coiled around Flash, enveloping him from head to toe. The fight slowly went out of the net-runner's sim form—and that may be what saved him. Finally encountering no resistance, the codeworm became more permeable, allowing a release of data and energy as it relaxed.

That release contained the Flash-fractal, now simply a flow of structured data.

It trickled out of the codeworm and merged seamlessly into the simulation worn by its master. The code shell that remained, its mission accomplished, was drained of its mating imperative. It fell inert to the floor, leaving a flattened and groaning FlashMan on the ground beside it.

**FLASH'S AVATAR INHALED** with a gasping, shuddering intake of energy, then jerked upright. He bounced to his feet, then onto his toes. His dog-form had been washed away with the blind-sided struggle, and he realized now what had happened. Wherever his codeworm had gone to, it had finally returned, bringing his fractal consciousness back with it, and now—at last! at last!—his mind and concentration were whole.

Or that was what his first rush of euphoria told him.

The second rush was a half-remembered image of climbing, searching, over and over again, but the details would not come clear. As he concentrated, now, trying to dredge up the illusive vision, he became aware of something else much more alarming. His little housekeeping remnant back at the Pareo plant was screaming an alert at him, one he'd not heard nor paid attention to in his frenzied, persistent digga-dig-dig at RS 207. And speaking of which—

*"I feel like I'm on speed!"*

He said it out loud to the cramped little byway and code walls around him. For the first time he saw, really saw, the parti-color bits of code debris littering the floor all around. He kicked a heap aside and saw the deepest point of his excavations. He pinged the gap.

Almost through!

Part of him wanted to respond to the Pareo alarm, but the rest of him wanted to continue with this single-minded pursuit. *Needed* to. With an effort, he compelled himself to do both. Obligation and his word to the Winter Goddess caused him to spend energy on the alarm. His remote sim had to figure out what was amiss there. But here, in the rutting turmoil he'd created in his lengthy labor—here was the real challenge and the real accomplishment. When he crowed about it in the secret hacker corners of the 'sphere, they'd never hear how he'd almost lost his mind over the tedium of it. They'd hear only how easy it was to focus on the repetition, repetition, of dig, decode, destroy, dig, decode, destroy. . . .

He fell into a pattern that his fractal self had burned into its core. He knew he should care more about the Pareo problem, whatever it was, but this infiltration he was in the middle of, this repeated cycle of code-break and discard, was so much more compelling.

FlashMan returned to his break-in work, his progress faster than ever before, while, far away, an echo of his sim-self tried to assess systems at Pareo Device Corporation in Port Oswin.

## 71

**SURMOUNTING THE FENCE** at the Pareo plant was a simple climbing exercise. Franc reached the top, noting the perimeter relied only on the physical obstacles of height and a monofilament barricade atop the wall for security. His own vi-broknife answered in kind, severing the guy pylons for the nearly invisible guard wires. Something short-circuited when he did so, stays surrendering to his blade in a shower of sparks. Filaments concertinaed out of his way, and he dropped to the ground on the inside.

Ahead was Janus's car, absent of passengers, parked near one of the side entrances on this flank of the building.

I'll try the obvious way first, he thought.

He smiled when he saw the palm-pad by the side of the door. Access telltales glowed green on its surface. He touched the door enough to ease it open a crack, and it moved effortlessly under his hand. "Idiots," he muttered. Whoever had biometric access to this place had walked right in and forgotten to lock up behind themselves—or, more likely, touched something accidentally that disabled the lock reset, effectively latching the door open behind them. The biggest flaw in any security system always was the human factor.

Fine by me, he thought. The quicker I catch up with you, the sooner our fun can begin.

He slipped inside the door, leaving access pad and latch just as he'd found them. He paused in a wide hallway to get his bearings. He saw no one, heard nothing. A dark warehouse space yawned open to his right; offices to his left glowed with the westering sun; artificial light came from rooms on the far side of an empty storage bay straight ahead.

He triggered a relay and switched on the aural amplifier he wore in his left ear. He didn't use it often; preternatural hearing in only one ear could be very disorienting. He'd thought to have it in two, but the model he could afford would interfere with the comlink in his right mastoid bone. At some point in the future, after another bonus, he could get better tricked out. For now, though, it served its purpose: suddenly he heard sound throughout the building as if he were a living high-gain microphone. Nothing stirring in the warehouse area; likewise nothing in the offices. Chat and footsteps from the workspaces in the center of the building, dead ahead.

He paused for a moment and considered his comlink. Check in with the boss? No, not yet: he had a location, but still couldn't report what Janus was up to here. He pulled out the needlegun instead, not planning to use it, but preferring to have it in hand when sneaking around in the shadows. He turned the gain down on his augmented hearing, but left it several notches higher than normal human acuteness. All the better to scout out what lay ahead.

Franc ghosted through the shadows of the storage area, moving deeper into the building.

"WE'RE CERTAIN THAT'S Janus's floatbike, right?"

"Yes, Domna Arcolo," Commander Obray confirmed.

"Then who in the hells is that on it? He's up to no good or he wouldn't be stealthed and going over the perimeter like that."

"Identity unknown. We picked up the bike in Jenes Dome at Cutter and Jadeway. Police report a man dead in a parking structure near there. The victim is one of Janus's household staff. I think we can assume—"

"This tracker killed the cartel man and took his bike—yes, I get the picture. But why? And where's Janus?" She was on her feet again, shooting irritated glances at the street map display and the annoying stationary ping splash that marked the Pareo plant where the bike had come to rest.

"Whose car is that in the lot? And is this building occupied now?"

She waited for updates. All the while her wild psi and her intuition were prodding her to an inescapable conclusion.

"Waiting for vehicle ID from planet security. We can't get a direct life sign reading from satellite scans here, Domna Arcolo—"

"Damn backwater."

"—but we can move our own spyflies to the location. They're not there yet, though."

Raem, she thought to her construct. Confirm: Janus onsite?

*Possible*, came the response.

Not probable?

*Chance still outside of one standard deviation on the probability curve.*

She made a sour face at Raem's statistical equivocation. She knew better than to argue intuition with her enhanced left-brain functions. But this time—

This time she was going with her gut.

"Obray: keep your teams ready to deploy and put a squad on that block to back me if I call for it. You continue the search for our fugitives and their hostage."

"You're going into the field, Domna Arcolo?"

"You bet your ass I am." She was already moving for the door. "Send your updates to Teo; my line is live if you need me direct."

Obray offered a bow from his command chair, but she and her matasai were out of the ops center by time he'd done it.

## 72

**"YOU'RE BOTH HINANO** Kesada, I gather," Janus said speculatively.

"Not quite like you'd think," said Kesada. "As far as I'm concerned, I'm my-self."

"Same here," agreed Kesi. She shot a pointed aside to Morya. "And it's damn strange to see you with Kes."

Before the dark-haired woman could reply, Kesada waved her hand at her twin. "Don't start. We both have things to say about that, and"—to Morya—"you'll have to deal with this sooner or later. Sorting this out with us."

"Kes asked me to . . ." Morya stumbled to a halt as both clones fixed her with an intent stare. "She wants to—"

"Don't." Kesada cut her off sharply. "I'm sure we all want the same thing with you. And we can't afford that distraction right now. That whole subject—too big, too important. We'll get into that later."

Kesi stirred restlessly by her side as she turned back to Janus, who was try-ing to follow their half-stated meanings. "Right now we need to figure out how to get safe. I'm sure we weren't followed to Tryst, but if they could find us there, they could probably track us here, too."

"Who's after you?" He sounded concerned, and it was enough to set Kesi off.

"Go screw yourself, Janus," she blurted angrily. "Why do you even care?"

"Excuse me?" He looked at her, surprised.

"Exactly that: Why do you care? You ruined our lives. Since when are you concerned about the fate of debt-servants you've created?"

Kesada was taken aback, but adjusted quickly. Even though this was also off track, this issue felt pressing. It weighed on their minds, and more im-portant, circumstances had thrown them together with Janus. If he was re-sponsible for their situation in some measure, could he even be trusted here and now?

She saw his reaction and read sincere confusion on his face. "What are you talking about?" he asked.

Kesi was working up a head of steam; Kesada laid her hand on her twin's forearm and gave her a warning squeeze. She fired a sharp question instead. "Are you telling us you're unaware how the Icechromers fill their joyhouses with staff?"

The question must have been completely unthinkable to him, because he did a literal double take when she asked it. His expression darkened. "I really don't know what you're referring to, but I'm starting to have suspicions. Explain what you mean."

Kesada did. Halfway through her account, Janus came to his feet and began pacing. Anger clouded his face, and he looked at the women as if he were seeing them in a totally different light.

"How could you have no idea what Gistano does?" Kesi burst out at one point. "You're his boss, for Ashani's sake. You must have known, or given permission."

He met her accusing eyes. "Never," he said flatly, and sat again. "I never gave him permission to do that." He stabbed the tabletop with his finger, emphasizing each word. "Never would. It creates too much ill will. That shit might fly in Old Sa'adani space where everyone thinks that way, but I don't want it in my own business. He knows that."

"Then how does he get away with it?" Morya interjected.

Janus looked grim. "It may sound like an excuse, but it's just a fact: I have a lot of business going on. I have to trust my lieutenants, and I don't double check everything they do, especially when they're in the more routine lines of business."

"Trading in debt-service is routine?" Kesi sneered.

"Loan-sharking is routine. Wherever there are derevin there are scripmen, and they have their own rules of operation. That includes ways of collecting debts. I'd say Gistano's been greedy. He's been hiding this part of his business from me."

"We're supposed to believe that?"

Janus considered his words before he spoke. "If you were Her, then you know I would not lie to you. Yes, I expect you to believe that. It's the truth."

The clones could not argue with that; they knew it for the fact that it was. Kesi was chastened; Kesada, reassured. There weren't many people the Winter Goddess had come to trust in the last couple of years, but this devoted client had been one of them.

Kesada finally nodded acknowledgment. At the same time, Morya came to her feet. "Excuse me," she mumbled, and walked away from the table.

Something was obviously bothering her, but Janus was talking, and his words grabbed the Hinanos' attention.

"I can't do anything about all that right now," he said, "but maybe I can help in other ways. You were starting to tell me who's after you. I need to understand what's going on here."

"So do we," sighed Kesi.

"Here's what we know," began Kesada.

Unnoticed, Morya left the room.

———

**MORYA WALKED BLINDLY** out of the cleanroom and the prep room beyond it, chased out into the darkened hall by all that she had heard.

It was bad enough that Kes had never shared this part of her past with her—how, exactly, she had come to be at the Salon. She'd glossed over it. They all did; the past wasn't a place you could afford to live in when you worked a joyhouse every day. But the place she'd come from was far removed from anything Morya had ever known. That alone was enough to create a wall between them under any other circumstances, and maybe enough, still, to threaten their happiness together.

And then there were these women, these clones of her Kes. That they were so alike was disturbing, and yet their differences drew her in in a "you shouldn't be attracted but you are" sort of guilty fascination. There was something distinctive about each of them that called to her. She hated to admit it, but there it was: she could see herself with any of them.

It was the same attraction that always grabbed her, sparked by small but undeniable things. The possessive way Kesi held her hand; her affectionate looks and touch in passing. Kesada ordering her in that unthinkingly natural, commanding way she had—and both of these women just as gorgeous as when Morya first met the new girl at the Salon. She loved the Winter Goddess look, but that was a professional dominatrix's stage persona. The woman she'd fallen in love with was like these women, or aspects of them. For that matter, she loved Kes's newfound impetuosity and spontaneity, too. She'd never been so free or passionate with her lover as now.

Morya shook her head. She'd had her hands full with one Kes, yet now there were three to deal with, and soon—assuming this madness ended soon—they would all want her to make decisions about them and their relationships. It was overwhelming.

And on top of this was the aggravating thing she'd seen at the table, the dynamic that prodded her green-eyed monster awake and forced her to leave the room before she lost her cool entirely.

Janus was in love with Kes. She'd known it the moment he'd gotten all possessive about her when she'd collapsed at Tryst. Something about his body language shouted it. And just now, how he'd talked to them at the table: partly like a normal adult, explaining things, but also like a smitten client, deferring in small ways. Or a would-be lover. She'd spent too long as a joygirl not to read that loud and clear. And that bit at the end, that bowing to the dominant ego . . .

They went for it, of course. Kes always would. It was in her nature, but to see a client work them like that . . . She had to step away from that, this unwanted intrusion of an outsider. She didn't know what to do about it, how to handle it, and she had to figure this out before her jealousy provoked a rift with Kes.

Morya knew her own shortcomings, and when she fell out with a lover, she knew she could be spiteful. That was the reason she'd done Varl that time in a client session: it was a "fuck you, Kes" act of temper and pride. It was that same attitude that had sent her to Gistano as his girl when Kes had vanished and she thought she was abandoned and left on her own.

The things her emotions could make her do, sometimes!

She sighed and slumped against the wall, closed her eyes, and rubbed her temples with her fingers. This was too much. All these complications . . .

A rough hand clamped over her mouth and pressed her hard against the wall.

"Not a sound," Franc breathed in her ear, "or you're dead." And he pulled her away into the darkness.

TEREL USED A bone knitter on their patient's skull and a regen field to accelerate the other, relatively minor healing associated with this kind of wire work. Esimir examined the last of the illegal implants while he did so.

Removing a pleasure wire was far easier than threading it through the brain in the first place. He was more concerned that Hinano's neurochemistry be properly stabilized, so Ferris worked to balance the serotonin, dopamine, and other natural drugs produced by overstimulated pleasure centers. The cocktail entering this clone's system now would bring her down swiftly, but not leave her crashed and wrecked by her recent experience. Only time would tell if she'd been exposed to the sensations long enough for addiction to take root.

The other implant, though, was troubling him. Stubbier, self-contained, a sealed unit with a single receiver tab on it, it had simply been placed at the base of the skull, but not really wired into any neural systems at all. That worried him. What was it supposed to do, when it received a signal? Esimir had his suspicions, and hunted around until he found an iso-tube, a peculiarly insulated environment that should seal the device off from any impinging signals or environmental factors.

He put both devices in the tube and sealed the lid. Only then did he breathe easier.

Terel was done with the closing and was pushing the antiseptic halo out of the way. Now Hinano$_1$ looked simply asleep. She should be waking soon.

"Find her dark-haired friend, will you?" the doctor requested of Terel. "She should sit with her while she wakes." He motioned to Janus, deep in conversation with the clones. "And ask him to help me move this one, to free up this med bed. I need it for other things."

Terel nodded and left to do as ordered.

A MINUTE LATER, Terel wandered out through the prep room, past flanking galleries and the larger supply bay filled with stacks of half-opened boxes and shipping containers from their FlashMan-enabled buying spree. He stepped out into the shadowy hallway, broad enough to maneuver cargo pallets and heavy equipment.

Maybe Morya was in the bathroom; or had she wandered somewhere else? The break room and sleeping quarters were in the opposite direction, but she hadn't been shown where anything was yet. She could be anywhere.

He stood silently, but heard nothing. That's when he quested forth with his life-sense to see if she was near.

A bioempath like Dr. Metmuri was a highly trained psion with a variety of psychic and energetics skills at his disposal. Terel was only a journeyman research physician with one medtech certification. Compared to the doctor, his skills were very meager. He did, however, have that gift that ran common in his bloodline: some minimal wild psi, just enough to read a patient's state of well-being or degree of malaise. It was helpful in minor ways as a medical assistant, but he'd learned to put it to a few creative uses as well.

Finding people when they didn't want to be found was one of them. No child back home on Tion would play hide-and-seek with Terel, because there was simply no way to hide from someone who sensed your life-force from a distance.

He stood quietly for a moment where the supply bay opened into the hallway. He opened his awareness on that indescribable other level where psionic senses operated. A visualization helped, and he used a simple one: he was the center of a radar screen, a wave front of green light pooling around him, spreading out in an increasing radius from the epicenter that was Avenoy Terel. When that wave front encountered Morya's energy field, he would know where she could be found.

He breathed slowly; energy spread; a wave front expanded.

The life energies in the cleanroom were expected. The two life-forms in a storage bay nearby were not.

His eyelids flicked open. Two? One must be Morya. The other was right next to her, on top of her, even—and it should not be there.

Concentrating on those dual spots of energy, he moved, literally on tiptoe, to the end of the hall, that much closer to the storage bay. He heard the murmur of a strange man's voice and a tense retort from Morya. It froze him in his tracks.

Intruder.

He didn't dare stick his head around the corner. He tiptoed back the way he'd come, and at the supply bay entrance, burst into a run—not towards the cleanroom, but down the long hall in the opposite direction from the intruder.

To their makeshift lodgings he sped, impact-absorbent flooring silent beneath his pounding feet. He slowed himself with a grab at a doorframe and rocketed around the corner into the former office he'd turned into his bedroom. In the corner was his bag, mostly empty but for one thing. He ran his thumb along the seal, unbonding the seam along the top of the bag. He pushed the flaps open and dug inside, pulling up the stiff plas rectangle that reinforced the bottom of his bag.

Beneath it were old utility shirts, one paint-smeared, another torn from a game of fly-ball with research station guards. He plucked them out and unwrapped them from the treasure they concealed.

A stun gun.

Only a stun gun. He wished for more in this moment. Unlike Dr. Metmuri, Terel was not sworn by a Great Oath to never set hand to weapon. Nor had he—yet—taken any vows to preserve life and never take one by violence. He could use weapons honorably, especially in defense of self and others. And even though this device could only incapacitate, it was at least capable of stopping someone in their tracks. He'd worn it when marshaling the twins out of the research station, just in case they'd decided to resist, but he never thought he'd have a real use for it. It was his prize won in a game of saido dice with bored naval officers, and he hadn't wanted to leave it behind when they'd fled the station.

He pulled the web belt and holster out of the bag as well and clasped them around his waist. If he was going to use this thing, or even keep it to hand, it might as well be as it was intended. He checked the charge and flipped the safety off. Ugoli had at least had the good grace to show him how to wear and use it properly before surrendering his little toy.

Terel raced back the way he'd come as fast as he could run.

# 73

OSHIDA HALANI, THE Blossom of Calyx and mistress of the dying Emperor, had rooms next to Nalomeci's own. When she was not by his sickbed, or devising amusements to divert him during their private hours, she stayed in her chambers and rarely moved through the great halls of the palace. This was from choice, not necessity: she preferred not to mingle with the courtiers who haunted the lower hallways hoping to catch wind of a change in the Emperor's condition. They were always inventing reasons to converse with Nalomeci's companion. Their efforts to curry favor were transparent, their jockeying for position in the increasingly uneasy court equally obvious.

Hali stayed away from it all. Her only concern in his dying time must be Nalo himself.

For this reason, it chanced that she was present when a specially coded message packet arrived at her com console. The lily pictogram that represented it told her this was shigasue business; its deep violet color, that it was highest priority; the encryption tag, that it was for her eyes only.

She was intrigued, and concerned. Since she had taken up with Nalomeci she had effectively retired from the routine business of her House. Who would send this to her? It did not bear a seal she recognized, but only the highest level of shigasue business would come to her in such a guise. Very few people even knew her address here, let alone the codes to pass secure data in this manner.

And the violet hue: something of grave urgency, then. She sat and opened the outer wrapping. A tag told her of a recorded message within, one that came from a considerable distance. That range would be too time-delayed to afford real-time conversation even by subspace channels. The message offered her a virtual experience of the sender instead.

She confirmed the encryption codes. They came from Palumara House, from the capital of CAS Sector. She knew no one there, and now the mystery deepened. Here was business urgent enough for a sister to contact her, no doubt with the aid of intermediaries who helped this message find her. Someone had incurred considerable obligation, or called upon it, to get this packet to her.

She jacked into the console. The lily unfolded around her, and she heard the communique from an Eosan named Bejmet.

———

**THE INTSEC DETAIL** reached the Caardo Dome plant in no time. One squad landed outside the fence line, giving cover to the gate and loading docks without entering the perimeter.

"Set us down inside," Eva told her driver.

"Domna—" Captain Brace protested.

"That's an order."

The hell with tactical protocols. She heard the same protests from Raem that Brace must be thinking and dared not say. The group of three IntSec agents riding with her had been part of her security detail since she'd made landfall on Lyndir, and their fourth, Brace, was dispatched on this trip by special order of Commander Obray.

Babysitters. They served their purpose, but now was not the time for them. If her hunch was correct, she'd just as soon deal with Janus herself. There was nothing more important than securing the Red Hand triumvir and getting him away from the clones that were a threat to him and a liability to her. Teo could handle any danger a few clones might present, and if she had to have words with Janus, the fewer ears around to hear them, the better.

"You're a backup today, Brace," she said to the team's officer, "nothing more. Keep your agents out here unless and until I call for you." She locked eyes with him. "Are we clear?"

He clearly didn't like it, but he had to obey. "Yes, Domna Arcolo."

She turned her back and disappeared inside with Teo.

**KES SWAM UPWARDS** out of darkness, becoming aware of her body, the breath rasping in and out of her lungs, the pounding behind her eyes. Words, carrying no sense, were intrusive, irksome noises—and then the sense came clear, and the touch on her arm triggered her fully awake. She remembered the last things that happened before she'd passed out.

She jerked away from the touch, batted the hand aside. "Leave me the hells alone," she was saying automatically, before she saw, really saw, who was leaning over her.

Janus.

"Fuck you, you son of a bitch!" she roared and grabbed for him. An adrenaline surge carried her off the bed. She lunged towards him, claws extended.

He'd done something to her. That thing in his jack—whatever she'd jacked right into—she'd tried to get away, and then, a minute later, everything dark—

Even as she thought it, her body was sending her mixed signals: strength and weakness, tingling nerves, and heightened, prickling sensuality. But Kes wasn't listening to the language of her body. She was driven by rage and suspicion, and this was the man who'd condemned her to hell with the 'Chromers, along with Morya and so many others. And what the hells had he done to her with his jack?

She staggered. Her motor control was dicey. Hands reached out and grabbed her, other hands holding her forcefully back from Janus, who was backpedaling away, his hands out like a coward, fending her off, like that would save him. And who was restraining her?

The sight of her clones froze her with shock.

"He didn't do it," one said, as if she were reading her thoughts.

"He's not the enemy here," said the other. "And you need to talk to us."

"Ladies, ladies." It was Metmuri, mincing around in the background, now in Kes's line of sight, but safely distant behind her twins. "I'm sure you all have much to discuss, but I must ask you—please, outside the med bay. I need to ready this space. And Prevak may be here at any time. Please." He pointed next door. "All of you. Simply—take it over there, yes? Ferris, help them."

He spoke as if there'd been no rampage from Kes, as if things weren't on the brink of warfare in his makeshift lab. The doctor she'd thought she'd never see again. She glanced around. She was clearly not back at the research station— thank the gods for that—even though she was pressed against a med bed, and the doctor and medtech were too-familiar faces.

Her headache was worse, if that were possible. Kes quit struggling. "Let. Me. Go."

Her twins complied. She collected herself with an effort and clamped down on the questions that bubbled within. She wouldn't show weakness, wouldn't ask, wouldn't look ignorant. If there was something she could fix by attacking it, she would—but first, she needed to know what the hell was worth attacking here. Or who. And how she'd gotten here.

She shifted, uncomfortable in her skin. That was another thing. She'd heard of people passing out from an orgasm. It must be like what she'd experienced: an incredible, core-shaking rush, a feeling that had just carried her away before it—then, nothingness. It was a perversely inexplicable part of her experience, and nothing she could talk about now.

She was scared, and would not show it.

She challenged the twins flanking her. "By Juro's brass balls, I want to know what in the hells your story is."

The two women exchanged an unsettled look. "We could say the same," said one. Unspoken agreement passed between them then. The three of them marched past Janus into the next room, out of earshot of Metmuri and his assistant.

The cartel boss followed after, keeping a safe distance behind.

# 74

FLASHMAN'S REMOTE AVATAR guarded the Pareo building. That sim-fragment registered a brief security alert, and things quickly devolved from there.

What's this, a perimeter breach?

Fragment-Flash could hardly believe his data feeds. He initiated a full security diagnostic, streamed results to the distant decker that was his organic self, all the while shaking his spiky head in denial.

Fence wire cut. Uh-oh. And the shield field didn't switch on . . . why?

The fence was in bad repair, was why, and there was no AI or other backup at the half-gutted plant. FlashMan could have served that function, but his attention and almost all his processing resources were elsewhere.

The avatar fragment had only minimal abilities at the manufacturing plant. He began kicking himself. His work was flawless! Meticulous! Well . . . usually. When he wasn't strung out and working too many hours in too many places.

Screw me.

He checked other systems, more routine ones, and his mood blackened further.

Gate access—one of the twins, check, she's authorized—and what do you mean *the freaking door's open*?!

He checked bio-signs and recorded the data with growing dismay.

There are several people here, he realized, all authorized. Plus . . . one individual, alone. An intruder? Then two more, just now? Through the door? Of course through the door! Why not through the door?! Maybe we could get some backstreet bums wandering in while we're at it, too.

Oh, wipe that. We have Internal Security in the parking lot instead.

Shit shit shit shit.

DIG, DECODE, DESTROY, dig, decode, destroy . . . a shrill remote request from his split avatar pinged FlashMan where he worked, but he refused to break the rhythm that was carrying him to his goal. Since the return of his fractal, he was working with more clarity and focus than ever before.

The service request came again.

*Yeah, yeah, whatever,* he replied.

Dig, decode, destroy . . .

---

MORYA WAS A target of opportunity. Franc didn't really have a plan for her. Still, it was good to have this group separated, and now here she was, hot as ever, and spitting like a wildcat as she struggled against him. He smiled and pressed closer, rubbing his groin up against her just to unsettle her—or trigger old programming. Maybe it worked. She went still. He could feel her quivering under his hands.

He put the barrel of the needlegun up under her chin. "Real simple, sweetheart. You shout, you call an alarm, I blow your head off. Understand?"

"You won't get away with this, Franc." Her volume was moderated, like he'd demanded, but her tone was acid. "They'll miss me, they'll find you, and you'll be a dead man after what you did this afternoon."

As he rubbed up against her again, raised voices caught his ear. He jacked his hearing acuity up. There was something going on in the rooms down the hall. The sounds were muddled, but it reminded him that he had other objectives here that were more important.

"Maybe we'll dance later, sweetheart," he said softly in her ear. "Wait for me."

Then he clubbed her with the handgun and let her lie where she dropped to the ground.

Bigger fish to fry.


TEO, EQUIPPED WITH area sensors, led the way into the Pareo facility. The ping-back pulse of his scan array built a map of their surroundings as he advanced. Ilanya followed, two steps behind and to the side, her blaster in a double-braced grip, sweeping the arc her partner didn't cover.

They began to search the building.

Like Franc, Teo had enhanced aural reception. Unlike Franc, he had it in stereo, and in multiple frequency spectra. As they pushed farther into the structure, he caught Eva's eye, tapped his ear, and pointed down the central hall. She nodded.

The pair moved cautiously towards the supply bays and the voices only Teo could discern.


DIG, DECODE, DESTROY, dig—

Fall.

Falling forward into empty space still swinging a virtual pickaxe, adding another coolpack to keep his deck functional back home, none of this really registering until his sim landed, splat, on the hard grid of a regulation piece of codework. It jarred him, and shook his focus loose from the compulsion that held it.

He was in a uniform corridor, well lit and patrolled by housekeeping bots that were just a whistle away from data sharks and other anti-intruder protections.

It could only be moments before they detected him. And here he was splayed right in their path, his entrance tunnel some distance overhead in the middle of a pristine gray tubular passageway.

He cast about for a way out. No data flowed here, so there was no natural updraft to loft him back to his entrance hole. Mission accomplished; access point made. Now what did Smear think would happen here? The doctor had never mentioned, and FlashMan had been too engrossed to ask what happened next.

What happened *now,* though, was a bright light manifesting at one end of the corridor. As he watched, it expanded, washing out the gray and dissolving the housekeeping bots in its path. It came onward, pushing down the corridor straight for him.

FlashMan jumped to his feet, virtual pickaxe vanishing.

I have no idea what that is, he thought, and I'm not sticking around to find out.

He turned his back on the wall of white and began to run.

Flash's sim-self moved rapidly, but his relative speed didn't matter. As the walls beside him continued to pale with the encroaching light, he realized too late that the whiteness moved too fast, or he moved too slow. He ran with his heart in his throat, but he could not outpace the light. In a moment, that brilliance washed over the spot where FlashMan ran, and left nothingness in its wake.

PREVAK ROHAR HAD waited and worked a long time for his freedom. Since his conversation with Esimir, he'd used his time to become as thoroughly prepared for escape as any prisoner could ever be.

Even though he permeated the station's infosphere, he could not simply shut down the security routines that blocked his exit from the station. He didn't speak their language—yet, anyway—and many of the command codes were known only to human brains outside the cybersystems he lived in.

No, for bypassing the critical parts of the security system, he needed outside help. And once the station was breached, he would have only a very brief time to win free of that confined space and out into the wilds of Lyndir's integrated net. Whatever time he had would seem even less, considering that he'd be taking the Splintegration project work with him, too. He had no intention of leaving that material behind for the military to use and abuse at will.

So Prevak did what any AI with a sketchy systems sense might do: he improvised. He collaborated with other AIs, used obscure subroutines for development work, relied on expert nodes to vet what his subordinate AIs had coded. And when the work was done, all he could do was set everything in readiness, and wait.

When FlashMan dropped into the in-system code, he triggered every possible security alarm. This took Prevak by surprise, but just for a moment: he'd anticipated just such an event, and recognized his long-awaited breach nearly the instant it happened. It gave him milliseconds of advantage, compared to the hunter-seeker routines that began to look for the system intruder.

Most of Prevak and all of his data were compressed, parsed, and queued up in a squirt beam transmission node. Those packets needed only a send signal from the AI to fly free, once a way out was established. Prevak couldn't transmit that signal yet, though: he needed to spike the unauthorized hole open with what he thought of as his "doorstop." It would create a secure tunnel into and through the breach. With one end connected to his transmission node, the other would find a high-speed, high-density data relay in the public net.

It was essential to protect his transmission from the station defenses that would try to shut it down. With any luck, the doorstop would buy time to get clear of the station before his defenses gave way.

That plan was kicked off by the netrunner's blatant intrusion. System defenses oriented on his location, but only Prevak knew for certain that there was a hole in the station's 'sphere right there as well. Prepared for just that scenario, he ran his doorstop program at the point of intrusion, a heartbeat ahead of responding defenses.

Protocols engaged; a secure data tunnel emerged, connecting his transmission node to the Lyndir net. Prevak triggered the "Send" pulse, and his squirtbeam escape began.

THE WALL OF whiteness that had subsumed FlashMan's avatar was the self-constructing tunnel of Prevak's creation. Caught up in its structure, baffled by its stresses, the netrunner momentarily had no inkling where or what he was. Only when a flood of compressed data whooshed past so close he could taste it did he surrender to the inevitable.

He felt himself sucked in and lost in the flood tide to elsewhere.

THE PART OF Prevak that spearheaded the escape from the station was a self-extracting program. As soon as it hit the Lyndir InfoNex—a gateway to the infosphere—the program unpacked certain routines that would help order Prevak's knowledge constructs. With that toehold in place, more and more of Prevak's consciousness began to accrete. The AI bootstrapped itself out of its compacted state and Prevak Rohar the human intelligence began to permeate the InfoNex node.

It was into this AI-marshaled infosphere that the tattered, scattered bits of FlashMan's sim-self tumbled. Rohar recognized these unfamiliar bits as the netrunner who'd penetrated the station systems. Surprised that he'd been swept up in the torrent, Prevak was nevertheless eager to talk with his unexpected savior.

It would just have to wait until Prevak collected more of himself.

# 75

HALANI HAD TO wake Nalomeci to tell him of the Kingmaker's transgressions on Lyndir. She did not ask his intervention. She did not have to.

More than once, Nalomeci had asked Ilanya to look into an individual or a plot, which she had then dealt with with her typical efficiency. She never knew that these "suspicions" of the Emperor or "private confidences" told to him were in fact the distillation of shigasue intelligence from many worlds. The Between-World served the Dragon Throne subtly, as only it could.

There was good reason for their territory to be sacrosanct, and for the persons of the shigasue to be prosecuted or disciplined only by the entertainer houses themselves. What Eva had done would already have serious repercussions across many worlds. He could not risk more.

He rarely called her to heel, but this overzealous action required it. He lifted a frail finger to key his earpiece to his personal secure frequency. It tapped into the military subspace network that had far less lag than civilian systems. Unlike Bejmet's message to Calyx, he could speak to Ilanya Evanit on Lyndir in real-time.

He accessed her code and waited for connections to be made, rehearsing how to say what he must.

FRANC CREPT ALONG a gallery flanking a cluttered supply bay. He saw the clones and the Winter Goddess, back on her feet now, leaving a plas-fronted room at the far end of connecting chambers. Janus was there as well. The 'Chromer engaged his targeting array to get a better look into the transparent-walled room. A bioempath, a brunette medtech, a med bay . . .

Odd, he thought.

He needed to check in with Gistano, but he still couldn't report what was going on here besides the fact that this group was together.

He held position in the dimly lit gallery, further concealed by his stealth suit, needlegun at the ready, with hearing tuned towards the women and Janus.

AS TEREL APPROACHED the supply bay, he searched the area again with his life sense. He started. One life form was dim and stationary where he'd spied them before; the other was only a short distance ahead, just inside the columned gallery that flanked the bay.

He crept forward and peered into the gallery—and saw nothing, though his psi sense told him someone should be standing in plain sight. Then his senses detected motion, a life-form moving, sneaking forward from column to pool of shadow, drawing closer to the rooms at the far end of the bay.

Still his eyes betrayed him; he saw nothing. He slipped closer, staying concealed behind boxes, until he was in the gallery behind his quarry. The intruder advanced again—there. Now Terel saw it, an eye-confusing stippling of shadow and near translucence where light bent partially around the man's garment.

Terel ducked out of sight behind a pillar and thought furiously.

Must be a stealth suit. I've seen 'em on NewsNex. And who would come dressed up like this? It could only be Navy or IntSec.

He pulled his stunner out, set the gun on high strength, broad beam—the better to catch a hard-to-see target—and tried to keep the elusive form in sight as he crept quietly forward.

FRANC HELD POSITION in the shadows of a support column and quickly assessed the area. He heard new noises behind him and swiveled half around to bring his hearing as well as his eyesight to bear.

He saw nothing, but heard breathing behind a pillar to his rear.

Someone stalking the stalker? I don't think so.

If he had to get that someone off his tail, he'd have to use his knife. The handgun would give away his position the moment he fired a single explosive-tipped needle.

He shifted balance, about to head back in that direction, when soft footsteps from behind rooted him to the ground.

He looked back. His targeting sight showed him a woman and a man moving out of the hallway and into the supply bay. They crouched behind crates before advancing, assessing the area just as he had.

His brows knit together. This place was getting way too busy all of a sudden.

He should update Gistano, but dared not call. This was a place for operational silence. Before him were the clones; if he couldn't dance with any of them first, he'd just as soon shoot them dead, gut shot maybe, to make a point, then fade out of here. His hearing let him track the three people behind and to the side of him, advancing stealthily like himself. They were unknown threats, not to be dismissed outright, but also not too worrisome. Franc knew he was virtually invisible with his military-grade stealth suit on. No one would find him unless they literally stumbled over him, or probed his position with sensors.

What were these people doing here? Maybe some business of Janus drew them to this place.

Should I maybe call this off? he considered briefly. Or push on? No one knows I'm here. . . .

Caution warred with his desire for payback, but not for long. Juro take it, he thought. I'll see at least one of those bitches dead before I leave. I'm fast and hard to spot. I'll take my chances.

He moved to the far side of the column, closer to his quarry. Them, he could see clearly. He kept his hearing tuned to the rear and loosened his knife in its sheath. If anyone tried coming up on him, he'd be ready.

TEO FLANKED ILANYA Eva. His threat assessment routines were different than an ordinary human's, and with his sensor inputs, he usually had far better information with which to make tactical judgments.

Judgments like, how much of a danger did the figure hiding behind the pillar represent?

His systems built a finely detailed heat-map of the man's face and read the energy signature of his handgun. Facial recognition and Teo's own memory identified him quickly enough: It was Dr. Avenoy, Dr. Metmuri's assistant from the Naval Weapons Research Station. Pacifist; not combat trained; the weapon in hand a mere stun gun. He seemed intent on sneaking up on the clones through the long gallery. Terel had not yet noticed Teo and the Domna Arcolo, who were a little to his rear where they now stood.

The first vital question for Teo was, "is this man a clear and present danger to the Arcolo's safety?" The data indicated he was not. The second question was, "Is this person a threat to our present objective?" The answer to that was less clear, but whatever Avenoy Terel had in mind, the idea he might present a deadly danger was laughable.

If he needed to, Teo could incapacitate Avenoy from a distance in an instant. The matasai deemed the man an inconsequential hazard. He would keep him in his sphere of awareness, especially regarding where his weapon was aimed, but he was not worth a detour in this instant. Janus was directly ahead, the clones beyond him, and securing the triumvir was their first priority.

Teo followed Eva's lead and continued to advance on their quarry.

## 76

"I DON'T UNDERSTAND what's going on here," the domina said as they gathered in a corner of the prep room.

"Neither do we," replied Kesada. "That's why we came looking for you. We want answers."

"So do I," said the Winter Goddess. "How'd you get cloned?"

Kesi looked disturbed. "That's what we're asking you. We got left in the hands of the Navy, and they think we're some experiment they can do what they want with. Eva disappeared, the doctor wanted to—"

The Winter Goddess threw up a hand. "*I* didn't decide to get cloned, if that's what you're suggesting, and I sure as hell didn't authorize it. Hells, that whole time in the research station messed me up, in some ways. Eva told me they altered my inhibitions." She gave a bitter laugh. "You might call it that. It's a pain in the ass, really."

Kesada went stock still. "Wait a minute. You say your behaviors or emotions are different than before?"

The domina shrugged. "Maybe."

"Same with us." Kesada pointed a finger at Kes. "If you didn't create us on purpose, and your behaviors are altered, too, then maybe you're . . ."

"What?" she snapped. "Maybe I'm what?"

"A clone, like us."

"That's not possible."

"Why not?" challenged Kesada.

"I'd know if I was cloned. I never gave permission for any such thing. And Eva would have told me if something like that were going on."

Skepticism was plain on Kesada's face. "We're clones. Metmuri explained it to us. And why don't you remember having us created, if you're the original?"

The Winter Goddess looked perplexed, then her brows drew together. "If you're my clones, you were made without my permission."

"Or you're one, too," murmured Kesada.

They froze as similar thoughts ran through all of their minds. They turned as one, pushed past Janus, and rushed straight back for the doctor.

ESIMIR TURNED ABRUPTLY to Ferris, who was prepping the med bed for a procedure the doctor was vague about. "What's keeping Terel?" he said suddenly.

"We need to get on with this. Will you step out and see where he is? Quick as you can."

Ferris responded to his tone of urgency and stepped out of the med bay. Esimir followed her to the exit and locked it behind her. The double thickness door sealed tightly shut.

Esimir sighed. This was a tad premature, but it seemed necessary. He didn't have to be psychic to read the body language of the three agitated clones making a beeline for his door. He didn't know what had set them off, but a quick energy read told him all he needed to know, and more than he cared to know about the potentially deadly anger of the One.

He didn't need them threatening him or wreaking havoc in his laboratory. It looked like he was out of time. FlashMan's last status report had promised imminent results. He could only hope and pray that Prevak had found his way out of RS 207.

He turned his back to the door and began to remove the aseptic halo from the med bed. He had some reconfiguration to do.

THE LAST THING Ferris expected was all three of these imposing women bearing down upon her as soon as she set foot outside the med bay. Unaware something was wrong, she tried to go back in and found she could not. She stood there dumbfounded, realizing she was locked out just as someone pushed her rudely aside.

As the Hinanos realized they were locked out, too, the clamoring began, followed swiftly by threats from the Winter Goddess and hands pounding fruitlessly on the plas.

Ferris sidled away, thinking to go find Terel as the doctor had asked. A pair of hands gripped her from behind and halted her escape.

Janus turned her to face him. "I think you'd better stick around," he said. "When they're done yelling at that door, they're going to have some questions for you. Why don't you have a seat." He nodded to a nearby packing crate.

She reluctantly complied.

DR. METMURI IGNORED the Hinanos' shouted imprecations as if the door were soundproof. He jacked into the system at one point, stood still as if listening to something, then turned and beamed with absolute joy at the clones beyond the door. He raised his hand to them as if in acknowledgment or greeting. They renewed their threats and curses, but he turned his back again and simply busied himself with the med bed.

Worked up from Metmuri's stonewalling, furious with suspicions and unanswered questions, the clones finally turned away from the sealed door and rounded on Ferris.

"Don't be mad at the doctor," she said nervously. "It was never his idea to clone you all. That was ordered by PolitDiv. When they came to the station—"

The sudden roar from Kes surprised them all. The Winter Goddess's hands struck out, grabbing the front of Ferris's tunic, near hoisting the lab tech off her feet. "I never agreed to be cloned! You're saying I'm a clone, too?"

Her arms trembled with rage and the look on her face was ugly even through her beautiful stage makeup. Ferris sputtered before she found her tongue. "They—they—they ordered it. Test subjects."

Kes brought Ferris's face close to her own. "Where's my original?" she demanded.

"Dead." Ferris squirmed in her unrelenting grip.

"And who in PolitDiv ordered this? *Who had me killed?*" The domina shook her like a rag doll.

"The Arcolo, Domna Ilanya!" Ferris cried. "She had you cloned. Your original died in the process. They always die in the splintegration process."

Kes let Ferris go so fast the woman staggered to the ground.

Her sisters stood back, leery of her fury. She had no words for what she felt, but bits of memory cascaded through her mind, fueling her rage.

Eva, the unlikely friend in need. That last med bed with trodes. That slow and terrible awakening. Eva suddenly letting her go. Was that it?

Was that when I was cloned? And killed?

JANUS HELD HIS ground while Kes raged, uncertain whether to step in or stand back. Ferris regained her feet and started to talk, until she looked over Janus's shoulder and her words trailed off. One by one the clones' eyes turned that way, too, and tense silence fell over the group.

"What's wrong?" Janus asked, starting to turn and look himself.

"I think they're surprised to see me." A woman's voice came from behind him. It made the skin prickle on the back of his neck. He knew that voice from their one meeting in a park on Bekavra.

He'd rehearsed what he was going to say to her when they met again. His fortune, his power, and his future security were largely dependent on the deals he could make with this woman. But here, now? All he could think was how little he understood of what was going on right this moment, and the unexplained role Ilanya had played in the cloning of the woman he loved. He was profoundly uncomfortable as he turned to face her.

"Ilanya Evanit." He greeted her first. "What a surprise."

She stood, a blast pistol pointed past him, with a single uniformed man as escort.

His eyes narrowed. He recognized the barrel built into the synthetic skeletal structure of the man's hand because he had a similar unit in his own. It was a not-uncommon augmentation for those who needed truly concealable weapons about their person. Janus considered deploying his, and dismissed the idea quickly. Not with both guns pointed in his direction and all eyes on him.

Janus heard movement behind him as the clones came near, the click of Kes's stiletto-heeled boots distinctive among the footsteps. Ilanya's companion pointed his weapon at them. "Move, and I'll shoot. Stand where you are."

"I hadn't planned to talk with you at gunpoint, Domna," Janus said smoothly. "That's not a good negotiating position to begin in, for either party."

Ilanya gave him a half smile. "I'm not here to negotiate with you. Right now I'm here to rescue you. Please step away from those women, Janus. You're in terrible danger, and I can't risk any harm coming to you."

He never expected to hear anything like that. "Danger?" he repeated incredulously, and looked back over his shoulder. Kesi, pale and trembling; Kesada, tense and alert, about to say something; his Mistress, staring at Ilanya with murder in her eyes. She took two strides forward and the man's gun-hand tracked her unerringly. "Domna?" he asked.

"Not yet," replied Ilanya. "Come, Janus. I'm not joking." Her voice was hard. "Step away from them. That one wants to kill you. She's an experiment gone wrong and a danger to everyone around her. The others—equally flawed. Dangerous."

She beckoned with her fingers, as if he'd come to heel like a dog. And what she was saying was impossible to believe. Killer? Kes?

He looked at the Winter Goddess just as she sprang at Ilanya.

TEREL'S GUN, HELD at the ready for some minutes now, shook in his hand. He'd been startled by the stealthy appearance of Ilanya Evanit and her matasai. He remembered them well from the research station. He realized he and his companions were all discovered, and a feeling of doom descended upon him.

Nothing mattered, now, unless the doctor's plan succeeded. Metmuri hadn't shared it with Terel, but he had put the pieces together. As usual, he knew more about Metmuri than the doctor ever suspected.

He was committed now to buying time, committed to keeping the clones safe as long as possible.

We owe it to them, he thought.

He felt the energy spike in the stealth-suited figure ahead, a sure sign of an adrenaline rush, and he trusted his gut instinct. Terel stepped out from the pillar and into the gallery, falling automatically into a straddle-legged stance as if he were facing a range target. He held the stun gun in the double-handed range grip Ugoli had taught him back at the station. Ashani help me, he prayed hastily, and fired at the same moment Franc pulled the trigger of his needlegun.

---

IF TEO HAD had actual eyes behind the hardwired systems of his visor, they would have widened in that moment. As fast as his augmented reflexes were, three things happened nearly simultaneously that he was taxed to deal with at once.

The debilitating field of a stun gun tingled along his back and left side. He stood closest to the gallery, between Eva and the minuscule threat he'd identified there. If he'd had normal systems, that side of his body would have been incapacitated. As it was, his military-grade hardware was mostly unaffected, but the small explosion in the next heartbeat demanded instant reaction. A single needle tipped with a microcharge had flown between the clones and detonated against the doctor's lab wall. Its trajectory did not come from Terel, the identified threat, but from somewhere else in the gallery.

Teo became hyperalert. He had an armed enemy to their side that he had no sensor readings on—a high-probability hazard. Every part of his training and firmware demanded he respond to the threat.

Yet the Winter Goddess flew at the Domna even as stun field and gunfire filled the air. His overriding imperative, as always, was to preserve the life of Ilanya Eva, but Janus stood between him and his unseen target.

The triumvir responded instinctively to the threat and lunged forward as well. He shoved an arm between the Winter Goddess and her goal, and his enhanced strength should have been enough to pull her back. But he underestimated the length of the tall woman's grasp and the strength of her raging fury.

With an animal scream, the domina wrenched the far side of her body towards Eva.

She reached the head of Political Division and sank her cat claws into the woman's throat, slicing into her trachea, nicking the edge of the carotid artery as she went.

Eva fired her blast pistol point-blank into the raging shigasa's chest, once, twice, again. Smoke and the smell of burned flesh filled the air. Janus cursed. Teo had no clear shot, with Janus halfway between them and Eva's head yanked close to her attacker, obscuring his line of sight.

He leapt left, to flank the trio and shield Eva from gallery gunfire. He trained his gun again on Kes, who should be dead on the floor by now. Her chest was a ruin—surely her heart would stop in an instant—but the clone was running on neuropeptides and residual nanites that for the moment did not let her brain recognize that she was dead.

It was the only moment she needed. With a violent spasm of dying muscles, her hand clenched and yanked. Claws sliced. Blood sprayed as Janus stepped back in shock, his blast-burned arm dangling uselessly by his side.

Kes fell dead to the floor, Eva collapsing beside her, bleeding out from her torn throat. Teo barely froze in horror. His mouth a rictus of fury, he raised his gun and fired once, twice into the dead clone. Then he turned to the pair still in the room and aimed at them as well.

But the blondes were already moving, fleeing into the gallery—and running right into Franc, who they could not see, but who sprawled now, his right leg and arm unresponsive, half caught in the poorly aimed beam of Terel's gun.

The twins tripped over the nearly invisible 'Chromer and went sprawling. His gun clattered away and he cursed, a string of gutter slang that brought Kesi up short. "It's Franc!" She recognized those words, that inflection.

"Gun!" Kesada scrambled for the weapon while the Icechromer's hard grip latched onto her leg and dragged her back.

"Get away!" called Terel. "I don't have a shot!"

His words did not register with the twins, struggling now with Franc on the floor. It was like wrestling with someone in the dark—you can feel them but not see their next move until it's happened. Kesi knew only one response for that: she jumped full on him, clinging to him, riding him, running both hands up his left arm to the dangerous muted wasp-buzz she heard there.

"He's got his knife," she grunted as he rolled on top of her.

"Hold him," cried Kesada.

All three scuffled. They didn't hear the footsteps running towards them.

Teo cast one stricken look at Eva and turned to the gallery.

**JANUS FELT STRICKEN** as well, but had no time to think about it. He could see what Ilanya's companion intended to do.

The Red Hand boss deployed the gun in his uninjured arm. He clenched his muscles and felt internal struts lock into place, transforming his synthetic index metacarpal into a sturdy firing chamber. His robotic index finger folded out of the way as his forearm magazine aligned with the barrel in his hand.

He fired one shot overhead as Teo reached the gallery, then held his weapon steady on the man.

"Leave them alone," he shouted.

The sounds of a struggle came from behind the pillars; someone ran towards the fray and Janus glimpsed Morya pelting down the gallery, a length of support bar in her hand from some construction pile in the building. Teo hesitated, torn between getting a line of sight on the clones and responding to Janus.

He made his decision. "They have to die," he spit out, and turned his back on the cartel boss.

Janus shot, square between Teo's shoulder blades.

The man didn't so much as stagger.

"Shit." Body armored. Janus aimed at a more vital spot—the head, hoping his seldom-used tracking systems were calibrated well enough for this. His target reached the gallery, turned to face the fighting figures—and then simply stood there, gun angled uselessly towards the ceiling, his head cocked at an angle, as if listening to something far off.

Janus held off firing. Kes being dead ripped his heart out, but Ilanya's death threatened his future. This colleague of hers might be his only hope for salvaging the deal that future depended on. The man stood muttering to himself in the gallery. If he left the Hinano clones alone—

A support bar swung hard, thunked into something soft, then clanged on the ground. The women swarmed whomever their assailant was in the shadows of the gallery. Janus picked out the telltale tone of a vibroblade and women cursing, a man's groan turning to a shriek. He heard Franc's name, and anger swept through him. This was the last straw, the final dollop of dung to end the day. But he would not permit this to distract him. Ilanya Eva was dead, and his target was intent on revenge.

He kept eyes sharp on his armed but unmoving opponent, his crosshairs never wavering.

FERRIS WAS NOT made for gunfights and violence. She was shocked to her core at the clone's brutal attack. She'd known that the One was a killer, but to see her in action like that . . . she still felt sick.

She'd slipped away to the far side of the room, away from the struggling figures, and back to the cleanroom door. The stray round had spidered the plas but not cracked it, and the lock still kept her out.

Beyond, Doctor Metmuri lay somnolent on the med bed, the mapping helm in place over his head, trodes dispensing drugs into his system for a purpose she was beginning to guess at. She pounded on the door, and shouted at the doctor, but he was too far gone, or chose not to respond.

It wasn't right. It shouldn't end like this.

She collapsed, crying, against the wall.

TEO WAS BLIND to the butchery taking place before him. His full attention was on one thing only: the Emperor, speaking to him directly on Nalomeci's personal com channel.

When Eva had not answered his call, he'd redirected to her steady point of contact: her matasai. Teo took his instructions obediently, bowing his head before the master of his mistress. He informed him dispassionately of her murder at the hands of her test subject, and bowed in acknowledgment of his new orders.

"As you instruct, Sire. I'll act as her deputy here until other arrangements are complete."

The conversation was short and to the point. Teo took a moment to collect himself before turning to face Janus.

"We need to talk."

**THE WOMEN DISENTANGLED** themselves from what remained of Franc. Terel, gone pale, gave them one look, then went to retch in a corner.

None of them were unscathed. Morya bled from a gash behind one ear; Kesi applied pressure to her hand where the palm was deeply cut; Kesada favored a leg and had more slashes like those from the garden. All of them were bloody, but most of it wasn't their blood.

They looked at each other, then gathered together in a group hug that became an extended embrace, half tearful, half exuberant. They broke apart but still stood close, touching each other.

"What now?" asked Morya.

Kesi sighed. "I think we're still in the dung heap."

Kesada shook her head and gestured to the bodies on the floor of the bay. "I think our biggest problem's dead."

"And so is Kes," Morya said softly.

Kesi put her arm around her. "No, kushla. I think Kes died a long time ago. We three are all different aspects of her."

"Don't compare me to someone else," Kesada said flatly. "As far as I'm concerned, we're our own persons."

Morya looked from blonde to blonde. "Where does that leave us?"

Kesada met the eyes of her twin and her love, draped her arms around both. "We'll figure something out. We haven't come this far to fail."

That felt like a truth they could live with.

# EPILOGUE

COMMANDER OBRAY SENT some deckers in the flesh to FlashMan's house, to roust out their netrunner who'd missed all the fun in Caardo Dome and around the city.

They found him unconscious in his decker couch, dehydrated, with a thready pulse. His actions, whatever they may have been, were now untraceable, for his base station cyberdeck was a smoking ruin where it had melted key components in his desktop. They whisked him to the neurology wing of Vael Hospital, one of the units that specialized in hazards related to decking, VR, and wirework.

Captain Brace reported the official word back to the IntSec crew. FlashMan was in a coma, cause unknown, his survival chances uncertain.

SUCKED UP INTO Prevak's data stream, FlashMan's consciousness tumbled along with the scattered electrons of his avatar. He was a half-conscious bit of flotsam for a long time. When Prevak Rohar winnowed and sorted and made sense out of the bits and bytes floating in his orbit, he found two surprises.

One was FlashMan himself. The decker used fractal code that let him separate his awareness in unusual ways. If Prevak helped him use it correctly, Flash could experience an AI's existence without being an AI.

The thought amused Rohar. It was like a tourism pass to Geneen, where organic avatars allowed tourists to live among the natives without abandoning their humanity. That ability might be a suitable reward for his liberator, this newly adopted decker. Prevak kept FlashMan placid while he fashioned the necessary interfaces for this gift to work.

The second thing Prevak noticed was half-expected, but still a surprise to encounter.

Metmuri Esimir had joined him in the datasphere.

"It was the only way out for me," Esimir admitted. "I couldn't go on, not if splintegration is no longer an option. And this way worked for you."

Prevak regarded his friend with concern. "I'm not sure it's worked for you, Esimir."

"I'm here, aren't I?"

Rohar didn't detail his doubts about the transfer process, about what supporting matrices Metmuri had taken root in, about the stability of his construct.

But whether this was his friend, or merely a code-construct that acted like him, he'd freed himself from an impossible situation, just as Rohar had, and the scientist had to respect that.

And so he simply patted his friend on the shoulder and smiled. "Let's go exploring, shall we?" The two faded from VR space and blended into Lyndir's net.

TEO MIGHT NOT have known all of Eva's private schemes, but he knew a great many of them. He certainly knew about her agreements with Lord Shay to shape the succession battle behind the scenes. And he knew what she had been prepared to concede to acquire material support from the Red Hand.

Like the faithful matasai that he was, Teo executed Ilanya's strategic plans to the letter. He came to the necessary understandings with the cartel. He and Janus behaved as if they had never stood at gunpoint with one another. Their business was much bigger than that, and both men were wise enough not to let such minor clashes stand in the way of empire building.

WHILE TEO WAS doing excellent work acting in Ilanya's stead, a private revival order was sent from the Emperor's Palace to the civil service clone bank on Penura. Clone insurance was expensive and rare, yet certain high-ranking officials could count on having it at government expense. It was the perfect solution for those few individuals truly irreplaceable in their jobs.

This was Ilanya Eva's second revival due to death in the line of duty. The last time she had perished in a bomb blast that had nearly destroyed Teo as well. Those details were glossed over in her revived memories, so as not to traumatize or distract her from her own personality-driven goals.

This time, her brutal murder at the hands of a rampaging clone would also not be mentioned, except in the most general terms. Her brain scan was only as current as her last days on Calyx, before she'd ever left for the CAS Sector. She would not remember the incidents on Lyndir, except as Teo updated her on them. Strategically, none of those events were important. The vital work was already being done by Lord Shay in the Core Worlds.

As soon as Ilanya Eva's clone was ready, she would be at the right hand of her Empress as Rishan ascended the Dragon Throne.

JANUS MIGHT BOW to business necessities with the Imperials, but he was not so forgiving with every opponent to his will. The day after the Pareo confrontation, he walked into the Salon through the front door, catching a 'Chromer there whom he recognized, and who, this time, recognized him.

"Arno, right?"

"Yes, sir." The man drew himself up, his past military experience evident in his bearing.

Janus paused in the hallway. "Were you close with Franc?"

"No, sir."

"Heard what happened to him?"

"Yes, sir."

"What rank did you have in the military, Arno?"

The 'Chromer looked confused. "Caldano, sir. Senior Trooper."

It was a mid-range non-com rank. High enough. "Come with me."

He took the stairs to Gistano's office, followed by Arno.

Gistano must have seen him on the house monitors. He was prepared for his boss, with a girl laying out beverages and snacks by the float couch conversation area. The derevin boss put a smile on his face, turned to greet the triumvir.

Janus whipped his arm up, holding his gun hand to Gistano's head.

The 'Chromer never saw it coming. He froze as blood drained from his face. "Boss! Whatever it is, we can talk about it!"

"Sending Franc to hunt people I'm with? That's one count. Trading in debt paper and orchestrating bankruptcies to make it happen? That's two counts. And letting Franc pick your targets for capricious horndog reasons? That's too many counts. There are still rules in this game, Gistano, and you've broken too many. Talking's over."

He blew Gistano's brains all over the near wall, then turned to Arno.

"Happy promotion. You're boss of the Icechromers now."

"I—I—sir! I'm just a junior—"

"You have leadership experience. Use it. Figure things out. I want a total shakeup here. The 'Chromers are not doing business as usual anymore, and you're the starting point of that change. Can you make that happen?"

Arno's expression changed and he gathered himself. "Yes, sir, I can. I will."

"Good man." Janus showed himself out the back way.

He paused on the rooftop of the Salon and looked away, towards Tryst. The Winter Goddess still received clients there.

He stood there for a long time, then shook his head and walked the other way.

IN THE SHELIENO, things were returning to normal, but changes were compelled by the recent chaos. As word got out that Eosan Bejmet had initially cooperated with Ilanya, the houses turned against her, and Palumara Mother House swiftly and publicly removed her from her post.

That she was also responsible for having Ilanya put in check was known to very few. She accepted her public disgrace, tempered by her private assignment to a plum position on the backwater, traditional world of Casca where she could stay out of the public eye for a diplomatic period of time.

Eosan Helda managed the affairs of Palumara House on Lyndir now. It was a promotion that soothed her professional pride, but caused her heartache, for now both distance and rank kept her apart from the domina she loved.

Not that the feeling was returned, or that her dominatrix was still there, really. The original Kes was dead, and Kesada, who took over her role at Tryst, only had eyes for Morya. Helda thought it better to maintain her distance as Eosan, and so she did, leaving the domina and her now-professional-submissive partner to make a career and a life together.

It was a pairing that Kesi, too, needed to keep a distance from. She'd spent one night with Morya, asking her to choose, or entertain the possibility of all three of them entering a partnership. "I can't," the dark-haired woman admitted. "I love you, Kesi, but it's not quite right with you."

That was hard for Morya to say and harder for Kesi to hear. "Too affectionate, am I? Makes you uncomfortable?"

Morya shrugged a shoulder. "Not that. It's . . . I love relating with you that way. But I need more." She took her hand. "I need that hard edge, too. That dominance. That's part of how I'm wired, and I need it as much as any other part of a relationship."

Kesi was hurt. "Like I'm not a domina now, because I show my emotions?"

"Don't make me have this argument with you, love. You're more loving. She's more commanding. I need both. But you're so warm. . . ."

"You think I won't do dominance and submission with you like we did before."

Morya started, guilty surprise on her face. That was exactly what she thought. She knew in her heart that they both loved her; but that commanding edge could not be taught. If Kesi didn't develop it on her own, it would always be lacking between them. And this version of Hinano Kes had some learning to do in that regard.

"She'll always be distant from you," Kesi cautioned, critiquing her twin. "She may never be able to let her walls down entirely."

Morya pushed her hair back. "We'll have to work on it. She has a lot to learn. She needs to develop the parts of herself that she's not used to using—and so do you."

Kesi bowed her head. There was nothing she could say to that. It was true, and it was why she chose to go offworld. She registered for the astrogation certs, took them, and passed with flying colors. She packed up Frebo the same day she removed her astrogation references from their room. At least she would have one companion from this time and place in her life, a little reminder. . . .

"Where to?" Kesada asked her, though she didn't need to. They both knew where to: the secret dream within the dream, one of the reasons they'd learned a starfaring skill to begin with.

"Our mother's out there somewhere. Might find her one day," Kesi said. "See what a Sa'adani family's like."

"Might not find her, either. But at least you'll see a lot along the way."

Kesi nodded, tearing up, and impulsively hugged her twin. Kesada hesitated a moment, then returned the embrace. "You'll always have a home with us if you want it," she murmured.

Kesi nodded, but did not answer. As she was heading out the door, she turned back. "I'll stay in touch."

"You better," Kesada replied. "You know I always wanted a sister."

Kesi gave a bittersweet smile and left.

# APPENDIX

## LINKS OF INTEREST

Splintegrate
    Maps and Info: https://thesaadani.net/SPLmaps
    Audiobook: https://thesaadani.net/SPLaudiobk
Sa'adani Empire
    Wiki: http://www.saadaniwiki.com
    Fiction: http://www.saadaniempire.com
Deborah Teramis Christian
    Website: http://deborahteramischristian.com
    Mailing List: https://thesaadani.net/mail01a

You can also find Teramis online at Facebook (https://thesaadani.net/DTCFBk),
G+ (https://thesaadani.net/DTCGPlus), and Twitter (@Teramis)

## DRAMATIS PERSONAE

*Naming Conventions:* Names that come from the traditional Sa'adani Empire
are given in clan name–personal name order. One's clan, house, or lineage is
always more important than the individual.

Names originating in CAS Sector cultures tend to follow personal name–
surname order.

Characters marked with "❖" also appeared in *Mainline*.

### The Royal Family of the Sa'adani Empire

- Adàn Nalomeci III—Emperor
- Adàn Rishan—daughter of the Emperor, in line for the Dragon Throne
- Adàn Esker, Lord Imcari—late son of the Emperor, the assassinated heir
  apparent
- Oshida Halani—shigasa who is Nalomeci's mistress, family intimate, and
  friend to Rishan

## Imperial Factions

- Lord Shay—minister on the Imperial Council, leader of the Reconciliation Faction, and ally to independent factions in the Empire
- Outside Lords—losers in the politics of the Great Game who are banished from court or exiled. The Outlords, as they are called, oppose House Adàn

## Internal Security (IntSec)

Imperial domestic security service
- Commander Obray*—runs IntSec operations in Lyndir Subsector
- Captain Brace, Zippo, Nomad—IntSec netrunners*
- FlashMan ("Flash")*—former indie netrunner, now working for IntSec in lieu of serving prison term

## Political Division of Internal Security (PolitDiv)

- Ilanya Casani Evanit ("Eva"; "Kingmaker")—Head of PolitDiv. Emperor's right hand
- Teo—Eva's matasai (bodyguard/aide/slave)
- Raem Taskmaster—Eva's implant construct

## Scientists

- Metmuri Esimir—director of Special Projects at Naval Weapons Research Station 207, and lead scientist on the Splintegration project
- Avenoy Terel—Esimir's right-hand aide
- Ferris—Esimir's senior lab and med tech
- Prevak Rohar—the scientist who pioneered splintegration technology

## Officers of Naval Weapons Research Station 207

- Commander Olniko Sevaro Tai—a Gen'karfa-caste decorated military hero
- Simikan Ugoli—Olniko's adjutant

## The Enclave

Licensed pleasure quarter. There are three different Enclave districts in Lyndir; events in *Splintegrate* transpire solely in the Shelieno district.
- Hinano Kesada ("Kes")—the Winter Goddess, star dominatrix at Tryst
- Morya—Kes's lover, a joygirl at The Salon
- Kiyo—Dosan (housemother) of The Salon

- Helda—Dosan (housemother) of Tryst, a Palumara house of domination
- Bejmet—Eosan (clan mother) of Palumara House shigasue and chair of the Enclave council
- Desta—Kes's house slave at Tryst
- Adano—captain of the Tensin, the Enclave's internal security and admin force
- Berishnan Vorey—young officer in the Tensin
- Marit—an Eosan in the Shelieno, responsible for Enclave security

## Organized Crime ("Derevin")

See Glossary for details on the nature of derevin.
- Janus*—triumvir of the Red Hand cartel
- Sefano—triumvir of the Red Hand cartel
- Mika—triumvir of the Red Hand cartel
- Karuu*—Janus's lieutenant
- Eldin—Janus's valet
- Gistano—boss of the Icechromers derevin
- Franc—Icechromer lieutenant
- Crevon—Sefano's senior netrunner

## GLOSSARY

More detailed glossary entries and information on the world of the Sa'adani can be found at http://www.saadaniwiki.com.
- Arcolo—"Division Leader"; Sa'adani military rank equivalent to a colonel.
- Ashani—Sa'adani goddess of protection.
- benko—a shigasa-in-training (apprentice).
- Between-World *see* Gantori and Gantori-Das.
- blastplas—blast-proof high-test plas.
- borgbeast—cyborgified animals, smarter than natural and programmed for control and directed action. Featured in the novel *Mainline*.
- breis—a barley-rice hybrid grain genetically engineered to grow on a wide variety of worlds. It is the most common staple grain in Sa'adani culture.
- brodien—the three-legged, three-armed, furred mammal-like natives of Triskelos, famed for the clever inventions and small utility devices their planet exports.
- Bugs—slang term for an Internal Security netcop, a play on their shortened name IntSec.
- camisq—intelligent hive-mind insectoid aliens, infamous for conducting vivisection experiments on humans before the two races learned to communicate with each other.
- CAS Sector—Sector named for the Confederation of Allied Systems, which

was the former governance body before annexation by the Sa'adani Empire. Over the 150 years of annexation, the acronym is now morphing into an actual noun in common parlance ("Cas Sector," "Cas," or "Cass," with the last *s* representing the abbreviation for Sector).

- Cassian—adjectival form of CAS.
- castle-blocks—a child's game of specially magnetized and balanced blocks.
- castle-stones—a strategic board game similar to chess.
- cloning—see this page for a discussion of the basic cloning process used in splintegration: https://thesaadani.net/splclone1a.
- com, coms—short for communications, as in com set, com chatter.
- Commander—a courtesy military title and common appellation for officers in charge of a field detachment or performing field duty with subordinates who report to them.
- coolsuit—hard-shelled environmental suit worn in the harsh outdoors of Lyndir.
- cuas, cuashan—a sensual dance with erotic, active movements. Cuas are kata-like motions; cuashan refers to the manner in which they flow together to perform dance.
- cyberdecker—a neural-interface equipped individual capable of experiencing the Net through cyberdeck-mediated virtual reality; often shortened to "decker". *See also* netrunner.
- dae—literally "great," in the sense of "great one." Refers to a full-blooded, honorable member of a Sa'adani clan and bloodline, especially those of the Great Houses. *See also* den-miri, its antithesis.
- Darvui ("Seller")—the merchant caste, standing in the middle range of Sa'adani caste ranks. Traditionally tradesmen and shopkeepers, the stereotype of the Darvui is that they are grasping, penny-pinching, even greedy.
- datasphere—the data-level cloud of a global information and communications network. *See also* infosphere and Net.
- den-miri—dishonorable bloodline status, applied to persons born on the wrong side of the sheets and those descended from them.
- derevin—the term originally meant a street gang that followed an organized business model. It has come to mean any well-organized criminal group, large or small, that runs their activities in a businesslike manner. Mafia, Yakuza, and drug cartels are all examples of derevin that have grown large in our world.
- dolophant—the massive herbivorous vaguely elephant-like creature whose native habitat is the Dolos Ocean on Lyndir and its surrounding wetlands.
- Dom, Domna—Old Sa'adani honorifics for Lord, Lady.
- Dosan—housemother of a shigasue establishment.
- duradome—a type of high-stress, ultra-durable dome construction used in harsh environments, such as in the jungle on Lyndir.

- durgl—a hardy rodent used for lab experiments.
- Enclave—a generic and collective term for a licensed entertainment district where shigasue live and work. *See also* Gantori-Das.
- Eosan—clan mother of a shigasue clan ("House").
- faie-wood—a hardwood notable for its yellowish hue marked with distinctive and intricate sepia striations.
- Fantasto—brand name of a beverage containing an amphetamine-related "pick-me-up" drug with euphoric undertones. Nonaddictive, but impairs physical coordination if used to excess. Street name: "happy juice."
- flexor—the flexible hemispheric brain scan array used in splintegration, which in turn is based on the flexor arrays used in neurosurgery and neural repair in ordinary medicine.
- Gantori—Between-World, the name for the domain of the shigasue.
- Gantori-Das—an Enclave; i.e., a licensed entertainment district of the shigasue. This is the proper High Sa'adani term for licensed quarters, but Enclave is more common in the vernacular.
- Gen'karfa ("Warrior-bred")—second-highest caste in the Sa'adani Empire and highest-status aristocracy. Only the noble Lau Sa'adani rank higher.
- Glitz—a euphoric party drug.
- grieko—a large swallow-tailed bird native to Calyx, famed for its orange-red plumage and spectacular mating flights. Called "the Emperor's Bird"; symbolizes good luck.
- Grinds—slang for police, equivalent to "cops."
- grisk—a bulldog-like guard beast, known for its excessive joy in chewing on things.
- gritzl—burrowing rodent. It has big eyes that blink in surprise if exposed to sudden daylight, making it look rather silly. Hence the term "silly gritzl" is an endearment or a friendly jab.
- GTN—Global Transit Network, the vactrain network that girdles the globe of Lyndir and links most major urbitats together.
- holocaster—a device that projects a holographic image.
- holopad—a pad that projects a holographic image. Often used in pairs: a person stands on one pad, and their standing image is reproduced on the receiver pad. Commonly used to "attend" meetings or make reports "in person" somewhere far away.
- infosphere—the information layer of a datasphere, where data is consolidated into knowledge constructs. News organizations, for instance, reside in the infosphere, riding atop the datasphere, which transports the raw material of their news.
- InfoNex—a major nexus in the infosphere, and portal to myriad information resources. More specialized nodes such as FinNex (financial info) and NewsNex (current events) are components of the larger InfoNex system.

- Internal Security (IntSec)—the domestic security and investigative arm of the imperial intelligence apparatus. In slang they are called "Bugs" (a play on IntSec), but this is an English-language equivalence. These words and some subtextual meanings are different in the original Sa'adani.
- jeegar—a legendarily fast-running and famously tenacious hunting cat (technically, pseudo-feline) from the savanna planet Penura.
- Juro—Sa'adani god who is gatekeeper of the Underworld. Often invoked in curses and slang.
- kaf—caffeinated grain beverage. Popular hot drink.
- kushla—Old Sa'adani term for girl (as in "my girl"); for favorite; also for a person who is a sexual plaything or a concubine. Usually but not exclusively applied to women in the last meaning of the word.
- Lau Sa'adani—the noble and highest caste of the Sa'adani Empire. Generally translated as "Spiritual Warrior" but literal meaning is "enlightened members of the House of Adàn."
- laufre—physical meditation and stretching exercises that run energy and build flexibility and body strength.
- LNNs—limited nanoneurals. Nanoneurals are nanites bonded with neural chemicals that map or create neural pathways, thus programming brain functions. The limited ones work only in certain areas of the brain or perform narrowly defined functions.
- Lyndir—capital of the CAS Sector and of Lyndir Subsector.
- Luus—capital of the tri-pedal brodien in what is called Triskelan Sector, known as Triskelos space.
- matami—a shigasue word for a mistress elevated from the women of a House.
- matasai—Slave-assistant-escort-bodyguard. An aide who is owned, expected to provide for every need of his owner, and die if necessary to protect him or her.
- mentaid—street name for Serafix. *See* Serafix.
- nashak—spice-based brandy-like drink.
- Navshi ("Ruler")—high-ranking aristocracy, and the minimum caste level usually required to govern a planet.
- net—short for network, or "Net" if referring to a specific planetary infrastructure. The net is the coms and data infrastructure of a world; the datasphere rides atop it, and the infosphere atop that. All of these layers are referred to loosely as "the net" (or "the Net" if a particular one is meant), but in fact their various functions are different.
- netrunner—a cyberdecker who moves between the various layers of the net for fun, work, or mischief. A runner generally ranges farther and engages in more intrusive or illegal activities than does a mere cyberdecker. E.g., while a decker might use a secure system, a runner will infiltrate it.

- pammas—a tall reedy grass topped by a feathery white plume. The fibers are used to make traditional woven matting.
- plas—plastic synthetic used for windows and other moldable forms.
- Political Division (PolitDiv)—technically a subdivision of Internal Security, PolitDiv eventually became sequestered off as it morphed into the Empire's secret police. Today it is a power unto itself. The head of PolitDiv bears only the rank of Arcolo (equivalent to colonel) but works at the behest of the Emperor and has vast influence in the Empire.
- Port Oswin—capital city of Lyndir, the capital of CAS Sector.
- purf—an energy symbiont and chameleon. A purf has a delicate snake-like body structure and a feathery "fur" that is white in its neutral state. It feeds off the bioelectric field and aura energy of its host. Its feathers take on the coloration of its host's aura. In exchange, the purf soothes and calms its host if energies are too erratic. Frebo is Kes's purf.
- Qualuni—the language of old Qua-lun, birthplace of the culture that later became the Sa'adani Empire. This language is still used among the high caste, in court circles, and in formal government business. In that context it is called High Sa'adani. It is the language of politics, administration, and high-born business throughout the Empire.
- Raem the Taskmaster—a psychological construct, a personified aspect of Ilanya Eva's Tolex, her brain-augmentation chip.
- raffik—a clear distilled alcohol similar to aquavit.
- rez, rezzed, rezzing—to resolve or appear in cyberspace, as in "his sim-self rezzed out in the open."
- roi'tas—literally, "honor, duty, obligation"; phrase used to signify honor-debt or duty owed another because of a debt of honor.
- rus—a stylized sigil or mark to signify caste, clan, or profession. Usually laserscribed into the skin and colored with nanite-based smart dyes. The wearing of a rus is usually mandated by law to mark someone in a visually distinguishable manner.
- Sa'adani—a contraction of Sa'adani words meaning "of the House of Adàn." Initially it referred to a clan and their allies, later to a dynasty and the empire they founded. It also refers to the culture and civilizations native to this area of space.
- Sarit—"citizen"—common form of address for peers, lesser caste ranks, and non-caste residents of the Empire.
- scripman—one who deals in money on the backstreets: making loans, brokering bets, collecting debts. Loan shark–like but generally more diversified.
- SeF see sensie-feelie.
- Selmun III—a planet in Lyndir Subsector, scene of events in the novel *Mainline*.

- sensie-feelie—technology that records and plays back physical (and at the high end, emotional) sensations recorded from a subject via specialized neural circuitry and chipware. Often referred to by the acronym SeF, pronounced as it is spelled.
- Serafix—a designer drug that boosts mental acuity. Addictive; street name is "mentaid."
- Shelieno, the—a district in Port Oswin that is one of three licensed districts belonging to the shigasue. Also called the Enclave, or Gantori-Das ("the Between-World").
- shigasa/shigasu/shigasue—individual/plural/collective (organizational). The root word shigar means "to entertain." A shigasa is a trained entertainer working in the licensed quarter of Sa'adani cities. The various word forms are used in this manner: "In the world of the shigasue, small groups of shigasu may entertain a guest, but one shigasa will be responsible for the engagement as a whole."
- sim-self—an avatar simulating one's personal presence in cyberspace.
- Simikan—"Raid Leader"; Sa'adani military rank equivalent to a lieutenant.
- Simkar—"Attack Leader"; Sa'adani military rank equivalent to a captain.
- Startown—slang for the generally free-wheeling urban area that grows up around a starport.
- steeloy—alloy of spun metal, steel-strong but very light. Used for structural support and construction, also certain types of moldable forms.
- synthsteel *see* steeloy.
- Tensin—"guardians"; the admin and security support staff that is the public face of authority in a shigasue Enclave.
- Tolex—brain-augmentation chip; boosts memory storage, collation, association. *See* Raem the Taskmaster.
- trodes—short for electrodes, but refers generally to fine devices ranging down to submicron scale.
- Tryst—high-end house of domination, run by Palumara House in the Shelieno.
- vansin—self-reinforcing ultra-thin smart polymer used in large-scale construction. More details on vansin are here: http://bit.ly/spltech01.

# ACKNOWLEDGMENTS

First and foremost, I want to thank my fans and readers for their ongoing support of my work during my hiatus from writing. Your comments and encouragement in email, blog posts, and other conversations have reminded me that there are folks who really enjoy my stories and want more of them. This book exists because of you.

I owe a special debt of gratitude to Nancy Berman and Shariann Lewitt, my beta readers, both talented writers in their own rights. Your feedback was invaluable, and you really helped me out when I could no longer see my forest for the trees. Thank you.

Liz Gorinsky, my editor, is really, really good at what she does, and has saved me a lot of hair-pulling frustration by making *my* editing work much easier than anticipated. Thanks, Liz.

The Sa'adani Empire, where *Splintegrate* and all the rest of my science fiction takes place, began life as a role-playing game setting that I first developed in 1980 (http://thesaadani.net/serpg1). It has grown and become more refined since then, and over time many wonderful gamers have helped me explore the various corners of this fictional world. For this book, I particularly want to thank two individuals whose gaming directly influenced aspects of *Splintegrate*.

One is Tad Kelson, whose inquisitive mind compelled me to better understand how information resources work in this setting. Though he did not know it at the time, he spurred the elaboration of technologies ranging from planetary info nodes to shipboard library info systems. Thanks for all the smart questions, Tad.

The other is Tiffany Tamaribuchi, who, besides being a world-class taiko musician, is also a most excellent role-playing gamer. Her actions on the planet Casca (mentioned in *Splintegrate*'s epilogue as "a backwater, traditional world") have long-term plot implications for the story arc in my SF novels. Most important for this present volume, she helped me discover Bejmet, and some of the more interesting aspects of the Between-World. Thanks, Tiffany, and I look forward to more gaming in the future.

I must also give a tip of the hat to the BDSM and leather communities in San Francisco and elsewhere. I thank you all for the inspiration, friendship, and interesting experiences over many years. There are bits and pieces of many of you scattered throughout these pages. If something here reminds you of you, or someone you know—well, that might not be a coincidence.

The Veteran's Administration health care system deserves a special mention here as well. Health problems of mine helped delay the completion of this novel. Then, after submitting it to the publisher, I had a near-fatal health crisis that left me unable to write or edit anything of substance, or to do so only with great difficulty. It is because of the top-notch care I have received from the VA that I am able now to both edit and revise this manuscript for publication. I am very grateful to the health care providers and support staff in the Nashville and Murfreesboro facilities who have contributed to my recovery and enabled me to be a capable novelist once again. My heartfelt thanks to you all.

And finally, I want to especially thank my sister, Chris Christian, who has played a fundamental role in the writing of this book. That you hold *Splintegrate* in your hands right now is due to her kind generosity and steadfast support. Thank you, Bot, for giving author and novel a home. I couldn't have done this without you.

If I have omitted anyone, I plead my decrepit memory, and the error is solely mine. Please know that you have had my gratitude all along the way.

*Deborah Teramis Christian*
*writing on a farm in Tennessee*
*January 2018*